*Joyce
this to . — , — joys
all the joy
(Graduated w/her
in 1960 — Durend
High School*

Promise at Daybreak

By

Elizabeth Wehman

Summit Street Publishing

*Trudy~
Best
wishes,
Elizabeth
Wehman
Ro 34:8*

PROMISE AT DAYBREAK
Published by Summit Street Publishing
131 West Grand River
Owosso, Michigan 48867

ISBN 978-0-9905580-2-6

ISBN 978-0-9905580-3-3 (electronic)

Publishing in the United States by Summit Street Publishing, Owosso, Michigan.

Library of Congress Cataloging-in-Publication Data
Wehman, Elizabeth
Promise at Daybreak/Elizabeth Wehman-1st ed.

2015912513

Printed in the United States of America
2015

10 9 8 7 6 5 4 3 2 1

Promise at Daybreak is dedicated to the special relationship of sisters, but especially to my precious sister of my heart, Christie Ann (Martin) Habermehl. You taught me the value of sisterhood, the sweetness of having a sister as a best friend, and the precious patience of a big sister...if only for a moment. Our relationship will always be my favorite. And also, to the prime example of forever sisters: Jeanette, Esther, and Mary.

Acknowledgements

Could I do it again? Could I possibly come up with another idea, outline, draft, plot or characters which could exceed the first published manuscript? Upon voicing this concern to one of my dearest writing friend, his words included: "Yes you can, now get busy!" Thank you Ed. I will never forget your prodding or you.

Thanks to my husband, David, who read the book early to give me the 'thumbs up' before hitting the publish button. Your tears in certain chapters makes me know why I love you so much.

To my daughters and their relationship and how some of this book is inspired by the rivalry and sustenance of these two sisters. How many times I told them, "I'd love to have a sister," and their usual response, "You can have mine." You both bring me joy!

To my son who encourages me by trying new things with a spirit of a winner. He's shown me how to keep going, even when there isn't a muscle in his body to keep pedaling. I love your spirit.

To every single reader who bought my first book, and left me speechless with their generous, encouraging words. For those who wrote a review, sent me a note, e-mailed me words of inspiration...thanks. Sometimes I do get writing right.

Special thanks to my awesome, amazing editor-in-chief, Kathryn Frazier. Not only is she amazing with any manuscript, her talent surpasses highly paid professionals. She encourages me with constructive, honest, and sincere comments. I couldn't do any of this without you. You make me shine.

Thanks to my cover hand models Doris Adams and Esther Atkinson for taking time to help me as well as manicurist Renee Dugan of "Hair We Are."

This opportunity to write my second book is beyond my dreams. For that I cannot leave out the God of my heart who truly gives us the 'desires of our hearts.' May all the credit be given to You and Your abundant promises. Without You, I can do nothing!

Elizabeth Wehman

Psalm 34:8

Chapter 1

Irene Fredericks glanced up from her recliner to see her mother's photo. She'd picked out an ornate, gold frame for it nearly twenty-five years before. The eyes in the photo reflected her real mother's real soul. Kind and endearing. That is the mother she remembered, the woman the illness stole. The change had been gradual. As dementia infiltrated her mother's brain, her language altered, her common sense disappeared, and then came that stare. That blank, clueless look. No one knew her after that. No one came to visit, not even to give Irene a break. She shuddered remembering how lonely it left her.

Seeing Mother's photo always prompted Irene to begin her daily recitation. *Telephone number: 288-5793. Zip code: 48429.*

Where did she live? She looked out the window, "*Durand, Michigan.*" Irene nodded as she recited it in sequence, just as she'd done numerous times before. Her friend, Edna, had recommended she get busy playing Scrabble again. *X and Z give the best points, but nothing is better than a J on a triple space.* Perhaps they'd play a game together, on Edna's next visit.

A rumble outside distracted Irene from her recitation. She stopped to listen. It sounded like thunder, but the heavy snow-fall suggested otherwise.

There it was again. Thundersnow? She often had a hard time distinguishing the difference between railroad cars cracking together at the far end of town, and thunder in a snowstorm. When she heard the rumble a third time, she decided to get up from her chair to investigate.

Thundersnow wasn't typical for Durand, but neither was this particular storm.

Grabbing for her cane, Irene struggled to right herself from the recliner. Blasted cane. If she wasn't so dizzy, she'd manage without it. Where was the television remote? The news only frustrated her anyway. As she stood, the remote fell from her lap. She sat back down, removed it from the folds of the blanket now at her feet, and hit the off button.

"That's enough of that." Standing again, she dropped the remote onto the coffee table, causing her cat to jump in response. "Oh, sorry Max." She steadied herself and picked up the calico, now stretching after his afternoon nap. "I just can't take that nonsense anymore." Irene looked into his face, Max meowed in response. He felt heavier now than even the day before. "That's right. You understand, don't you?"

Placing the cat back on his perch, she looked out the window. Snow swirled outside, coating the windowpane with a fresh layer of white. "Oh my, it's getting miserable out there." Irene picked up her cane and shook it at the cat, "You need to thank your lucky stars you are an inside cat." The cat responded with a slow lick to a paw.

A distant train whistle sounded. "Must be the afternoon chemical train." Bare trees caused the whistles to sound as if they were right outside her door, even though the closest track was blocks away. Floor boards creaked as Irene shuffled through the living room and made her way down the hallway toward the kitchen. She stopped for a second in the foyer to look at herself in the mirror. With just a glimpse, Irene shook her head in disgust. She smoothed down her tangled gray waves, long overdue for a haircut. The weather wasn't helping her get to the salon, she tsk-tsked as she continued into the bright, yellow kitchen.

She'd asked Brian, her son-in-law, for the brightest shade of sunshine he could find to paint the room. Michigan winters could be hard to get through, without some kind of reminder that the sun would shine again. She smiled at her choice as she made her way to the tea kettle on the stove. Max slinked in behind her and coiled around her ankles.

A squeal of train brakes pierced the air as Irene put water into the kettle for a fresh cup of tea. Visitors often startled at the village railroad sounds, but Irene was used to the distant rumble of trains connecting and the screech of heavy metal brakes in her little town. "Oh my," she glanced out the window over the kitchen sink at the snow accumulating in white drifts around her garage. "It's piling up fast today, Max."

Irene filled the tea kettle full, set it on the stove, and switched on the burner. "A cup of tea is gonna be just the ticket." She nudged Max with her foot. "You gettin' hungry, Max-a-million?" Irene took a tin of cat food out of the cupboard and removed the plastic bag keeping the food moist. The wrapper helped her remember whether or not she'd fed him each morning. Max seemed to be going through the cans too fast, causing her annoying, additional trips to the store.

"How 'bout a little snack with me this afternoon?" Reaching down by the oven door, she found Max's silver dish and placed the leftover food in it. Her phone rang and, Irene jumped.

"Oh goodness, gracious!" Irene shuffled to the opposite side of the room, sat down at the table, and picked up the receiver. "Hello?" No reply at the other end. "Hello?" Irene put down the phone, turned up the volume on her hearing aid, lifted the receiver back to her ear and tried again, "Hello?"

"Mom!"

"Hello?"

"Mom, it's me, Kathleen."

"Kathleen, is that you?"

Laughter erupted from the other end, "Yes, Mom."

"Who are you laughing at?"

"No one." Her daughter seemed to stifle a giggle, "Mom, are you staying warm?"

"Yes, dear. I have the furnace up. Quite the storm, isn't it? I think I just heard a rumble of thunder."

"I think it was thunder. The weatherman said we may have a bit of that in this storm. Funny to hear this time of year."

"I thought perhaps I was dreaming." Irene felt better knowing her daughter heard the rumblings, too.

"Brian wanted to know if you need anything. He's headed home from work and can stop if you need him to."

"No, Max and I are fine. Still have milk." Irene looked in the direction of her refrigerator, as if to prove herself correct. "I think."

"Okay. Call me if you need anything."

"I will, sweetheart. Thank you for thinking of me. I'll pray Brian gets home safely in all this mess."

"Thanks, Mom. Take care."

As Irene placed the phone back on the receiver, the tea kettle set off its high pitched whistle. She snatched at her hearing aid and turned the volume off. "I'm coming. I'm coming." Irene dropped her cane as she stood up. "Oh dear." She gripped the edge of the counter, thankful for it, while pouring herself a cup. She breathed in the aroma of the fresh tea brewing in her cup. Nothing like a berry blend on a cold February afternoon.

Irene reached down for her cane, righted herself, and then carried her tea into the living room. The heat from her cup warmed her hands. Settling back into her chair, she placed the steaming cup beside her, then leaned over to gather up the blanket at her feet, and her worn, leather Bible from the coffee table. Reading scripture always gave her a renewed sense of security. Church bulletins and sheets of paper with prayer requests fell into her lap.

She began reading in Matthew. *Thou shalt love thy neighbor as thyself.* She'd read that verse many times, but eased back into her chair to think about the words. She closed her eyes and thought of the handicapped boy next door, and his elderly mother. Then her thoughts trailed to the young family two houses down, and for Edna and her painful back. She whispered short prayers for each one. She prayed for the grandson of one of her dear friends, stationed in Afghanistan.

She smiled to herself. She'd never had a problem loving others. She might have a little temper from time to time, and an occasional worrisome spirit, but she was sure those were her only sinful issues these days. Despite the occasional loneliness, nothing felt amiss in her spiritual heart. She praised God for His faithfulness to her, in helping her to remember important things. *Telephone number: 989-288-5793.*

Irene never admired those who blamed God for their trials, yet she often wondered why God chose certain people to have to endure more severe trials than others. She believed consequences were a part of bad life choices, but sometimes bad things happened to good people through no fault of their own. Like her mother. She shook her head. Dementia was like that. It didn't care who and when it would rob a person of themselves. It just didn't care.

Irene sipped her tea while she asked the Lord to give her more love for others, Max jumped up into her lap. Startled, she watched the cat turn around on her lap to find just the right spot to settle. A ritual Max enjoyed. Once he did, she began to feel his warmth soak into her lap. Resting her head on the back of her chair, she closed her eyes to pray.

A pounding caused Irene to stir from her unexpected nap. She opened her eyes, but didn't move. Perhaps she'd heard it in a dream, or maybe it was just another rumble of thundersnow. A loud rap woke her up more fully. It sounded like someone pounding on her kitchen door. Pushing a sound-asleep Max off her lap wasn't an easy task, but she grabbed for her cane to right herself out of her slumber and her chair. The pounding grew louder, more intense.

She called into the kitchen, "I'm coming. I'm coming. Hold yer horses!" An odd stuffiness filled the room.

"Irene!" The call sounded loud and urgent. That's when she recognized the voice of her elderly neighbor, Violet. "Irene? Are you in there?"

A poignant odor came from her kitchen. Looking into the room from her foyer she noticed a cloud of smoke filling the room quickly. She uttered in astonishment, but walked faster into her now foggy, smoky kitchen.

More pounding. "Irene! Please! Where are you?"

Irene rushed into the kitchen to open the door for her neighbor. Once the door was opened, smoke billowed from the room and poured through the opening. Violet, wrapped in just a sweater and wearing bedroom slippers, hobbled into the kitchen. "Is something burning on your stove, Irene?"

Irene shuffled to the other side of the kitchen, fanning at the air and coughing as she went. As she reached the stove, she realized she'd forgotten to turn off the burner on her stove after pouring her tea. "Oh for Pete's sake." Her eyes began to burn. She pulled a tissue out of her pocket and placed it over her nose and mouth.

"Don't touch the handle. I'm sure it's hot." Her friend left the door open and rushed toward her.

"It's a wonder it didn't go up in flames. I wonder how long I've been sleeping?" Irene snapped on the exhaust switch over the stove. The fan pulled more smoke from the room.

"I think we caught it just in time."

Irene nodded to her friend. "Max and I must have fallen asleep. Oh goodness." Coughing now, she snatched up a worn potholder and gently removed the blackened tea kettle from the burner. "It's a wonder I didn't burn the house down around me."

"Greg saw the smoke from his bedroom window and ran downstairs to tell me about it. I was washing dishes and just ran over here as fast as I could." Violet now stood beside her with slumped shoulders shaking, her breathing deep and heavy. "I don't move as fast as I used to."

"Oh Violet, I'm so embarrassed. Please sit down. I'll get you a blanket." As Irene left the room she heard something about Greg calling the fire department. Pulling her hearing aid out of one ear, she turned up the volume, turning back she asked, "Did you just say you called the fire department?"

Just then, the blare of an emergency siren filled Irene's front room. She rushed to a front window, pulled back the curtain, and looked out. There sat a bright, red fire engine, with 'City of Durand Fire Department' etched on the door. Heavily dressed men were unwrapping a fire hose from the inside of the truck. "Oh dear." Irene let the curtain drop, covered her mouth, and turned to open the front door. How could she have let this happen? She was mortified.

When she opened the front door, snow began to hit her face. She waved frantically to the firemen headed toward the kitchen door. Coughing a bit, she tried to shout, "Boys, boys!" One by one, the men turned to her voice. "It's okay," she called. I have it all under control now." She started coughing so hard, she had to put the tissue back over her mouth.

The fire chief came up onto the porch. "Mrs. Fredericks, are you okay?"

Irene shivered as the cold of the snowy afternoon penetrated her house coat, and dampened her hair. "I'm fine. Just fine. Kitchen's a little smoky, but that's all."

"I'll meet you at the back." Irene recognized the fire chief as one of Brian's friends. He left her on the front porch and headed for her kitchen door.

She closed the front door and headed back into the kitchen, waving at the air with a dish towel. The mishap would soon be all over town. She hoped Edna hadn't seen it. If she did, photos of Irene's smoking house would surely end up on Facebook.

The men inspected her stove and the tea kettle for a few moments, then left, but not before leaving wet boot tracks over her formerly, clean floor. She waited to hear the truck start up, and prayed a silent prayer that there wouldn't be additional sirens, before she shut the door. Her shiny, new yellow paint now ashen and sooty in color. She sighed, and another cough escaped.

Irene sat down in the chair opposite her caring neighbor. What would she do without Violet and Greg? They always cared for her from their windows next door. "Thank you."

Still shaking, Violet rose from her chair. "No worries, Irene. Thankfully, my son is always on the alert for things, not quite right. I need to head home. Are you okay now?"

Irene nodded. "I'm fine. Thanks again."

Before she went out the door, Violet turned. "Perhaps you should tell Kathleen about this."

Irene stood and headed for the door. "No, no. Let's not bother her. She'll just fret and worry. And with all she has going on in her life, she definitely does not need to worry more about her forgetful mother."

"Well. I think you're getting a bit too forgetful. Maybe I should call her?"

"Oh no, please no, Violet." Irene began to panic. "I know I've been doing some odd things lately, but I'm old. You know how that can be." Irene hadn't told Violet about Kathleen's recent suggestions that she might be suffering from a memory illness. Not everyone needed to know her business.

"I do, but Irene..."

"I'll mention something to her about it. Please let me."

"Okay." Despite a look of doubt, Violet turned again to leave, "My it's so cold out here," she shivered.

"Watch for ice, Violet. Be careful."

As Irene closed the door, she knew without a doubt that Violet was right. Her illness was making it difficult. She'd forgotten to close the door to the garage many times, which was never a habit she'd had before. Once last week she nearly overflowed the kitchen sink. She'd started the water to do dishes, then totally forgot she'd turned it on. Her thoughts seemed so jumbled on certain days, but what could you expect from an eighty-four year old? She shook her head. "Gracious! How'd I get so old?"

She couldn't believe she nearly burned her house down. What would be next? She prayed Kathleen and Brian would never find out. They'd worry themselves sick. Over and over again she'd asked the Lord to keep her from becoming a burden to her children. Yet, as of today, she was beginning to even bother the neighbors. She thought of Louise in Florida. Perhaps it was time to let her sister know of her condition. Their mother had done many of the same things Irene now did, but she'd never almost burned down her home.

Shaking her head, Irene determined to be even more careful. More observant. Less irresponsible. She gazed out into the snowy afternoon again and thought again of her sister. A shiver ran up into her arms and she shuddered. Irene closed her eyes and breathed a short, 'help me,' prayer. Would her sister remember? Would she fulfill their promise? Worse yet, would she even care? The strain on their relationship over the past few years may have changed the course Irene had set for her life. Another clap of thunder erupted outside. Of all days to almost set a fire. She'd try to prevent Kathleen from finding out. But how would she mask the smell of smoke now permeating the entire house?

Chapter 2

The room smelled of antiseptic and bleach. A doctor's office always made Louise Williams feel vulnerable. Medical terminology and scientific dogma didn't merge with her world of literature, art, and frivolity.

"This will not work." Doctor MacKenzie looked over her chart on the electronic gadget he tapped with his finger. He sat down on the rolling stool opposite her.

"Of course it will." Louise smoothed out the white sheet spread underneath her noticing her need for a fresh manicure. Raising a shaky, swollen hand she picked at last week's leftover purple polish. The manicure hadn't lasted as long as her usual ones. That new nail tech must be the problem.

"You don't understand this illness. Before long you won't be able to accomplish simple tasks. Walking to your car after leaving a grocery store, shopping, even going out to get the mail will become more of a struggle for you."

Louise whispered an expletive and muttered, "My mailbox is attached to my back door."

The doctor looked up from his new-fangled contraption. "Doesn't matter. Everyday activities will take more time. Simple activities, a struggle. I'm sorry."

Louise sighed.

"Your life will change dramatically soon, Louise. You need to find a caregiver."

Louise laughed him off. "A caregiver? Are you serious?"

The doctor nodded. "More than ever. Where's your family?"

"I live alone."

"I know that, but do you have family who can come stay with you or even take you into their home?"

"No. Nor would I ever do that to them." She almost laughed to herself, thinking of her sister in Michigan. Irene could care less about her after their last quarrel a few years ago. She sat up straighter on the examining table and folded her hands in her lap.

"Do you have the resources to get into an assisted living facility?"

Louise nodded. "For now. But not enough for a long-term situation. This illness could last awhile until the rest of my body decides to call it quits, right?"

"Straight answers, Louise?"

"You know how I like it."

Her doctor nodded. "You need to make plans."

"How long?"

"It's different with everyone, but maybe a year. And sometimes, your heart gives you little warning and as you just said, it decides to call it quits."

Louise struggled to get off the examining table and stand upright. Louise Williams always faced problems head on, proficient in finding plausible solutions. She'd figure this out.

The doctor wrote out a prescription and handed it to her. "Here. Start taking this tomorrow. It will take a month to six weeks to start working, but once it does, you'll feel better. For a time."

She grabbed her purse strap and thrust it onto her shoulder. Of all things life could dish out. Was this really her future? She couldn't believe this was her it. Her death sentence? Why couldn't she die, without warning, in her sleep, like the fortunate few her same age? At eight-two, surely she had at least ten good years left.

"I'm sorry." The doctor turned to leave. "I'm serious about the living situation, Louise. You need to get some help. You shouldn't be living alone." He left the room as if the sentence had been dealt.

God found it convenient to interrupt Louise's life. He rarely bothered her, until her life began to get interesting and exciting. Today wasn't any different. So what if her feet and hands were twice their normal size? Lacking the ability to walk across the room without becoming weary and short of breath was just a normal part of her day. Yet God decided to have this happen just when Howard Phillips started showing more interest in her.

She struggled to stand tall, despite the ache in her back. She raised her chin and walked out of the room. She'd been on her own forever and she knew one thing. She could take care of herself. She'd done it for years and she wasn't about to stop now.

Chapter 3

Irene purposely checked the tea kettle, burners, and oven before she left the kitchen for a few minutes. Now raps on the back door startled her, and caused her cane to fall next to her chair. Why couldn't she keep that thing from falling to the ground all the time?

Just bending over already got her short of breath. Cane now in hand, she shouted from her chair, "I'm coming!" She rose slowly, then waited by her chair for a few seconds to gain her balance. The rapping continued.

"Oh gracious," Irene hobbled to the kitchen, bumping Max as he trotted in front of her. "C'mon Max, move."

She reached the kitchen and sniffed the air. A bitter odor, like burnt toast, still hung in the air from the day before, but it wasn't as intense. She breathed a sigh of relief to see her good friend, Edna, peering into the kitchen, her nose plastered to the window and her hand cupped over her forehead. It made Irene giggle.

She unlocked the back door, and smiled at her friend, who came in with a flurry of snow and cold air. "Edna, mercy me, can't you wait for a person to get up out of a chair?"

Edna gave Irene a stern look. "What in the world were you doing? Were you on the toilet?"

"No." Edna pushed past her with a bag in her hand. Tracks of snow followed her. Irene would have to mop the floors again, as she'd done after her friends from the fire station left yesterday.

"Come in, come in." Edna was one of her best friends, but she lacked tact. Max scurried off to his hiding place between the cupboards and refrigerator.

"I don't want to stay long, but dear, I'm worried about you. Violet told me about the house fire."

"House fire? I did manage to leave the tea kettle..."

"She said the firemen were here and everything."

"Well, yes. They were here, but..."

Edna shook her head and put a pensive finger to her mouth, "Irene, the firemen came."

"Edna." Irene shook her head. "Listen. It wasn't a big deal."

"Well." Edna placed a shopping bag onto the kitchen table.

Irene shut the door. If she didn't change the subject, Edna would never get over the minor interruption from yesterday. "What do you have there, Edna?"

Edna turned to her and held up the bag. "Irene. After having your house nearly burn down, I brought you something."

"My house didn't nearly..."

"Oh, I know. I know." Her friend waved her hands. "That memory of yours is just getting worse. So I thought this would help. I've had it in my house for years and have never used it." She pulled a kitchen timer out of the bag. "It will be perfect. See? Watch me as I set it for you." Edna motioned for Irene to come closer.

Irene approached her friend. Edna always emitted a distinct odor of bologna. The snowy footprints from the floor began seeping through her slippers. Wincing, she answered, "I'm not sure I need a timer. I have one on my..."

"No, no, this one is different. My son got it for me. Now watch. You set it like this," Edna turned the handle with a twist, "And voila!" She set the timer down and slapped the counter. "See? No need to worry about causing another fire. Set it each time you put something on the stove. As a reminder. And it's small. You can carry it with you into the bathroom, or set it beside you in the living room. It will fit into your pocket." Edna smiled as she removed her woolen hat to reveal matted white hair. Always hard to keep a nice hairdo in the middle of a Michigan winter.

Irene sat down. She knew her friend's visit would stretch long into the afternoon. She also knew that if she rejected the gift, she would not only hurt Edna's feelings, but she'd hear about the refusal of help, week after week, at church. Every. Single. Sunday. "Thank you Edna. This will help, I'm sure."

"Yes, I agree. I would hate to hear that you didn't use something like this and then sat in the chair of yours in the living room while the house burned down; all around you. It does still smell a bit musty in here." Edna waved at the air. "Oh, if we could open a window or two. This winter is just atrocious. Did you hear it thundering yesterday?"

"Yes, it surprised me. Only when those storms come out of the East, do they bring thunder with them." Irene picked up the timer. "It was thoughtful of you to bring this to me. How about a cup of tea while you are here?" Irene wondered if this time would be any different than the other bi-weekly visits from her friend. Full of helpful ideas, sprinkled with hints of scolding and reprimands.

17

"No, no. I'm on my way to take care of Mrs. Arnold. She's getting so frail."

Irene sighed in relief. Her friend would never consider herself as elderly, even though Irene was pretty sure she had her by two years. Caring for others was her gift. She loved everyone. Volunteering her time to drive around those who found it hard to get out or didn't have available transportation, caring for others, this was her contribution to the world. The small town would miss her when she was gone.

She sat down across from Irene. "I will stay a moment though. So...how did it happen?"

"What?" Irene grasped to remember the topic of the current conversation.

Edna laughed, "Oh my, you are worse than I thought."

Startled a bit, Irene laughed along. "Worse than whom?"

Edna stopped laughing. "It's a serious matter, dear. I've been watching your decline now for almost a year. I hate to see you like this."

Edna was always succinct. "Please keep it to yourself, Edna. I don't want the world feeling sorry for me."

"I mean, remember last fall when you totally forgot about where the kitchen cabinet key is kept at church. Then, you totally forgot Margaret's birthday. Remember that?"

Irene nodded. She didn't, but if she said otherwise, Edna's list would grow longer.

Edna reached for her hand, "Listen to me. I'm sorry."

Irene was rarely harsh to others. She tried her best always be patient and kind, but this whole visit was starting to perturb her. "Sorry? Sorry for telling me I'm losing it? Or for making me feel inadequate and unable to even take care of myself anymore?" She felt bad for the words as they escaped, but it was too late. So much for loving others. She'd have to confess now. Work harder on loving. Sin was a never-ending succession.

"Oh. I see I'll have to be a little more careful what I say to you from now on." Edna folded her arms.

Irene shook her head. "No, I'm sorry. I know I'm having memory issues, but what can a person do? I'm eighty-four. Not getting any younger. I want to think straight, not be forgetful, but I'm afraid it will happen whether I want it to or not." She looked out a window, turning her face away, afraid her friend would see her blinking to forbid tears from falling down her cheeks. It will be for me just like it was for my Mother. Edna's visit meant that Kathleen would know soon. She needed to confess the incident before her daughter found out through Edna's Durand grapevine. Or even worse, through Facebook, of which Edna was queen.

Edna patted her hand. "I know. I know. We'll all help you. Violet and I. The rest of the girls."

Irene smiled. "Thank you. Can you please not put it on the Internet?"

"Oh Irene, I wouldn't do that to you. But honey, you have to just try and be as careful as you can. Can you do that?"

Honestly, Irene wasn't sure she could. It grew harder each day. Her brain just seemed tired. What was she going to do? Zip code: 48429. Social security number: 362. The pity showing in Edna's eyes distracted her. Irene attempted to divert the conversation and she knew the exact way to do so. "Did you hear about Mabel?"

Edna's eyes grew wide. "No. What?"

Louise Williams prided herself on her resourcefulness. Flirting came naturally, but asking a person to become your husband, well that was something else. It was her one and only hope, as long as her question didn't give the unsuspecting man a heart attack.

What was wrong with looking her best? But what if her best wasn't good enough? She did her best to apply lipstick directly on her lips, but her shaking hand made it almost impossible. The whole smear mess reminded her of all the elderly women she used to make fun of who looked like their smiles had been painted on by a precocious four-year-old. Now she was joining their ranks and there was nothing she could do about it.

A bit of rouge on her cheeks brightened them against her pale, wrinkled skin. She used to pinch her cheeks. Now it only caused her skin to wrinkle more. It was almost impossible to apply mascara anymore. The last time she'd attempted it, she looked as though she had chicken pox, only with black dots. Her eyes shown bright blue, though. She hoped they were enough to entice the opposite sex.

Looking down, she adjusted her clothes as best as she could. Low-cut shirts just hung on her shoulders now. Droopiness replaced perkiness. Louise sighed. She could stuff. Cocking her head, she looked over at the roll of toilet paper beside the stool and then decided against it. With her luck, the tissue would escape, and she'd look like a thirteen-year-old going to a dance with the evidence trailing out from under her shirt.

She wasn't sure who she was trying to fool. The only man to glance at her twice these days was Howard. Rating the others, most couldn't hear, or were too busy talking about themselves to listen. Others could barely remember her name. Despite that, it was almost impossible to keep her flirting in check. It really wasn't anything she wanted to change, anyway. She was sure none of the eligible bachelors could perform if she did took them up on the lewd comments they spewed at her every afternoon in the coffee shop. She never wanted that to stop. If it did, she felt she might as well stop, too.

Her hair still looked fashionable. It wasn't the brassy gray color that most women her age deal with, but rather a shiny, chiffon white. Sure, it had grown sparse in places, but Louise knew just how to cover the bare spots. She always checked the back with a hand mirror before leaving the house. Holding the mirror in one hand and a comb in the other allowed her to reach any protruding cowlick, and fix it with a squirt of hair spray.

Putting on a pouty face, she looked into the mirror for one last adjustment. High heels would go great with this outfit, but could mean suicide. Temporary water weight gain replaced those with a size triple- E shoes. So she slipped on her plastic, hot pink, sandals, complete with multicolored fake gems. Thankfully, designers honored the elderly with a more sophisticate style. The shoes matched her white cream shirt and hot pink pants almost to perfection. Louise pulled her silver charm bracelet from her jewelry box. Each charm held special meaning for her, from the Eiffel tower to the tiny wine bottle replica from California. Traveling had been such a thrill for her. Despite her struggle to get the clasp snapped, Louise hated to leave the house without that bracelet. She'd spent a fortune on every dangly bobble. Adjusting it on her oversized wrist, she headed into the kitchen for her purse.

Louise found Howard at the far end of the restaurant. She smoothed back her hair, stood tall and crossed the room. Among her many talents was her ability to get the men to look her way. It always helped her feel beautiful and important. She may be old, but never too old to flirt.

Howard looked over his newspaper, scooting out of his booth seat to stand for her. "My, my, my, Louise, you look beautiful today."

Louise lowered herself to sit opposite from him. She smiled. "Why thank you, Howard."

He scooted back into his seat, leaned forward over the table, and in a hushed tone said, "No, I'm serious. You look exceptionally beautiful today."

Batting her eyelashes, she remembered her mission. "Oh Howard, you know how to make a girl feel..." the word seemed to linger on her tongue a little longer than she wanted, "...simple." That wasn't right, but it was out before she could change it.

"Simple!" Howard laughed, "No dear, you should feel beautiful, just like you are." He picked up her right hand and started to kiss it. She jerked it away quickly, for fear that he'd notice its swollen size and question her. Her bracelet jangled. He looked up at her. "What was that?"

"What?"

"It's like you didn't want me to kiss your hand."

Louise sighed. "No, I did want you to." She knew she needed to change the subject quickly. "Howard, I was wondering. Are you tired of being single?" She remembered to be tactful too late. But what the heck? She wasn't getting any younger or healthier waiting on this man.

Howard sat back in his chair, picked up his napkin, covered his smile, yet laughed. His eyes crinkled and sparkled. "Sweetheart, why are you asking me this now?" He again reached for her hand, but she had neatly tucked it into her lap. His smile disappeared and he began tapping the table with his index finger, like he always did when he was nervous.

"I need to know."

Howard's forehead wrinkled. His demeanor changed to a stern etch of concern. He picked up the newspaper he'd been reading and folded it. "Do you want some coffee or something?"

Her heart jumped. He wanted to avoid the subject. Yet she continued, "Just answer the question."

Silence. Howard avoided eye contact. Finally, he leaned across the table, "Louise, you are a great companion to spend time with."

"Don't end a sentence with a preposition." Louise felt like a teenager about to spend the evening holding a box of tissues, and a carton of double fudge ice cream. More likely, she'd go to bed lonely and clutching a bottle of antacids.

"You're a beautiful woman. I'd be stupid or blind to not see that, but dear one, I imagined you smart enough to know one thing about me."

"What one thing?" The thought struck her hard. "Are you gay?"

Howard blushed. "No."

"You don't want to marry me, do you?"

He shook his head, "I can't."

"What do you mean, you can't?" Louise leaned back and folded her arms.

"Louise, this is not how I wanted to tell you."

Louise raised both hands. "What? Just say it." She waited to hear about her looks or his need to be alone. What could it possibly be? She was a catch. Any reasonable, available man would know that.

"I'm married."

She never saw that one coming, after a whole winter of flirtings, shared coffees and companionship. She blinked. "You're what?" It came out a little too loudly.

Howard hushed her. "Sorry, I should have told you sooner." He looked down, wiping his hands on his pants. An intense sadness seemed to creep over his face.

Louise stood up. Not as quickly as she needed to make her point, but as fast as she could manage. Maybe she could reach for his coffee and throw it in his face. Yet with her luck, she'd miss or splash it all over the table with her shaky hand. She reached out to slap him, and as she did, Howard took hold of her hand. Unfortunately, she didn't jerk away this time.

"Sit down."

"No."

He pulled her hand, purposely moving her back to her chair. He looked nervously around the restaurant. "Please?"

She pulled away, sat down with a thump, and looked out the window of the shop. The Gulf of Mexico loomed just outside the door, waves churning onto shore as an oncoming storm approached. Her eyes grew moist. Fighting tears as much as possible, she blinked. Hard. This was not how she kept her dignity nor her spunk for life.

Howard reached again for her hand, but she held it tight in her lap, gripping her skirt. "Louise, look at me. I need to explain."

She glanced back at him. He looked sober and shy. He was just so handsome, even at the age of eighty. He'd caught her eye at a New Year's Eve party at the club house. He'd smiled at her across the room. Priding herself on always having an eligible man to kiss on New Years, she'd smiled back. Soon he was across the dance floor. He kissed her on the cheek as the clock ticked midnight.

"I haven't told you because she isn't here with me anymore. She's in a home across the state. Close to my son, his family and my daughter and her children. They all live there."

"Why didn't you tell me?" Louise gulped back emotions forming a lump in her throat and tears trying to slip down her cheeks.

"And ruin our times together?" Her friend now smiled that familiar, boyish-like grin. "I loved sharing coffee with you every morning. Walking on the beach in the afternoons. Playing cards and watching movies with you each night. Your company is superb. I thought if I told you, you'd put a stop to all of it." He rubbed his mouth and smoothed down his mustache. "I'm sorry for not telling you."

Anger now replaced the ache in her heart. "Where's your wedding ring?"

Howard reached around his neck and pulled up the chain he always wore under his floral shirts. Up it came, a gold wedding band. "I don't wear it. I'd rather flirt with beautiful women like you." He flushed, "Which says a lot about me."

"That's morbid!" Louise folded her arms. "You're a tramp."

"Perhaps," Howard slipped the ring back under his shirt. "Or maybe the truth is, I'm just lonely. She's had dementia for ten years now. She doesn't know me or her own children. I get away from her for a few months to get a break."

Louise's anger subsided and she really looked into the brown eyes of a man now fighting his own tears.

"My son, he's good to her. He takes our grandchildren to see her. But it's no use. She knows no one. She's turned from a sweet, dear lady into a maniac. She's mad at me all the time. It's just tiring and frustrating. When the disease started, she blamed me for everything, from the food tasting horrible to the construction she imagined going on around her room. She often told others I cheated on her, even when I would come to visit her every day. I grew tired of her bad-mouthing me. It was hard to think of what the nurses and her caregivers thought of me. Now, she doesn't even know who I am. She stares off in the distance. Our conversations are one-sided. I often wish she would complain to me again, instead of the silence I now face when I go to see her."

Louise had heard similar stories from other friends. "I'm sorry."

"It's okay. I shouldn't have kept it a secret. But to be perfectly honest, I lost my wife completely five years ago to this horrible disease. I know she needs me. I need her. But not this woman she's turned into. I'll go back soon, after a month or so, to take up the task of caring for her again. I've so enjoyed spending time with you that I added an extra month to my normal time away." Howard shook his head, "But, she's safe. My son is good to her. I need breaks from time to time."

Louise nodded. "I think I understand."

"I'm sorry to have led you on. It was wrong."

"Getting old isn't for sissies." Louise thought about her own mother and how the illness had caused many of the same symptoms Howard's wife experienced. She thought of her sister. Had Irene grown tired, like Howard, of caring for their mother? No doubt she had. For her, it was a full-time job. Louise always felt guilty for not helping her more.

Howard laughed. "That's for sure." He looked at her with pity, but with a smile, "So why are you wanting to get married this fine February day? Valentine's Day has passed. I gave you flowers."

Louise looked out the coffee shop window again. She wasn't sure how to answer him. At this moment, he was her only hope. Glancing back at his sweet, brown eyes she smiled. "I'm not needing flowers. I need help. The doctor says more care. And soon." She sighed, blinked hard and added, "I should probably go visit a few homes in the area."

"A home? Like assisted living?"

Louise nodded. "Unfortunately." Now she fought back tears of sadness with everything she had, "I'm not going to get any better." She felt a tear slide down her cheek, and quickly wiped it away.

The sweet man she'd grown to fondly love sat across from her with a new sadness in his eyes. He reached for her hand and this time she didn't refuse. As his hand warmly grasped hers, she suddenly realized he'd never held her hand like this, except to offer support going down stairs or getting into his car. The only kiss they'd shared was on New Year's Eve, and that was a peck on the cheek. He'd been faithful. She'd just hadn't realized how much until now.

"Oh stop it. It happens to all of us, sooner or later."

"Hey, I know. Let me help you find a home. I could drive you."

27

Louise smiled at the man with whom she'd grown so close over the past two months. At their age, time passed quicker, and she knew it had been her who was falling in love. "Thank you."

The timer went off in Irene's kitchen. She'd used Edna's gift, knowing full well that if she didn't, she'd hear another lecture. But why was it going off now? Had she put dinner in the oven? Had she forgotten to feed Max again? She pulled her robe closer around her, adjusted her cane, and walked toward the sounding alarm. After silencing the buzzer, she looked into the oven, but could find nothing ready to remove. She looked back at the timer, as though it might tell her why it went off.

Feeling a bit bewildered, she left the kitchen and looked around the living room then out the window onto the front porch. Perhaps it had been the doorbell she heard. She opened the door to nothing but a blast of cold air. Shivering, she shut the door and returned to the kitchen. She'd been trying so hard to keep things in order, not to forget things on the stove or laundry ready to be put into the dryer. What possible reason could she have for setting the timer?

The clock read ten past ten. Why would she set an alarm for such an odd time? She shook her head and went to draw water for a bath. Stepping into the bathroom, she slipped on a puddle of water and nearly toppled into the stool as she grabbed the towel bar to avoid falling. Water brimmed the edge of the tub, spilling on the floor.

"Now why would I have left the water running?" She held onto the edge of the tub, and turned the faucet handles, sloshing and spilling more water out onto the floor as she did. "I've nearly flooded my bathroom." Sitting down on the stool, Irene sighed. Her memory wasn't getting any better. Soon she'd forget something worse than the bath water. She shivered to think about how many things she might already be forgetting, without even realizing it.

It seemed as though Kathleen's daughter had so many events relating to her upcoming marriage. She was sure Kathleen had told her there was a bridal shower each week until Taylor's wedding. How many bridal showers did one bride need? She'd been blessed to have just one, given by her mother. Wait. Had Kathleen told her which day was the wedding? She'd have to remember to ask next time she visited.

Irene undressed, and slipped into the tub, causing more water to spill onto the bathroom floor. Exasperated, she flipped the stopper down to allow the water to descend to a more appropriate level, then flipped it back up. She lay back and let the warmth penetrate her tired bones.

Closing her eyes, she thought about the timer. She wished she could remember why she'd set it. Surely her memory wasn't any worse than every other elderly woman her age. Was it? Her thoughts drifted to the horrible days she spent watching her once-active mother turn into a walking zombie--ugly, foreboding memories that she thought she'd been able to erase. Her eyes popped open. Was she becoming like her mother?

For ten years, Irene put her life on hold while she cared for her mother. She went from being an active member of the community almost into obscurity while her sister, Louise, lived an active life in Florida and refused to come back to Michigan to help. That decision so strained their relationship that now, almost twenty years later, she still held hard feelings. They rarely visited each other or even spoke on the phone.

Kathleen had been in college, then newly married, during that time. Caregiving prevented Irene from helping with and planning Kathleen's wedding, but her mother never even knew how much she gave up. When she buried her mother, with her sister by her side, she made a vow. Right there, standing next to their mother's grave at daybreak, she made Louise promise, too. She would never ruin the life of her child like her mother did to her. It wasn't fair.

She dipped her head under the water and felt the water soak into her hair. She'd wash it today, because she couldn't remember if she'd done it the day before. She sat up, put a dab of shampoo in the palm of her hand, and started scrubbing her hair. Soap dripped down into her ears and her eyes. It was too sudsy. It didn't quite smell like shampoo either. She wiped her eyes with a washcloth, then picked up the bottle and looked at it. She'd put body wash in her hair instead of shampoo.

Time stood still. Tears formed in her eyes, not from the stinging soap, but from the fear rising within her heart. Soon she'd probably be using the shaving cream in her hair, or even some kind of tile cleaner. Her life was no longer her own. It was her malfunctioning brain taking control. The misfires, the forgetfulness... it was just like her mother. Edna was right. She couldn't stay by herself much longer.

She got out of the bathtub and wiped her body with a fresh, laundered towel. She patted her face dry and looked into the mirror at her wrinkled cheeks, bloodshot eyes, and her matted, dull, gray hair.

She found her robe on the back of the bathroom door and, wrapped it around herself. She needed to call Louise. Despite their differences, she needed her sister's help. Is that what she wanted? Did she even have a choice now? The thought sent fear through her heart. Could they possibly set apart their differences and live together? Worse yet, what if Louise refused?

Irene grasped the doorknob. It stopped before opening the door. She turned it the other way. The same thing happened. She jiggled the knob back and forth. The door didn't open. Trying not to panic, Irene leaned her cane against the closet door beside her and tried the knob again with both hands. The door refused to open. She felt her heart beat faster, harder. She started to hyperventilate as perspiration broke out on her forehead. After fiddling with the door for a few minutes. Irene grew tired. She was locked in her own bathroom. She couldn't get out.

Chapter 4

Kathleen kissed Brian on his red, cold face as he entered the back door, "I'm so glad you are finally home."

Brian took off his gloves and slapped them together, putting snow all over the kitchen rug. "It's miserable out there. So cold. Cars were in ditches all around town this morning. I'm glad to be home. Tell me again why we live here?"

Kathleen took her husband's coat and shook it over the back door rug. "Get your wet things off. I have dinner ready."

Brian made his way to the stove and held out his hands over the burners cooking his dinner. "Oh that feels good. I think temps are down as well. The roads are sheets of ice under the snow cover."

"Sit down and I'll get you a plate. And, while we are on the subject, we live here cause it's close to my mother."

"Speaking of her, have you talked to her today?"

"Yes, as I do every single day." Kathleen scooped a bit of chili in a bowl for her husband and added a piece of cornbread to a plate placed under it.

"Talked to Roger today."

Brian picked up the mail bundle and shuffled through it.

"Roger? Fire Chief Roger? How is their daughter? I know she's been sick since Christmas."

"We never got around to talking about Jennifer. He wanted to know how mother was."

"Mother? " Kathleen took another bowl out of the cupboard. "That was nice of him."

"He asked about the smoke damage in her kitchen."

Kathleen stopped putting chili into her bowl, "Smoke damage?"

Brian sat down and moved his bowl closer. "I guess Violet called them the other day because your mother left an empty tea kettle on the stove and forgot to turn the burner off."

Kathleen sat down with her half bowl of chili. "What?"

Brian nodded. "Yup. I think we need to talk to her about it. Roger said she begged him not to mention this to you.

"Are you kidding?"

Brian ate a bite of his dinner. "We knew this day would be coming."

"How are we gonna manage this whole dementia thing? Your job is taking all your time. My job has been insane with evening home showings and such. The wedding is this summer and..."

Brian nodded. "I know what kind of life we lead, Kathleen. Going to most of Jade's games, Taylor's wedding. There isn't much time for us, let alone your mother."

"Perhaps I should quit my job."

"You don't want to do that. You have a clientele now. Returning customers. No. We need the income. Retirement is looming."

Kathleen shook her head and began eating her chili. "We have to have other options."

"We could hire someone." Brian reached for another piece of cornbread.

"Yeah. I suppose, but that could get expensive. Mother would have to sell her house." Kathleen gazed out the dining room window at the snow falling hard outside. "She could move in with us."

"What about Max?" Brian shivered. "I get itchy by just saying his name."

"He can't come here. You'd sneeze continually." Kathleen sipped her tea.

"Does anyone at church need a home? Someone who could live with her, be her companion?"

"Unfortunately, they all have issues with taking care of themselves. Ida is starting to have her own memory lapses, and Florence is diabetic. Mother would never have the right food in her house and she can get so snippy from time to time."

"Maybe you could put an ad in the newspaper."

"Brian, no stranger is going to live with my mother. It would upset her if they didn't believe as she does."

"Yeah, in this day and age, I would agree." The wind howled, rattling the kitchen door. "It's getting colder out there. Tomorrow they're predicting even fiercer winds."

"There is one thing I have been thinking of."

Brian sipped his coffee and glanced at his wife, "Well, let's hear it."

"Aunt Louise."

Brian set down his cup and roared, "Louise? Are you crazy? They'd kill each other. Literally. And when was the last time you heard from that floozy?"

"Brian!"

"Well, it's the truth. She's probably too busy sleeping with all the wealthy, elderly men in Florida to care about her sister. When's the last time she called Mom?"

"She got a Christmas card from her."

"I mean audible speaking. Like a phone call."

Kathleen shrugged her shoulders. "What's the alternative?"

Brian shook his head. "The only other thing would be to put her in a home."

"She could never afford that. Not without selling the house." Kathleen's bowl now empty, she stood to get a little more for herself out of the pot on the stove. "I can't do that to Mom. Probably in the future it will be inevitable, but not now. She's still pretty cognitive. And what about Max. She'd have to find him a new home."

"If she stayed home, she could keep Max."

Kathleen nodded as she came back to the table. "Maybe I'll call Louise tomorrow. Who knows? Maybe she'll understand and want to help us out. Help out her sister."

"Possibly. When Florida freezes over."

As Brian got up to get something from the counter, his phone rang. "I'll be right back," he called and left the kitchen. Kathleen could hear him talking in the other room, but he was too far away to understand. Must be someone from work.

While finishing her dinner, Kathleen thought about her mother and aunt living together. Shaking her head, she knew her husband was right. Something drastic had to happen before that could even be a possibility. And her mother would never give up Max. They'd been companions for years.

35

Kathleen loved her mother. She wanted only the best for her. Did it mean she needed to do the same for her, as she'd done for her grandmother? Taylor would be married in the summer. She wanted to be a major part of those plans and to be there for her. Houses were selling again in Michigan, and she wanted in on the new sales team. Was it wrong to want her own life, take care of her own responsibilities. Guilt began to seep into her soul.

Brian entered the kitchen, still talking on his cell phone. "I understand. No, don't worry, we appreciate the phone call. Thanks for calling, Violet. Yes. Of course, we'll call you when we find her. Uh, huh. Goodbye." Brian turned to his wife. "That was Violet. I think we need to head over to Mother's house."

"Why?"

"Violet hasn't seen any lights on at your mom's."

"Maybe she's napping in the living room."

"I don't know," Brian set his phone down on the countertop. "Violet appeared fairly upset. She said Greg went over and knocked on the door, but Mom didn't come to the door."

Kathleen knew that was odd. Mom always answered the door. "Is she sure she's home."

"Said she never left. Violet would know. That woman is always on the lookout for your Mom's welfare."

Kathleen nodded. "We better head over there."

They both looked out the kitchen window to the scene of swirling snow and shook their heads.

"All I wanted to do tonight was put my feet up and watch that basketball game I recorded." Brian said.

"Well, why don't you? I can check on Mom." Kathleen stood up and washed out her chili bowl.

"No. The weather's too awful. I'll drive you."

As the couple grabbed their coats and bundled up, Kathleen had only one thought: Perhaps she wouldn't have any choice. Sick parents, children marrying, and a housing market didn't wait for a perfect time. Life happened. She looked up at Brian, now grabbing his cell phone and handed him her keys. "Let's take my car. It does better in the snow."

Chapter 5

Violet was right. Mom's house was totally dark. Not even a reading light in the living room shown from the windows as they pulled into the driveway. She knew that was unusual. Her mother could be in the bathroom, which didn't have a window, but it was still odd to not see even a kitchen light on over the stove. She rarely turned that off.

Brian stopped the car and turned it off. "Maybe she isn't home."

"Brian," Kathleen pulled on her mittens again to head outside, "She rarely leaves the house this late. It's almost eight."

"Do you have the key?"

"It's that one." Kathleen pointed to the key chain in his hand. "The long one."

Brian nodded. "Let me get the door open and then you can come in. No sense both of us freezing."

Kathleen agreed. The wind had to be blowing at below zero. It hurt her face to be out in it. She watched Brian go onto the back porch, remove his glove, and unlock the door. He motioned for her to come.

The wind hit her so hard as she got out the SUV, it nearly knocked her to her knees in the driveway. Her head hurt from the blast of cold as a gust of wind swirled around the side of the house. She could hear Brian calling for her mother through the wind as she approached the doorway.

"Irene? Mom?" He called into the house as he held the door open for Kathleen.

She got into the kitchen as Max met them at the door. He meowed a greeting, but didn't stop. He was agitated about something. Kathleen called. "Mother?" No answer. She tried louder, "Mom?"

Brian stomped snow off his boots by the back door. "I don't think she's here."

That's when they heard her. It was a weak call, but it was her mother. Kathleen rushed toward the sound, calling again as she went. "Mom?"

A weak, but audible voice answered, "Kathleen." It sounded as if her mother were crying. "Where are you?"

Brian followed close behind and pushed past Kathleen, "I think she's in the bathroom." He tried the doorknob. "Mom?"

"Brian. Is that you?"

He looked back at Kathleen. "It's locked."

"It's us, Mom. What's wrong? Unlock the door."

"I can't. It won't open."

Brian shook his head. "Blasted door." He turned the knob harder and put his weight against the door.

"I was in here taking a bath and the door locked. I can't get out."

"How long have you been in there?"

"I don't know, Kathleen. But I'm tired and hungry. Get me out, Brian."

Brian continued to lean into the door and monkey with the knob. It wouldn't budge.

"Can you break it down?"

Brian looked at her over his foggy glasses, "Right, Kathleen. I'm just a bean counter, not a body builder."

"Mom, do you have a key to this door?"

"I don't think we've ever had a key to this door, Kathleen."

Brian stood back and folded his arms. "I may have to take it off the hinges. I'll go out to the garage to find the tools." He began putting his gloves back on. "Tell her I'll be right back."

As Brian left, Kathleen moved closer to the door. "Mom. Did you lock yourself in there?"

"I don't think so Kathleen. How would I know?"

"You know the lock switch. You have to push it one way or the other to unlock or lock the door. Remember?"

Kathleen saw the knob move, then she heard a click. She grabbed the knob, turned it and the door opened. Her mother was on the other side, tears streaming down her face. "Oh Mom. It's okay." She took her mother into her arms and hugged her. "It's okay. Come over here and sit down."

As she put her mother in a living room chair, Brian returned, covered in snow, shivering, with tools in hand. He looked from Kathleen to her mother. "How'd you?"

Kathleen knelt by the chair. She picked up a blanket and covered her mother with it to calm her shivering. "Are you okay now?"

"I've been locked in a bathroom for hours. No. I'm not okay."

Kathleen reached for the tissues and pulled one from the box. "Here, wipe your tears. It's okay. We're here. It's over."

Brian gently set the tools down by the opened door, removed his gloves and perched his foggy glasses on the end of his nose. "How'd you get her out of there?"

"She unlocked the door." Kathleen smiled at Brian. "That door has always had a touchy lock. It locks by itself, but usually..." She eyed her mother blowing her nose and wiping her face, "...we've been able to get out by just unlocking the door."

"I tried, Kathleen." Her mother blew her nose again.

"I know, it's touchy."

Brian sat down in a dining room chair and sighed. Kathleen looked over at him and mouthed an apology. He shook his head and smiled. "She's okay now?"

She rubbed her mother's leg. "She'll be fine. In a minute," she said, even though, deep in her soul, Kathleen knew she wasn't okay. It was time to make a decision regarding her mother's care.

"I've wasted your time today." Louise looked over at Howard in the driver's seat. "I'm sorry."

Howard took her hand. "You aren't a waste of my time. I told you, I have enjoyed every single moment with you. You are attractive and sexy. A little stubborn, but then, that's good for us old people. Sometimes it's all we have left."

"That's the truth." Louise squeezed Howard's hand. She'd told him about her congestive heart failure. She didn't have to hide her hands from him anymore.

"You're right there, dear."

41

"What will you do now?"

Louise shrugged. "I don't know. I really don't. I can't afford any of these monthly fees. Even if I sell my house, that would only keep me one or two years in a home. If I can stay home for a few more years, it might come down to that, but right now…"

Howard nodded. "I understand. Keeping Dorothy in a home has sucked me dry. I need to stay as healthy as possible or my poor kids will have to pay for my care, too."

Louise started to open the car door but before she did she leaned over the seat and kissed Howard on the cheek. "You're a doll. I'm sorry your wife is sick. You're an amazing man."

Tears formed at the edges of his eyes. "You're a dear. Thank you."

Howard nodded as Louise got out of the car and slammed the door behind her. She laughed as he backed out of her driveway and sped down the road. The old man was a daredevil driver, yet that was one of the things she liked about him. He wasn't afraid to take chances.

Once inside, Louise turned up the thermostat on the air conditioner. Her condo was cold. She set her purse on the table, opened the sliding glass door, and went out on the porch. She lay down on a lounge chair and closed her eyes. She should make herself some lunch, but she wasn't hungry. Anyway, fixing herself something to eat had become such a chore. She often became exhausted just opening a can. The new medicine, that the doctor assured would help her, just made her sleepy.

A seagull squawked over her head, swooping down for nibbles of food from the sandy grass of her yard. Sometimes their brazen calls were just downright impudent. The Florida afternoon sun warmed her. Maybe she could just take a little nap. Sleep helped her escape life and her problems, just for a little while. Sometimes, though, trying to relax, striving to breathe comfortably, was even harder than moving around.

A musical ringtone erupted from her kitchen. She opened one eye and tried to decide whether to ignore her phone or get out of her comfortable position. Perhaps it was Howard again. She didn't want him to think her rude, so she shifted to rise up from the lounge chair. The music continued to play as she made her way back to the kitchen and picked up her phone. A bit breathless, she answered. "Hello."

"Hello Aunt Louise?"

Louise's heart sank, as she recognized her niece's voice. "Yes, hello."

"It's Kathleen, Aunt Louise. Did I catch you at a bad time?"

"No. No, dear." Thoughts of her sister flooded her mind. When had they last talked? Did she forget a Christmas card? Was she ill? "How are you?"

"I'm fine. How are you?"

Should she tell her? Lay it all out on the table? Louise sat down. "Well, okay." Her breathing came in staggers. She hoped Kathleen wouldn't notice. "Is Irene okay?" Did she have the right to ask? Really, did she even care?

"Well, that's what I'm calling about."

"What's wrong?" Louise closed her eyes, fearing the worst.

"Oh nothing really. Old age. She's been having some memory issues."

43

Louise sighed. *"Memory issues?"* That single word thrust her back to her mother's graveside, brought fear into her heart. She did love Irene. They'd been mostly peaceable, up until the argument a few years ago. "How bad?"

"The doctor predicted it would get worse and it is."

Louise thought of Howard's wife. "So, she's been diagnosed with it?" She asked, still struggling for breath, "You know, dementia?"

"Yes. Like your mom."

Louise refocused. "How bad is it now?" She was certain Kathleen knew nothing about the promise she made to Irene, at their mother's grave. Irene had sworn her to secrecy.

"Louise, she needs someone to be with her. Stay with her. Help her remember to turn off the stove or get back and forth to the grocery store."

"Can you hire someone?" Louise pretended as if there was an alternative, but she knew in her heart, there was only one thing to do. She'd made a promise. The realization brought with it sadness for Irene, but also a possibility for herself.

After a long pause, Kathleen said, "Yes. But we thought maybe you could think about coming back to Michigan. For a short time. Brian and I are so busy with our jobs and Taylor is getting married this summer."

"She is? How wonderful!"

"The wedding is coming quickly. I want to be there for her. If you could just stay through the wedding, then maybe we could find an alternative solution."

"Of course, dear. I understand." She understood almost too clearly. Louise concentrated as carefully as she could. If she could keep Kathleen thinking this was her idea, things might go better. "But, I think you've forgotten one thing, my dear."

"I know. I know. You two don't get along very well."

Louise mumbled, "That's an understatement." Silence permeated the phone line. Louise had to stop herself from thinking out loud.

"I'm sorry, Aunt Louise. If there was another option right now, I'd have made it. I just can't see having a stranger come into the house. I guess..."

"What?"

"I thought perhaps you'd put your differences aside to help your sister."

Louise knew this was it. This one way she could make up the past to Irene. They could finish their lives well. Together. She'd always felt guilty for leaving Irene with all the care of their mother. She realized not only what she might be turning down, but also her obligation. She'd promised.

"Kathleen. I need to think about it. I love Florida. You know that."

"I know."

"Give me a few days."

"Okay."

"I'll call you back."

"Okay, thanks Aunt..."

Louise ended the call, and put her face into her hands. She wasn't certain she and her sister could put their differences aside. One thing was for sure, this would help her as well as Irene.

If she didn't know better, she'd have thought God somehow planned it all. Why would He do anything like that for her? She'd had fun nearly all her life. Lived life to the fullest. She had been selfish. Perhaps it was time to put someone else, before herself, for once.

She left the kitchen and headed back to her warm chair on the porch. The afternoon sun hovered over that side of the condo. She relaxed now.

Their argument had been a silly one. Irene had been doing her usual thing of trying to convince Louise to 'stop living without God.' She'd never been good enough for Irene. Irene saw life through those religious blinders, but Louise looked at life logically, and at times, philosophically. She'd told Irene that she believed there's more things in life than God. What started out as a discussion, had ended in a full-blown fight. When Irene wouldn't let up, Louise had told her to mind her own business. And in her typical way, her sister continued beating her over the head with Bible verses.

Half-jokingly, Louise said Irene had never been free enough to let alcohol soothe her soul, or a man's touch thrill her with a late-night escapade. She'd only said it to make Irene madder. It worked.

For some reason, Louise loved playing make-believe with her sister. Pretending her life was just like Irene imagined made her laugh. She drank wine, and even whiskey from time to time, but she didn't jump into bed with every man who came along. Most were not worth her time. She'd rather sit at home and read the latest best-seller or walk the beach at dusk .

That is, until Howard came along. She could truly see herself becoming closer to him. She'd imagined them growing old-well, older-together, walking the beach and staying home watching movies late into the night.

Until he'd told her the truth. She'd had her future all planned out again only to have it dashed on the rocks like the late night-breakers after a storm.

Now it came right down to her pact with Irene, made at their mother's graveside that dreadful day. Would Irene forgive her? Give her another chance? She wasn't sure, but at that moment before she drifted off to sleep, she decided she'd go to her sister. It was the least she could do for her, after all the grief she'd been to her down through the years. She hoped Irene would accept her help. Perhaps then, she could convince her to change her mind.

The next morning Louise dialed Howard's number. When he answered she spoke just a few words, but then asked, "Howard, I need a few favors. Could we meet this morning?"

Howard met her at the coffee shop and agreed to all the issues she had left to settle in Florida. He would help her with a garage sale, be the liaison in helping her sell her house.

"You're a doll."

Howard reached for her hands again. "I know you'd do the same for me."

Louise leaned back in her chair. "You know, my sister and I are opposites. She thinks everything can be solved with a prayer and a Bible verse."

"Oh my. She is wicked."

"It's worse. She has a cat. I hate cats."

"Well now, little Louise, I happen to love cats."

"Oh my. Good thing you're a married man." Louise folded her arms and looked out at the beach. "I'm gonna miss the beach so much. I hate Michigan. I hate the winters. All that white stuff piling up in mountains all around your house. Winter days are cloudy and the sun rarely shines. I'll have to sit in a chair in the living room and never leave the room until June first and then my tan will diminish and I'll turn to a pale, death-like color."

"You could go to a tanning place." Howard sipped his coffee.

Louise nodded. "I could." She leaned in close. Do you think they get naked on those tanning beds?"

"Maybe." Howard giggled.

"Sounds sexy, doesn't it?"

Howard roared. "Oh how I will miss these conversations."

"I have one more request."

"What's that, my dear."

"Let's have sex before I go."

Louise watched her friend's face pale.

"Are you serious?"

Louise then laughed. "No. I think I'd give you a heart attack anyway. And then who'd take care of my condo?"

Howard laughed again. "You are quite the lady, Louise. I haven't had sex in years. It is quite a tempting idea."

Louise winked at him.

"But I can't. My wife is a blubbering idiot in a home many, many miles away from here, but I promised her. For a lifetime." Howard lowered his head.

Louise picked up his hand and shook it. "You are perfect. She is one lucky woman."

Howard squeezed her hand. "No. She could do better. A husband like the one on that Nicholas Sparks' movie...What's that title?

Louise giggled, "*Moment in time...*No. *A Life to Remember.*"

They both laughed then.

"I should be with her. All the time. Yet for now, that's all I can give her. She has no dignity left, but she does have my faithfulness."

Louise again looked out at the blue ocean water. "I wish we could take a walk. We won't have many more times we can do that."

"We can walk slow and not very far. Let's go."

The waves foamed over Louise's feet as she and Howard walked on the beach. He had never held her hand as they walked, always keeping his hands deep in his pockets. She now knew the real reason.

Pulling her sweater closer over her shoulders, Howard asked, "Are you okay? Warm enough?"

She nodded. If she brought up the subject to Howard, how would he respond? He knew the heartache of dementia first hand.

"Howard, can I ask you a question?"

He put his head back and laughed. "I'm not sure I'm ready for another life altering question, but what now?"

"No, I'm serious this time."

"Okay."

"My sister and I went through some horrible things when my mother died. She had dementia just like your wife."

"Bad?"

"Yes. She was always afraid. Always skeptical of what we were doing for her care. Much like your wife, her personality changed so much."

Howard nodded.

49

"We decided we never wanted someone we love to have to go through it again. So we made an agreement."

"An agreement?"

Louise nodded and pulled her sweater closer around her. "If it were to happen to us."

"What's the agreement?"

Louise remembered the pact. The *entire* pact. "You know, I promised I wouldn't tell a single soul about it. I'm not much of a person, Howard. I'm not proud of many of the things I've done in my life, but your dedication to your wife has taught me one thing."

Howard reached out for her hand for the first time. "What?"

"To be faithful."

Howard smiled, but let go of her hand as they stood on the beach looking at each other.

"But I just wanted you to know. If you rarely hear from me after I move to Michigan, I need you to know. It won't change my friendship with you. Okay?"

Howard smiled, "Okay."

They continued on their walk. Louise knew she'd almost given away the pact's most important rule. No one was to know. No one. She just thought if she could lay out the plan to Howard, he'd tell her it was a horrible one. To forget about it. But one thing she knew about her sister. She'd never forget. She'd want to go through with it, no matter what. She was the one with a daughter, after all, not Louise.

###

50

It was past ten o'clock on Tuesday when Kathleen's phone rang. It was Aunt Louise.

"Can you pick me up at Detroit Metro next Thursday afternoon at two o'clock?"

"Well, hello, Aunt Louise. I think I can."

"Good. Don't be late. I'll be coming in on Delta."

"Okay."

"Thanks." *Click.*

"Oh my word!" Kathleen put down her phone. "The nerve of that woman."

Brian sat up in bed and propped up his pillow. "Who was that?"

"Aunt Louise."

"What'd she want?"

"She's coming."

"Here?"

"Yes, here. Next Thursday. I have to pick her up at the airport."

Brian leaned back on his pillow. "Oh no." He laid his book down on the side table. "What now?"

"Well, our problem is solved, but I gotta tell Mom."

"She's gonna kill you."

"Thanks," Kathleen got up from her side of the bed and went to the window. She folded her arms and sighed. "We had no other option."

"It'll be okay." Brian tried to sound confident.

"No it won't. They'll kill each other."

"No. They're too old for that."

Kathleen was quiet. She didn't quite know what to say. She feared calling her mother and telling her who was moving in. She had a little over a week to break the news.

"But, a civil war could break out."

Kathleen nodded. "Civil war. That's it. The South meeting the North. The North has no clue it's coming."

"The battle of Phillipi."

"Where was that?"

"Virginia."

"It'll make history, that's for sure."

Chapter 6

Kathleen deposited her purse and a small bag of groceries onto the kitchen table as Brian called from upstairs. "Kathleen!"

Kathleen called up. "What do you need?"

Where are all my white shirts? I need one for my presentation in the morning."

"Oh Brian. Can't you wear a different color tomorrow?"

"It's important. Last week the boss told me that white is the only option for this client. He's older and insists that accountants have only white shirts to look professional."

"They're all in the wash. I'll run a load."

"Can you iron it tonight?"

Kathleen groaned. "Of course, but I also have a house showing. I'll see what I can do." It was Tuesday. She had spent the week showing houses late into the evening, editing a work speech for Brian, and she had yet to tell her mother about her upcoming 'visitor.'

As she headed for the laundry room, the phone rang. She answered with a winded voice. "Hello."

"Mom. I need you. This veil doesn't look like the one I picked out, but I ordered it such a long time ago, I'm just not sure. Can you come to the bridal shop?"

"Right now?"

"I'm sorry. You probably just got home from work, but if you could…?"

Kathleen looked up at the clock. "Okay, sweetheart. I'll be there in five."

"Thanks, Mom."

She picked up her purse again and headed back out the door. Maybe she could visit her Mother after dinner tomorrow.

The next day, Kathleen trudged through work, thinking of the conversation she'd have to have with her mother that evening. Her friend, Ruby, approached and asked about her day.

"Do you really want to know?"

Ruby entered her cubicle and took a chair by the desk. "What's up?"

"My mother. I have to go to her house tonight and talk about my aunt coming to live with her."

"Well, that will be nice. I'm sure she will appreciate that after her bathroom episode."

"No. She won't."

Ruby stopped. "Why not?"

"Her sister and her get along like water and oil. The wicked witch and fairy godmother. Cinderella and her step-sisters."

"Ugh. Really?"

"Yeah. And tonight I gotta go tell my mother who her new roommate will be."

"Pity you." Ruby rose to leave.

"I'll trade you the lake house for the double wide on the west side if you go tell her."

"No chance. But, that's a great lot."

"Exactly." Kathleen turned back to her computer. She'd give away her firstborn to get out of this task.

Checking her calendar, she saw she'd made appointments for every night that week. None could be cancelled. But somehow, it was easier to work than to go face to face with General Grant.

A knock startled Irene out of her thoughts. She looked up to see Violet standing at the back door. Picking up her cane, Irene made her way to the door.

"Irene, dear. I made you some cookies." Violet held out the plate.

Irene loved cookies. "Oh Violet, they smell wonderful. Come in, come in. I'll make you a cup of tea."

Violet came in and sat down at the table. "Looked like you were deep in thought."

Gathering up a tea a bag, and spoon, Irene set it down in front of her friend. "Well, many things going through my head today."

"Can you share?" Violet took her tea cup, ripped off the paper, and put it in her cup before Irene poured in the hot water.

Irene sat down. "I was thinking back to when my mother was sick."

Violet scowled, "That was such a hard time. I remember how you gave up nearly everything for your mother."

Irene nodded. "That's what's bothering me."

"How so?"

Irene knew she could trust Violet. Violet was a quiet, sincere woman. She'd never tell a soul about the pact, if Irene revealed it to her. Irene looked into the sweet, kind eyes of her dear neighbor, pondering whether to tell her. Maybe just the minor points. "My sister and I..."

Violet met her eyes over the table. She knew then that she couldn't reveal it. Not even to Violet. If she did, the whole pact would unravel. For the first time in years, Irene doubted whether or not their graveside promise was a good thing. "I think Louise and I might have to make up for some of our issues as of late."

"Making up is always a good thing. Sisters need each other."

Irene nodded. She knew that, but Violet really didn't know her sister.

"I think she might come and stay with me, if I ask her."

Violet smiled. "Irene, that's wonderful."

Irene shook her head, "I'm not so sure. You see, she's pretty..."

"Pretty what?"

"Contrary. To how you and I believe."

"Well good. We'll convince her otherwise." Violet nodded. "Oh my. Irene that's wonderful that you have a sister who will come and be with you right now."

"You know," Irene added, "I think I might be having memory issues."

Violet smiled, "Irene, I know."

"You do?" Irene sat back in her chair and looked at her friend.

"Of course."

"Did Kathleen tell you?"

"No," Violet patted Irene's hand, "It wasn't hard to figure out. We've just been keeping a more vigilant eye on you, Greg and I."

Irene was certain that Edna had spilled the beans. But what difference did it make? Soon everyone would know.

"So your sister could help you. Greg and I watch, but it's much better to have someone with you in your home. What if I'd gone to bed the other night and not called Kathleen when your lights didn't come on? You'd still be in your bathroom."

Irene nodded. She wondered what bathroom episode Violet was referring to. "I know my sister could help me. But she's quite different than I am. I'm sure she will do things, just to embarrass me."

Violet shrugged. "I do things all the time to embarrass myself. I think having your sister here to help you and protect you, is a good thing. You need to thank God for her."

Irene knew her friend had great faith. Violet always pointed her in the right direction.

"It will be fine. We'll all welcome her here. With open arms. Right?"

Irene thought and then nodded, "Yes."

"And maybe, just maybe, we can be a witness to her. It's never too late to share your love of God with others, is it, Irene?"

Irene methodically nodded. But Violet didn't know her sister.

Chapter 7

Irene held up the mittens for size. The local shelter recently publicized the need for warm accessories for some of their residents, and İrene had set to work with her knitting needles. She'd knitted for years. It helped her to be busy doing things for others. Loving them through her needles.

She studied her next stitch. She froze with her knitting needles in her hands. Frustration bubbled as she couldn't figure it out. In her lifetime, Irene had made hundreds, if not thousands, of mittens for the homeless shelter, for the children in the neighborhood, for the city mission, and for her grandchildren. Why was she finding it almost impossible to knit?

The clock on the mantle chimed five o'clock. Irene set down the half knitted mittens and grabbed for her cane. She wasn't quite sure what she'd have for dinner, but she'd find something. Dinner sounded better than making her mind figure out the next twist of her needles.

Shuffling into the kitchen, Irene stopped to look at herself in the mirror. She tucked a stray gray hair behind her ear. She'd never gotten around to making that hair cutting appointment. The weather of these past few weeks kept her at home. She'd venture outside more, come April. The birds were returning, despite the lingering cold of winter. She heard new chirping birds each morning.

Gazing into the refrigerator, she wondered how much longer she could go without heading out to the grocer. Last time she went to the grocery store, she was pretty sure someone stole her car and moved it to the other side of the parking lot. Why would someone do that to her? She pulled out plastic containers, but couldn't find anything very appealing. She closed the refrigerator and opened the pantry. She'd made due with leftovers the night before. Maybe soup would work for tonight. As she reached into her pantry for a can of potato soup, the doorbell rang, followed by a knock. Kathleen usually made that kind of greeting, but she always used the kitchen door.

Puzzled, Irene shuffled out of the kitchen just as the front door swung open. Kathleen stood at the door with a suitcase and a nicely dressed older woman. Irene stopped in her tracks, still holding the can of soup, and gazed at her guest.

"Look at you!" her sister smiled and held out her arms. "Miss me?"

Irene looked at her sister, then her daughter. Kathleen was too busy putting down the suitcase and taking off her scarf and hat to look up. Irene was pretty sure this would prove beneficial to Kathleen.

"Well, come here. I need a hug, I'm nearly frozen to death." Louise looked skinny, but still all tan and smiles.

Irene shuffled toward her and held out her left arm. "What are you doing here?"

As they produced an adequate hug, her sister announced. "I'm here for a visit."

"In March?"

Louise shrugged. "It's almost April, Florida's getting hot."

Irene stepped back and again tried to make eye contact with her daughter who now looked up and over her foggy, glass lenses. Irene gave her the look that only a mother could when her child misbehaved. Kathleen looked down at the floor and patted her Aunt Louise on the back.

"Come in, Aunt Louise. I bet Mom has dinner on."

Irene couldn't believe her ears. Not only had the visit been a total surprise, but now her daughter expected dinner on the table. Irene turned away from the pair and shuffled into the kitchen before they could see what she was holding in her hand. She set the can on the counter and, she turned to her guests. They were whispering.

"She knows me, right?" She heard Louise ask. Kathleen nodded.

"The house looks marvelous, Irene." Her sister assessed, looking around. "Hmmm, always so clean."

"Let me take your coat." As Kathleen performed formalities at the door Irene sorted through what she could produce for dinner, other than popcorn in the microwave. The world would have to come to an end before she would serve half a can of potato soup to a guest, especially her sister.

She opened the fridge again. If only she hadn't cleaned it out last night. "Have you eaten?"

"Not since lunch at the airport."

Kathleen must have finally sensed her mother's agitation with the dinner comment, because she said, "Don't worry, Mom. Brian's coming soon. He can bring dinner."

Irene felt her shoulders slump. She could finally breathe a little easier and turned to her two unexpected guests. "Really, what are we having?"

"Umm, chicken," announced Kathleen as she made her way into the kitchen. "How's Kentucky Fried sound?"

60

"Greasy!" Louise went to a chair and pulled it out to take a seat.

"Well." Irene turned to her daughter, who she now envisioned putting into a barrel and sending over Niagara Falls. She quickly brought out her Sunday morning personality. "That will be nice. When will he arrive?"

"I'll check with him about his late meeting. I'll be right back." Kathleen grabbed her phone out of her purse. "You two get reacquainted while I make the call."

"If we're gonna do the Kentucky chicken thing, order me the grilled kind," Louise yelled after Kathleen. "I can pull the skins off myself."

Irene knew well and good that her daughter hadn't planned on having Brian bring dinner. It was her way of appeasing her mother for dropping by, not only at dinner time, with a guest, but worst of all, with her sister. She looked at her sister and did her best to plaster on a fake smile, the kind she always gave Matilda, the town gossip.

Her sister seemed to shiver at the table. Her hands were shaking in a miserable way. Even worse, they were horribly swollen. Irene had forgotten her manners completely with the arrival of the sister she hadn't even talked to since. She had no clue when. "Um, would you like some tea?"

"Got anything stronger?" Her sister grabbed at her hands, which looked almost purple compared to her suntanned arms.

Irene knew the comment was a dig about her lifestyle, but she wasn't about to let her sister rile her. "Coffee."

"Yes, that would be fine," Louise sighed. "Make it black. As black as you can."

Irene saw her sister eye her cat at the far end of the room. Max slinked closer to her sister's legs, tucked under the table.

"Okay," Irene made her way to the counter. "So, what brings you on a visit? In the middle of winter?" Perhaps keeping Louise in a conversation would distract her from Max.

Louise coughed. "It isn't the middle of winter. It's nearly spring."

Irene took down the instant coffee jar from the cupboard.

"Don't you have the real thing?" Louise asked.

Irene turned and leaned against the counter. "No. You know I don't drink coffee. I just keep this on hand for the kids. Brian likes coffee."

"Well, make a big pot. I'm gonna need it." Just then Irene saw her sister look under the table and eye Max. "There you are, cat!"

"I can only make one cup at a time with instant. You know that." Irene sighed again. Her angry tone wasn't going to be the best way to begin this visit. She turned to the sink, filled the tea kettle, placed it on the stove, and turned on the heat. Moving to the table, she pulled out a chair, sat down, and eyed her sister. "No really. This is a complete surprise. What in the world are you doing?"

Louise seemed distracted by Max. Irene hoped the water heated quickly. She needed to stay at the table and protect the cat.

"Are you in trouble?"

Louise turned back to her. "I think we are bit past the age of getting into trouble, don't you think?"

"Not that kind of trouble." Irene began to wring her hands. They were past their ages to 'get into trouble,' but she was just unsure of this visit. Her sister's visits were usually heralded months in advance. By phone call after phone call to prepare each other to be together for a few weeks. And it was never in the middle of winter. Never. "Are you broke?"

"No." A burning look welled up in Louise's eyes. "I am not broke."

"Then?" Irene deserved an answer. Even though the visit was something she knew probably would happen soon anyway, she was shocked it happened today. In winter.

Louise looked up from the table and into her sister's eyes, "Can't I come and visit my sister? We can talk about it later." She motioned a finger toward Kathleen in the dining room making a phone call.

Irene nodded. "You are...always welcome in my home." Now that was a good answer. More godly. More sincere. She felt a bit of her angry spirit subside, murmuring a silent 'help' message to the Almighty.

Kathleen burst into the kitchen. "Brian said he can be here by six. Is that soon enough for you ladies or do you want me to head out and get something sooner?"

The sisters did not look away from one another. Irene knew her sister too well. Was this really a surprise visit, or was it something that had been planned? Had Kathleen told her about it? She'd never forget someone telling her of Louise planning to visit. Would she?

Louise answered, "Six is fine. Thank you. As soon as I get some coffee into me, I'll feel better."

Kathleen pulled three mugs out of the cupboard. "What're you fixing, Mom?"

"Hot water for coffee." Irene turned to her daughter, "Tea for me, though."

"Coming right up." Kathleen added a teabag to one mug and spoonfuls of instant coffee into the other two.

"Do you drink the hard stuff now, Kathleen?" Louise laughed. Irene studied her sister. She knew why she was laughing and it wasn't funny.

63

"I tried to buy mother a Keurig for Christmas, but she has never liked coffee. It would have been more for Brian and me than her." Kathleen took off the whistling tea kettle off the stove and poured hot water into the mugs. "So, what brings you to Michigan, Aunt Louise. In the winter?"

Irene glanced at her daughter. She must be in the dark about this whole visit herself. She nodded to her sister.

Louise stirred her coffee and tried to take a sip, but lowered it. "Ouch! Too hot."

"Sorry, that's what happens when you boil water." Irene knew it sounded mean as it came out. She would need to be a little more careful. She hadn't had a chance to prepare her spiritual heart for a sister visit.

Louise laughed, "You are so right, sister." Silence hung in the air as the women just looked at one another. "I'm uh…"

"It's just that, we don't normally see you in the winter months." Irene added.

Louise nodded, "You're right. I couldn't wait until spring this time."

Things just weren't making any sense to Irene. She knew that Louise must have an extremely important reason, and that she needed to be very cautious as she maneuvered her way through this mine field. Surely, her younger sister wasn't to help her. Was she? Louise had always been smarter than her, but she couldn't have known about her recent mishaps. Her forgetfulness.

Above all, Irene knew she needed to keep her sword close and ready for battle at any time. Where'd she'd put her Bible?

###

Kathleen wiped the grease from her fingers and proceeded to clean up the table. Brian stood to help her.

"Thanks for bringing dinner for us, Brian." Her mother commented as she held up her paper plate.

"Yes dear. It was…" Aunt Louise sounded as if she were trying to act grateful. "Different. Haven't had fried chicken in ages. I hope it doesn't give me heartburn tonight."

Brian laughed.

"Oh honey, you just wait. You think I'm kidding," Aunt Louise sat back in her chair and folded her arms.

"I know you aren't kidding, Aunt Louise, I'm keenly aware of heartburn pain."

"You have heartburn, too? You're too young for that, Brian."

Brian shook his head and opened the cupboard door to dump trash into the container. "No, I'm not. You forget, I have a daughter getting married soon."

"Yes, yes, we are all getting older. It's hard for me to believe you two are old enough to have children getting married." And how do you feel these days, Irene?"

Kathleen sat down to hear her mother's answer. She wondered how her mother would explain her health issues of late.

"I'm fine. Max and I do fairly well in this big old house," Her mother patted her hand. "The kids are good to me, too. They help me get groceries when I can't get out." Kathleen smiled. The newness and surprise of the visit was starting to wear away. She was sure that the fried chicken dinner appeased her mother. Kentucky Fried was Mom's favorite eating out place.

"Have you told her yet?" Louise looked at Kathleen.

Kathleen shuddered. This wasn't the way she wanted her mother to hear about their concern over forgetfulness and need of care. Yet she had been the one shirking her duty, by not telling her of Louise's visit before she came.

Her mother looked at her. "Told me? Told me what?"

Louise leaned over the table and patted her sister's arm. As she did, Kathleen noticed her aunt's swollen hands. She remembered how out of breath Aunt Louise had seemed when she helped her walk through the airport. They'd had to stop several times for her to catch her breath. She'd told Kathleen, "That happens when you're eighty two years of age."

"I'm here to help you," Louise said.

Irene looked at Louise and then at Kathleen. "What? Kathleen? What have you told her?"

"Well, you see," Kathleen looked down and fumbled with her napkin.

"Why would you do this to me?" Her mother looked at Louise, "I don't expect you to drop your own life to be here. For me."

"I'm sorry, Mom. I should have gotten over here earlier to tell you."

"What? Kathleen, why wouldn't you talk this over with me before calling your aunt?"

Aunt Louise pushed back her chair. "You know what? I'm really tired. Is it okay if I just go up to my room? I want to unpack a little and then take a shower. Would that be okay?"

"Wait a minute. That's why you're here?"

Kathleen knew Mom was trying her best to keep a calm look on her face, but she also knew she had gone behind her back.

Her mother must have noticed her and Brian exchanged glances. "Brian, did you know about this, too?"

Louise interrupted, "Irene, can I have my usual room?"

Her mother nodded, but didn't take her eyes off of Kathleen. "The room on the right, just up the stairs."

Aunt Louise pushed in her chair, "Thank you, Brian, for a nice dinner. And Kathleen, thank you for picking me up at the airport on such short notice." She left the kitchen.

Kathleen put hand on her mother's back. "Mother," she whispered, but her mother looked down and stared at the table.

"Mom, I didn't know she was coming until a few days ago."

Her mother looked at her now, her face revealing hurt and betrayal. Kathleen knew how much her mother hated anyone to see her crying, especially her daughter. She had always maintained a strong front.

"Why I don't mind that you think I need help. I mind that you couldn't talk that over with me. I needed to be ready for Louise. You know how we struggle to get along."

Kathleen nodded, "I know. I know. But Mom, we are just worried about you. Aunt Louise is here at least until Taylor's wedding. Then we'll discuss the situation again, but right now..."

"You know Louise and I have been having disagreements lately. Why wouldn't you ask me first?"

"I know, I know. I'm sorry I didn't call you and let you know she was coming. But the other ladies at church are in the same boat as you. None of them could move in here to help you, and it was less than a week after I called her." She knew she was rambling, but rambled on. "Violet and Greg do their best to keep an eye on you, but, Mom, listen. I'm not sure why she came," she shook her head, "Let alone so quickly. But let's try to make the best of this. She's here. See how it goes. If it's…"

"It is pretty surprising she'd come at all. When did you say you called her?"

"Just a few weeks ago."

"Sorry. If it's bad, we'll figure something else out. But please let her help you until after the wedding."

She rose from the table, got the tissue box from the counter, and handed her mother a tissue.

"I just can't believe it."

"What?"

"Number one, that you called Louise and asked her to come without consulting me. But by the looks of her swollen hands, I don't think my memory issues are the real reason she's come here. I know my sister. There's always a motive behind what appears to be good intentions. I bet there is a whole 'nother reason why she's here."

Chapter 8

After she'd taken a hot bath, the floor boards felt even colder, and Louise's thin, linen, pajamas held little insulation against the evening temperature of Michigan in early spring. She pulled her cell phone out of her purse, got into bed, and pulled up the covers as she punched in Howard's number.

"Hello?" The familiar voice caused Louise's eyes to well up.

"Howard?"

"Louise, did you make it to your sister?"

"I'm here." Louise sighed. "Although I'm not exactly sure why."

"Yes, you do. You know why."

"She hates me."

"That's silly. Sisters don't hate sisters."

"Do you have one?"

"No."

"Then how in the world would you know?" Louise heard Howard burst out laughing at the other end of the phone. She so wished she was there with him now.

"You silly woman. It will wear on her, you being there."

"Ya think?"

"Yup. You both will get used to one another again. Did you tell her?"

"Tell her what?"

"About your illness?"

"No."

"I'm sure it's obvious that something's up."

Louise nodded, "Yes, I'm sure it is. She's just so proper." Louise pulled the covers up to her chin, "And Howard…"

"Yes."

"It's colder than a menopausal woman here."

Again, laughter erupted from the other end. "What?"

"Well, minus the hot flashes."

"Ah Louise, I miss you already."

Louise smiled. "I will miss you. Did you get some more boxes, for the dishes?"

"Yup. Today at Publix."

"And…"

"I won't kill myself packing them all up, but I'll work on it here and there in the next few days, just as you suggested."

"Good man."

"You sound like my wife." Howard added, "I sent the first fourteen today. You should get them within the next four days."

"Ready or not, guess I'm staying."

"Didn't you decide that yet with your sister?"

"No. I went to bed early. I think I may have caused her to have a mini-stroke just by showing up like this."

"What will happen when the boxes arrive?"

"I'm not sure, but one thing's for sure. She'll know I'm staying then."

Howard laughed again. "Be a good sister and tell her. Tonight."

"Tomorrow."

"Okay, tomorrow. Now get some rest. You've had a long day."

"Howard?"

"Yes?"

"Thank you for being such a dear. I'll never forget your kindness."

"You're welcome. Now talk to your sister. Be brave. You can do this. She's gonna understand."

"She's never understood anything but the gospel."

"Then, she'll have to take you in, like a good Christian."

"Yeah, but just so she can tell me I need Jesus."

"We all need Jesus." Howard chuckled. "Good night. Sleep well." He hung up before she could answer.

Louise looked down at the phone. *Why in the world did he have to be married?*

"Well, that went well." Brian gripped the steering wheel. "These roads are slippery again tonight. I'm so ready for spring."

"That did not go well." Kathleen winced, "It was horrible."

"How was your Aunt Louise when you picked her up?"

"Strange." Kathleen rummaged through her purse for a tissue as tears streamed down her face. "I feel horrible. My life is too busy. Why couldn't I have called or talked to Mom before she arrived?"

"You tried. We're just swamped right now."

"I should have tried harder," Kathleen blew her nose. "I'm a horrible daughter."

"You're not a horrible daughter. How did you know Aunt Louise would take you up on the suggestion to stay with your Mom so quickly? Why did she act strange to you?"

"I don't know. The whole ride to Mom's house was weird. We had to stop several times on the way to the car at the airport. She was so out of breath. And her hands, did you see how swollen they were? Maybe she's had a stroke or something."

"Ya think?" Brian looked over his shoulder to see if he could merge.

"Something was wrong."

"Well, they're together now. There isn't much we can do."

"I'll check on them tomorrow. Mom seemed to think something was wrong, too."

"She would know. She is her sister."

Kathleen nodded. "It all just happened so fast. It was as if…"

"What?"

"As if Aunt Louise needed Mom, too."

"Aunt Louise hasn't needed anything. From anyone. Ever."

"I know, that's what so strange. She's always been the most independent, stubborn woman I know, but today she seemed like a sad, frail, old woman. As if…"

"As if what?" Brian didn't take his eyes off the road as he maneuvered slowly down their street.

"I don't know." Kathleen wadded up her tissue and threw it into her purse. "I'm glad I'm an only child."

"They definitely have their own personalities. Such complete opposites."

Kathleen shook her head, "They've been that way ever since I can remember. Mom said their mother would have fits over their fights. She told them both, she wished someday they would both have daughters and see how it felt to be consistently waving a white flag. When Aunt Louise would say cold, Mom would say hot. They would argue over who had the prettiest hair, and who they thought Grandpa loved more. It's an old, familiar thing for the two of them."

"Who knows," Brian said, "Maybe this will be the time they work things out."

"That would be a miracle. If..."

"What's that?"

"If they don't kill each other first."

Chapter 9

Brushing her dentures the next morning, Louise sorted through ways to tell her sister that this time, she wasn't here for a visit. Every scenario played out and wiser than the truth. If she told her sister the truth about her heart condition, she'd get unwanted pity. She hated that. And it was also true that she came to help Irene. To fulfill her graveside promise.

Leaving the bathroom, she heard her sister making her way down the creaky steps. *'We need to carpet these stairs.'* The thought startled Louise. She actually believed there was a possibility of living here for quite some time. She stood taller.

Taking one last glimpse in the mirror, she puckered up. What good was it to produce an attractive face each morning? There wasn't anyone here to entice.

Stairs were getting harder and harder for Louise to manage. Her condo was designed purposely without stairs. Going down was bad, but going up was nearly impossible. She'd had to stop several times on her way up last night. The downstairs bedroom served as Irene's sewing room. Was her sister sewing much these days? Throwing out ideas on how to change her sister's home would need to be done with skill. As much as Louise loved change, Irene abhorred it.

She heralded her entrance into the kitchen with a flourish, "Good morning." Irene just looked up and smiled. "Got any orange juice?"

Irene shook her head. "I don't. Sorry. If I would have known you were coming, I could have bought some."

"What's a morning without freshly squeezed orange juice?"

"Michigan."Her sister pulled out a frying pan. "In winter."

Louise knew Michigan didn't have oranges growing on trees right outside the window, but the stores surely sold them. Something citrus. Then it struck her. Her sister's comment was meant to give her a hard time. "Good for you, Irene."

"What?" Irene sat down at the table with her hot cup of liquid, slopping a little as she set it down. "Oh my. I hate when I do that." She turned to look for something to wipe it up.

Louise reached for the towel, and handed it across the table to her sister.

"Oh no, that's one of my nicest towels. Get me a piece of paper towel."

Louise turned to look for a roll. She found one just above the sink on a stand. She ripped off a section and handed it to her sister.

"What you have there?"

"Tea." Irene turned with the paper towel and handed it back to Louise. "Throw this away. Would you rather have another cup of instant coffee?"

Louise always associated tea with fuddy- duddy old Baptist ladies. A tall glass of orange juice or a smoothie was her choice of a morning wake-up beverage.

"What kind of fruit do you have?"

Irene bowed her head quickly, and then started in on her tea and toast. "It's Michigan, Louise. And it's March."

"We don't ship up good things from Florida anymore?"

"Probably, but I do quite well on toast and tea in the morning."

This whole conversation was sliding down the proverbial winter slope on a sled. Louise looked around the kitchen. "Not even any bananas?"

Irene shook her head. "If you haven't noticed, we've had bumper-to-bumper snowstorms lately. Kathleen's been so busy with this upcoming wedding and her other important things, she hasn't been able to take me to the store."

Louise realized her sister's health issues were preventing her from her normal gadabout around town. Perhaps even preventing her from driving.

She sat down opposite her sister. "Irene, I'm sorry." She took a deep breath. She hated apologizing, but more importantly, she despised apologizing to her sister. "I didn't mean for our time together to start out this way." Louise looked over at her sister who was slowly munching on her piece of toast and sipping her tea.

"What did you mean it to be?"

Louise sighed again. "A time to catch up. A time to get reacquainted."

"Good try." Irene wiped off her mouth, "Really, Louise. Do you think I woke up yesterday and assumed I'd get a surprise visit from my sister? The sister who rarely calls me. Only visits in the summer when there's a reunion."

Louise wanted to choke the woman. Each scenario she planned out as she brushed her teeth was slowly going down the bathroom sink drain, just like her over-applied denture cream. The only way to win her sister over was to bring up a fond memory. Something they once shared and enjoyed.

She wasn't sure if she should say anything about the graveside promise just yet.

"I noticed the garage has recently been painted."

"Greg did it for me. This past fall."

"It's a nice color. Matches the house quite well." Louise hadn't really paid any attention to the garage, but could now see it out one of the kitchen windows. "Do you remember the time we used to scare Daddy when he was out working in it? We would get on our bikes and slowly pedal up to the garage door and peek around the side to see what he was doing. He rarely heard us, due to the board he was cutting on his saw or something. It's a wonder we didn't cause him to cut off a finger when we would scream."

Her sister smiled, "He somehow acted as if he knew we were there. His reactions always seemed planned."

Louise smiled as well, "Yes, they did. I saw you have one of his desks in the foyer. It looks nice there."

Irene went back to munching on her bread. "It's been there for fifty years, Louise."

"Yes, well, I guess I just noticed it then."

Irene wiped off her mouth and folded her napkin. She put both arms on the table and folded her hands. "Louise, how long do you plan to stay on this surprise visit?"

Should she come right out and say it? Louise eyed her sister. She was staring her down now. She wanted an answer. "As long as you need me here."

Irene glared back at her, "I don't need you. I don't need anyone. Max and I are just fine. By ourselves."

77

"Kathleen doesn't seem to think so."

"Kathleen needs to mind her own business."

"Maybe so, but honey, we both know that minding each other's business is essential today. We forget why we left a room. We forget if we subtracted the monthly power bill from our social security checks. Sometimes we even forget to turn off things. Important things."

Irene's glare flashed into despair. "She told you?"

Louise leaned forward. "That you are forgetting things? Yes. But not how much." She grew more courage. This could work. "Would you like to share?" She had always been a master at pretending.

Irene picked up her cup with a shaky hand and grabbed her cane to stand, "It hasn't been that bad." She shuffled to the sink, placed her cup in the sink and threw her folded napkin away. "There's been a few times when I do find myself doing silly things."

"Like what?" Louise knew the sympathy tactic would work with her sister. "I forgot my key the other day and locked myself out of my house."

Irene turned to face her, "I forgot to turn off the bath water a few weeks ago." She pointed to the stove. "I try and set the timer to remind myself and then," she looked down at the floor, "I then forgot why the timer is set."

Louise nodded. "I've done that, too."

"Well, wonderful. Now the person called on to help me is doing the same thing. Between the two of us, we'll both burn the house down. Which...I almost did last week." She folded her arms and, leaned against the counter.

The two sisters looked at each other. Without missing a beat, they had always known what the other was thinking.

Louise rose from her chair and went to stand beside her sister. She hadn't done anything like this in a long time, but she slowly put her arm around her sister's bony shoulders and squeezed. "Maybe together we could become one," she raised a shaky finger, "a whole person. You're still my big sister. I could help you, just like when we were little." That sounded better than, 'you know what this means.'

"Oh yes. Let's do that." Irene pulled a little away. "Let's go back to you bossing me around."

"If that's what it takes," Louise shrugged her shoulders. "Sorry, but you do know, I have always been smarter than you."

Irene's angry face turned to a more playful state, "Oh right. Who'd you vote for in the last election?"

Louise shook her head. She knew this trap, and the first day was not the day to bring up politics, but she couldn't let the dig go unnoticed. "He's a good man."

"For what?"

Louise turned from her sister, left the room and called back, "For change."

She heard her sister laugh from the kitchen. Changing the subject was imperative or she'd be kicked out of this house faster than a dead mouse in a trap.

Louise looked around her sister's hobby room and called, "Hey Irene, how much do you like your sewing room?"

"A lot. I like it a lot." Irene followed her into the sewing room. "Why?"

"Well, I was thinking that maybe we could move it upstairs in the room I'm staying in now and then you could have it closer. I could use this room as my bedroom."

"I don't like that idea." Irene chided. "I like things just the way they are."

"I know, I know." Changing the subject was again imperative. Louise inspected the dark, cluttered room. Walking over to an open sewing machine she asked, "Is this Momma's old machine?" With a shaky hand, Louise felt the rough black texture of the Singer sewing machine. She'd watched her mother sew all kinds of clothing on this machine, from many of her childhood dresses to even her wedding dress.

"Yes, it's Momma's. Remember, you didn't want anything like this from her estate."

"Of course not. I don't sew. You needed it more than I did." Louise scanned the room a little more, sizing it up for her bedroom furniture. "Do you still use it?"

No answer. Louise turned to her sister, "Irene, don't you use it anymore?"

Irene looked down. "I can't thread the blasted needle." She shrugged her shoulders, "I can't see the eye."

"I can't either. I have to take clothes to my neighbor, even to have her sew on a button for me. It's a pain, but not too costly. She loves my lemon tree and takes lemons on a regular basis."

"Well, that seems like a fair trade."

Louise nodded. "Yes, it is. Except when there aren't enough left for lemonade when I want to make some. It's a nice room. I'm sure you have enjoyed it as your sewing room."

"I'm not in here all that much, I usually take my sewing to my chair where the light is better. As you can see," Irene held up her cane and waved it over the room, "It's my free-for-all room now." Irene sat down on the sewing stool. "I've been thinking of moving my bedroom down here and shutting off the upstairs heat." She nodded and smiled, "It would save on the winter heating bills."

Louise hesitated for a minute but thought this breakthrough would be a great transition to tell Irene the news of her permanent move. "We'll work something out with that. I can share the costs with you. Of heating, food, air in the summer, even taxes."

Irene looked up at her. "What?"

Louise moved to the window and, pulled on a dusty blind to let in a little winter morning sunshine. "Yes. Did you think I was here to freeload off of you?" She wished she could open a window. The room smelled musty. Dust was everywhere.

Irene slumped on her stool. "Are you planning on staying longer than a few days then?"

Louise moved closer to her sister and pulled out a chair next to the window. "Maybe." But she didn't look in her direction.

"Oh Louise," Irene shook her head, "Are you sure about this?"

"What's wrong? We're sisters," Louise did her best to elicit confidence and security into her reasoning. "If we can't get along…"

Before she said another word, Irene raised her hand and stopped her, "Whoa, whoa, whoa. Are you crazy, Louise? We have never gotten along."

"We have to. We'll have to try harder. You need me. Don't you?"

Irene sighed. "I do. I was going to call you, but Kathleen beat me to it."

"You were?" Louise couldn't believe her ears. "Really?"

"Yes. My memory is getting worse. I can feel it. Sense it." Irene folded her arms.

Louise went to her sister. "It will be okay. I'm here. I will do whatever you want me to do to help you. Even..."

Irene gave her a puzzled look.

"I promised you. Remember?"

Irene nodded.

Chapter 10

"Who's that?" Louise picked up her fork and motioned to the man standing at Irene's garage door.

"Oh," Irene grabbed her cane and shuffled to the kitchen door, "that's Greg."

"What's he doing?" Louise munched on her lunch.

Irene opened the door and shouted, "Hello Greg. Is it going to be too big of a job?"

The man made his way to the back door to greet her, "No."

It was clear to Louise, by the look of his face, that the man had in intellectual disability.

Awww, Irene." He reached out and hugged her sister. He peered into the house. When Louise met his eyes, he grew quiet. Turning, he shouted over his shoulder, "I'll have this done in a jiffy."

"Thanks, I'll add it to your tab." Irene shouted out to him, over the scrapes his shovel now made on the cement.

The man laughed, "Okay, thanks Irene."

Irene shut the door and shuddered, "Oh wow, it's a cold one today." She looked out the window at the man shoveling in a constant motion. "I hope he doesn't work too hard."

When Irene sat back at the table, Louise wasn't sure if she should ask or not. "Is he…?"

"Mentally handicapped?" Irene smiled, "Yes, but quite capable."

"Is he bad?"

Irene looked up at her sister, "Bad?"

"As in, severe?"

"Severely?"

"Handicapped?" Louise couldn't believe how she sometimes had to pry things out of her sister.

"No. Greg and his mother live next door. I give him odd jobs to do around the house. Shovel snow, trim bushes in the summer, paint the garage. He'll even run into town for me and get me a gallon of milk."

"He can drive?"

"Yes. Quite well. He hasn't had a ticket in twenty years. He'll tell you." Irene speared a piece of chicken and put it in her mouth. "They are great neighbors. Violet, his mother, is slow and doesn't get around much. She wouldn't know what to do without Greg."

"They live together?"

"Yes. Greg probably couldn't live much on his own. It's convenient for Violet to have him, too. He's a big help. She'd have to probably be in a home, if it wasn't for Greg."

"Well, it doesn't often happen that way. Usually children with disabilities are a lifetime burden."

"I'm sure Violet had a time raising him, but he does many things she wouldn't be able to do on her own."

Louise took her bowl of soup to the sink and washed it out. She hated doing dishes. Rinsing and putting it the strainer was as far as she would go. She returned to the table. "What about the sewing room?"

"What about it?"

"Can I have it as my room?" Bold. Succinct. To the point.

Irene sat back in her chair, "You don't sew."

Louise rolled her eyes, "Not for a sewing room, Irene. As my bedroom." Irene seemed to have forgotten all about their talk that morning.

Irene sighed. "What's wrong with the room upstairs?"

"It's upstairs."

Irene now shuffled to the sink, filling it with hot water and a squirt of dish soap. She picked up Louise's bowl and added it to her pile in the soapy water.

"I already washed that."

"Uh, huh. I'm not sure I'm ready to give up my sewing clutter room just yet."

"You said yourself you don't often get in there to do any sewing anymore."

The dishes clanked in the sink as Irene added more to the water. "I know. I know. But it will take a month of Sundays to get it all cleaned out."

"I'll help."

Irene turned to her sister and frowned, "You will, will you?"

Louise nodded her head, "Of course. Maybe Craig, or whatever his name is, would come over and even do a paint job for us."

Irene looked out the window at her neighbor. "Greg. His name is Greg, and he can do many things. He once came over and fixed my water heater. We had so much fun that day." Irene went back to wiping down the dishes, rinsing them off, and placing them back into the strainer. "I like my rooms painted well. I'm a bit picky."

"Then, we'll hire someone else."

Irene turned to her, wiping her hands on a dry towel. "Louise! I am not made of money, you know."

"I don't expect you to pick up my cost."

Irene looked at her with disgust, "Your cost?"

"Of course. I will pay half the housing bills. What do you pay?" Louise began counting off the possibilities on her fingers. "Heating, water, power…what am I missing?"

"Taxes, lawn care, and what about food?"

"Yes. All of it. I'm in."

Irene folded her arms. "So that's it. No questions? No formalities?"

"Such as what? Do you want to do like a pre-nup or something?"

"A pre-nup? What on earth?" Irene turned back to the sink, rung out the dish rag, and started wiping down the kitchen counter. "Are you sure this whole thing is going to work?"

Before Louise could answer the question, the doorbell rang, Irene grabbed her cane and shuffled to the door. "I wonder who that could be?"

Louise wasn't budging. The sun was hitting her back perfectly, warming her tired old Florida bones. It felt heavenly. She could hear her sister's movements perfectly as she ambled through the foyer and opened the front door. She wondered why the woman couldn't pick up her feet more.

"Is this the Irene Frederick's residence?" Louise heard a gruff, masculine voice ask. She heard her sister answer affirmatively.

"These packages are for a Louise…um…Williams."

Louise closed her eyes. She couldn't believe how fast they had reached Michigan. She suddenly couldn't remember how many Howard told her he had sent. Had he told her twelve or fourteen?

"All of these?"

"Sign here, please."

Louise got up from her chair and walked to the doorway of the kitchen. She could clearly see the front door from the kitchen threshold. The delivery man handed her sister a monitor-type device and indicated where to sign. As she did, Irene called, "Louise!"

"I'm right here. What's the matter?"

Irene motioned to the boxes now being carried into the front room. "What is this?"

Louise walked into the foyer a little ways. "Did you order something?" She might as well act dumb. She wasn't sure how this conversation would end up.

Irene bent down and looked at one of the box labels. "From Florida?" Her sister's voice began to rise in the same way that it used to when they were in high school, and Louise listened in on Irene's phone conversations with her boyfriend, or used her makeup without asking.

"Okay," Louise got closer to the four boxes now stacked in the foyer. "They're mine."

"Boxes?"

"Well, what would I ship my belongings in? Toilet paper?"

Her sister's voice rose even higher, "Your *belongings*?"

Just then, the delivery man dropped the last box he had on the pile. "I'll be right back, have about ten more in the van."

"Ten more?" Irene screamed now. Her face turned red and the veins in her neck began to bulge.

Louise cringed as she stepped closer to her sister.

"I can't believe you were so sure I would say yes to this move-in situation. What if I had refused to allow you to stay here?"

"I guess I didn't think that was a possibility."

"You are always so cocky! So sure of yourself!"

"Irene, wait. Now wait." Louise tried to follow her sister as she made her way up the stairs, but she couldn't. She didn't have enough breath left in her body.

Chapter 11

Irene slammed her bedroom door. She didn't care if Louise could hear it. In her heart, she knew she actually wanted her to hear. They shouldn't have planned this without her. This should have been at her request, on her terms. Her daughter's betrayal was more than she could bear. Kathleen should have talked to her. They could have talked at length about whether Louise would be able to move here, to move in her 'belongings.' She wished it had been her to call, instead of Kathleen, to see if her sister really wanted to come. To see if Louise was still willing to put their promise into action.

She went to her chair by the window, sat down, and looked out at the snow. It was a beautiful winter day. The new snow glistened and sparkled in the sunshine, and caked on the pine tree branches, weighing them down like a scene from a Christmas card.

Irene sighed. The sun illuminated a tiny bird perched on a branch just outside the room. She looked up into the blue sky and prayed. *'Lord…I know this is what I planned, but do you think we will be able to live under the same roof. I think she's going to drive me even more insane.'*

She often talked to God like that. Over her eighty-plus years on earth, she knew God had reasons for everything. He worked all things out for our good, despite how we felt while going through them. She'd trusted Him more times than she could imagine. She'd learned the trust issue many years ago when she found herself a widow at the age of fifty-five. The next few years had been hard. She learned to trust God as never before, thankful for

His care and loving kindness. She rarely questioned Him, and when she did, she had good reason. Today was one of those days.

She called the old patch-work fabric rocking chair, her 'morning place.' It was there she started off her mornings. Glancing over at the worn Bible placed on the table right beside her, she knew she'd feel better if she read for a little while. She eyed it for a moment, but then decided God probably wouldn't want her reading it with this horrible anger in her heart. *'Come unto me, all you who are heavy burdened,'* she remembered. *'I will give you rest.'*

So she picked up her worn Bible. It had been her husband's. After he died, she couldn't think of parting with it. He'd underlined so many verses. She opened it to the section she'd been studying for the past few weeks. Loving your neighbor. Her shoulders drooped. "Love," she whispered to herself. She shook her head. She'd proven love for others in many ways. Greg and Violet next door always helped her, but she tried to help them from time to time. She volunteered many Sundays in the church nursery, and even baked cookies for the children in the neighborhood. On and on she went, making her case, recalling all the people she'd done her best to love.

Then she remembered her mother. She did love her mother. More than life itself. She thought maybe that's why God took her husband so early, to help her give those ten years of her life to care for her mother. Halfway through the ordeal, she had wondered if it began to be a curse. Louise had lived in Florida. She would only come back to Michigan for a week during the summer and also around Thanksgiving. The job of caring for her Mother was her lot. Her burden.

Toward the end of her mother's life, Irene had grown angry and frustrated. Her mother didn't even realize the care she was getting. Due to her mother's wandering, Irene couldn't sleep well, and that left her even more irritated and upset during the daylight hours. Irene had to take her mother along, wherever she went. Her mother would throw temper tantrums, like a child, in the grocery store. People would avoid her because of the uncontrolled behavior.

She looked out the window again, resting her head on the back of the chair. This time the sun was darkened by a stray cloud. The shiny snow now turned dull and shadows lingered over her yard. Perhaps a nap this afternoon would help her. She lay down on her bed, and pulled an afghan over herself. As she shut her eyes, she thought about Louise. Would she willingly come to Irene's rescue? They had made a promise at their mother's grave, but abiding by promises had never been a trait that Louise possessed. Why would she do that for her?

Could she allow Louise the chance to try? Through the years, whenever she trusted her sister, it had not ended well. But if Louise stayed, she could help Irene remember things. She might even prevent her from burning down her house. But most of all, when the time came, would she still agree to fulfill their graveside promise?

Before she could analyze it any longer, Irene drifted off to sleep.

Louise did her best to push, shoving with her foot, to move boxes filled with her life, into the sewing room downstairs. It really wasn't in her heart to make her sister mad by putting them there, but she knew without a doubt that she'd never manage to carry them all upstairs. Leaving them all in the foyer would probably just ensure another outburst of anger from her sister. Entirely winded and tired, she'd managed to only push two boxes into the sewing room. She'd have to finish the job later. She fell into a living room chair. Her body throbbed. Her head hurt. She longed for her porch back home, where she could sit and watch the waves lap on the shore of Clearwater Beach.

She could barely catch her breath. Possibly, the boxes had done her in. She breathed deliberately, in through her nose and out her mouth. Sitting up in the chair she stretched upward, but the breath just wouldn't come. She started to panic. What if she couldn't catch her breath? Perhaps she'd faint right here.

She closed her eyes, concentrated on breathing. Just breathing. Nothing else. Her head throbbed. Her mouth grew dry.

Even though she was nervous about this attack, she was glad Irene couldn't see her struggle for a breath. She didn't want pity.

How ironic it was that her sister needed her at the same time as she needed her sister. She wasn't really sure why she thought it was a good idea to keep her illness a secret, but she did like the pretense that she'd come to help Irene. Somehow it gave her power, strength to deal with her own inadequacies. For her own dignity, she needed to keep that intact for as long as she could.

She clutched at her chest, which grew tight. Her lips felt numb. She'd had two other bouts like this, and each time brought her new fears. What if she fainted? What if no one found her for awhile? Or she couldn't get to her purse for a pill? The worst fright of all was this time might be her last.

Chapter 12

"Mom!" Kathleen yelled as she opened the front door of her mother's house. Max came first. He drew up close to her legs and wrapped himself around them, meowing his own greeting.

Kathleen bent down to pick him up. "Hey, Max." She scratched the top of his black head. Max contorted his neck backward, begging for more scratches. A stack of boxes lined the foyer. "How's Gettysburg?"

"Kathleen!"

The voice sounded like Aunt Louise, yet it sounded so weak.

"Aunt Louise?" Kathleen set Max down and walked into the living room. Her Aunt was sitting on the edge of a chair, pale, with wide eyes. "What's wrong?"

Louise closed her eyes and breathed in deeply and then out through her mouth. "I can't....seem to..."

Kathleen knelt beside the chair, "What can I do to help you?"

"My purse." Breathing in and out slowly, her Aunt pointed toward the kitchen.

Kathleen hurried to the kitchen, searching for the purse. She found it hanging on a hook by the back door, and rushed back, handing it to her Aunt.

Louise rummaged through her purse and found a little white pill. She slipped it under her tongue.

"Do you want a glass of water?"

Her Aunt shook her head.

"What's wrong? Do I need to call an ambulance?"

"Boxes." Her Aunt motioned to the boxes stacked in the foyer. "I pushed them."

"Exhausted." Her aunt took a deep breath. "Oh," she cried. Another long draw. "Oh my!"

Color began to come back into her Aunt Louise's face. Whatever pill she'd taken, it slowed her breathing.

"Oh my," she kept saying. "Oh my!" Perspiration now dotted the old woman's forehead, and her breathing slowed even more.

"Where's mother?"

"I think she's sleeping or something. You better check on her."

Kathleen rushed upstairs to find her mother sleeping.

She rushed back downstairs, maneuvering through the boxes set by the front door. "What was that?"

Louise looked fine now. Her breathing labored, but steady, "What was what?"

Kathleen shook her head. "Aunt Louise. That was some kind of attack. What's wrong?" A bit of drool dripped from her Aunt's mouth, "Let me get you a napkin."

Before she could turn and head for the kitchen, her Aunt wiped her mouth with the back of her hand. "No." Another deep breath. "Fine."

Her Aunt's face returned to a normal shade of pink, and her breathing settled into a normal rhythm. She acted as though she could now talk.

Kathleen made her way back to the front door. "What are all these boxes?"

"Sewing room."

"What are you doing in Mom's...?"

Before she could finish the sentence, her Aunt jumped in, "They're mine."

"Where did they come from?"

"Florida."

"Well, I know, but..."

"Look Kathleen," Louise interrupted again. "You asked me to come help your mother."

Kathleen held up her hand, "Aunt Louise, I know I did, but I guess I just didn't see you coming this fast. Or..."

"Moving in?"

Kathleen nodded, "Okay. That's fine, if it's okay with my mother."

"Does she really have a choice?"

Kathleen looked at her Aunt, who now waited for an answer. She shook her head. "No."

"But Aunt Louise, what's wrong with you?"

Louise looked down at her hands. "Since, about last summer."

"Last summer?" Kathleen asked.

"Yes. Last summer is when it got bad. But now, it's even worse."

"Aunt Louise, what's wrong?"

Her aunt look up at her with sadness in her eyes, "Kathleen, I have congestive heart failure."

Chapter 13

Irene woke from her nap. Pushing off the blanket, she looked around the room trying to get herself together. Why was she sleeping? She sorted through her thoughts. A nap seemed to always bring her around to having to deal with memory issues.

It wasn't like her to fall asleep in her bedroom. Most of her naps were in front of her television. Just after lunch. Had she had lunch? She didn't feel hungry.

She got up from bed, held on to the footboard and stretched to reach her cane beside the rocking chair.

She went to the mirror and smoothed down her hair. It must have been a long nap, because her hair was going every which way. She picked up her comb and tried her best to fix it. She didn't think she had to go anywhere that day, so she placed the comb back into a drawer and walked out of her room.

The top step creaked as she made her way down the stairs. Kathleen was at the bottom step looking up. "Mother?"

"Who else would it be, Kathleen?"

Kathleen crossed her arms, "You must have had a good nap."

"What time is it?"

Kathleen looked at her watch, "Just after four."

"Can you stay for dinner?" Irene made it to the last step and looked at the stack of boxes in her foyer. "What are all these?"

"They're Aunt Louise's." Kathleen gave her a quizzical look. "I thought Aunt Louise said you were here when they arrived."

"Aunt Louise? How would she know?" Kathleen gave her another puzzled look. "What's wrong?"

Kathleen shook her head, "Nothing," then turned and headed into the living room.

Someone was sitting in Irene's chair. She pressed down the front of her shirt, "Do I have a visitor?"

Kathleen touched her back, "Aunt Louise had a bit of an attack."

Irene looked at her daughter, "Why do you keep mentioning my sister as though she were..."

Louise turned in her chair and glanced at her.

"Louise? What on earth are you doing here?"

Louise sighed. "What do you mean?"

Irene turned to her daughter, "Kathleen, what is your aunt doing here?"

Both women were silent.

Irene went over to her sister, sitting in her chair. "When did you get here? How long have you been here?" She turned to Kathleen again, "Why didn't you wake me up to tell me my sister had come for a visit?"

Louise was shocked. Irene didn't remember her being there. At all. It was as if they were greeting each other again for the first time.

"When did you arrive?"

"Two days ago."

Her sister looked at her with a puzzled look, "I've been sleeping for two days?"

Louise shook her head and looked at Kathleen.

"Um, Mom, are you hungry?"

Irene looked at her daughter and then back to Louise, "I don't know."

Louise stood up, "Why don't you sit here? In your chair. Kathleen and I," Louise took Kathleen by the hand, "We'll go and fix you something to eat. Are you hungry for anything special?"

Louise led Kathleen into the kitchen as Irene sat down in the living room chair. "She doesn't know I've come."

Kathleen nodded to her as they made their way into the kitchen.

"I can't believe it. She doesn't remember me arriving." Louise said in a hushed tone. "At all." They stood in the kitchen and looked back at Irene. "She's getting worse."

"I told you." Kathleen folded her arms. "That's why I called you."

"Let's fix dinner." Louise went to the refrigerator and peeked inside. "We can have leftovers from last night. We fixed a nice casserole. All we'll have to do is heat it up."

Kathleen nodded as she opened a cupboard door and pulled out some plates. "I was hoping you could come and help her through this hard time. But are you going to be okay? You have a few issues of your own."

Louise set the casserole dish on the cupboard, "I'm sorry Kathleen. I never imagined I would be sick at the same time as your mother. I want to be here. To help. I really do."

Kathleen pulled the aluminum foil off the dish and began scooping out the chicken and stuffing casserole onto their plates. "What did the doctor tell you?"

"To get help. To not live alone."

Kathleen sighed.

"I think I can do that. But," Louise looked at her niece, "I think I might need help getting Irene's sewing room changed around. I can't manage the stairs."

"We can help with that." Kathleen put one plate into the microwave. "Why didn't you just tell me?"

Louise looked down at the counter. She shook her head, "I guess I was embarrassed."

"Embarrassed? Because you're sick?"

She nodded, but didn't look up. "Would you have been so eager to have me come, if you'd known?"

Switching a cool plate with the warmed-up one, Kathleen shook her head. "I don't know, but I do know that I have a wedding to plan. My son is graduating from college this summer. I have clients begging me to show them houses and after five years of a horrible economy, things are finally starting to perk up." Kathleen leaned into the counter, "I need your help."

Louise could tell she was just about to burst into tears. "I know. I'm here."

"But for how long? How long can you keep this up?"

Louise shook her head, "I don't know, but I'll do the best I can. I promise. I have to remember to take my medicine each day."

"I'll take this plate into Mom. She'll be fine eating there. You and I need to sit down in here and talk about this. We need to have a plan." Kathleen left the room.

Louise knew what the plan would have to be now. Irene's plan. She was here to fulfill a promise, and at this moment, it seemed to be the only solution to all of their problems.

"Is that like COPD?" Brian looked at Kathleen with a puzzled expression.

"I don't think so. Congestive heart failure means just that. Her heart is failing."

"Is she dying?"

Kathleen nodded. Brian sat down at the kitchen table and pulled his laptop closer to him. "I wanna Google that. What are the symptoms?"

"I don't know." Kathleen sat down at the table with him. "Being out of breath has to be one of them."

Brian nodded. "That's understandable."

Kathleen buried her head in her hands. "This is crazy. Aunt Louise has always been so healthy. I've never seen her sick. Mom always said she was too stubborn for it."

"Well, Kathleen…," Brian typed. "Rarely, do we see the woman. We have to remember, these two women are not young anymore."

Kathleen nodded. "That's true." Wringing her hands, "Now what? We wanted her here to help care for Mother. Not the other way around."

"Well, now wait," Brian didn't take his focus off the computer screen in front of him. "Let's look this up to see what we are up against here."

"She could have it for years. Like...a long time."

"She hasn't been here that long to know which stage she is in."

"Are there stages?"

Brian clicked off the site. "Who knows? I'm no doctor." Brian leaned back in his chair and folded his arms. "What now?"

Kathleen shrugged. "You tell me. Care issues have now doubled. I don't even know if the woman I've assigned to help my mother can even take care of herself."

Brian sighed, "Perhaps we shouldn't have called Aunt Louise."

"Too late now. Instead of helping, I've added another thing to my long To-Do list." Kathleen left the room mumbling, "Just exactly what I need right now."

Chapter 14

Irene had been brooding about finances all day. This was a viable subject. More viable than her usual rantings about wanting ice cream for supper. With her short-term memory sharp, for at least this hour, Louise decided to bring up the subject of the pact. Just after dinner, she said, "Sister?"

Irene looked up from her plate. A stray piece of cheese dangled from the corner of her mouth.

Louise handed her a napkin. "You have a piece of cheese," she pointed to the corner of her own mouth.

Irene wiped at the cheese.

"Irene, we need to talk about my moving in."

Irene nodded. "You have all of those boxes in my sewing room?"

Louise nodded, set down her fork, and folded her hands over her plate. "I know your memory is bothering you." She wasn't sure how many things she'd have to ask over again for Irene to understand.

"You forget things, too, don't you? Wasn't it just last night you struggled to remember the cat's name?"

Louise nodded. "Yes, but I don't set the house afire."

"When did I do that?" Irene gave her a puzzled look.

"Irene, do you remember a conversation we had at mother's grave? When she died?"

Irene gazed at her. Louise began to see signs of the disease in Irene's expressions. Occasionally, she would just stare off into space. Her facial movements random. This was one of those moments. "You don't remember, do you?"

Irene shook her head quickly, then stopped. Then slowly began to nod. "You're here for me, aren't you? Will you follow through? With our plan?"

This was it. She felt so empowered, pretending the real reason was because of Irene's memory. She could lie to her sister or tell the truth. Louise nodded. Which would it be?

Irene bowed her head, set down her spoon, and gazed into her bowl of soup. "I didn't think it would be me. I mean," she fumbled with her napkin in her lap, "I thought probably it would be, but Weezie, you never really believe it," she looked up at Louise, "until you almost burn your house down."

Louise felt sudden pity for her sister. It was one thing for an illness to take over your body, but to take over your mind. She knew the fear of the first, but had only heard about the other. Now she was seeing it first-hand. It helped her understand Howard a bit more. She reached over and patted her sister's hands. "It's okay. I'm here now."

"But you hate me."

Louise was taken aback. Yes, they had their differences, but hate? She didn't hate her sister. She really didn't. "Irene, I do not hate you."

"What do you mean? We've never gotten along. We made that pact, but neither one of us thought it would ever come true. Did we?"

Louise knew that to be true. She shook her head.

Her sister tried to stand up. Louise stopped her. "Sit down, Irene. We need to talk this through."

Her sister eased back into her chair, but looked away.

"Irene. Look at me."

She appeared to Louise like a two-year-old caught eating a cookie before dinner.

"We can make this work. I know we can. We are grown women. We have lots in common." Louise couldn't believe how much. "We'll make it work. I want to be here for you."

"What about the pact?"

"I need to know, right now, what you want to do. Do you want it to still happen? I need to know, before it's too late and you can't tell me for sure."

Irene looked up. Tears slipping down her cheeks. "I don't want to be a burden to Kathleen or Brian. Ever."

"Just like we promised?"

Irene nodded. She picked up a napkin and wiped her face. Tears flowed freely now.

"Are you sure?"

Irene nodded again. "Yes."

"Then we'll make it work. It will happen. We don't need to talk about it any further. Okay?"

"What if I forget?"

"Are you thinking clearly? Right now?"

"I think so." Irene sighed. "It's time. Promise me again. Promise me it will happen just as we promised each other that morning at daybreak."

Louise grabbed her hand. "I promise." Perhaps they'd been wrong. Perhaps they could get along better than they thought. Louise needed to clarify one more thing before she lost Irene again. "And from now on, until it happens, we'll live together as peaceably as we can." She gripped her sister's hand. "Okay?"

Irene nodded.

For the first time in a long time, Louise felt peace. Fulfilling this promise would not be easy. She'd have to be careful to keep herself as healthy as possible. And they'd have to go forward with plans soon. But if she could keep this promise to her sister and fulfill her wishes, in some way, she could erase the wrongs she'd done to her. She sat back in her chair and smiled at her sister, "Everything will be okay. I promise." And she meant it.

"You need to tell her."

"I know, Howard" Louise switched her cell phone to her better hearing ear. "I just don't want her pity."

"Her pity? How do you think she feels, Louise?"

"I hate having people feel sorry for me. It was hard enough telling you."

"But now Kathleen knows. If you don't tell Irene, she might..."

Louise had to change the subject. She wasn't sure Irene would remember if she told her anyway. "How's your wife? Have you heard lately?"

"She's fine. Having a few medical issues. She gets UTIs on a regular basis. It makes her even crazier."

"Poor dear."

"I hate to think of this being your future, too."

"It won't be." Louise had let it slip out before she realized it.

"What?"

"Nothing. The first boxes arrived, did I tell you?"

"Were they okay? Did I pack them well?"

"To be perfectly honest, I haven't looked yet." She had no intention of telling him about her episode.

"I hope they are okay. I didn't want anything to break."

Louise shook her head, "Howard, you have been so wonderful. Thank you again for all you've done."

"Just stay well and warm up there in cold Michigan."

Louise laughed. "The weather report is saying we'll have a few warm days soon. By 'warm' they mean at least in the forty-degree range."

Howard laughed. "That sounds horrible."

"Howard, darling, you have no idea."

"Want to try and get out today? You've been saying you need a haircut." Louise passed the gallon of milk to her sister across the table. Birds were beginning to sing outside. Despite the closed and locked windows, their bright songs gave Louise hope that the weather would soon change.

"I do need a haircut."

"It'll be fun." Louise knew it probably wouldn't be, but she needed a day out, and, Irene seemed to be having another good day. "I'm getting tired of staring at these walls." They'd made a couple of trips to the grocery store, but other than that, the sisters hadn't had any other outings. "I think

106

it's supposed to be forty-two degrees, if the weatherman was right this morning."

"It's better than twelve, that's for sure." Irene smiled.

Louise agreed. "Where do you usually go for a haircut around here?" She ran her hand over her own hair.

"The usual place."

"Is this a trick question?" Louise squinted at her sister, who shrugged her shoulders.

"Changes."

"I know, Irene. That's what we need, a change," Louise grew exasperated. "But where do you go to get those much-needed changes?"

Irene smiled, "I just told you."

Louise got up and picked up both their cereal bowls. "No you didn't."

"Louise, my beauty parlor's name is Changes. I've been going there for years. Do you want to see if we can get in today or not?"

Irene had a harsh tone in her voice that Louise hadn't heard in quite a while. It made Louise laugh. "Well, Changes it is. Do you have their number?" Louise placed the bowls in the sink and rinsed out the leftover bran flakes and milk.

"288-3812."

Louise turned to her sister. "Are you sure?"

"Sure is rain, sister." Irene got up from her chair. "I told you. I've used them for years." Irene shuffled out of the room, just after putting the milk jug back into the refrigerator. "Ask for Deb or Lori. We probably should get milk, too. We're almost out."

"A change might do us both good." Louise placed the rinsed-out bowls in the strainer.

###

Louise let her drive. Irene was shocked, but thankful. She hated to think she needed to give that up now, too. She'd had to convince Louise she could do it and tell her exactly where the salon was located. Louise handed her the keys before they left the house. Could she ever get lost in Durand? She'd lived there her entire life. She walked back and forth to school all the way through high school, then walked Kathleen to the elementary school each day. She went to church in the town, volunteered at the historic Union Station. Above all, she'd been to Changes once every few months. She could get them to the beauty parlor.

The car started right up. Irene and Louise waved at Greg who had just come outside. "Where you two girls goin'?"

They'd told him their need for haircuts. He waved to them as he headed in the opposite direction for his morning walk.

Irene owned a Chevy Impala. She'd had it since 2008. The color was dark blue, Irene's favorite color. She pulled out into traffic and headed south.

"Are you sure you know where you're going?" Louise fidgeted in the seat beside her. She'd had a horrible time getting her seat belt fastened.

"At least I know how to fasten my seat belt." Irene closed her eyes for a bit after saying it. She didn't need to be rude. "I'm sorry Louise."

"You are right. I had a devil of a time getting that thing fastened. I hate wearing a seat belt. It wrinkles my pants."

Irene gazed out the front window. "This car needs a bath. I can't see out the window very well."

"Are you sure you don't want me to drive?"

Irene smiled. "No. I can still drive."

"Can you drive a little faster?"

"You in a hurry?"

"No, but I don't think the speed limit is," Louise leaned toward her in the seat and looked at the speedometer. "Ten."

"Oh for pity's sake, I'm not going ten." Irene wasn't sure how fast she was going, so she pressed a little harder on the accelerator. The car lurched.

"Mercy, Irene! Take it easy."

"Make up your mind, Louise. Do you want to go fast or slow?"

"I want to get there in one piece."

"That will happen," Irene stared at the pavement in front of her car. "Be calm."

Louise wasn't sure if it had been a good idea to let Irene drive. She drove like a snail, but surprisingly, she appeared to know where she was going. If they ever got there.

Irene found a good spot right in front of the parlor. "This is it." She slammed on the brakes and Louise jerked forward in her seatbelt.

"You're gonna kill me."

"I didn't want to miss this good parking space." As soon as the car came to a stop, Irene turned the key.

"Irene! You have to put it in park first."

"I did."

"No you didn't. Look!" Louise pointed to the dash.

Irene squinted at the letters in front of her. "C'mon. We'll fix it later."

"No. You have to fix it now. You don't want your car going home without, do you? Turn it back on, but keep your foot on the brake."

To Louise's relief, Irene did what she was told while Louise fumbled again with her seatbelt.

"Now come on." Irene opened her car door and maneuvered her cane out before her. "I can't wait for you to meet the girls. They know everyone in town. You can ask them about anyone."

"I don't know anyone, Irene."

"Oh. You'll be surprised."

They held hands as they made their way into the beauty parlor, so neither one would fall on the icy sidewalks. Louise wasn't sure if they could actually keep each other from falling, but it still gave her a sense of safety.

A bell rang as they opened the door. Louise jumped. "Oh my!"

A perky brunette sat at the reception area at the front. "Well hello, ladies. Irene, is this your sister you've told us about?"

Louise grew tense. What on earth had Irene been telling strangers about her?

"Yes it is." Irene turned to Louise and grabbed her arm, "This is Louise. My sister."

The receptionist got up from her chair, came around the desk and smiled, "Hello Louise. We're so glad to have you here today." The woman was shouting a bit.

Louise stood back. "I can hear just fine, miss. Thanks for the welcome though."

Irene smiled at the woman. "My hearing isn't so good, but Louise can hear just fine."

The woman blushed and covered her mouth, "I'm so sorry."

Louise shook her head, "It's fine." The shop was cute and seemed welcoming.

A blonde woman approached them from the middle of the room. "Hello Irene. Who do you have with you today?"

After the formal introductions to almost everyone in the parlor, the sisters sat in chairs right next to each other.

One hairdresser's name was Deb and the other Lori. The ladies worked in unison, sweeping up hair from previous cuts, then putting white paper collars on the sisters and covering their clothes with black capes.

Lori smiled at Louise, in the mirror. "What are you wanting today, Louise? Just a trim?"

Soon the pair were getting their hair dampened at the sinks, and tottering back to the swivel, hair-dressing chairs.

"How long have you been in town?" Lori asked Louise, from behind the chair.

Louise answered, but the questions kept coming. She asked her everything from how she liked Florida to what kind of shampoo she used. Did she go to school here in Durand? What year did she leave? Did she have children? In between the questions, Louise could hear Irene chatting with Deb. They laughed. Changes was a pleasant place to get hair cut. This had been a good idea.

Suddenly, another woman from across the room shouted, "Louise? Louise Williams? Is that you?"

Louise jerked her head so hard that Lori dropped the scissors. Who knew her here?

Lori turned Louise's chair around to face the woman now limping toward her. The stooped-over lady with gray hair and manicured nails didn't look familiar at all. "You don't remember me, do you?"

Louise shook her head. "I'm sorry."

Irene was facing the woman, too. "Sarah, is that you?"

Sarah? Louise thought of every imaginable older woman she could think of, but she couldn't place the name anywhere.

Then it happened. The woman stood tall in the middle of the beauty parlor. She put her hands on her waist and swayed her hips. "We are the Railroaders, mighty, mighty Railroaders! Every-where we go, oh, people want to know, oh..." Her black cape was flapping and her arms were flying in opposite directions. That's when it hit Louise.

"Sarah Michaels?"

The woman continued, grinning and nodding, "...Who we are...so we tell them." She pumped her fist into the air. "We. Are. The. Railroaders!"

Louise looked on to see if the woman would do a jump, just like they used to do in high school. But she just stopped and moved to take one of Louise's hands. It *was* Sarah. She hadn't seen her in almost sixty-five years, but she could never forget her smile, nor her laugh.

"How are you, Louise?"

They greeted each other with a hug. After a few questions about Louise living in Florida her whole adult life and Sarah staying in Durand, the two parted ways. Louise couldn't believe she'd found a high school friend after all these years.

It was hard to believe this woman was actually Sarah Michaels. Sarah had been one of the best gymnasts in Durand High School back in the

1940s. Her jumps had been amazing. She was head cheerleader for almost every year of her high school career. But the woman who greeted Louise was old. Her hair silver. She limped.

Louise looked at herself in the mirror as Lori sprayed her hair. She'd done a nice cut. Louise liked it, but all she could think of was her reflection. Did she really look as old as Sarah? She knew she did, but hopefully a little better. Unfortunately, reflections never lie. Despite the fact that she wanted to get up and cheer, right along with Sarah, she'd grown just as old. Still in her heart, she was once again a Durand Railroader cheerleader.

The sisters shuffled out again, holding hands until they got to the car. After that they were on their own to get into their designated seats.

"Don't forget," Irene called out. "We still need to stop and get milk."

Louise shook her head. *'I bet she doesn't know what we had for lunch though.'*

"I need a cart." Louise stumbled toward the grocery cart corral at the front of the store.

"I do, too." Irene followed her sister, heading directly to the corral herself.

"We don't need two carts," Louise scolded her. "We're just getting milk."

"Maybe not, but I can't manage to get through this whole store without holding on to one." Irene jerked at the cart closest to her. "I hope this one doesn't squeak."

The sisters maneuvered their way down the middle aisle. "We're quite the pair, sister." Irene laughed.

Louise waved her hand with a grin. "Go behind me so people don't know we're together."

Irene faked a scowl, "Oh, pulleeese."

"Where are the mangos?"

"Mangos?"

Louise turned around. "Yes, you know they're green on the outside and orange on the inside."

Irene shrugged her shoulders. "Oh." She slipped past her sister, who was now stalled in the aisle. "I always start in the dairy."

"Dairy isn't good for you."

"Of course it is. Milk, cheese, yogurt."

"Well, I do like yogurt," Louise now took the lead with her cart.

"Your tire squeaks," Irene declared, suppressing a chuckle.

"Go find me some WD-40 then," Louise grumbled. "I don't care." She headed straight past the pop toward the dairy section.

Irene tagged along behind her. "You don't want any pop, do you?" Irene hated to ask. She rarely had any in the house, unless she knew her grandkids were going to visit. Then she'd buy Vernor's.

"Pop. You mean soda?"

"Welcome back to Michigan, sister." Irene put a carton of cottage cheese in her cart and headed to the yogurt section to see what kind sister was getting.

"I like Greek yogurt." Louise loaded up her cart with the odd-shaped packages.

"How many do you need?" Standing shocked, Irene watched her sister pile in the cartons.

"It's cold out. We need to get enough for two weeks," Louise looked over the one package after another, and kept placing them in her cart. "One every morning."

Irene shrugged and scooted past her sister, "Okay…but you have to pay for whatever is in your cart."

"What do you think I am? Stupid? Of course I pay for whatever is in my cart." She moved her cart ahead from the side and began to push again.

"There's the milk."

"Yes." Each sister grabbed for a different kind of milk. Irene grabbed 2 percent and Louise started to place skim in her cart.

"That's nothing but water," voiced Irene.

"It's better for you than that one," Louise pointed to her sister's jug.

A man pushing cart sauntered by and looked toward the sisters. As he reached them, Louise said, "Hello," with a sultry voice and a wink.

Irene couldn't believe the audacity. "Louise! Concentrate."

Louise looked back at the milk jugs. "Why don't you get what you want and I will get the kind I like."

"We don't need a whole gallon of milk."

"Then get a half gallon." Louise placed her choice in her own cart.

"Louise, I know math class was a long time ago, but a half gallon for both of us is...," Irene held up her jug.

"Oh, yeah. Do they have quarts?"

"I've never bought one. I always buy this size." Irene placed her choice in the cart.

"You drink a half gallon, so will I." Louise scooted out into the aisle again. "Where are the oranges?"

Irene pointed down the main aisle to the opposite side of the store. "We get that last. We have an entire store to get through before the produce section." Irene took a side aisle. She asked her sister, now following her, "What cereal do you like?"

"None. I like yogurt for breakfast. And mangos."

"Okay, well I like cereal." Picking up a box of cereal, she leaned down for a bag of popcorn. "Do you still like popcorn?"

Louise smiled. "Oh yes. I love popcorn still. Do you have an air popper?"

"A who popper?"

"Air?"

"I do it on the stove."

"Wow. Nothing like being old fashioned."

"It's best that way."

Another older man approached the women. "Do you pretty ladies know where I can find the hamburger buns?"

Irene smiled, "Down the bread aisle. Which I think is over there."

"Thank you," the man dipped his head, pushing his cart in the direction Irene pointed.

Before he could get very far, Louise hollered to him. "Uh sir, I think the bread aisle is this way."

"Way to point the man in the completely opposite direction, sister."

"I did?" Irene coiled in frustration, "I was just trying to be being nice."

"Right," her sister moved past her again. "But make sure you know which way to send someone first."

Irene and Louise rejected and accepted items, one by one, as their investigation of the grocery aisles took place. Soon the sisters found themselves at the produce section. Louise filled her cart up on fresh produce, but not before picking up each one and mumbling under her breath about how bruised they were.

"The stuff comes from the southern states. It's a long trip up here."

"I miss Florida."

Irene knew her sister loved the southern state with its sunshine and beaches. She often envied the fact that Louise got out of the cold northern state of their childhood. Yet when spring came to Michigan, she always remembered why she never left the state for a warmer climate.

"Ready to leave now?" Irene made her way to the check-out lanes.

"I suppose. Although…" Irene watched Louise scan the room.

"What do you want?"

"I can't tell you."

"Why?" Her sister began to walk in a completely opposite direction. "Where are you going?"

"Just go. I'll meet up with you at the exit."

Irene didn't have a good feeling about this. But her sister was her own person. She headed to the shortest line and resigned to ignore the secrecy.

The long, tube-like paper bag was hardly noticeable in Louise's cart. She stuffed it lower before she reached Irene waiting by the door.

"You ready?" Her sister didn't look into her cart, for which she was truly thankful.

"Yup. Let's go."

"Did you get everything you need?"

"They didn't have a fresh coconut."

Irene scowled back at her. "You eat fresh coconut?"

"Of course."

The air outside the store hit her and sent a shiver up her spine which she hadn't endured in years. Even though the temperatures were now rising in Michigan, she still couldn't get used to the frigid breeze. She buttoned her coat higher on her neck and wrapped her scarf tighter, as she labored to catch her breath.

"I'll unload my groceries first." She pushed past her sister and made her way to the car.

She put the long bottle in the car as her sister struggled with her cane to unlock the doors. She tucked it behind a few of her own bags and then proceeded to the passenger car door to get in. Why did she feel wrong? Why did she feel like she was hiding her purchase from her mother? Being a grown woman, she had a right to purchase anything she wanted.

Getting into the car, Louise mourned her beloved Florida. If the doctor hasn't insisted on her getting help sooner than later, she would have at least waited until May to return home. Early in March was too soon. She snuggled down into her sister's coat a little deeper, putting her gloved hands to her face and blowing on them.

"Why didn't you turn on the car?"

"Sorry, I didn't think of that," Irene told her sister as she turned on the ignition.

"Hurry up. Crank up the heat." Louise said.

"You gotta wait for it to warm up."

"Ugh!" Louise shivered more.

"Want to head to the clothing store?"

"No. Let's just go home, where it's warm. Please?"

Her sister smiled. "Okay. You can use some of my sweaters until you can get to the store."

"When does it warm up here?"

"June," her sister giggled as she pulled out into traffic.

"Great." All Louise could think about was the warmth she'd find from the bottle in the trunk of her sister's car.

"Irene, why did you go past that street?"

"What street?"

That one back there." Louise pointed over her shoulder.

"Why would I go down that street?"

"That's your street."

Suddenly, Irene hit the brakes. Louise felt like she was about to go through the front windshield. She swore. "What are you doing?"

Her sister looked at her as though they were standing before God. "I don't know."

Louise looked out the windshield to find them sitting, motionless, in the middle of the street. "Irene?"

"Should I take this street?"

Louise realized her sister wasn't sure where she should go. So much so, she wasn't driving at all. "Oh my word."

"What?"

"Take a left here," Louise motioned down the next street. They nearly hit the curb as Irene turned abruptly. "Sister! What are you doing?"

Irene's face turned red, her motions slow.

"Irene, pull over." Louise saw her sister freeze in fear. She pulled at the wheel. "Over here. Pull off to the side."

Irene managed to stop the car. In the middle of the street.

"Good thing we live in a small town." Louise unbuckled her seatbelt a little quicker than before. "Get away from that steering wheel." She pulled her scarf closer around her neck and handed Irene her cane. "Switch seats. Hurry, before another car comes."

It took what seemed like ages as the sisters gathered their canes, got out of the car, and switched places. Once back in, Louise cranked up the heat and buckled her seatbelt again. Irene was just pulling her cane into the seat with her. "Buckle up, sister." She reached over to help Irene get her seatbelt strap pulled long enough to go around her. "You need to lose some weight."

As she finally turned to face the front, she realized that no cars had stopped because of their switch. Her sister shouldn't be driving anymore. "Do you know the way home?"

Irene looked out the side window. "I have no clue."

Louise began to laugh, at first with giggles and then with a gut-busting cackle. She looked over at Irene who now stared back at her.

"Why are you laughing?"

"We just did a Chinese fire drill. Do you remember the kids telling us about those?"

Irene then began to smile. "Chinese what?"

"Fire drill."

"What's on fire?"

Louise began to laugh harder, tears now dripping down her face. "Oh sister. Stop."

At that comment, Irene began to laugh as well. "Let's go home."

"Yes. Before I wet my pants."

Chapter 15

The last swig of alcohol Louise had taken was the last night she spent with Howard. They'd shared the last of her vodka, knowing her sister wouldn't allow such things in her home. Louise convinced herself she needed the bottle only for the extreme shivering she had each night before going to sleep. A little vodka would warm her up helping her with good sleep. It always had.

"You still hate alcohol, don't you?" Louise finally gained the courage to ask that night before dinner.

Irene glared at her sister, "Is that what you went off to buy by yourself?"

"Focus on carrying those trays to the living room, Irene." Louise motioned. "Don't have a cow." She knew this would happen if she even mentioned 'the "A" word' in her sister's home.

Irene didn't say a word.

"I need it."

Silence.

"It's too cold here. I'm not used to these arctic temperatures."

More silence. Irene headed into the living room.

"Irene?" Louise grew more agitated with the situation. "You don't have to participate in drinking it."

"I don't like alcohol in my home."

"I know," Louise let out a sigh, relieved that her sister was finally talking to her. "But technically, the alcohol isn't yours. I spent my own money on it. I will keep it hidden."

"In your own bedroom."

Taking a deep breath, Louise added, "Okay. My own bedroom."

"I do not want you coming to a meal...intoxicated."

"Geez, Irene. Why would I do that? It's for warmth. I can barely get to sleep at night. I'm so cold. The house is freezing."

"For goodness sakes, Louise! It's not January."

"Well, I'm not used to it. That's all I'm saying. I thought a little nightcap would make it a little easier. My bones hurt so."

Irene put her napkin in her lap as she sat down to eat, "I never want to see it."

"Okay."

"Never."

"Okay!" Louise folded her arms and decided changing the subject was the better idea. "Do you think the snow has stopped? Have you heard?"

Irene shook her head. "It's Michigan. We've had snow in May before. That's why we're watching the weather report on television."

The next morning, Louise woke up to a house which seemed to have been plucked straight out of Alaska. If she didn't have to use the bathroom so badly, she would have stayed put the entire day. Slipping into her slippers at the foot of the bed, she grabbed her Florida robe and headed to her bathroom. Her teeth chattered and her body shook with cold. When she left the bathroom, she went to the window and pulled back the curtain. So much for yesterday's forty degree temperatures. A couple of inches of snow now blanketed Irene's yard.

"Michigan weathermen still can't seem to predict snow."

Louise headed out of her bedroom, noticing a slight hesitation as she took each step. It was as if her limbs just wouldn't cooperate. As she made the last few steps, she heard people talking in the kitchen.

"I'll get it done, Irene."

"Oh Greg. What would I do without you?"

"I don't know."

As soon as Louise entered the kitchen, Greg looked at her and scooted out the back door. "Gotta go."

Louise stood and watched him leave. "I must scare that man off every time he sees me."

Irene jumped and looked over her shoulder, "Oh Louise! You scared me."

Louise walked to the counter to pull a coffee mug out of the cupboard, "I know I look bad in the morning, but geez."

Irene came up behind her and must have seen her shivering. "Louise, are you cold?"

"A tad. If you haven't noticed, there's snow on the ground."

"I'm going to get you another robe. That slinky Florida thing won't keep you warm."

While her sister left the kitchen, Louise filled her mug full and stood at the window watching handy-man Greg shovel more snow from around the garage. "That boy sure gets that done in a hurry. Smiles and all." Greg waved and smiled at her. "Well, there we go. That's a start."

Louise gulped the hot coffee. A few days earlier, she'd pulled out her own coffee-maker, and yesterday at the store, bought coffee grounds to brew. She couldn't stand that instant stuff any longer. Even though the heat burned her tongue, the taste was magnificent.

Her sister came back into the room with a heavy robe. She draped it around Louise's shoulders. Louise leaned forward in her chair so she could tuck it in behind her.

"Thank you."

"You're welcome. Hungry?"

"Let me warm up with this coffee first."

"What time is it?"

"I think around seven ten."

Louise took another sip of her drink, "He's up early to help."

Irene poured hot water into a mug over a tea bag, then pulled the bag up and out of her drink. "You know what's funny. He's not one to get up so early. Many times his mother comes by and Greg isn't out of bed yet and it's ten o'clock, but when it snows, or when he has a job to do, Greg is usually up early. Like it gives him some kind of purpose or something."

"I think it's sad."

Irene sat down at the table, "What's sad."

"Greg."

"Why?"

"I'm glad women can prevent things like that from happening now." As soon as it came out of her mouth, Louise closed her eyes, waiting for the fireworks.

"What are you saying? Greg shouldn't have been…?"

"Taken care of." This hole was getting deeper. Why couldn't she just keep her mouth shut?

Irene's face grew red and rigid. "How dare you say something like that."

Louise scrambled for something substantial to back up her comment. "I'm not saying he isn't worth anything. Look, he seems to be quite the worker. But he must be a hard drain on his mother. She's old. There probably won't be anyone to take care of him after she's gone. He'll probably have to go into some kind of institution."

"Over my dead body!"

"What? Are you gonna take him in?"

"I might."

"Irene. Really?"

"Yes. Abortion is wrong. Completely wrong."

"So you think if a woman finds out, for a fact, that her child is going to be intellectually disabled his whole life, that she would, in her right mind, want to have a child like that. Number one: She'd have a massive burden for the rest of her life. Number two: We have to pay for people like that. They are on disability their whole lives. It's better to take care of the issue before they are born. That way, no one has the burden to carry."

"Greg is not a burden."

Louise chuckled, "I know you think I'm a dimwit, Irene, but really."

"Dimwit is a good term. I think every human being is precious in the eyes of God. All of them. Especially those like Greg."

"Well, of course they are. God loves everyone. But some people, like Greg, are a burden to society."

"Greg has never been a burden to me."

"Of course not. You haven't had to raise him. But I guarantee,"

"No. Violet, his mother, she loves him."

"I'm sure she does. But at least now, we have a choice whether we feel we can handle a child, like him, or not."

Irene slammed down her tea cup so hard, Louise was sure it would shatter. "There are a whole lot of people I know, people *you* know, that God has given a full-thinking mind, who are a much larger drain on society than mentally handicapped people like Greg!"

Louise couldn't really argue about that, but she wanted to get her opinion in. "I'm just happy that women have a choice now. To do what they feel is right."

Irene pushed her cup aside. Louise could see the invisible soap box boosting her up, right in her chair. "This whole 'woman's choice' thing gets my insides churning. A woman who chooses to have an abortion has made a whole lot of other choices. All of those choices lead up to a child. An innocent human being. What rights does that child have? None." Irene folded her arms as the flush in her face slowly died down. But soon, out came the pointing finger, right at Louise. "If a person can make choices on their own, I would suggest they make choices to not, in any possible way, get pregnant in the first place. Especially if they are pretty sure their choice would be to not have to deal with a child."

Louise wanted to bring up rape or incest, to bring the conversation back to the issue of a disabled or sick child, but she knew better. Her sister had definite answers for most of her objections. Women's rights had come a long way since they were younger. Louise heralded it as progress. Good things. As her sister stood up to leave the table, she found herself gazing out on the man now almost finished shoveling their driveway. As she did, Greg raised his hand to wave at her. Perhaps he was an exception. He seemed to be fairly handy at many things, including getting all that nasty white stuff out of their way.

Chapter 16

Louise sat down on the bed and went through one of her boxes, deciding where she'd put her things. Brian had come over that weekend and he and Kathleen moved all the boxes right where Louise could easily access them in her sister's room.

Howard had carefully packed everything neatly and wrapped her glass items in paper. Unwrapping each layer made her miss him even more. Memories came with each thing she unwrapped. She'd gathered all kinds of unique items during her travels down through the years. Linens from Norway. Exquisite marble figurines from China. Even though she'd sold many things, she had kept those that brought fond memories of her travels. She remembered getting each one, from the person she'd purchased it from, to the shop which sold it.

Soon she realized the more boxes she opened, the more things would clutter the room. If Brian painted, she wouldn't want plant splatters ruining her precious treasures. She rewrapped some of the things and put them back in the box.

Irene had told her that morning that she would ask Brian to come over and paint. If he couldn't do it, perhaps Jade, her grandson, would. She'd even suggested a few colors, and Louise actually loved her ideas. Besides their alcohol issue after the store, the spat about a woman's right to choose, and her reaction to Louise's suggestion that they make Max a garage cat, her sister had continually shown her a generous and loving side. Irene could always be gracious. She could also always please their mother.

No matter how many times Louise had tried to please their mother, the stricter parent by far, she always came up short. The sisters often went on bike rides through the neighborhood, and Irene always picked the perfect flowers for mother on those rides. Louise never understood why her flowers always seemed wilted and ugly compared to her sister's by the time they handed them to their mother. Irene always got better and higher grades in school, where Louise always had to work extra hard for her top grades. Irene always had her nose in a book, whereas Louise wanted to run to the dime store for a soda, to meet the other cheerleaders for ice cream or shopping. Socializing had always been her favorite thing.

Irene had loved going to church. Louise didn't mind going, but she was always being reproved there for her endless wiggles and whispering to her friends.

Max came into the room. Louise looked down at the cat. Why couldn't her sister be in love with a dog? Not that she would love having a dog in the house, but at least he would be a little more compliant and could chase a ball. The cat slinked towards her legs and Louise immediately began kicking at him. "Go away you stupid ol'e thing." The minute she said it, a sneeze took hold of her body. She grabbed for the tissue box on the small table nearby. "Stupid animal."

As if sensing her displeasure with him, Max slinked off into the other room. "Wish that thing would go play in traffic."

"Why do you hate Max so much?" Irene stood at the sewing room door.

"I don't hate him." Louise hated getting caught saying nasty things about Max. Why did she have to talk to herself?

"How's the unpacking going?"

"Okay. I guess. I don't think I better unpack much until we can get Brian here to move things around a bit."

Irene entered the room, walking around picking up odds and ends. "We can clean out the closet first and then you can start storing some things in there."

Louise looked up from her seat on the bed, "Thank you for allowing me to use this room. I know it was a good room for your sewing projects."

Irene smiled. "It's okay. Better clean it up now. I'd hate to leave this disarray for Kathleen to have to take care of, after..."

Louise pulled out her Chinese marble figures from one of the boxes again. "Have I ever shown you these?"

Irene sat down beside her on the bed. "They're beautiful." She held one delicately in her hands.

"I got them in China. Remember when I went? Shortly after graduating from University of Michigan, I wanted to see the world. I was poorer than a church mouse, but I found this attractive young co-ed..."

"I remember the trip. Mother hated to think of you going with a man."

"Nothing happened. Truly. We just went as friends."

"Still sticking to that story?" Irene glared at her sister.

"Believe me or not." She took the figurine back from her sister. "It was a long time ago."

"Louise, will you answer a question for me?"

"What?"

"Why are you really here?"

"To help you."

Irene crossed her arms and gave her sister a look. The look of unbelief. Louise knew this was the dementia talking. Their conversation about the pact, long forgotten.

Louise looked into her sister's eyes. She decided to be honest. Perhaps she'd forget all the facts by tomorrow. "Ironic, isn't it? They thought they were helping you get help when they called me. In actuality, it was a godsend for me. The doctor just told me last month that I needed to find a place to live. Someone to be with me for awhile."

"Are you sick, too?"

Louise nodded. "I have..." could she really let it out? Tell her sister? Louise saw the pity instantly hit her sister's now softer eyes. "Congestive heart failure."

"Congestive what?"

"Heart failure."

"Is it bad?"

"Not yet, but I've known for awhile now. It will gradually get worse. The doctor wanted me to start living with someone. I have these attacks. I can't breathe. Once I take a pill or sit down, I'm usually okay, but sometimes they catch me by surprise."

Irene reached over and took her sister's hand and gave it a squeeze. "We're gonna be quite the pair. One of us won't remember an appointment and the other won't be able to get to it."

"I would have never imagined us doing this together. Would you?"

Irene shook her head. "Never. In a million Sundays. Although, I think I remember Momma saying this would happen one day."

"She did? When?"

"She'd often tell me," Irene picked up her finger and pointed it at Louise, "You'll need your sister. One day you'll understand that. I thought she meant it as a warning, not as an inevitable solution to our problems."

"Yeah. Me, too."

"You know this is their old bed."

"It is?" Louise smoothed down the comforter with her hand. "You know, they had sex in it."

Irene stood up. "Louise!"

"Well, it's true."

"It might be, but I don't think you need to bring that up."

"They were married. God says sex is a good thing when you're married."

"Oh, Louise. Stop it."

"You've done it before. You know I'm right."

Irene continued out of the room. "But I don't want to talk about Momma and Daddy doing it. Stop."

Louise laughed. She loved bringing up uncomfortable things around her sister. She laughed louder as her Baptist sister tsk-tsk-tsked her from just outside the room.

Irene's shuffling stopped and Louise heard her return to the doorway. "Louise. We have to go through with it."

"What?"

"You know what." Irene's hand shook on her cane. "The pact. It's happening. What we didn't want to happen is now reality."

133

Louise nodded. "But,"

"But what?"

"Can't we change it a bit? Things not so final?"

Irene shook her head. "You agreed."

"But."

"No. "

Her sister turned and left the room. Louise needed to remember the details now. Although, there were some things she'd never forget, especially the bottom line of the pact. She wondered where Irene might have hidden the agreement. She needed to find it. Before it was too late and she couldn't tell Louise where she'd put it.

One Saturday, Kathleen and Brian came to the ladies rescue and shuffled around furniture. Their children came with them and not only washed walls, but painted the room, a dusty blue color. Louise's things began to be put around the room and soon she found it to be quite pleasant.

Irene came to the doorway one morning and peeked into the room. "It's looking nice in here. I like how you put the table in the corner like that. Your china looks pretty on it."

"Thank you," remarked Louise.

Irene came into the room more and looked around. "I think it would have been better painted green though." And she walked out.

"Green? Everything in your house is green."

Her sister called from the next room, "My point exactly."

"Let's eat by the television tonight," Louise looked around her sister's kitchen, "Got any trays?"

"I think I have TV stands around here somewhere." Irene put food on their plates.

Louise made her way to the living room. Looking behind the door, she found the trays resting against the wall. "Oh, these are nice."

Her sister came in with a plate, "Oh good you found them. They should be nice, you bought them for me."

Louise looked up after snapping together one of the tables, "I did?" She took her sister's tray and placed it on one of the open stands.

"Yup. With that Walmart gift card you sent me for...Christmas? My birthday? It was a few years ago. "

"Well, that was worth sending you." Louise snapped together the second stand. "I'll go get my plate."

Louise was so relieved that her sister agreed to this type of eating situation. She'd always eaten in front of the television in Florida. Watching the evening news was a favorite part of her ritual. Returning with her tray, she picked up the remote and switched the television to a local station. "What time is it, Irene?"

Irene hollered from the kitchen, "What?"

"Time?"

"Why do you need a dime?"

"I never said I need a dime. I said, time!"

Irene came in with some napkins. "I don't have a dime right now. If you need one, get my purse."

Louise shook her head. "Never mind."

Louise looked at her sister's ears, Irene had forgotten to put in her hearing aids after her nap.

They each had their respective chairs now, almost like having their own space. Louise had pulled the second recliner from the other side of the room and put it next to Irene's shortly after arriving. Irene had fussed a bit, but now she was fine with the chairs sitting next to each other in front of the television. Irene had her knitting bag beside her chair and Louise had books beside hers. Now if they could only get used to sharing the remote. Louise insisted on having control of it. Irene could seldom figure out how to work the thing.

"Are you going to make me watch the news again? It's always so depressing and liberal."

"You can watch Judge Judy when it's over. Hurry and do your prayer, cause I'm hungry and I don't want to miss anything." The prayers before dinner were a ritual for her sister. She'd agreed to participate, but, she rarely closed her eyes. As soon as "*amen*" was uttered, Louise pushed the button on the remote.

Irene's lack of hearing aids caused her to talk even above the television broadcaster, "Turn it up louder, Louise. I can't hear it."

"It's 'cause you don't have your hearing aids in." Louise felt as though she were screaming to her sister sitting right next to her.

"What was that?"

Louise pointed to her own ears. "Hearing aids." Irene gave her a puzzled look.

Irene put her finger in her right ear. "Oh my. Oh my." She pushed her tray away from her chair and left for her bedroom. "I'll be right back."

Louise sighed. Now at least she could watch the opening news stories in peace without her sister's constant commentary.

Irene soon returned and sat down, pulling her tray back in front of herself.

Louise tasted a spoonful of mashed potatoes. "Better?"

Irene nodded. "I don't know why I keep forgetting to put those buggers back in after my nap."

A mass shooting today left three dead in a shopping mall in Miami. Police say the gunman walked into the Rose Brook Mall and opened fire on customers.

Irene shook her head, "How horrible!"

As police surrounded him, he turned the gun on himself.

Louise took a bite of her meatloaf. "This food is delicious, if I don't say so myself." She'd spent nearly Irene's entire nap fixing the food. They'd have leftovers for several days. She noticed her sister devouring her plate of food. "Slow down, honey. There is more on the stove."

A dab of potatoes was on Irene's lip. She pointed to her own mouth. Irene got the hint and wiped her mouth with a napkin. Louise wondered if her sister even paid attention to the broadcast.

Hollywood actor John Newton and long-time partner Andy Carter were married today in Los Angeles.

Louise again peered at her sister, who seemed more interested in the green beans than the news.

"That's wonderful," Louise cut up her meatloaf and put a piece in her mouth.

"What could possibly be wonderful about that?" Irene stopped eating.

Louise stopped in mid-chew. "Because, sister, if you haven't noticed, it is a new day. The time when each one can decide for themselves the type of life they want to live, and we, as American citizens, shouldn't have old laws on the books forbidding others the right to love whoever they want to love."

Irene stopped eating and sat back in her chair.

"What?" Louise wasn't sure she should ask her sister the question, but what the heck? "You don't still believe all that Sodom and Gomorrah crap coming from your Baptist church, do you?"

Irene sat up in her chair now and pushed her tray away. She fumbled with it and stood up. Just then the sound of train cars buckling outside shook the house. Louise jumped.

"Those blasted trains. I don't think I'll ever get used to that noise again." She looked on as her sister managed to get up out of her chair. "Where are you going now?"

"I can't sit here and watch the evening news with you."

"What? Why not?"

"Cause I hate the news. It just angers me."

Louise shook her head. "We need to be informed."

Irene turned around with her tray and eyed her sister like she was about to storm her own fire and brimstone down on her head.

"Go ahead," Louise acknowledged. "Leave me in my own abyss. I'll be fine."

"Call me back out when Judge Judy comes on."

Louise shook her head. 'If Judge Judy was the one show her sister wasn't upset over as a better moral compass of our country, they were in even bigger trouble than the evening news.'

Chapter 17

As Irene sat alone in her kitchen, she thought about one of the last times her and her sister had gotten along. She might be forgetting where things were these days, but she would never forget their discussion that morning. Taking a bite of the delicious food Louise prepared, she thought back to that cold October Michigan day, when they stood by the grave of their mother.

"She would have liked this day," Louise had said. A slight Michigan wind blew crunchy, rust colored leaves around them as their hand grip tightened. It wasn't customary for the sister's to hold hands. They had rarely gotten along at all. But that day, they actually needed each other. For support. "She would have loved the flowers," she added. "Pink was her favorite color."

Both sisters had nodded.

Irene had been wanting to bring up the subject. What better place than right there, that moment. "Louise, I want to talk something over with you." She had turned to make sure Kathleen, Brian and their children were still standing beside the black funeral home limousine. Finding them in deep conversation, she had turned to Louise.

"These past few months, even years, have been so hard."

Louise had raised her hands, as if in surrender. "I know, I know. That was horrible of me. I should have been here more."

"That's not it." Irene had shaken her head. "You have a life. I wouldn't have wished these past few months on anyone. Not even you."

"But I was her daughter, too. I guess I just didn't realize how hard it was."

"It was hard. The worst was how she ended up treating me."

"She didn't hate you."

Irene had laughed. She'd looked at the flowers, covering her mother's casket, and said, "I know that in my head, but my heart tells me otherwise."

"Look at how you dropped everything. Even quit your job for her. You did well."

"Stop."

Louise had turned toward her. "What? What's bothering you?"

"I need you to promise me something."

She remembered Louise grabbing the fingers on her left hand with her other hand. "What?" She had looked petrified.

"Help me."

"Well, I do need to be back in Florida in about..."

"No. Not now."

"Then, what?"

That's where they made the promise. Right there. Louise had fussed and told her she'd change her mind, but still promised. It would be their secret. Their agreement. No one else would know anything about it. No one.

"What if it happens to both of us? At the same time?"

Irene had shaken her head. "It won't. And I'm almost certain, it won't be you. I'm the most like Mother's side of the family. You favor Dad more. I need you to make it for me." A cool breeze had blown through the cemetery that morning, heralding the onset of another Michigan winter. The sisters had pulled their sweaters tighter around their shoulders. "We've talked about this long enough. Will you do this for me?"

Louise had sighed. "Kathleen isn't stupid, she'll figure it out."

"It doesn't matter. If she figures it out, you are out of the pact. Okay?" Irene had begun to grow impatient. She'd rarely asked her sister to do anything for her, but it had to be decided. That day.

Like they used to always do as little girls, Irene had said, "Louise, do you swear on your life, as my sister, that you will honor me with this pact? Today? At the grave of our beloved mother?"

Louise had nodded, sighed, and said, "I do."

Irene knew her sister wouldn't deny her. She would always keep this pact, with a Sister Promise. She wouldn't break a sister promise when they were children and she wouldn't do it now.

That had been nearly fifteen years ago. She hadn't forgotten it, but at the time it seemed much more dire than now. Yet she was on the verge of needing that graveside promise to come to fruition. Would it cause more harm than good? She thought about the heartache left after caring for her dementia-ridden mother. The hurt, the loss, the fear in her mother's eyes. Those images brought tears to her eyes. Despite the years which had gone by since the day of the promise, she agreed in her heart, the pact still needed to be fulfilled.

Chapter 18

Louise woke to the sound of a bird. She blinked her eyes a few times, caught another chirping song and smiled. It had been at least a month since she'd heard such a sweet sound. She could hear a distant train headed into town and the drips of water off a nearby gutter. They'd opened the windows last week amid unseasonably warmer temperatures, and the fresh smell filled her sister's house like air into a balloon. The sound of one train buckling into another erupted after the ding-ding of a railroad crossing. With the windows opened, all the train sounds were now even louder. Despite being raised in the train town, Louise was still getting used to the daily railroading sounds.

The thunderous train sounds reminded her of Florida on a rainy day. Oh, how she missed her home. The May sunshine streamed into her room as bright as the sound of the bird. She'd endured the last two months, but now warmer temperatures allowed her to leave her window open just a crack.

She wasn't always an early riser, but she loved daybreak. The sounds, the sight of the sun rising, chasing dark shadows to brighten the room. A sign of a new day beginning.

The next week was Easter. Her sister had talked about the Easter service at church. Perhaps she'd go with her next week. It wouldn't hurt her to attend church, especially at Easter. She wasn't a heathen. Perhaps she'd wear her pink suit. It would be perfect for the day. That is, if she could find it. Her wardrobe from the past two months had included all of her long pants and sweaters. Now she could unpack her summer clothes, shorts, short sleeved tops, and even a pair of sandals. A suitable and encouraging reason to get out of bed.

Getting up, she thought it odd she didn't hear her sister rummaging around in the kitchen. Irene always was the first one to get up in the morning. The creak of floor boards down the staircase or into the living room often woke her up. She was usually reading her Bible or praying in the living room chair by the time Louise managed to get herself up and around. Today, the house was oddly quiet.

Louise grabbed the new house coat she'd recently purchased, which gave her a little more warmth than the light one she'd used in Florida. She went into the kitchen and found the back door wide open, with the screen door the only barrier to the outside. Even that was unlocked. Louise looked out into the back yard. Her sister had said something about turning the ground in her flower beds yesterday, but they had both decided the ground was still too hard for that. The garage door was still shut. Would Irene try to go somewhere by herself? She jumped at the thought. Did she have the car keys or did Irene have them?

Rummaging through her purse, she found the car keys and sighed in relief.

Louise headed to the bottom of the stairs. She stood there for a few seconds and listened for Irene. A few creaks came from her sister's bedroom floor. But why was the back door wide open?

144

Louise went to the door and shut it. She pulled a sharp knife from the butcher block on the counter and an orange from the refrigerator. She'd been making her own orange juice for the past few weeks and enjoyed each one. The oranges weren't as sweet as the ones she got in Florida, but the fresh taste always made her smile.

As Louise picked the seeds out of her morning drink, Irene entered the kitchen. She still had on her robe and slippers.

"Good morning sister. You've been up awful early today," Louise greeted her.

"I hate sleeping in."

Louise eyed her sister suspiciously. "Sleeping in? It's only nine thirty."

Irene reached for the tea kettle and began filling it with water from the faucet. "Nine thirty isn't sleeping in?"

"Why'd you go outside this morning?"

"Outside?"

"The door was open. I thought..."

"The door was open?" Irene turned and looked into the living room. "Is someone here?"

"Why no," Louise laughed. "I think we're alone."

"Didn't you shut the door last night?"

Louise remembered last night's conversation clearly. She'd told her sister she was going to bed, and as they both got up to do so. Irene headed into the kitchen with her snack dishes. "You were the last one in the kitchen last night."

"I shut the door."

"Are you sure?"

Irene sat down with her cup, appearing a bit lost.

Louise saw this look in her sister's face more and more lately. Irene often appeared lost in her own kitchen or living room. She'd head into a room and quickly reappear to tell Louise she wasn't sure why she had gone into the room in the first place.

Irene lifted her cup to take a sip as the tea kettle's whistle erupted on the stove. Louise reached for the kettle. "You need water with that tea bag, don't you?"

Irene's eyes twinkled as she giggled. "Water would be beneficial."

Breakfast went without another glitch or memory issue. Louise sat across from her sister. With Irene's condition worsening, Louise could see now why her sister needed her. What would she do when things got worse?

"Sister?"

Irene looked up from her toast, jelly dripping down her chin. "Hmmm?"

"Your memory is getting worse."

"Just because I left a door open?"

"What if we'd been robbed?"

"We're in Durand. What kind of possible larceny could happen here?"

"A convict could get out of the Ionia prison and make his way here."

"That's a bit of a stretch, even for your imagination."

"Your memory is getting worse."

Irene looked up again with sadness in her eyes. "You just said that. I heard you the first time."

Louise nodded. "About that. I've been meaning to ask."

"I know what you are about to say."

"You do?"

Louise took her sister's hand. "Where is the pact?"

Irene sat back in her chair. "I've been thinking about that."

"You have."

Irene nodded. "I don't remember."

"Where would you think you would have put it?"

"Oh, lots of places."

"Maybe we should look for it. Go over it again."

Irene nodded. "Before it's too late."

The two sisters spent most of that day looking into every possible spot in the house for the pact. Louise was confident it was in some kind of office envelope. She hoped Irene hadn't accidentally gotten rid of it. Irene seemed to lose interest as their search progressed through the day. Louise had to keep reminding her what they were looking for and why.

"Irene, think through your most important places again."

"I have."

They ended up agreeing to just have lunch instead of looking. It was gone. Or hidden so well, they'd never find it. Perhaps it was a sign from God. Louise said, "I was hoping that this day would never come."

"You were?"

Louise nodded.

"You know how I feel about this pact."

"We have to do it." Irene looked at her sister with pleading in her eyes. "I keep remembering the hard times with Mother. The pain, the heartache.

147

I grew so tired, I was actually happy when she passed away. Isn't that awful? It's awful for a woman to be happy when someone she loves so much passes away. I will have the guilt of that for my entire life. I don't want Kathleen or Brian to have to suffer with that grief. Ever. You have to promise this is how it will go, Louise. Swear to me."

"I will. If you still think it's the best plan."

Irene nodded. "I think so."

"Are you having second thoughts?"

"About what?"

Louise went into the kitchen. "C'mon Irene, let's get some lunch."

Louise headed into her room to rummage through her boxes for more seasonable clothes. Irene had gone upstairs for a nap. She wondered if those papers, written by Irene after their mother died, still existed. Irene had told her she stored them in a safe place. If they didn't find them, perhaps Louise would be off the hook.

Knowing one of the boxes would be too heavy to lift to her bed for easier access, Louise pushed it beside the bed and sat down.

The box had come in the mail just the day before. It was probably the last of her belongings, hopefully filled with the summer clothes she'd encouraged Howard not to send until the end of his time in Florida. Why flirt with the option of wearing her favorite Florida clothes in the dead of a Michigan winter?

She opened the seals and looked in. On top of some of her hot pink, dusty blue, and minty green clothes laid an envelope. She flipped it over to find her name scrawled on the face. Opening it, she recognized Howard's handwriting. His first words brought tears to her eyes. I miss you Louise.

Talking to Howard every few days was a highlight to her life. She'd grown attached to him, without even really knowing how much, while in Florida. Now that he was no longer in her life on those mornings, lunches, and walks on the beach, she soon realized how much she loved this man. Despite the fact he was married. Perhaps it was a good thing her illness had sent her to live with Irene. He hadn't called her for about a week now. She knew he was busy packing and cleaning his van to head home.

It's a beautiful day here. If you were still here, we'd be walking on the beach. It would be our last visit together before I'd have to head home to my wife. There are moments when I think of what could have been with us. I so enjoyed your company. You are a funny, intelligent woman. But so was my wife. Funny how things work out.

Headed home today. I do miss my wife when I'm gone. Not the new woman she's turned into, but the old memories of how she used to be. If I don't concentrate on those memories, my endurance fades. I've never shared that with anyone but you. For some reason, I can't imagine anyone else understanding. Even my son thinks I just get worn out. He encourages me to take these two months away. Now that April is almost over. I have to return.

I dread the eight months to follow. Isn't that horrible? This disease is so hard on so many. I can't imagine what my wife feels being trapped in her body. Do you think they know? Sometimes I imagine her being deep inside her brain somewhere, screaming to get out. She's just so fearful and angry. Each time we visit, she looks at us as strangers. I see the face of my familiar wife. I know each wrinkle line and I remember when they weren't there. I've watched her eyes lose their glow to pools of stares. She gazes at me as though I were invisible. I guess that's what hurts the most.

Gonna walk on the beach just one more time this morning. Pack up my van and leave the beauty of my condo for the prison of my life back at home. Thank you for understanding me. Thank you for listening and not casting opinions on why I run away from her for months each year. I should have been honest with you from the beginning.

For some reason I am pretty sure you would have understood my secret.

I won't be able to call you anymore. Or talk to you once I get back across the state. But I'll think of you. For the next few months, you will be the memories I go to which will bring smiles to my face. I just wanted you to know that.

She placed the letter in her lap and sighed. No more calls. No more conversations to keep her sane here in her sister's home, a home which would probably never feel like her own. Would she be able to survive without talking to him for ten months? When he could talk again, it would be winter. She needed to get busy. Find something to distract her from her new life. She thought of the burden Howard carried. Would her burden with Irene be any different? The letter scared her for her own future. Would Irene turn mean? She couldn't imagine it.

Lifting the letter, she read the last few lines quickly.

Please do not call me unless it is an absolute emergency. I can talk while home each evening but often I have a grandchild or someone staying with me. I don't want them thinking I have even considered another woman right now. I hope you understand. Perhaps in January, you could come and visit again. I will look forward to it. Holding on to that thought, it will keep me sane until then. Good bye dear friend. Stay well.

Chapter 19

"You've thought about this, haven't you Kathleen?" Louise brought Kathleen into her bedroom after sharing supper with her and Brian that evening.

"Well, Aunt Louise," she shook her head, "Not really."

"My friend, in Florida, his wife is going through it right now. She's much worse than Irene, but he says she's mean and angry. All the time."

"Mom won't..."

"I've seen it before. I've seen the changes happen to people in my neighborhood. Many say that the main caregiver is the one who they become angry with. That's me." Louise shook her head. "Maybe, both of us."

Her niece who seemed to grow agitated with the conversation. "I've heard of this, but I've been so busy, I guess I haven't really thought about it." Kathleen now sat down in the other chair in Louise's room.

"Perhaps we should prepare ourselves more. Learn more about the illness. Maybe," Louise hated to even voice her next sentence. "What if I can't be well enough to care for her like you need me to?"

Kathleen shook her head. "It's okay, Aunt Louise. We'll figure it out."

Louise nodded. "You know, I thought my disease was going to be the worst." She kneaded her hands until the pain in them made her stop. "Maybe, I was wrong."

"I'll call the hospital tomorrow. I know they told me there are programs set up for caregivers. Maybe we can find out a little more. Make some plans. Just in case."

Louise nodded. She couldn't tell Irene's daughter that some of their plans didn't include her. There were some things left unattended. "Kathleen, perhaps you better take over your Mom's finances. Do you know where the will and such is? Does she have a power of attorney?" If Kathleen were to know the location of these papers, perhaps it would lead Louise to the pact documents as well.

Kathleen got up, "It's all ready. We took care of that last year."

"Where are the documents?"

"At the bank. In a safety deposit box."

"What about her checkbook?"

"She hasn't given me that yet. She wouldn't let me."

"I'll take care of it." That was all it took. Louise now knew how to get a hold of the papers she needed, but in doing so, she'd now be in charge of her sister's money.

"My checkbook?" Irene nearly dropped her cane. "I don't think so."

Louise knew this would be an issue. She needed to carefully select her words.

"You've stormed into this house..."

"I don't think I stormed into anyone's house. I just came to help you."

"No! Without any permission from me, you've come into my home." Her sister began to shake and her face turned red. "To help me? I was doing just fine without you. No warning. No 'Hey sis, can I stay with you?' Nothing. Now, you want to take over my finances, too?"

"Irene, sit down. You're gonna have a stroke."

"I just might." Irene sat down hard in her chair.

"Calm down."

"Calm down? Calm down?"

Louise nodded. "Yes. At least breathe."

Irene became rigid and silent. She folded her arms and gazed out a window.

"Irene, listen to me."

As a single tear caressed her sister's face.

"Irene, don't cry."

Without turning toward her, Irene said, "I never thought this is how my life would end." She shook her head. "Never in a million years. I prayed that one day I would go to bed and miraculously..." another tear slid down her cheek, "...wake up with the Lord. I always hoped I wouldn't lose my mind before going."

Louise got up.

"Where are you going?" Her sister looked at her as if she were the only person left on earth.

Louise patted her sister's shoulder, "I'm getting you a tissue."

"I have one." She pulled out a semi-used one from underneath the end of her shirt sleeve.

Louise still reached for the tissue box from the counter. "I might need one, too." Returning to her chair, Louise held out the box. "We never can chose how we leave earth. You know that."

Irene nodded, took a fresh tissue and blew her nose. "I know. But I thought living a good life. Honoring God..."

"Would get you an option? Name that scripture, sister. Maybe I would have tried a little harder."

Irene started to stand up from her chair, "I can't talk to you about this."

"Sit down, Irene. You forget one thing about me."

Irene turned back to her. "What?"

"I know what the Bible says about death. I'm not a total heathen."

"When's the last time you went to church, sister?"

"Well, it's been a while, but that's not the issue. I do own a Bible. And..."

"What?" Irene sat back down.

"I do read it from time to time. And," Louise raised a finger. "I was planning on going to church with you on Easter."

"No." Irene's face now changed. "You were?"

"Of course."

"You can't wear those low necked blouses."

Louise couldn't believe how she had to defend herself. "I own appropriate church clothes. My goodness!"

Irene's face brightened. Her eyes started to sparkle. "You really are going to church with me?"

Louise sighed and nodded. So much reaction from the mere mention of her attendance at the little Baptist church down the street.

If she would have known this would have been Irene's reaction to her deciding to attend church at Easter, she would have started with that. "Now...let's get back to the more important topic. Like your checkbook."

When Louise got back to her room, later that night, she glanced through her sister's checkbook. She'd found it on Irene's desk, stuck between some unopened bills. The last entry was in September. That was the last time a running balance had been totaled. Checks had been written since then, but some were missing important information. Most didn't have dates. Her sister's immaculate handwriting had now turned to illegible scribbles. The last check written was around January. Surely, bills were going unpaid.

She needed to talk to Kathleen right away. Kathleen needed to know this. Her niece was busy with the upcoming wedding and all, but this lack of attention was negligent. It was a wonder the electricity hadn't been turned off.

Tomorrow she'd look for bills. Bank statements. She had watched her sister take bills out of the mail. Had she looked at them?

Louise had been giving her sister money to partially pay their bills. She'd asked countless times to find out how much money to give her, but Irene never gave her the same number twice. Now she realized, she probably didn't have a clue.

For the first time since her diagnosis, she grew thankful. Her sister was right. It was a tough way to go. This would help to get through her own issues. Now she realized the pact was exactly perfect. She needed to be sure it worked.

"Let's go for a walk." The morning had presented itself warm and inviting, and Louise helped Irene put on her sweater.

"We won't get very far," Irene muttered. She'd been in an ornery mood for the past twenty four hours. Louise wasn't sure what was wrong.

"We'll go just around the block."

Irene grimaced.

"Oh, c'mon. It'll be good for you."

Irene picked up her cane. "What about Max?"

"He'll be fine. Let's walk down to the park."

Irene turned back to her sister. "I have a better idea. Let's go see the depot."

Louise smiled. This is exactly what would turn her sister's mood. She knew it. She followed Irene out the kitchen door.

Louise nodded. "Okay. But we can't get super close by walking."

Irene turned. "You're right. Let's drive."

"I'll drive." Louise had dropped her keys into her pocket after locking the door. Pulling them out, she thought to go back for her purse, then decided to leave it. What could hurt? They were just going down the street.

As they drove up to the ornate building Irene smiled, "I love this place."

They pulled into a parking space just outside the building and Louise instructed Irene to get out of the car. "Can we go inside?"

"What day is it?"

"Tuesday," Louise answered.

"I think they are open on Tuesdays."

As the sisters got out of the car, they gazed up at the slate roof of the Durand Union Station built long before they were born.

"I remember playing my clarinet outside this place one year."

"Wasn't it Fourth of July?" Irene glanced up at the dark, brown building. "Do you know they have it registered now at the National Register of Historic Places and the Michigan Register of Historic Sites?"

Louise smiled, "I'm impressed, Irene."

"We needed to memorize that when I volunteered here to show visitors through," Irene smiled, "Surprisingly, I remember quite a bit."

"Well then," Louise motioned to the heavy door in front of them, "Give me the tour."

"See this?" Just inside the door, past the oak woodwork, Irene ran her hand down one of the walls. "This is Tennessee marble. It's in the corridors, gift shop, waiting room, and restrooms." The sisters looked into the gift shop and then turned toward the ticket office at the north end of the building. Decorative wall stencils and frescoes adorned the large room which once housed waiting railroad passengers. Louise sat down on a bench in the middle of the room, to catch her breath. "I can never get over the beauty in this room."

Irene sat down beside her.

"This was one of the largest train stations in the nation in 1903 and 1904. It was home to the Grand Trunk Western Railroad, and the main line of the Ann Arbor Railroad. They shared the building. Upstairs," Irene pointed above her head, "were the offices of general officials, dispatchers, operators and Western Union."

Louise pointed to a corner of the large room, "I remembered a post office slot right there."

Irene nodded, "Remember when Mother would give us mail and we'd come up here and put it in that slot?"

"It's a miracle we weren't kidnapped or something. You couldn't allow two, little girls to do that now."

"You know there was a fire here in 1905, just eighteen months after the depot was dedicated." Louise didn't know that. "They say it started in the basement below the baggage room. The firemen were fighting the fire, but they had to cut their hoses to allow a train from the east to go through without delay."

"That sounds about right." Trains in the small town always had the right-of-way and often prevented residents from getting to their destinations on time.

"By the time the train went through, the fire had gotten out of control. These sidewalls remained intact," Irene pointed to the walls in the room, "but the fire destroyed all the woodwork. This part of the depot was spared. The loss was estimated to be about seventy five thousand dollars."

Louise shook her head, "That must have been devastating."

Irene nodded. "But they re-opened again on September 25 of 1905. Tile was used instead of slate to cover the roof. It changed the appearance of the building from a Chateauesque style to Romanesque."

"When did passengers stop coming through here?" Louise asked.

"About 1974. But before that, around 1912, Durand was often called 'Little Chicago,' because nearly forty-two passenger trains, twenty two mail trains, and seventy-eight freight trains came through here every twenty-four hours." Irene's face brightened and her eyes grew wide, "Can you imagine?"

Louise shook her head.

"In 1938, four out of five families in Durand were supported by a Grand Trunk employee." Irene smiled. "Like us."

"Yes. How long did he work with them?"

"Only a few years."

Irene nodded. "Remember during World War II, when troop trains were a regular thing. We used to stand on the sidewalk, waving our hankies at the young boys on the trains."

Louise nodded. She noticed a ticket machine in the corner, "Do passengers come through here now?"

Irene nodded. "Amtrak goes through. I think Edna's son used to get on here and go back to college after his spring breaks."

"I'm so glad they didn't tear this place down." Louise smiled.

"They almost did. Remember in 1976 when we had that Bicentennial celebration in town?"

"We had a big picnic that year. At the park." Louise nodded.

"Mother was so excited I'd come home for it."

Irene nodded. "That was the beginning of saving this old place."

Louise got up and went to see a few of the framed photos on the walls. Each depicted either a train heading into the depot or a railroad worker doing his job. Peeking into the ladies' room, she found the sitting room, just outside of the ladies' room, furnished with old furniture and decor that made it appear as it had been when she was a child. "I remember this room."

Irene called out to her, her voice echoing in the large room. "Let's take the elevator upstairs. There are some wonderful photos in the hallway up there."

Louise nodded. "I'm so impressed, Irene. Your memory is good today."

Irene laughed. "You memorize facts like this to point out to visitors all day long. Hard to forget those kind of things." She stood and pointed her cane toward the back of the building. "The elevator is between here and the gift shop."

The sisters shuffled to the door. "These," Irene pounded her cane into the floor, "Are terrazzo floors. Aren't they beautiful?"

Louise nodded. "Gorgeous."

The sisters took in each photo on the walls lining the hallway upstairs. Many brought back memories about her hometown that Louise had almost forgotten.

A rumble began as a quiet, yet fast approaching thunder. Louise looked at her sister, "Here comes one." Irene smiled, "Come in here," and led Louise into a large room with windows to the ceiling encircling the room. "Watch."

The rumble now turned to a roar. Irene pointed toward the east. A train headed down a track right in front of the grand building. "This is the best place to see this." Louise had forgotten the joy of seeing a train pass the old railroad station. The top of the train visible from the window they now peered out.

The roar of the train was only over-powered by a whistle alerting the town of the oncoming western-bound locomotive. Irene grinned and pointed. "Watch the tracks."

Louise peered out above the train to see the crossing bars lower and the lights flash, as car after car stopped for the train crossing through town. It could be a long wait.

Looking back from where they first saw the train, cars extended out of view. "Remember Mother would get so mad when we had to wait for these things before church, because we'd always be late?"

Irene giggled. "She'd nearly lose her salvation every single time. She would always say that, even though she knew it wasn't true."

"I'm sure she confessed once she got to church." Louise laughed.

The sisters stood and watched the caboose come into view, and the train headed out north of town. Louise reached down and held her sister's hand. "I will never grow tired of seeing that."

Irene squeezed her hand. "Me neither, sister. Me neither."

Leaving the depot, the sisters were smiling and laughing. Louise had grown hungry. "Let's head out for lunch. My treat."

Irene turned to her as she opened the passenger side of the car. "Didn't we just have lunch?"

Louise opened the driver's side door and got into the car. With all the facts her sister knew regarding the depot, you'd thought she'd have known whether they had lunch or not.

Chapter 20

Only one friend could help Irene with the confusion now haunting her days. Edna. She decided to go for a visit. Her friend lived just down the street a few blocks. It was a beautiful spring afternoon. She'd walk.

Louise was transfixed in reading a book. Many afternoons were just like this one. Irene would often just sit looking out over the yard. It was such a joy to see her flowers emerging from the frozen soil of winter. It was as if they had to peek out with their perfectly green leaves to see if it were safe to grow taller. She loved seeing the brown dirt give way to new plant growth.

She pulled her scarf around her hair, tightened her purse to her shoulder, and headed out, breathing in the fresh air of the day and the warmth of the sun on her shoulders.

"The checkbook?" Edna poured her friend another cup of tea. "That's a bit harsh, isn't it?"

"I'll say." Irene took a sip of the hot tea, burning her tongue. "Ouch."

"You okay, dear?" Edna touched her shoulder.

"Burned my tongue." Irene shook her head, "I just don't think it's fair. I've balanced my checkbook for years." She started to laugh.

"What?" Edna sat down opposite her. "Why are you laughing about that?"

"It never balanced. Never. Ever since my husband died."

Both ladies laughed.

"Perhaps she'll get it to balance. She's always been good at books."

"You know, Irene, God never gives us more than we can handle. This illness of yours."

"What illness?" Irene grew suspicious.

"Well, dear. We all know you aren't remembering things well."

"We all have those issues, Edna. Even you."

"But the kitchen fire?"

"What fire?"

Edna grew quiet now. She glanced at her like she wasn't quite sure what to say next.

"It's Louise who is sick. Not me. Not sure why they keep being suspicious of me. They must just want my money."

Edna took her hand. "No, that isn't it. They just want to keep you safe. Keep your money safe."

"By taking my checkbook?"

Edna smiled at her. "Now. What about that new woman going to church with us? Do you know her?"

Irene shook her head. She had no clue.

Louise wasn't sure how long Irene would be gone, probably just taking a walk around the block, but she immediately went to the desk in the living room in search of bank statements or unpaid bills. She found the bills fairly quickly. Each one had been written on with Irene's hen-scratching marks. Nothing made sense. Most were just a month or so off. The bank statements were missing. Part of the pile was unopened letters. She found cash, layered between some unopened Christmas cards. It must be some of the money she'd given Irene over the last few months. She'd wait for Irene to get home and then show her.

Shuffling through the rest of the piles, she remembered how much she hated her sister's pack rat habits. Nothing was organized. Not one paper in any of the piles made sense from the others. She found an unopened house insurance bill from October. *Good thing she didn't burn the house down a few months ago.*

For fear her sister's funds were too low, and without bank statements, Louise decided to just pay the overdue bills herself. She had plenty of funds now that her condo sold in Florida. Hopefully, money would never be an issue for her again. One less burden.

After organizing the bills, she decided to look in one more place for the pact papers. Irene's desk was a mess. She liked things in their places. Piles and piles of papers made her crazy. She remembered back to the time when she and her sister shared a bedroom. This had been an issue even back then. Looking into a small drawer in the desk, she found a key sitting on top of a tiny manila envelope. It was a small key, not made for the house or the car. She pulled out the key with its tiny envelope and read the name, *Sagelink Credit Union.* The words underneath were exactly what Louise needed to see, *safety deposit box.* This was it. This had to be where the papers were located. She'd go visit the bank tomorrow.

She didn't often get peace and quiet in the house, so she decided to nap for a few minutes. She scooted the cat off the sofa, wrapped up in a blanket, and lay down. Once Irene got home, she'd start dinner.

Drifting off to sleep, she thought of Howard. She missed their talks.

"Are you sure you will be okay going home?"

Irene didn't understand the question. "Walking home? Of course."

"Thanks for the lovely afternoon. I love your visits. Give Louise my best. I can't wait to see her in church."

Irene waved over her shoulder. "I will. Goodbye."

A bird chirped over Irene's shoulder with a sharp, high-pitched noise. In succession. As if no one were listening to him. Irene felt his pain.

She walked down the south street heading toward the depot. Irene loved the building. She'd spent countless hours volunteering her time, going through old boxes of artifacts and maps. Many of the activities held at the building required volunteers to man tables, decorate, and help with the fundraising. Volunteers like Irene, down through the years, were responsible for creating the beautiful building which the community admired and loved. She'd have to take Louise there one day. She'd probably like a tour.

A train whistle sounded off to her right, startling Irene back into her walk. Looking in the direction of the whistle, she became a little disoriented as to where she was. She stopped in the street. The red house to the right was totally unfamiliar. Looking to her left, a white house with green shutters was also not recognizable. Irene's heart began to race. She didn't recognize the street or the location.

She walked a little farther down the street. Hopefully, as she kept going, something would look familiar. Tripping on a high edge in the sidewalk, she stumbled a bit and nearly fell. Her heart rate escalated. What if she never got home? Would Louise miss her and start looking for her? Louise had her checkbook now. Maybe she wouldn't need her any longer. Maybe this was a ploy to get rid of her all along.

Irene clutched her handbag to her side. What if someone tried to come along and steal it? Irene grew tired and hot. The sun was warm. Her sweater began to stick to her. She was breathing so hard, she could barely walk.

She headed down another unfamiliar street. This whole experience seemed so wrong. She lived in a small town. Every street should be familiar, each house filled with people she knew. Did she dare go up to one and knock?

She stopped at the end of a driveway and looked toward a house with blue shutters. The gardens looked clean and ready for planting. The house seemed inviting. Surely, good people would be behind the front door and she could ask them how to get back to her street.

Louise woke up to the phone ringing. She stirred and pulled the blanket off her legs to get up. Somehow Max had gotten on top of the blanket. He must have been sleeping on top of her. She scooted him off her legs, the phone continued to ring. "I'm coming, I'm coming."

Her sister still insisted on having a land liner in the house. She'd have to convince her to get a cell phone. Soon. She reached for the phone and rubbed her forehead to wake up. "Hello."

"Aunt Louise?" Her niece's voice helped awaken her more.

"Yes. Kathleen?"

"Is mother there?"

"Um, maybe. I just woke up. She went for a walk a few minutes ago. What time is it?"

"Five o'clock."

"Oh my. Are you sure?"

"Yes, I'm looking at my wall clock right now. Where'd mother go?"

"Oh Kathleen. Oh my."

"Aunt Louise, what's wrong?"

"She left. For a walk. At one o'clock."

"Irene? Irene!"

Irene turned around to find Greg walking toward her.

"Irene. Why are you here?"

"Oh Greg! Oh Greg. This kind lady was giving me something to drink."

"Yes, I live here. Do you know this lady?" Irene's new friend held her hand.

Greg nodded. "Yes, she's my neighbor."

Irene stood up and hugged Greg. She'd never been so relieved to see someone in her whole life.

"Why are you here?" Greg seemed to know she was out of place. "Do you know her?" Greg pointed to the woman who had been so kind to her for the past hour or so.

"No, but she's been very kind to me."

"I didn't think you knew her. Louise is looking for you. We all are. Where have you been?"

"She's lost. Can you help her get home?" The woman stood.

He smiled and agreed, "Yes. They're looking for her."

The woman nodded and said, "I'll go with you. I think she's gotten lost."

Irene spoke to the woman. "It's okay. Greg can get me home."

"Are you sure?"

Encounters like this were common to Greg. Violet had told her about them. People often assumed he wasn't someone to count on, but somehow Irene knew he was. She loved Greg. He'd always helped her.

"It's okay. By the way, what is your name?"

"My name is Connie."

"Thank you, Connie. Greg can get me home."

"Okay then." The woman backed away and let Greg take Irene by the hand and walk her down the sidewalk. He waved back at the woman.

"C'mon Irene. I'll get you home."

As Irene walked, hand-in-hand with Greg, she wondered how she could have gotten so lost. Thankful, Greg had found her. She clutched his hand tighter.

He looked up at her and assured her again, "It's okay Irene, I'll get you home. Don't worry."

Soon Irene recognized her street. Relief filled her soul upon seeing Brian, Kathleen and Louise in the driveway. Familiarity replaced her confused mind. Brian appeared to be leaving in his car; Kathleen had her walking shoes on. She shouted out to them from the corner, waving a hand in the air. "I'm here. Greg found me."

Greg smiled up at her. "It's okay, Irene. I'm getting you home."

Louise came down the sidewalk toward them. Her face was stern and tense, and lacked color. "Oh Irene. Where have you been?"

Greg announced again, "I'll bring her to you, Louise. Stop worrying."

Greg walked her up to the front of the house and placed her hand in Louise's. Louise sounded choked up and emotional, "Greg, where did you find her?"

Before he could answer, Irene chimed in. "I just got turned around on my way home from Edna's. A kind lady, back a block or so, gave me something to drink. I'm fine. Greg helped me." Louise squeezed her hand. It felt clammy and cold.

"I didn't know you went to look for her. How in the world did you find her?" Louise asked.

"God." Greg stood back, appearing proud of himself. "God helped me." Greg turned to leave but added, "See ya, Louise. Bye, Irene," before heading across the driveway to his house.

"Oh Irene, you must be starving." Louise tucked Irene's hand under her arm as together the sisters made their way back into Irene's home. Kathleen followed.

169

Chapter 21

That night, Louise cooked dinner. She'd asked Irene over and over what she wanted her to cook like how their mother soothed them when they were young. Irene thought the whole matter a God-send. Her sister seemed worried. It seemed as though Louise could burst into tears at any moment, jumping at the chance to help Irene with whatever she needed. Perhaps Louise was here to help her, not make her life more miserable.

Kathleen left after she and Louise cleaned up the kitchen. Irene went to her chair in the living room, thankful to be home. The fears from the afternoon were now replaced by thankfulness and a need for rest. How had she gotten lost in her hometown? She knew almost every street name, right where sidewalks began and ended, where cracks and uneven edges buckled the paths. God had even blessed her with a new friend. Connie hadn't run her off, but sat her down and tried to help her. Irene wondered whether she'd remember where Connie lived. Perhaps she'd stop by one day and thank her for her kindness.

As she settled into her chair, she sent up a quick thank you prayer for Greg. He was her hero. She needed to remember to tell Violet about how brave he'd been. Resting her head back, she wondered what she could do to thank him. She sighed and closed her eyes.

Louise walked in from the kitchen, "Is there anything more I can get you, Irene?

Irene opened her eyes. "No. Sit down, Louise. I'm fine."

Louise plopped down in her chair, "Oh my." Louise looked over at her. "My sister, you did give me a scare today."

Irene nodded. "I'm sorry, I didn't mean to frighten everyone. I didn't do it on purpose."

"I know. I know." Louise waved her hand in the air and then closed her eyes. "Put the fear of God back into me today."

"Well then," giggled Irene, resting her head again, "maybe I'll get lost again tomorrow."

"What?" Louise sat up in her chair. "Don't you dare. Are you stupid or something?"

Irene giggled again. Her sister was beginning to sound like herself again. "No sister, I might be forgetful, but not stupid."

The room grew quiet. The clock ticked louder than any other noise in the room.

"I've never been so scared," Irene sighed. "In my whole life."

Louise shook her head. "I don't know what I was thinking. What possessed me to allow you to go on a walk by yourself in the first place?"

"Louise, it isn't your fault. How were you to know I'd get lost in Durand, for goodness sake?"

"It was stupid, but not only that, I fell asleep for over three hours. I rarely sleep that long in a stretch at night. Let alone in the middle of the afternoon." Louise stopped rambling and looked over at her. "I'm sorry you were afraid. That must have been dreadful."

Irene nodded. "I don't want to do that again." The sisters sat quietly for a few minutes. "It might get worse for me, you know."

171

Louise looked over at her with the same fretful look as she had that afternoon. "Are you afraid of that?"

"Wouldn't you be?"

Louise nodded.

"I've tried so hard to remember well. Every day brings new challenges." She looked down at her hands. "Louise?"

"Hmm?"

"I'm glad you're here. With me. Helps me not be as afraid."

Louise smiled, reached over and patted her hand. "I'm so happy Greg found you. He must have been listening when I told Brian and Kathleen about you being lost."

"He's always been a joy in my life." Irene smiled. "Greg is a treasure."

Louise looked down and began to pick at her fingernail polish.

"God created him in the very image of Himself. No, his brain isn't perfect, but that makes him no less a person than anyone else."

"I know. I agree. Today, he made me realize that simple does not make you worthless."

Irene nodded, "If my getting lost made you realize that even more, then I would get lost all over again."

Louise relaxed in her chair, "If you need to teach me anything more, then by all means, do it. But can it wait until tomorrow. I can't handle any more today."

Irene smiled. "I'll do my best to get to my bedroom okay tonight."

"I'm here. I'll help you."

For the first time, since she arrived, Irene began to feel peace about her sister's presence.

Irene poured Louise's coffee.

"Smells heavenly."

"Mmm, hmmm." Irene sat down and began eating her breakfast.

"You are quiet this morning."

Irene nodded. She knew she needed to bring up the subject. Talk it over with Louise. "I do have something on my mind."

Louise's hand shook more than usual this morning as she purposefully set down her coffee cup. "What?"

"When will we know when it is time?"

"Time for what?"

"The pact."

Louise bowed her head. "I don't know." She peeled a napkin off the holder. "Perhaps, you'll just know."

"I don't think so. I think the decision will rest on you."

"Me?" Louise stared back with fear in her eyes.

"We've known this all along."

Louise sighed. "I know. But Irene..."

"Don't you dare change your mind about all of this."

"But..."

"No buts. I mean it."

A train whistled sounded in the distance followed by stilted silence.

Irene looked at her sister, "I saw fear in Kathleen's eyes yesterday when I came home with Greg. We can't let it happen."

"Okay." Louise set down her spoon and pushed herself away from the table. "I made the pact. I remember."

"Good. 'Cause who knows how long I will..." Irene watched her sister trying to get up to leave the table. "Please Louise, sit down."

Louise stood, but stared back at her.

"Sit down and eat your breakfast. It's okay."

Louise sighed and sat back down. She sipped a bit of her coffee. Another train whistle sounded across town. Same train, different tracks. "You know something?"

"What?" Irene munched on her toast.

"I thought it would be me. When we made this silly pact so many years ago, I thought you'd be the one to care for me. You've always taken care of me. I'd be the most likely to..."

"Why would you think it wouldn't be me?"

Louise shook her head, "Cause you're the good one. You've been faithful. You love God. You read your Bible. You attend church." Louise wiped off her mouth. "Faithfully. You've done so many things for others."

"Bad things don't happen to good people? That's bad theology. Bad things happen to good people all the time."

"Where does it say that?"

"It rains on the just and the unjust."

"Well, why? I just can't believe..."

"I look at it as another reason why we need Him. He is a jealous God. He wants our attention. He wants us to trust Him."

"Jealousy? That's a horrible reason to give us difficulties."

"Maybe. But it works. Someone who won't look to God when everything is going great, when they're happy, will often call on God when they're hurting and alone?"

174

Louise nodded.

"When and if you go through with it, I'll be all alone. "

"We can fix that."

Irene glared at her sister. "No we can't."

"Of course we can. It isn't set in stone."

"Louise. No. You agreed. To all of it." Irene waved her hand through the air. "All of it." She looked at Louise with intensity. Determination. After yesterday, she needed to be sure Louise would follow through. "You agreed."

Louise sighed.

"Finish your breakfast."

Kathleen had taken Irene to a dental appointment. Louise faked not feeling well and called her the previous evening to get the day to herself. As soon as Kathleen's car pulled out of the driveway, Louise got busy gathering all of Irene's bank statements. She got out the safety deposit box key again, and noticed that the bank was actually a credit union. This pleased her. Credit unions clerks were always helpful.

The night before, she'd thought through how she would gain access to Irene's deposit box. There was really only one way to legally access the box, but Louise had never been one to be bothered with sticky-picky legalities.

At the credit union, she zeroed in on the youngest clerk at the counter. Thankfully, no one knew her here. Smiling, she showed her sister's key to the young woman. "May I get into my safety deposit box, please?"

"Sure. May I please see your identification?"

Louise showed the clerk Irene's driver's license.

175

The clerk glanced at the card. "Okay, Mrs. Fredericks."

Louise smiled. Her nervousness disappeared.

"Do you have your key?" The clerk glanced back, shuffling through a ring of keys.

"Yes. Thank you."

As they entered the vaulted room, Louise felt the cold dampness in her bones. It took a few minutes for her eyes to adjust to the dark. The clerk pulled out Irene's box and placed it on the marble table in the center of the room. "Here's your box, ma'am. I'll be back in a little while to check on you. Feel free to call me if you finish before I return." She smiled at Louise as she left the room.

Louise opened the box. It was there. Tucked neatly inside a large manila envelope. With tears in her eyes, she opened it, and instantly flipped to the back page to see her own signature, along with Irene's at the bottom. It was still hard for her to believe she'd have to be the one to carry it out. She felt the bumps of the notary stamp. The papers were legal and legitimate.

She remembered back to the day when Irene insisted they type out the agreement. Neither of them could type well, but Louise was a bit faster than Irene. She'd inserted the paper into the whirring electric typewriter, and together they made out each direction in sequential order. They had to rip out and tear up several sheets of paper before the pact was worded correctly. In their frustration, both sisters had to stop and fume from time to time. She remembered Irene pacing around her as she typed out the signature lines.

When Irene insisted on having the document notarized, Louise had laughed. "Oh Irene. Don't you trust me?"

With her arms folded and a look of determination on her face, Irene had answered, "No, Louise, I do not. I want this perfect. Unchangeable. I want to know it is sealed in cement and cannot be broken."

"But if it ends up being you," Louise had teased. "If the disease hits you, .you won't know if I will follow through or not. Who's going to enforce it?"

Irene glared at her. "If you sign this, you'll have to follow through."

Louise leaned back in the chair, folded her arms, and smiled.

"Stop that. You're making me angry."

"I'm just saying."

Irene softened and pulled up a chair close to Louise. "Louise, if you love me at all, you will help me. You will do this. Please promise me."

Louise remembered that look. She'd seen it just a few days before, at the gravesite. As much as she would have loved to have taunted her sister with not doing it, she had known without a doubt that she had to do it. She had made many promises in her lifetime, but this was blood. Sister blood. Louise knew at that moment that nothing would stop her from following through.

So she'd promised Irene. Not only with her word, but with the signed document she now held in her hand.

Stuffing the envelope into her bag, she glanced through the other items in the box. There were keys, possibly to Irene's house or car. A few plastic-wrapped historic coins. And a jewelry box. She opened the box to find a gold wedding band. It must have belonged to Irene's husband. She needed to remember the ring. Perhaps she should take everything out now, in case she was discovered as a fraud. Would she be so lucky to get into the box again as easily? She shrugged and placed everything back in. It had worked once, it could easily be done again.

She closed the box and locked it. The clerk soon came back and returned the box back to the shelf.

"Did you get the items you needed?"

Louise nodded. "Yes, thank you."

"You're welcome, Mrs. Fredericks."

"What is your name, sweetheart?" Louise leaned toward the clerk and squinted at her name tag.

"Grace."

"I appreciate your help, Grace." Louise repeated the name to herself until she could get out to the car and write it down. Next time, she'd know which clerk to approach first.

When Louise finally reached Irene's car, she cussed as she rummaged first through her purse, then her coat pockets, before finding her keys. She turned on the car to get it warming, and pulled the envelope out of her purse. She opened it, gazing over the first few paragraphs of the agreement. She remembered going with Irene to the notary's office to talk him into putting his stamp on the papers. He'd hesitated until Irene insisted she pay him a little more for the authorized stamp. Louise remembered he shook his head and flinched as he crushed the paper between the metal stamping tool.

Louise flipped to the third page. Cringing at the words, now she shook her head. Seriously. Why was this so important to Irene? Then she envisioned herself trapped in Irene's body right now. She sighed. Considering the issues she'd been having with her own health, Irene's demand for the pact seemed reasonable. Could she do this, though?

Reading over the last page, she nodded to herself. It really was ludicrous, yet Irene was her sister. Louise had to make up for their disagreements and squabbles since Mother passed away. She nodded. This was the right course of action. She could make up for the way she'd treated Irene by fulfilling the pact. By honoring her sister's wishes. She just wondered if she'd be clever enough to pull it off without making Kathleen or Brian suspicious.

Chapter 22

Louise paced in her room, back and forth, to the window and then to the door. She needed to talk to someone soon or, she would lose her mind.

The windows were open and the spring breeze filtered into the room in spurts. Despite the warm temperatures of May, Louise still felt cold. Tired. The doctor had upped her medicine last week and that helped, but the weakness grew harder to fight. She'd never envisioned her needs trumping her sister's. This wasn't supposed to be how it turned out.

If only she could talk to Howard. Hearing his voice would calm her heart. He'd gone silent since February. She'd hoped he would call her from time to time, or at least write, but she guessed if his family found out, it wouldn't look good for him. Howard's integrity was as important to him as her loyalty was to Irene.

She didn't want to cause Howard issues with his family, but she couldn't avoid staring at his number on her phone. If she could just get his opinion regarding the pact. Talk it through. Make it clear in her head what might work or what wouldn't.

She selected his number on her contact list, punched the call button, and held her breath. Just hearing his voice would bring her joy.

After the second ring, she heard a tap on her door. She ended the call and exhaled.

"Louise. Are you in there?" Irene called.

"Yes. What'd you need?" She'd never told Irene about Howard. Her sister would cast that glance and ask questions. How would she ever explain she was in love with a married man? Just saying it in her head made her feel shameful.

"I think we need to go visit mother's grave."

"Flowers?"

"Yes. It's almost Memorial Day. Shouldn't we make it look pretty? I can't go by myself."

Irene rarely went out alone anymore, even for a walk. The family made sure of that.

"Yes, you're right."

"Where would we get flowers?"

"At the store. There should be some annuals out now."

"Yes. The store," Irene turned to leave, "annuals should be out now."

Irene repeated conversations over and over now, as if repeating it would make it clearer in her head.

Louise tossed her phone back onto her dresser. Why have a phone that never rang? Yet the thought of never talking to Howard again; made her never want to cancel her calling plan.

At her Mother's grave, out in the country north of town, Louise pushed her white-peppered hair out of her face. She should be used to the growing Michigan humidity. Sitting back on her heels, she watched her sister take the bucket and go for water. Her sister's slumped shoulders and the gait of her walk made her appear so much older than when Louise had arrived in February. This disease was wasting no time in taking, not only her sister's memory, but also her ability to perform simple tasks.

"Over there, Irene." Louise pointed toward the water spigot close to the road. "See it?"

Irene looked around and then headed for the spigot. Louise went back to digging holes. The white-tipped pink petunias they picked up at the store on the way, now danced in the summer-like breeze.

Louise waited for what seemed like forever. "Irene, you are slower than those pokey trains in town."

Irene finally returned with the bucket of water. She'd sloshed out most of it on the way. Together, they poured water into each hole then added the flowers. Irene knelt beside Louise and helped her stuff dirt around the plants. They both sat back to admire their work. Louise rubbed a gloved hand over their mother's headstone to remove remnants of grass cuttings and bird droppings.

"Mother would love these flowers, especially the pink ones." Irene smiled. "I miss her. Don't you?"

Louise nodded. "She loved pink." Louise looked over at her sister. "I miss her, too. It's hard to believe she's been gone so many years. You look a lot like her, Irene."

Irene shook her head. "I'm not as beautiful as she was."

Louise laughed. "Yes, you are. Stop it."

Irene seemed to want to cry. "I'm so thirsty."

"Me, too. Let's get home and make some lemonade. Okay?"

Irene nodded. "Ice cream sounds better."

"Oh no. Since staying with you, my figure is getting out of control. You're too good of a cook, dear sister."

"But what about an ice cream cone? Doesn't that sound delicious." Irene stood and gathered up their tools, putting them in her now empty water bucket. As she did, Louise noticed her wet shoes.

Louise groaned as she stood, "I can barely stand up. I haven't weighed this much in years. Good thing my pants have an elastic waistband. And now, you want more calories. We need to get you home and out of those wet shoes."

"Forget about an ice cream cone." Irene announced.

"Yes, let's just concentrate on the lemonade." Louise picked up the empty plastic flower bins.

"I'd rather have a hot fudge sundae."

"No. Now let's just head for home."

"Not until you promise me an ice cream sundae." Irene stood still.

"The warmth of the day was taking its toll on Louise. She adjusted her sunglasses. "Irene. You do not need a sundae."

"Yes I do. Promise me."

"Sister," Louise pushed back her hair with her arm, "Really?"

Irene folded her arms.

"Oh my goodness, Irene. You're a piece of work. Let's go get ice cream."

Irene smiled and started toward the car.

"You're gonna kill me early."

"Well, at least," Irene grinned, "you'll die with chocolate on your lips."

"And my hips."

After putting the gardening tools in the trunk, Louise went over to unlock Irene's door.

Irene turned to her. "Don't forget, sister."

"What dear? What did we forget?"

Irene pointed a finger in her direction, "You promised."

Louise sighed. "I know. I'm working on it."

That night, Louise decided to try another important talk with her sister. She decided the only way to make this real for Irene was to take her, to have her pick out her own things. Talk to the director for herself. She picked up the phone book and looked through the listings of funeral homes.

In the morning, Louise poured hot water into her sister's cup of tea. "Sister, I think it's time to plan your last day."

"Do you think?"

Louise rubbed her arms and nodded. "Do you think you can do that?"

"Tell me again what we decided."

Louise sat down across from her sister, who seemed a little more lucid today than the past few days.

"We need to make arrangements. With the funeral home and the director. Do you think you can make those kind of decisions today? I want everything to be like you want."

Irene smiled. "Thank you. But will they go along with this whole idea?" She was understanding.

Louise smiled. "We'll see. This whole plan may unravel if we can't encourage the director to do it with us."

Irene gave her a frightened look, "Oh Louise, it can't. It has to work. You need to make it work. You promised."

Louise shook her head. "I can't guarantee anything. But I'll try."

Irene sipped her tea with shaky hands, spilling a little on the table. "I hope it will work. I don't want to be a burden."

Louise patted her sister's shaking hands. "I'll do the best I can. Do you think you can manage to get yourself ready?"

"Where are we going?"

"I just told you. The funeral home." Louise hoped their plan would hold. Today would be a deciding factor.

Louise drove everywhere now. She wasn't sure if it was the right solution, but if she didn't, they'd be stuck at home. It was frustrating at times. She hated to think what could happen to her and Irene if she were to have an episode. She tried to not think about it.

"Where are we going?" Irene asked.

"We are going to plan your last day." Perhaps by putting it that way, she wouldn't startle her sister.

"Oh." Irene loved to go on car rides. She'd grew silent watching everything pass by her passenger window. She giggled when she saw a dog or a young child playing in a yard. She shook her head when someone drove fast by them, and she pointed to spots she recognized along the way. "We went there for a picnic when Kathleen was little."

Louise looked for oncoming traffic. "How old was she?"

"Two." Irene glanced at her with a puzzled look. "Maybe five."

"That's a long time ago."

"No. It was last week."

"Seems like that, doesn't it?"

Irene became silent again.

Louise wasn't sure if another funeral home was in Durand. She only knew of the one on the main street through town. Watkins. Edna had assured Louise that, outside of this one, the closet funeral homes were in Owosso.

"Here we are, Irene." She pulled into the parking lot and parked in the handicapped spot. "Are you ready?"

"Louise? Where's Kathleen?"

Louise threw her keys into her purse. "At work."

"It was a beautiful day, wasn't it?"

Louise nodded. "Yes. Now are you ready?"

"I think so."

"Not everyone gets to make these decisions themselves. I'm proud of you."

Irene nodded.

"Let me help. I'll get the preliminary things out of the way first. Okay?"

"Okay."

"Let's go."

The sisters crept up the walkway to the home. Louise shook her head. "We are quite the pair, sister." Irene nodded. "It sure is warm today. Reminds me of Florida."

The door to the home opened for them. "Good morning, ladies. Come in. Come in." A man about Brian's age held the swinging door for them, taking Irene's hand as she stepped over the threshold. As they made their way into the foyer, the man held out his right hand to Louise. "John Michaels. Are you my eleven o'clock appointment?"

"Yes," Louise shook his hand. "I'm Louise Williams. This is my sister, Irene Fredericks."

Irene held out her hand, "How do you do?"

Louise smiled. Her sister was behaving well and thankfully, the funeral director didn't seem to know Irene. This would be a good appointment.

"We can start our meeting in my office." He gestured to the set of five stairs. "Right up here. Use the handrail if you need it."

As the sisters sat down in the man's office, he offered them something to drink. Thankfully, Irene didn't want anything. Louise declined with a wave of her hand, her breathing still labored from the stairs. "No, thank you."

"Okay then," the man sat behind his desk. "I presume you are here to preplan?"

Louise nodded. "Irene is. I'm her sister."

"Okay then," the man pulled out a folder and opened his laptop. "Let me get a few details before we start."

"My sister has dementia. I may have to help with some of her decisions. Is that okay?"

John looked at her over his bifocals, "Um, sure. As long as she can sign at the end, we're good."

Louise nodded. The air smelled of stale flowers.

After giving Irene's home address, phone number and essential data, John typed it into his computer. "Now, I have a few questions concerning the service, what kind of funeral you'd like, about how many people you expect, things like that." He looked toward Irene. "Do you have an idea of what you'd like?"

Without skipping a beat, Irene spoke up, lucid and coherent. Almost so much, that it scared Louise a bit.

"I want to be cremated. And no viewing. So we will not need to look at caskets at all."

"That would be fine."

"I want photos. Lots of them. They are what made my life. Photos of me as a baby and my wedding. My daughter Kathleen and her husband Brian, and their two children. I have two grandchildren. Can we display photos somewhere?"

"Of course. We have boards for photos. That's fairly typical."

"I definitely do not want anyone looking at me in a casket. Why do people believe it's necessary to gaze at a dead body?"

The funeral director chuckled. "Some find it helpful in closure."

"That's silly. It's just my body. I won't be there anymore. I'll be in heaven. With my Savior. Do you know the Lord, sir?"

Louise flushed. Oh no. Her sister was proselytizing the funeral director.

"Um, I go to church."

"Going to church does not make you a Christian, sir."

Louise shifted in her seat. She hated to stop her sister. She hadn't talked like this in months.

"Sir, even the demons believe in Jesus. But for me, He's everything. He's my Lord and my Savior. Because of Him, I won't be in that casket at the end of my life. I'll be in heaven."

The director smiled. "So, you'll be wanting a Christian theme."

"My Savior will be with me through this entire ordeal. You know, I don't think clearly on certain days. I struggle to remember what day it is when I wake up in the morning. I forget to turn off the tea kettle. I don't remember my grandchildren on some days, but this I do know. My Savior lives. He cares for me, and on that day when others will come to mourn for me, I'll not be in a fancy box in a funeral home. I'll be with Him. Celebrating my life. If only other could have that same hope in their life. He's gotten me through the worst days of my life, and continues to keep me strong. I love Him more than anyone here on earth. He's my forever friend."

Louise sat back, shocked. She never imagined Irene could come up with thoughts like this anymore. Somehow the words spilled out. She smiled. She didn't care that her sister was sharing the gospel. It was more important that she was putting sentences together and they were making sense. Almost too much sense.

"Many of my clients tell me the same words, Mrs. Fredericks. I'm happy you have your faith to get you through hard days."

Irene nodded. "You can have faith, too."

The man smiled. "Okay, how about music?"

Irene patted the table. "Yes, lots of it. As much as you can filter into the place without it becoming a dance hall." She smiled.

Louise laughed. "Yes. Anything and everything that fills a church on a Sunday morning."

Irene smiled at her. "Thank you, sister." Then a puzzled look immediately came to Irene's face. "Except...those ones with seven words sung over and over and over again. You can forget those. I want just the oldies."

"Hymns. 'The Old Rugged Cross,' 'How Great Thou Art.' Like that?"

Irene's head bobbed, "Yes, all of those. I may not be here to hear them, but I want everyone else to. That, my young man, is my greatest wish." And she began to hum.

"Music it is. Lots of it." John tapped into his computer.

"We have flowers ordered, from a local florist." Louise added.

"Good. You're ahead of the game."

Irene seemed to wander off in her humming. She smiled, but didn't answer any more questions.

Soon the session was over, and Irene was almost asleep in her chair. Louise asked the director if she could talk to him outside of his office. She patted Irene's hand, "Dear, I'm going out in the hallway for second, okay?"

Irene nodded, "Are you going to tell him now?"

"Yes. I'll be right back."

"Okay." Irene went back to humming.

"Sir. I'm not sure if you'll understand what I'm about to tell you, but you need to help us." Louise leaned into her cane for balance. "Irene's made these last day's decisions many years ago. She now doesn't remember many things, but in this one thing she is adamant. We already made a deal with another funeral director across town to perform the cremation. We will bring you the ashes and the funeral will take place here. Is that okay?"

"Why, um, this is an odd request."

"I know it is. But you see, when Irene's husband died, the other place gave her something like a 'two for one' deal on cremation. But the funeral wasn't acceptable. She doesn't want that to happen in her case. So she wants to keep the cremation with the other place, because it's prepaid, but wants you to have the service here.

John pulled on his collar. "So, the other director will provide the death certificate and such?"

Louise rested her hand on the man's arm and smiled her best flirty smile. "Would that be okay?" It worked on most men. She hoped it would work on this young one.

"Yes. I'm sure it will be fine. We'll take care of it."

Louise pulled back her hand. "Thank you. This means a great deal to my sister. We'll be on our way now."

As Louise pulled out of the funeral home's parking lot, she looked across at Irene.

She wasn't sure how she could deal with all of this. It was one thing to plan it, quite another to carry it out. Could they manage it? Once Irene was settled and gone, could Louise see it through?

"Well, that went well." Irene was still smiling and humming.

This would unquestionably be the hardest thing Louise would ever pull off.

Chapter 23

Irene devoured her sundae, cherry and all. She smacked her lips as she dug into the bottom of the cup to clean it out.

Louise enjoyed seeing sister's enjoyment. "You're crazy, Irene." Why deny her something so simple?

Irene looked up with a sparkle in her eye. "So good."

They sat at a picnic table in the park. Nearby, swings squeaked in unison as children giggled. Louise loved hearing the children's laughter, but the grating of the swing's squeaky chains annoyed her. "Something needs WD 40."

Birds sang, the sun shone bright, and they sat in the shade. Someone, just a few yards away, was mowing the lawn. Louise close her eyes for a moment to take in the warmth of the day and the rich smell of freshly-cut grass. It'd been a long time since she'd felt so warm and alive. Could she take another Michigan winter? Michigan winters were brutal, but a summer day like this one made her almost forget the days of blowing snow and wind gusts which took her breath away.

"Are you about ready to leave?" Louise asked.

"No. We need to talk."

Louise nodded. "Okay. About what?"

Irene looked off toward a few kids playing tag nearby. "You know. Where will you put me? Have you thought about that yet?"

"*Put you?*" Louise was startled. "What are you talking about?"

"You know what I need to hear. Please tell me your plans."

Without a doubt, Louise had to talk to someone. Howard was the only one who could possibly understand what she was going through. She had to try calling him again. He might still ignore her, but she hoped their friendship would trump his need to keep their relationship a secret from his family. Perhaps if she called late at night, he'd be home. Perhaps alone.

One.., two..."Hello?"

Louise sat up in bed, shocked to hear Howard answer. "Howard?"

"Yes."

"It's Louise. Can you talk?"

"Louise." He hesitated. "Um, yes."

"Are you sure? I understand if..."

"It's okay. How are you, Louise?"

"Are you alone?"

"Yes. I just got home."

"I'm sorry, Howard. I know you didn't want me to call you."

"It's okay. I miss you, Louise."

Louise sighed. She just wanted to sit on the edge of her bed and cry for joy. "Thank you, Howard."

"How have you been?"

"She's bad."

"Bad?"

"My sister, Irene. Her dementia. All she wants to eat is hot fudge sundaes, she rarely remembers her medicine, and she's gotten lost in her own neighborhood."

"Oh Louise, I'm sorry. You were the one supposed to be getting the help. "

Louise loved hearing the sympathy in his voice. "I'll be fine. I will. But this whole thing with my sister is so hard. I knew you'd be the only one who could understand."

"Well, I do understand. I do."

A quietness fell over the conversation.

Louise sighed, "How's your wife?"

"Not so good. Her memory is as bad as ever, and her health seems to be failing more. She just stares off into space. I like to take someone with me so I have someone to talk to while I'm visiting her. Does Irene still know you?"

"Yes, she knows everyone."

"Be thankful."

"I'm trying. I'm just not sure how to handle all of this. I mean, I'm sure it will get worse. But what if she begins to not like me?" Louise laughed at the thought. "I guess that really wouldn't be too big of a change."

"She doesn't hate you."

Louise smiled, "I know. We've grown closer since I've been here. She wants," Louise hesitated. She'd never told anyone about their pact.

"She wants what?"

"She wants to go into a home."

"Right now?"

"Yes. And as soon as she gets settled, she wants me to,"

"What?"

Louise stopped. She wanted to tell Howard, but she couldn't. She'd made a sister promise to keep the whole thing quiet. From everyone. "Does it seem odd to you that she wants to go into a home?"

"A bit. But Louise, nothing that a dementia patient suggests would surprise me. It's random how it affects people. Sometimes gentle, quiet people turn wicked, and hateful. And the other way around. How is her temperament?"

"Actually fine. But she believes in God. She believes He is in control."

"Not a bad way to feel."

"Howard, I'm sorry to bother you. I know I promised I wouldn't call."

"Louise, it's okay."

Louise smiled. "Thank you."

"I do need to go though. Call me again later if you want."

"You are too kind to me."

"At least I can be a benefit to someone. Take care, Louise."

She lay back on her pillows. That short conversation made her long for Howard that much more. She just wished he wasn't so far away.

Irene studied her reflection in the mirror as she combed her hair. Did it look good or not? Her thinking seemed odd these days. Some days she woke up happy and feeling like herself. Other days she opened her eyes and felt scared. She thought about hot fudge sundaes. She dreamed about the peaks of whipped cream, and the way it all melted on her tongue. If she could eat a hot fudge sundae every day, she'd be happy for the rest of her life. Life wasn't so hard anymore. Until the fear set in.

What was she supposed to do today? Was it Sunday? Perhaps she should dress for church. She opened her closet and looked for a dress. She found a sandal, and she sat on her bed to put it on. Did this sandal have a match?

Louise would help her. She stood up, still wearing her sandal, and thought about what day it was. Maybe she didn't have any clothes to wear because it was Monday. Wash day. She picked up clothes around her bed and took them to the hamper in her bathroom. It was half empty. Did she wash clothes yesterday?

Her stomach growled. Maybe Louise would take her for ice cream. She found a sweater and put it on. Where could they get ice cream? The store. But she couldn't remember how to get to the store. Irene stopped. What if today were Sunday? She looked down at her house coat and sweater. This wouldn't work for church. Then she remembered. She needed to brush her teeth.

She walked back into the bathroom and went to the medicine cabinet. She looked at herself in the mirror. Perhaps she'd better comb her hair.

Heading downstairs, she heard Louise holler up. "Did you brush your teeth?" Irene rolled her tongue over her teeth. Had she brushed them? She went downstairs anyway. She had to talk Louise into taking her for ice cream.

"What would you like for breakfast?" Louise asked, still in her housecoat and pajamas.

"Hot fudge sundae. "

Louise turned toward the kitchen. "Not for breakfast, sister. Not for breakfast."

She was tired of hearing her sister say that. Irene thought about what she would like for breakfast. Her foot felt bare, so she looked down. She had on only one sandal.

Chapter 24

The asking for ice cream each day began to wear on Louise. It was as if that was all Irene could think about. Irene ate things other than ice cream, but the request just kept coming. Breakfast, lunch, afternoon snack...always the same request.

The days grew longer. The house grew warm now, and Louise often turned on the air conditioner. She hated shutting the house up to do it, but it was a warmer than usual June.

Finding an assisted living home for Irene grew more urgent each day. Louise didn't mind caring for her sister. It kept her mind off her own problems, but she knew it wouldn't be long before the summer would be over. She began to dream about Florida. If she could get Irene settled before fall, she could work on a plan to get herself back to the Sunshine State before Thanksgiving. Yet where would she live? She needed additional assistance herself.

It had to be the perfect home. Irene needed to be happy and comfortable. Perhaps if she found one that served ice cream for every meal...Louise shook her head. That's silly. Happy nurses and good caregivers were much more important.

They'd visited several over the past few weeks. But today, Louise was able to get Irene's mind off hot fudge sundaes long enough for her to pay attention to the retirement home they were currently touring. Irene seemed totally with it as they went through the bedrooms and explored the dining room.

"Irene, do you like this home?"

She nodded, "Yes, it's very pretty. I like this table." She ran her hand across it.

Louise wasn't sure why a simple end table caught her sister's attention, but she liked the home, too.

The rooms were bare, except for a few specific items like a bed, a sofa, and an eating table with chairs. And Louise loved that each room had an emergency pull cord. Winded from walking, she sat down at the table and accessed what else her sister would need. A television, perhaps a comfortable chair. Would she be able to get those things out of Irene's house without arousing suspicion? Perhaps she'd need to buy those items.

Louise sniffed the air. It didn't smell like an old folks' home. Some of the ones she'd toured in Florida, with Howard, had horrible odors. Even after leaving, she had continued to smell the odor. She had refused to live in one of those places, so why would she subject Irene to the same punishment?

When they made their way back through the home, many of the residents came to the doors of their rooms and offered a greeting or a smile. Some seemed lost, but others seemed quite sharp. They all seemed happy, which comforted Louise.

They sat down with the director in her office.

Louise hoped she'd be able to keep Irene from discussing the pact. It needed to stay secret, more now than ever.

"Do you have ice cream here?" Irene asked.

The director laughed. "Why yes, Irene, we do. Do you like ice cream?"

Irene nodded. "Very much. Especially hot fudge kinda dribbled all over it."

The director laughed again. "We have regular ice cream sundae nights. We'll be sure you get your share."

"Do you have whipped cream, too?"

Louise was thankful the Baskin-Robbins topic was more important today than the details of their visit. It would keep Irene from spilling details of the pact.

"Yes. We have cherries, too."

Irene smiled.

The director turned to Louise, "Do you have any questions for me?"

"Is care around the clock?"

"Of course. All the time. Doors are always locked from the inside. She won't be able to wander or leave the facility at any time, unless of course, you or someone else from her family comes to take her somewhere."

"We have no family." The pact was materializing. It was important that Louise got the details correct. She'd been reading the fine print each night. Taking notes. She opened her folder now and began scanning over the questions she needed to ask. "I live in Florida. Once I get my sister settled, I want to return to Florida."

The director's eyes grew wide, her face concerned. "Are you sure? Irene will need visitors. It will help her memory."

"I will return to see her each summer, but I won't be close enough to visit on a regular basis."

"You have no other family?"

Louise shook her head. "No one."

"Does your sister have friends in the area? People who could come and visit her?"

"Not likely. We've always been private people."

"Okay." The director made some notes on her paper. "What about clergy or even..?"

"There is no one."

"Well, we will need your contact information in Florida, so if there is an emergency we can call you."

Louise nodded. "Of course." Louise gave her a fictitious Florida address, but her real cell phone number.

After discussing finances, Louise realized she'd have to do some budgeting to keep the pact intact and workable, especially if she needed to start paying for an assisted living home for herself. She'd do her best to keep that option open. She hoped she'd have enough money to take care of them both. With her deteriorating health, she needed to watch her pennies, but she was tough and determined. She'd figure it out.

"Well, if you have no more questions, I guess we just need to know when you'd like to reserve a room. Do you have a particular time when you want your sister to move in?"

"Um, I need to call you about that. Would that be okay?"

"Our rooms are on a first-come, first-serve basis. I can't guarantee you a room when you call. We could go months without one open for you. If you give me a specific time now, I'd be able to reserve the room and hold it for you."

Louise nodded. "I understand, but I still need a little time."

"Sure."

"I'm thinking this fall, but it could be later."

"Okay, why don't you call me when you know for sure?"

"Of course."

"Louise?"

Louise put away her notes in her purse and turned to her sister. "What Irene?"

"I need to."

Louise stood up. "What?"

Irene stood, too. "I need to go."

The director immediately seemed to understand. "Here Irene. A restroom is over here. Can you follow me?"

Louise watched the director, with smiles and kind words, reach out her hand to help her sister. This moment of kindness convinced her. She knew this was the place, her sister's final home. She was sure.

As they drove home from the assisted living facility, Irene smiled over at Louise. Louise noticed it and smiled. "Did you like that place?"

She nodded and reached for her sister's shoulder, "They were very nice there."

Louise nodded. "I agree."

"That's it."

"Are you sure?"

Irene nodded. "I'm sure."

"Okay then. Let's go home. We have a lot to plan. Are you ready?"

"Yes." Irene squeezed her sister's arm, and nodded. Then asked, just a second. "But, can we have ice cream before I move?"

"I hate photos," Louise grimaced as she was again to pose for yet another one of Taylor's wedding photos.

It was an almost perfect day in July, though it felt more like August in Florida. Louise had managed to get herself, as well as Irene, ready. Irene wore a pink dress she'd found in the back of her closet. The style heralded a decade ago, but she still looked pretty in it.

Louise chose a light blue pant suit that she loved wearing on special evenings in Florida. No dresses for her, not with her pesky varicose veins. She wasn't sure why they kept telling her to get into the staged wedding shots. For goodness sake, the bride was her great niece, not her granddaughter. She soon told the photographer she had to use the bathroom. A surefire way to get out of having to fake a smile.

Irene seemed fine at the beginning of the wedding. She was escorted down the aisle by her grandson, Taylor's brother. Beaming as she sat down next to Louise, who had been seated just before her, she whispered. "Everything looks so beautiful. I'm so glad we could come."

Louise nodded. Her shirt felt damp against the pew. Sweat poured from the young groom's forehead as he faced the procession up the aisle. Louise always felt self-conscious and sinful at church, even on a wedding day. She loosened her scarf around her neck. "Doesn't this church have air conditioning?"

"I think it broke last year. We only use it in July and August."

"Well, it's July sister. Tell them to turn the blasted thing up." Louise grabbed up her program and began fanning her face.

Irene gave her 'the look.' She hadn't done that in awhile and it made Louise laugh. When it flashed a second time, she knew she'd better stop complaining. Louise kept silent from that point on. No sense causing her sister anxiety today. She glanced over at Kathleen who looked radiant as the mother-of-the-bride. Her facial features, from her pointed chin to her dark, glistening eyes, resembled Irene's and also their mother's. There was no denying the family resemblance. Her mother would have liked this day.

There really weren't any other relatives at the wedding. Their family consisted of Irene's children. Both Irene and Louise's husbands were gone, as well as a few of their cousins. They remained the matriarchs now. Louise wasn't sure she liked that.

The music came to a crescendo, and Taylor made her way down the aisle. Louise and Irene stood up just in time to see her pass by their pew. Louise thought back to her own wedding day. It wasn't quite an impulse wedding, but only six months had passed since she'd met her husband. Their love had been so fierce, they had decided together not to wait any longer. As her father escorted her down the aisle, it was the first time she wondered if she were doing the right thing, marrying the right man. Her parents and Irene had objected about her marrying him so quickly, but she was determined to have her own way. So much so, that even the warning signs she saw in him, she assumed would go away once they were married. Now she knew her parents and sister had been right. She hoped Taylor wasn't thinking those same thoughts. Her boyfriend seemed attentive and kind. It was horrible to question your motives at such an exciting moment. She thought of Howard and smiled.

As the minister began the ceremony, he spent an exhausting few minutes praying. Louise leaned on one foot and then the other. She grew weak and the temperature continued to rise. Sweat slid down her back. Before he finished, Louise sat down, despite the people still standing around her. She looked around and wondered if the wedding party would be fainting like pregnant women from the heat of their outfits. The heat made breathing hard. She longed to sit in their car and turn the air conditioning on full blast.

That's when she noticed it. The groomsmen weren't wearing tuxedos. Who didn't wear a tuxedo to a wedding? All they had on were shirts, with sleeves rolled up to their elbows and suspenders. She almost giggled out loud. In her day, suspenders kept pants from falling down, and these boys were wearing them as a fashion statement. Astounding things would never cease in this ever-changing world.

And what color were the suspenders, but a pretty, pastel pink. She nearly laughed out loud watching them shift from one foot to another during the endless prayer now claiming more victims as one of her sister's friends from church sat down, too. She wondered if Taylor had chosen the groomsmen outfits.

She thought back to her own father, always wearing overalls. He'd let one strap fall to his side and the other strap hold up his overalls. That was his style. Finally the prayer ended and Irene sat down and smiled at her. Seeing her sister happy felt good. She'd even remembered Taylor was getting married today as they sat down to eat breakfast.

"Are you warm, dear?" She leaned closer to her sister who only turned and smiled back at her again.

"I'm fine. Doesn't Taylor look beautiful?"

Louise nodded, "That she does. But sister...," Irene leaned closer, "What's with the suspenders?"

"Wouldn't father have a coronary seeing them?"

Both giggled until Kathleen turned around to them and gave them the eye.

"Dearly beloved. We are gathered here now in the sight of God and all present to witness the joining of Taylor Blankenship and Andrew Mik...," the Pastor stammered, "Mikel..."

The groom leaned closer to the Pastor and whispered.

"Mikeltomski." The pastor smiled.

"Why on earth didn't Taylor find a Green or a Smith?" Louise leaned again to talk to her sister. "Why not another German? We're all German."

Irene shook her head and hushed her sister. "I want to hear. Shhh!"

Louise sighed. She needed to remember why she was there. Irene needed this. For her, it would be the last. She looked over at her sister now. She did look pretty in her powder blue dress. They'd found a pretty white sweater with pearl buttons which just suited her rosy complexion. Her pink carnation corsage looked beautiful on it. Looking down at her lapel, she gazed at her own corsage. She tried to smell the flowers, but the only scent was Irene's lavished-on perfume. A bit overpowering. She'd have to hide the bottle.

She felt Irene lean into her. Her sister was crying, and she whispered, "I'm so glad I got to come to Taylor's wedding. Thank you."

Louise reached over and patted her sister's hand. They smiled at each other. She hoped this would be something that Irene would remember. Tomorrow.

Chapter 25

Irene wished she could think better. She blinked. Was it morning or afternoon? Her window was open. What day was it? Her pulse quickened, and she sat up in bed. The birds were chattering outside. It sounded like morning. A whistle signaled in the distance. It might be morning. Was she alone? She looked around the room. There was no one there.

Maybe she should put something on. But what? It must not be winter, because the window was open. She wore a light nightgown. She took her heavy winter bathrobe off a hook in her closet, and put it on. It felt warm. Maybe it wasn't summer. She felt cold so often.

She made her way down the staircase, and she listened at the bottom of the stairs. Her house was silent. Max came up to her and meowed loudly. She shuffled into her kitchen and filled the tea kettle with water. She turned to the pantry and gazed at all the cans. Row after row of cans. She wasn't sure why she had so many. Perhaps she wasn't keeping track of them. What if they were expired? They had to be. She hadn't been to the store in almost a year.

She reached for the trash bin and started filling it with the expired cans. Soon the waste basket overflowed, but the pantry still had more and more cans. Where had they all come from?

"Irene. What?" Her older sister came into the room. Startled, Irene nearly toppled the waste basket.

"Louise? What are you doing here?"

"No sister. What are you doing with our food?" Louise took Irene's hand out of the pantry and took the can away from her. "Why are you throwing cans away?"

"When did you get here from Florida?" Irene couldn't believe her sister had come for a visit and hadn't told her.

"I live here now. Remember?" Louise took her hand and led her to the kitchen table and pulled out a chair. "Sit down, honey."

Irene hesitated.

"C'mon."

"We need to keep better track of the canned goods. They have to be checked."

Louise nodded. "Yes, we probably should, but Irene, these cans are new. We just bought them. Remember?"

"No. Are you sure?"

Louise turned on the tea kettle and sat down across from Irene.

"I just did that."

"What?"

"Turned on the hot water."

Louise turned back in her chair to face the stove. "It wasn't on."

Irene was confused. "I don't feel well."

"What's wrong?"

"What day is it?"

"Tuesday."

"Are you sure?" Irene's head felt muddled and tired.

"Yes."

"Are you hungry?"

"Do we have any ice cream?"

Louise stood up and set out two cups. "Let's have some tea."

"Louise?"

"Yes, dear."

"What time is it?"

Louise turned around, looking at the oven. "Looks like nine. Did you sleep well?"

"It's morning?"

Louise turned back. The look on her face was solemn. She just nodded. Then she smiled, "Irene, let's get breakfast. What would you like?"

"Ice cream."

Irene shook her head. "No."

"What about chocolate sauce?"

"Have we paid the electric bill this month?"

Louise picked up the remote control and switched the channel they were watching to the news. "Yes. I paid it."

"Where's my purse? "Irene looked around. She was pretty sure Louise was stealing her money and spending it. Louise always got to the mail first and looked through it. She stood from her chair and went to the phone.

"Where are you going, Irene?"

"I need to call Kathleen."

"What for?"

"You know, maybe I left my purse at her house. What's her number?"

"Don't worry about it. We'll find it. As soon as the news is over."
Louise waved her hand at her.

Irene stared at the phone. She couldn't remember Kathleen's number.
She didn't even know the first number.

"Irene?" Louise turned in her chair. "Come here, dear. You're gonna
miss what happened at the debates. How will you ever fight with me? You
need ammunition." Louise giggled.

"Are you stealing from me?"

Louise stopped laughing and turned in her chair toward her. "Irene. I
am not a thief. I did not take your purse."

Irene stood up. She shook her head at her sister.

"Irene." Irene went up the stairs to her room. Before morning, she
needed to get a hold of her daughter. She couldn't live with her sister
anymore, especially if she were stealing from her.

"Irene!" She could hear her sister call from downstairs as she shut her
door.

Louise got up from her chair and went to get her phone. How could
Irene think she was stealing from her? She hadn't stolen from Irene since
they were six and eight, and she took Irene's cookie, after Mother said she
could only have one.

She punched in Kathleen's number. No answer. Where could her niece
be? With Taylor's wedding passed, what could be keeping her busy now?
She hadn't visited in over a week.

She looked up the stairs. Living with Irene grew stranger each day. This was the most confused she'd seen her sister, and the first that she'd accused Louise. Is this what Irene experienced with their mother?

If only she could talk to Howard. Howard knew about all the symptoms. He'd know if it was normal for Irene to forget where her bathroom is in her own house, to forget what day it was. He knew exactly what she was going through. She'd try to call him again.

Going into her room, she tried his number. Being later in the evening, there was a chance he'd be available.

"Hello."

Louise sighed in relief when he answered, "Howard. It's Louise."

"Louise. Oh it is so good to hear your voice."

"Am I catching you at a bad time?"

"No. Just got home from a long walk. I miss you most when I take my nightly walks."

"She's getting worse."

"Oh Louise, I'm sorry."

"Today she accused me of stealing from her."

Howard sighed. "It's inevitable."

Louise knew it. He'd told her. "What do I do?"

"Go with it."

"What?"

"Go with it. Agree with her."

"Agree with her that I'm a thief."

Howard laughed. "No. That's not necessary, but try to help her."

"How?"

"Look for the money?"

"That's it. There isn't anything stolen. In fact, I've been paying almost all of the bills myself. Saving her money for the home."

"Just pretend. Pretend you're trying to find it. Go along with things."

"Truly?"

"Yes. It is easier on them. They don't get so agitated."

Louise sighed. "I guess."

"How's your wife?"

"We've had a rough week. She continues to go downhill. I hate to say it, Louise, but I think we're losing her."

Louise was silent. What do you tell a man who is losing his wife? What words would she have to comfort him?

"Louise?"

"I'm here. I'm sorry Howard."

"I knew this day would come. I just didn't realize how much it was still going to hurt and how much I wasn't as ready for it as I thought. "

The next night at dinner, Irene said nothing to Louise about the missing money. She seemed herself again after a three hour nap. Almost like it was when she first moved to Michigan.

"This spaghetti is delicious, Louise."

"No it isn't. It tastes just like it came out of a can. We should get some of those pre-made dinners. Lasagna or some Alfredo chicken or something."

"I like these breadsticks."

"Out of a box. They're not bad." Louise glanced at her sister. "How do you feel tonight?"

"Fine. I must have not slept well last night to take such a long nap."

"Perhaps." Louise debated on whether to bring up the money subject again. Maybe it was better if nothing was said. "Irene? Can I ask you to do something?"

"What?" Irene looked up at her with a dribble of spaghetti sauce on her chin. Louise motioned for her to wipe at it with her napkin.

"Could you pray for my friend?"

Irene almost choked on her food. "Really?"

"His name is Howard. He's losing his wife." Louise couldn't get Howard off her mind since their chat. He seemed so sad.

"Of course. I will add him to my prayer list."

"He's a friend I had in Florida."

Silence reigned again. Just the television could be heard in the room. They were watching their regular show, Judge Judy. Louise loved Judy's spunk. She was never afraid to call a person an idiot. Irene could only comment on the stupidity of those wanting to get compensation for their own bad choices. The episodes often brought up heated discussions between the sisters.

Although instead of really listening to the show that evening, Louise could only think about Howard. She wished she could be with him.

###

Edna came into the house with her plastic bag on her arm, using potholders to hold a casserole dish. "Girls! Oh girls!"

Irene came into the kitchen blowing her nose. "Edna. What are you doing here?"

"Dinner." Setting the hot dish on the table, she scooted a potholder underneath it. "Chicken pot pie. Thought you two would like something nice for dinner. Are you hungry?"

Irene sat down at the table, "I'm always hungry. That is so nice of you, Edna."

Edna set the bag down on the counter. I also brought you chocolate chip cookies and some cut up vegetables. Does Louise like celery?"

"I think so. She'll be tickled you brought dinner. She's getting tired of being the only cook. Kathleen often brings us dinner, too."

Irene bowed her head. She felt like such a burden to others. It was just frustrating her. "Why did you bring us dinner?"

Edna turned, put her hands on her hips and said, "Why not?" She turned back to the cupboard, "Now, where are your plates and where's Louise?"

"She's taking a bath. She's so tired."

"Before dinner?"

"She says it helps her feel better."

"Are they here?" Edna opened a kitchen cupboard.

"Plates are..." Irene struggled to remember.

"Never mind dear," Edna smiled, "I'll find them." She opened more cupboard doors. "Here they are. Hungry?"

Irene nodded.

"Well, why don't I make you up a plate? I'll sit and chat while you eat."

"Won't you join me?"

"No. I have to go eat with Myron. He hates it when I don't get home in time for dinner."

Soon the steamy hot food and a cup of tea was set before her.

"There, now dear. How are you feeling today?" Edna sat down opposite from her.

Irene nodded as she began to eat her food. She burned her mouth on the hot meal and winced.

"Oh dear, it's too warm. Wait a moment before trying another bite." Edna held her hand over her mouth. "I'm so sorry. I shouldn't have put it before you before it cooled down a bit."

Irene patted her friend's hand, "It's okay. Guess I'm too eager to eat."

"So Irene, your house looks a little in disarray."

"We're sorting." Irene tried another bite after blowing on it for a while.

"Sorting?" Edna looked around, stood up, and gazed into the dining room. "Why?"

Irene gathered her thoughts. She knew there was something she needed to keep a secret, but she couldn't remember what. "We need to get things ready."

Edna turned back to her. "Ready? Are you having a sale or something? I like to do that in the spring. Sort through things to be rid of." Edna laughed. "I'm not very good at it. I tend to keep everything I find and then, next spring, I find it all over again."

Irene struggled to figure out why they were sorting. She just couldn't remember, but she added, "I think I'm moving."

"Moving?" Shock shown clear on her friend's face.

"Um, maybe I'm not moving. I don't remember." She took another bite of the food. It tasted just like something her mother used to make. "This is delicious."

"It should. I got the recipe from you."

Irene set down her fork, "I wish I could still cook."

Edna patted her hand, "You will dear."

Irene shook her head. "No. My cooking days are over."

"Has the situation with Louise gotten better? You know, is she leaving your finances alone?"

"No, I don't think so." She tried to remember if she'd paid her rent that month. She stopped eating trying hard to remember. Or did she have a mortgage?

"Are you okay?"

Irene looked up. "I think so."

Edna smiled back at her.

"I don't think they'll kick us out of here anytime soon."

"Irene, the flowers are dying by the walkway."

"Dying?"

"When was the last time you watered them?" Louise went to the counter, put her bucket in the sink and began to fill it with cold water.

"Last night."

Louise shook her head, "That's impossible. They are almost all brown."

"Maybe two days ago."

Irene didn't know. Louise was sure of it. She filled the bucket only halfway. If it were full, she wouldn't be able to lift it out of the sink and carry it outside. Irene and she had spent almost a hundred dollars in the spring on all of these perennials. August was too early to lose them all. The heat of the past few weeks was not only killing their flowers, but their spirits as well. Irene's house lacked central air.

Louise pulled back a strand of her white hair and put it behind her ear. Sweat trickled down her back causing her shirt to stick to her. Carrying the bucket to the back porch she found Greg standing at the edge of the sidewalk watching her. As she managed to get the bucket out the door, he approached her.

"Can I help you Louise?"

Louise stopped, almost all out of breath, slowly setting down the bucket. "Sure."

Greg took the bucket. "Where?"

"Here." Louise pointed to the wilted flowers by the back walkway.

"You need to water your flowers, Louise."

Louise folded her arms. "I know, Greg. I know."

"I'll finish these and then get my hose to do the rest. Okay?"

Louise nodded. "Thank you Greg. You are a lifesaver."

"Louise, you like me now. Right?"

Louise patted the young man on his shoulder, "Yes I do, Greg. You are always very helpful."

Greg went about his work, spilling water on each flower along their sidewalk.

Louise turned and waved over her shoulder, "Call me if you need anything. Okay?"

"Okay, Louise."

Louise went back into the kitchen to find her sister at the table now looking intently at a spoon. It was as if she never seen a spoon before. She had on her heavy, brown sweater. It made Louise hot to just look at her.

"Irene. You need to take off that sweater. If it isn't a hundred degrees, I'd eat my hat."

"Eat your hat?"

Louise waved her off as she sat down across from her. "It's just an expression dear. That's all." She looked out to see Greg pulling on a green hose from across their driveway. He was headed for the other flowers along the edge of the sidewalk. "It's four o'clock. It should be cooling off soon."

She looked again at her sister. "What are you doing?"

Irene set down the spoon. "Is everything ready?"

"Dinner?"

"No."

Louise took a napkin from the holder in the middle of the table and wiped off her forehead. "Ready for what, dear?"

Irene looked up and at her sister. "Are we ready now?"

Louise studied her sister's eyes. They used to hold such spark. Irene had laughing eyes. Now they just stared. Some moments Louise would look into her eyes and see nothing. Now they looked watery and red. She looked tired. "What are you talking about?"

"You know. Is it almost time?"

Louise was shocked. It had been a few days since her sister said much that made sense, but she was pretty sure, at this moment, her sister was asking about the pact.

"What do you think?" More questions would bring a true answer.

"Should we do it now?"

Louise sighed. She had no clue when it would be the right time. She'd put everything in order. All was ready. Everything but her heart.

Irene looked into her eyes with longing. She knew exactly what she was saying at that moment. Louise was sure.

"I'm worried."

"About what?"

"That it won't work."

"It has to."

"But what if it..."

"It will work. We've worked too hard to get to this point. We have a place. You know what you promised me, you'd do."

Louise nodded. "I know."

"Give it one month."

"A month? From today?"

Irene stood from her chair. "I need a nap."

As she shuffled out of the room with her cane, Louise wasn't sure she could react as she needed to. She'd be all alone. To figure out all of what was happening. Could she keep it all to herself? Pull off this elaborate pact of theirs and not feel guilty? And worse, could she do it alone?

"Irene?"

She watched her sister turn back.

"Are you still sure?"

"Yes. I'm tired."

It wasn't the answer she was looking for, but, it was the answer she needed to hear.

Chapter 26

Louise wouldn't be able to take much, so it was Louise's job to figure out what to take, but she wanted to separate the things Irene would need and like.

Perhaps her knitting bag, but then again, Irene hadn't had the sense to do any knitting since early spring. Photos. But which ones? She looked over at Taylor's wedding photo on the mantle. Photos. Would Irene like photos? Which ones? Everything she packed for Irene, would need to go unnoticed from Kathleen. Everything.

She found a stack of old photos in one of Irene's bookcases and asked her about them. "Irene, are these your photos?" One was of Irene's wedding. Her husband's high school graduation. One of Kathleen as a baby.

Irene was having a good day and answered cheerfully, "Those were mother's photos. I seem to have too of many of them now."

"We'll go to the store soon and pick you out some frames." Surely, Kathleen wouldn't notice extra photos no longer around the house. They'd be perfect for Irene's new room at the home.

Louise needed to do this with everything they took. Two of everything, so. Kathleen wouldn't pick up on anything missing.

The bigger items, she wasn't so sure about. A missing bed or an absent dresser would certainly be noticed. She'd have to go out and purchase those things and have them delivered to the home. It was imperative that Irene to have everything to make her new home feel familiar.

She hid the partially packed boxes in her own room. Kathleen rarely went into her room. They'd be safe there until the day arrived.

Chapter 27

Kathleen and Brian had begun coming over more often. With Taylor on her honeymoon, and now preparing to move away, Kathleen seemed to want to make up lost time with her mother. Her visits also gave Louise a bit of relief from caring for Irene.

Kathleen put her mother to bed and came down to the kitchen while Louise soaked up the sun in front of the kitchen windows. It was too warm to sit directly out on the patio.

"Looks like you're loving the sun today, Aunt Louise."

Louise smiled. "Reminds me of Florida. I miss it."

Kathleen pulled up a kitchen chair and sat down beside her.

"Hard to believe you've been here six months now."

"Isn't it?"

"How are you feeling? Is it too hard on you to be here with mother?"

"It's helped me to have you here more, dear. I love your Mom. I never imagined living here with her would work out like this, though. I wondered how we'd do. It hasn't been so bad. We seem to have gone right back to being little girls again. We giggle, we laugh. It's not all peaches and cream. She still wants to convert me."

Kathleen smiled. "She does have pretty strong beliefs."

"Yes she does. She could come into the twenty-first century a bit, but those beliefs of hers will keep her strong. To the end."

"Why Aunt Louise. I never imagined hearing you say that."

Louise roared in laughter. "It is pretty unbelievable, isn't it?" She sipped on her iced tea. "Our mother would've been proud of her. God was important to her as well. She loved church. The people in it. She cared for everyone around her. She took care of her neighbors and friends, like your Mom." She twirled her straw in her glass. "Irene reminds me of Mother these days. It's probably the disease, but other things as well. Hard to believe Mother has been gone so many years. I miss her. Being with Irene makes it easier. Somehow."

"Well, Brian and I really appreciate all you've done for her. We wish we could be here for you both more."

Louise looked over. "Kathleen, my illness isn't getting any better. I struggle to breath. If I don't take my diuretics, my day gets almost impossible to get through. I'm not sure how much longer I can hold off for her. I'll try."

Kathleen patted her hand, "You let us know if this gets too much for you. We'll make other arrangements. Don't think you have to handle this all alone."

Louise smiled at her niece. "I think we can manage. I just need to be sure I keep taking my medicine."

"If we can do anything for you, you let us know. If you get too tired, let me know. Or call me if you are having a bad day yourself."

Louise nodded. If only she could ask Kathleen to help her keep this promise to her sister. But this was all on her. There was nothing Kathleen or Brian could do.

225

That afternoon as Louise rested on the couch, her cell phone rang. When she saw who it was, she immediately swiped it to answer.

"Howard?"

"Yes, it's me. How did you know?"

Louise laughed, "No one else calls me, but, caller ID,"

"Louise, I need to tell you something."

Louise tried to sit up. Her breathing was labored today. "Howard, are you okay?"

"She's gone."

Louise righted herself on the couch. "When?"

"In the night." He began to sob.

She wanted to say something. She struggled to breathe. She sighed, heavily, then leaned back into the couch and just listened to her friend sob.

"Louise?"

"Yes, Howard. I'm so sorry."

"I wish you were here."

Louise knew she should say something comforting, but what could a person say to ease such intimate, fresh grief? There was only one way to break the moment. "Howard, I don't think showing up at your day and claiming that I'm your girlfriend would probably be the best thing to do right now."

Howard coughed and grew silent for a moment.

"Howard?"

"Yeah, probably not a great idea, huh?"

"Horrible." Louise laughed.

"I miss you." Howard blew his nose.

"I miss you, Howard. What happened?"

"She went in her sleep. Last night. We just returned her home."

"How's your family?"

"Sad. But okay."

Louise sighed. "I am truly sorry, Howard, for your loss."

"Thank you."

Then the phone went dead. He'd hung up. Louise rubbed her forehead and tried to take a full breath. For the umpteenth time since March, Louise wished she'd stayed in Florida. She wouldn't dare go to Howard's wife's funeral, but she'd be closer. He could come and visit her. They'd walk on the beach. She'd help him through this horrible time. Despite the fact the wife was not even buried yet, Louise would give anything to be with Howard right now.

The next day, Louise was being shaken in her sleep. She envisioned an earthquake or even a bad wind storm shaking her bed, but then awoke to Irene staring at her. She jumped in fright. "Irene, what are you doing?"

"Wake up. Wake up now." Irene grabbed at her hand.

"Irene, what's wrong?"

"Wake up. You need to get up."

Louise had never seen her sister so agitated. Frustration filled her heart. Now her sister wouldn't allow her even the privilege of sleeping in. "What's wrong, Irene?"

"I can't find Kathleen."

"Kathleen?"

Irene left her and went to the window. "She went off to catch the bus, but that was hours ago. I just can't find her."

Louise laid back on her pillow. "Irene. Kathleen is a grown up. She doesn't go to school anymore." This morning was going to be harder than she thought.

"She's lost. I know it. Maybe," Irene's hand went to cover her mouth, "she's been abducted."

Louise tried hard to breath well and sat up on the edge of the bed, "Irene. Sit down with me."

Irene began to pace in front of the window. "I can't. We need to go out and look for her. Call the police."

Louise stood up. "Irene come here." Her head began to spin. Lack of breath caused her to fall back on the bed. She needed to get up slower.

"Oh Louise, what will we do? You're too sick to help me look for her. She's just a little girl. She'll be afraid."

Louise motioned for her sister to come toward her, "Irene come here. Please."

Irene just kept pacing. "Oh my. Oh dear God, help me."

"Irene." Perhaps a bit of a demanding tone would work on her sister. "Come here." Louise sucked in a deep breath. "Sit with me, please."

Irene looked at her and then came and sat down. Louise immediately put her arm around her frightened sister and felt the tenseness in her body. She grabbed her hand, "Look at me."

Howard's stories of dealing with his wife filtered through her thoughts. "Now. I just woke up. You need to give me a few minutes. Let me catch my morning breath. Let me go to the bathroom. When I've finished, we'll go look for Kathleen. Okay?"

Irene stared at her with that confused, blank stare. Her eyes glassy. Far away.

"I can't breathe well. You have to help me."

Irene nodded.

"Give me a few minutes and we'll go find Kathleen. Okay?"

Irene nodded again, but tears filled her eyes. One single tear rolled down her cheek.

"I know you are afraid. What do you do when you're afraid?"

Without hesitation Irene said, "Pray."

"Well get to it sister. You tell me all the time He listens when we pray. Right?"

Irene nodded and bowed her head. Her lips moved but no words came out. Louise felt her sister's body begin to relax, despite the tears now streaming down her face.

She hugged her sister tighter. For the first time in her whole life, she understood her sister's faith. It was everything to her. Despite the fear and the dementia, she remembered how to pray. Irene's lips still moved, her eyes squeezed shut. Her breathing began to grow calm. Louise heard her say, "Amen," and at the same time her body relaxed even more.

She looked over at her. "I feel better."

"Okay. Now let me get my wits about me, get out of bed, and then we'll go look."

Irene nodded, turned away, and looked out the window.

Louise began to get up. She searched for her slippers under the bed and looked back to her sister.

229

"Why was I afraid?"

Irene had forgotten the fear, forgotten her lost child. She sighed. "Are you hungry?"

Irene nodded. "And thirsty."

"I'll be just a moment."

As Louise finished up in the bathroom, she returned to the bedroom to see her sister staring out the window again, "You ready for breakfast?"

Irene turned to her and smiled, "Yes."

Maybe God would help Louise get through this whole ordeal, after all. Louise was fairly sure He wouldn't be there for her, but it looked like He'd be there for Irene. She'd never be alone.

Chapter 28

"Howard, you have called me almost every night this week," smiled Louise.

"Do you hate me?"

"No. Of course not. Just surprised."

"I have more time on my hands now. It's been almost three weeks. My kids are all back home. I'm alone with nothing to do but sit here and think of you. So I figured, why not call you."

Louise smiled. She did like his calls. She wondered if Irene would grow suspicious. Howard called around eight o'clock each night. "I love hearing from you. I do."

"Then what's the problem?"

"Not sure I'm ready for my sister to find out about you."

"How is she?"

"Today, good. Tomorrow, who knows?"

"Welcome to my world. I mean, my former world."

"How are you?"

"Lonely."

"Make some new friends."

"How?"

"Bingo, shuffleboard, go on a walk."

"I only want you."

Louise smiled. "I wish you lived closer to Michigan."

"Me, too."

Both sighed.

"Howard, I wish I could tell you why I need to be here."

"For your sister I understand."

"It's more than that."

"Well, why?"

"I can't tell you. I can't tell anyone."

"It's almost September, Louise. Can you come back to Florida this winter?"

"Perhaps."

"Really?"

"I'm not sure yet. It might be a possibility."

"Oh my dear. Things will be different now. I've been mourning for ten years, but we can be together now. Really together."

"Howard, that sounds like heaven, but do you really want to get involved with another sick, old woman?"

"In a heartbeat."

"That might be all I have."

"Louise, I have a feeling your heart will live forever."

"Maybe, but it doesn't feel like it. I struggle to breathe every single day. The doctor upped my medicine. He says I need daily breathing treatments. I struggle to stay conscious some days. Who knows what tomorrow will bring."

"Do you think...?"

"What?"

"Do you think I could come and visit you?"

"Here? In Michigan?"

"Yes."

"Oh Howard, I don't know."

"I could stay in a motel. Just for a few days. I will try and not bother you or your sister."

"You'll bother my sister. She won't understand."

Howard sighed.

"Howard, it might not be long now. Perhaps we can be together again. Soon. We could live closer."

"Or together."

"Together? What are you saying?"

"Together. Why not?"

Louise sighed.

"Louise?"

"Yes."

"I'm serious. I want to be your husband."

"I don't accept proposals over the phone."

"Then let me come to Michigan. I'll do the whole works ring, roses, on bended knee."

"You'd never get up again!" They both laughed.

"Maybe not, but I'd do it. If I were there."

"Who was that?"

"A friend." Louise came back into the living room and sat in her chair, across from Irene's chair.

"You're smiling."

"Am I?"

"Yes."

"Did you ever think of getting remarried, Irene?" Louise wondered if her sister would be able to hold a complete conversation. Often she couldn't, but occasionally...

"No. Never wanted to, I guess."

"Ever?"

Irene shook her head. "I loved my husband, but I also liked being alone. Until you arrived, and then I realized maybe I was lonelier than I thought."

"We have had a pretty good time, haven't we?"

Irene smiled over at her as she leaned her head back on her chair. "Not bad for two old sisters."

Louise sat down the next day and reviewed her list. Everything was checked off. The funeral home, the assisted living home, the flowers, the photos, as much packing she could do without leaving evidence for Kathleen to be suspicious. Things were in order. Ready. All she had to do was pull the plug. Call it quits.

It'd be easy now. Now she had a plan of her own. Howard without a doubt would take care of her. She needn't worry about her own care. Things were falling into place as accurately as she could have ever imagined.

Perhaps this was God's plan. That's probably what was happening now. Her sister's faith. Her sister's legacy. She wondered if she could ever have the ability to claim God like her sister had. As a friend. As a person, someone important in her life. Perhaps she was too old for a change like that.

When would she launch their plan? She wasn't sure, but she smiled now instead of dreading it all. She'd fulfill her sister's wishes, and then jump on a plane headed for Florida. She hated to think of repacking all her belongings, but there wasn't much left. She'd leave the rest for Kathleen.

The focus of her life now was Howard. But before she could go to him, she needed to fulfill her promise to Irene.

Chapter 29

Kathleen decided to stop by her mother's house on the way home from work. The weather was cooler and it was raining. She debated on stopping, but knew the rest of her weekly appointments would forbid her to do it in the next few days. She rushed into her mother's home as drops started to fall. Soon the leaves from the large oak trees in the yard would loosen and fall, just like these drops of September rain. She dreaded to think of the upcoming cold season.

Her mother grew worse each day. Memories eluded her. Just last week, she'd asked Kathleen, about ten times if Taylor was excited about her upcoming wedding. Kathleen had put a photo album together for her a few weeks earlier, so every time her mother asked about the wedding, Kathleen showed her the photos. Even so, her mother often forgot she had the album, just as she forgot the wedding day.

She wondered how much longer Louise could handle the stress of her mother's illness. Dropping by more often made her realize the burden her mother was becoming to Louise. Louise wasn't getting any better either. Perhaps it was time to find an assisted living home. She hated to think of that. She wanted her mother to be able to stay home as long as possible.

Coming in the back door, she called out to her aunt and mother, but no answer met her. "Yoohoo! Mom?" She pulled off her coat and shook it on the rug by the back door, "Aunt Louise?"

Nothing. No noise. Not a return call out. She wondered where they had gone. It was six o'clock. Perhaps they were watching the news. The kitchen looked spotless, which was odd for that time of the day.

She called again as she walked into the living room. No television. No radio. Max came to meet her and rubbed against her legs. She picked up the limp kitty.

"Max. Where is everyone?" The cat purred a response. She set him down on his feet again. Kathleen glanced around the quiet room. She went to the bottom of the stairs and called up, "Mother? Louise?"

A bump came from her mother's bedroom. She ascended the stairs. "Mother?"

She heard it, but it was barely audible, "Hello?" The response came from her mother's bedroom. Quickly, Kathleen ascended the stairs and opened her mother's bedroom door. Her mother was just on the other side. "Mother, are you all right?"

"I was just taking a nap."

"Where's Aunt Louise?"

"Who?"

"Aunt Louise."

"Oh, she's in Florida. You know that."

"Mother, she isn't in Florida. Did she run an errand?"

Her mother shrugged her shoulders. "I just laid down for awhile."

It wasn't like Aunt Louise to leave her mother alone. Not since she'd gotten lost on her walk that time.

Kathleen left the room and went back down the stairs calling as she went, "Aunt Louise? Are you home?" She found the sewing room door closed. She tapped on it. "Aunt Louise?" No answer. Her mother came up from behind her.

"Why are you knocking?"

Kathleen shook her head and slowly opened the door to her aunt's bedroom. She found Louise lying on the floor by her bed. Running to her, she pulled her cell phone out of her pocket. She knelt down by her aunt who appeared to be breathing. Barely. She punched in Brian's number and then changed her mind, and called 9-1-1.

The paramedics knocked on the front door and Kathleen did her best to shout to them. Her mother wouldn't answer the door. She just sat in a chair in her sister's bedroom with a worried look on her face. Kathleen had placed her in the chair to ease her frantic state over the strange woman lying in her sewing room. "What's wrong, Kathleen?" she'd fussed, as Kathleen gently patted her aunt's cheeks and called her name. "How did this woman get in here?"

Kathleen held a cool, damp cloth on Louise's forehead, and cradled her aunt's head in her lap on the floor. She wasn't waking up.

The front door opened. "Ma'am? Hello?"

"In here. The bedroom. Far room on the right," she called out. As soon as they came into the bedroom, she heard the front door open again and Brian call to her. "In here, Brian."

The paramedics went right to work, lifting Aunt Louise onto the stretcher and giving her oxygen. Louise drew a long breath, and opened her eyes. Kathleen got up from the floor, went to her mother and held her hand.

"What happened, Kathleen? How did Louise get on my sewing room floor? " Her mother seemed agitated, yet concerned. "Did she hit her head on my sewing machine? That darn thing always trips me up." For a few minutes her mother grew silent, then she added, "Will she be okay?" She looked up at Kathleen with pleading eyes.

"I hope so, Mother. The men will take care of her."Kathleen looked at her husband as the paramedics pushed the stretcher out of the bedroom and to the waiting ambulance. "Can you stay here with Mother? I better go to the hospital with Aunt Louise."

Brian nodded, with a worried look. "Of course. Do you think she'll be okay with me here?"

"We have no other choice." Kathleen grabbed her purse from the kitchen table and called back to her husband, "Call Edna if she gets anxious. She can always calm her down." Brian nodded as he walked into the kitchen with Kathleen's mother.

"We'll make some dinner. How does that sound, Mother?"

"Good. I'm starved."

Kathleen kissed her husband's cheek before she went out to her car. The ambulance pulled away from the front of her mother's house. This wasn't in the plans. What would she do now?

Kathleen watched as Aunt Louise was pushed on a gurney down the hallway of the hospital. Her aunt's color had returned to her cheeks and she seemed to be stirring a bit. The doctor had kept Kathleen from following,

saying, "We'll let you know how she is doing soon. Let us examine her."
He'd then motioned for her to sit in the waiting room and Kathleen
complied.

Brian called her as she waited. "How is she?"

"Not sure. They're examining her now. How's Mom?"

"She's fine. I fixed her some food and she's eating now. Watching the
news."

"You're amazing." Kathleen smiled.

"I wonder how long Aunt Louise had been lying there. She looked
awful. Her face so ashen. Death-like."

"Poor Mom. I'm glad she slept and didn't have to find her. She
probably wouldn't have even looked. When I found her she was pretty sure
Aunt Louise was in Florida."

"Sweetheart, I think we need to look into a home for your Mom."

"I agree. The sooner the better. We'll go this weekend."

"I'm sure that's best."

"Brian, can you feed Max? Who knows when he last ate."

"Done. He purred. I thinks he likes me better now." Brian sneezed
into the phone.

Kathleen laughed.

"Haven't seen him since though."

"Poor cat. Might need to find a home for him, too."

"I'm sorry Kathleen."

"It's okay. We knew this day was coming." Kathleen saw the doctor
approaching. "Gotta go. Here comes the doctor."

"Call me back."

"Okay."

Kathleen stood.

"How are you related to the patient, ma'am?"

"She's my aunt."

"She'd bad, but we caught her in time. Her breathing was so low, I'm not sure she'd still be with us now if you hadn't found her."

Kathleen shuddered, rubbing her forearms. "What now?"

"We're gonna keep her on oxygen. She's kinda feisty. Keeps asking about someone named Irene."

"That's my mother. They live together. Tell her she's fine."

"Okay. Give us a few more minutes and you can come back to see her. We have her on heavy diuretics and that should give her some more relief. Good thing you found her when you did."

The doctor left and Kathleen sat back down. What would she do if she were to find Aunt Louise gone? Kathleen was so relieved she'd decided to stop to see them both. They couldn't wait any longer. She'd cancel appointments for the rest of the week and get to the job of finding her mother a new home. Perhaps she could put the two women together. Her life suddenly was changing. She was thankful the wedding and her son's graduation were now over. As her mother always said, *'Life's interruptions always come without asking.'*

Kathleen owed her Aunt Louise so much for caring for her mother this whole summer. The least she could do was care for her now.

###

Kathleen walked into the hospital room and saw her aunt hooked up to oxygen and an IV. She was breathing heavily, but with consistency. She approached the bed.

Aunt Louise was awake and her eyes grew big when she approached her. She patted her aunt's arm. "It's okay, Aunt Louise. Everything's fine. You just rest."

She mumbled something and Kathleen got closer, "What?"

"Irene?"

"She's fine. She was sleeping and didn't notice you gone."

Her aunt took a deep breath and closed her eyes, "You rest. Everything's fine now. I'm here. Brian's with Mom."

Just before her aunt went to sleep, she heard her whisper what sounded like, "Howard." Kathleen never heard her say that name before. She didn't know anyone named Howard.

What would she do now? She pretended to go to sleep. Kathleen probably wouldn't leave her side if she knew she was awake. If she faked falling asleep, she might get left alone. How could she have allowed this to happen? Everything was going well. She had decided to give it a month and then start the pact in motion. This had definitely not been in the plans.

She tried hard to recall the day. Had she taken her medicine? She rarely forgot because of how hard it was to get through a day without it. The medicine gave her relief. Helped her breathe. How could she have forgotten?

Going over the morning in her head, she remembered helping Irene most of the morning. It was getting harder and harder for her sister to do simple tasks by herself. Combing her hair, brushing her teeth, and cleaning herself was a slow, step-by-step process. Louise often sat in the bathroom with her, telling her what to do. She was thankful Irene could still take a shower alone, she just needed to be talked through the process. They'd had lunch. She watched Irene walk up the stairs to take a nap, then went to her room to do the same thing. That's all she could remember. She didn't remember getting out of bed or passing out on the floor as the doctor told her she had done.

She thought back through the morning. She hadn't gone to the bathroom much all day. That had to be it. She'd forgotten to take her medicine. Groaning, she opened her eyes for a few moments to find that she was alone in the room again. Kathleen had left. There wasn't anything more she could do. So she decided to go to sleep. Rest.

She needed her strength. Strength to pull off this whole promise. It couldn't wait a month. It had to happen soon. No. It had to happen *now*.

As she drifted off, she thought of Howard. He would never have known what happened to her. Her phone would probably die before anyone would hear it ring. It had to be sitting in her bedroom. She hoped, for just this one night, he wouldn't call.

Kathleen spent the night with her mother. She couldn't get over how much care her mother now required. She was lost without Aunt Louise. Kathleen had to help her get undressed and ready for bed. It was like putting a toddler to bed. She kept getting up and asking for a drink. Her mother seemed particularly agitated. Pacing back and forth.

Kathleen did her best to keep her calm. She wasn't sure what else to do. After her mother settled down and finally seemed to go to sleep, Kathleen was exhausted. She'd spent most of the evening in the hospital with her aunt. Brian had gone home about an hour before she tried to get her mother to bed. He had work to finish up and he needed to head back to work in the morning.

She found Max, picked him up, and placed him in her mother's chair. He did his usual turn around six or seven times before finally settling down in the cushion to sleep. She rummaged through the closets, looking for an extra pillow and blanket for herself. She found a quilt in the hallway closet, and headed into her aunt's room for a pillow. As she did, she nearly fell over four large boxes stored in front of her aunt's closet. She hadn't noticed them earlier, because Aunt Louise had fallen on the other side of the room. Other small boxes were stacked by a bed-stand.

She thought that was particularly odd as she grabbed for a pillow from her aunt's bed. Most all of the boxes were sealed with packing tape, but one in the corner appeared open. She peeked inside and found some of her mother's things in the box. Some hangers, towels, and a few of her winter sweaters.

Taking the pillow back into the living room, Kathleen reflected on the box. Why did it contain some of her mother's possessions? Perhaps Aunt Louise was sorting through their possessions to take to the consignment shop, but why were her mother's things in Louise's room?

As Kathleen finally settled down, she turned on the television and watched a bit of the local news broadcast before shutting it off to go to sleep. She'd have to call her boss in the morning and explain why she needed a few days off to get things settled for her aunt and mother. Perhaps her co-worker would take a few of her accounts for a few weeks. She hated to lose the money, but there really wasn't another option.

Kathleen couldn't take her thoughts of the boxes in her aunt's room. Perhaps her aunt was making plans of her own to move her mother to a facility. Surely she wouldn't do that without consulting her.

Irene awoke. Looking around the room, she tried to remember if she had been taking a nap or if she had slept all night. She looked toward her window to see if the morning sun was peering through her curtains. Picking up the edge of her cover, she looked down to see she was in pajamas. It must be morning.

She pulled off the covers to face a slight chill in the air. Thinking hard she thought about the time of year. Pulling off the house coat off the end of her bed, she slipped on the slim, lightweight fabric which felt silky to touch. Must be summer.

Everything seemed fuzzy in the bathroom. She had to squint to see herself in the mirror. After using the bathroom, she called out for Louise. She knew she wouldn't come up the stairs for her, but she called to see if she was home. A woman came into her bedroom. Irene backed away from the door.

"Mother, what do you need?"

"Who are you?" The face seemed familiar.

"Mom. It's me."

The woman went to her bedside table and picked something up and placed glasses on her face.

"Do I wear glasses?"

The woman laughed and patted her, "For years, Mom."

"Kathleen?"

"Yes, Mom."

"What are you doing here?"

"Aunt Louise is in the hospital. Remember?"

"What's wrong with her?"

"It's her heart. She forgot her medicine yesterday. She's fine now. We'll probably go get her tomorrow."

"Who'll fix my breakfast?"

"I'm here. I will."

"Don't you have to go to work?" Confusion filled Irene's thoughts. Her stomach growled. She passed gas. "Eww, sorry."

Kathleen giggled, "It's okay. Are you hungry?"

"Yes. I'm always hungry."

Kathleen held her hand and led her out of the bedroom. "What would you like me to fix you?"

"Do we have any ice cream?"

"Ice cream for breakfast?"

"That's what Louise always fixes me. I love hot fudge sundaes the best."

Kathleen stopped and looked at her mother. "Aunt Louise would not fix you an ice cream sundae for breakfast." Kathleen laughed.

246

Irene remembered, "No. She wouldn't. But sometimes she does. Louise has been very good to me."

Kathleen laughed again.

After spending the morning with her mother, Kathleen knew things weren't as comfortable as she'd imagined. The care her mother now needed was astounding. She was surprised Aunt Louise hadn't complained about it. While eating breakfast, Kathleen realized her mother needed a bath. The unpleasant odor prevented her from eating all of her own breakfast.

After giving her mother a shower, fixing her hair and changing her into clean clothes, she realized her care was far more than she'd imagined. Some of her care was even beyond Kathleen's abilities. She was afraid Mother would fall in the shower. She needed to have Brian install some safety bars. Some were needed by next to the toilet as well. Gagging, she did her best to wash her mother's dentures. Even the stairs were almost too hard for her mother to navigate safely. She had to keep reminding her to use the handrail.

That night at dinner Kathleen asked Brian, "What do you think? Should she stay in the house or should we just take the initiative and find a home for them both?"

Brian wiped off his mouth and set down his coffee cup, "Whatever you decide, I think we need to move quickly. You can't continue to be there for them all the time. Look at you tonight. You're exhausted."

"Maybe we could find a home for both of them. Together."

Brian took another bite of his meal, "That would be good. Help them both transition better."

Kathleen was exhausted. She'd cleaned her mother's room and also much of the downstairs. It was dusty. She washed a few windows but then noticed dust on the curtains.

"I've neglected them."

"You didn't know," Brian looked up as she blinked away tears.

"I should have paid better attention."

Brian patted her hand. "We'll get this fixed."

Kathleen looked over at her mother who now slowly sipped her soup. Some dribbled down her chin. Pulling a napkin out of the holder in the middle of the table, Kathleen handed it to her mother, then motioned to her own chin. "You're leaking, Mom."

Her mother looked up at her and smiled, "I'm sorry." She seemed oblivious to their conversation.

"It's okay. We all drip from time to time."

"No." Her mother shook her head, "I'm becoming a burden. I don't want to be a burden to you and Brian."

Kathleen blinked and wiped her eyes, "Mother, you are not a burden to me."

"Yes I am. I don't remember."

"It's okay."

"No. Aunt Louise promised."

Brian looked up with a puzzled look on his face. "What did she promise, Mom?"

"To help me. Take care of it."

Kathleen put her hand on her mother's back, sitting beside her. "We'll help you now. What do you want taken care of?"

"Me." Her mother was adamant and spoke loudly.

"We're here to take care of you, mother."

"No. Louise promised."

Her mother grew agitated, wringing her hands. Tears filled her eyes.

"Mother, what's wrong?"

"I need Louise."

"I know. She's been a huge help to you."

"When is she coming back?"

Kathleen sighed, "Tomorrow. We hope."

"Good. We need to fix this."

"Fix what?"

"Me," her mother shook in her chair. "Now."

Kathleen helped her mother get ready for bed. The room smelled so much better. Her cleaning did wonders. She tucked her mother in bed and kissed her cheek. "Have a good night sleep, mother. I'll be downstairs if you need anything."

"Okay. Thank you dear."

"You're welcome." Kathleen stood off a bit and watched her mother close her eyes and almost immediately breathe heavier. She covered her mouth with her hand and blinked back more tears. Life had changed. She was now the caregiver, tucking her mother into bed. It had taken a few minutes to calm her down after dinner. Brian seemed to be better at it than she.

Turning off the light, she left the door open a crack to hear if her mother did call for her. She wished she didn't have to sleep on the couch tonight, but there really wasn't any other option.

Brian had stayed and was watching television in the living room. She needed to let him go home. At least one of them could get a good night's sleep.

"Why don't you head home, honey. It's Friday. You must be super tired from the week."

"Me? What about you?"

"I'll be fine." Kathleen picked up Max out of Aunt Louise's chair. "Max will keep me company."

"I've been hearing a noise coming from Aunt Louise's room. Is her cell phone in there?"

"I don't know." Kathleen dropped Max back on the chair and went into her Aunt's room. "I don't hear anything."

"Give it a second," Brian called from the other room.

Kathleen stood in the middle of the room. Soon she heard what sounded like the chirp of a dying cell phone. It came from her aunt's bed-stand.

Turning on the light she headed for the sound. Her aunt's cell phone was under an opened book on the stand. She flipped it over and turned it on. A dying battery button shown in the dark room. She looked around for a charger cord. It was amazing to think of her aunt having a cell phone. It was even a smart phone.

She found the charger and plugged in the phone. Leaving the room, she came back to find Brian putting on his coat. "I hate to leave you."

"I'll be fine." She stopped and helped him button his coat and then kissed his lips. "I think I'll get busy calling homes tomorrow. Can you help me by going to look at some tomorrow? Perhaps we can get Violet to sit with Mom for awhile."

"Then we'll go and get Aunt Louise in the afternoon."

"Sounds like a plan." Brian kissed his wife. "I love you."

"I love you more," she smiled as she responded in her usual way.

"Don't worry. This will all work out."

Kathleen sighed and folded her arms, "I hope so. Call me when you get home."

A chill in the air made Kathleen shiver as she let Brian out the kitchen door. Shutting the door she waited for him to get into his car and then back out of the driveway. She missed home.

Returning to the living room she thought about what she'd watch on television as she pulled up a blanket. Max headed right for her lap. He jumped up on it and then did his usual circle on her lap trying to find a comfortable spot to land. They both settled into a warm position and Kathleen pushed the remote to find a suitable show to watch.

A cell phone began to ring in her aunt's bedroom. Kathleen looked down at Max all comfy and starting to purr. "Oh Max. Should I get that?"

The cat didn't move, but the phone continued to ring.

She sighed. "Get off buddy. I better get that. It might be the hospital."

Kathleen pushed the cat onto the floor. He looked up at her and arched his back.

"Hold on. I'll be back soon."

Kathleen hustled into her aunt's room and flipped on the light. She went to the night stand and picked up her aunt's phone. She swiped at it and answered, "Hello?"

"Louise?"

"No, I'm sorry. This is her niece, Kathleen. Can I help you?"

The caller hung up. "Well, okay then." Kathleen glanced at the caller ID as the phone call ended. *Howard.*

'Howard? Who's that?' Kathleen then remembered her aunt had said that name the other night before she'd left her hospital room to return home.

Whoever Howard was, it was quite evident, he didn't want to talk to anyone but her aunt.

Louise wished she'd been conscious when leaving in the ambulance. She'd have picked up her cell phone. She desperately wanted to talk to Howard. She had always prided herself on being independent. Self-reliant and assured. After spending the day in the hospital, she felt helpless and old.

Several times, the nurses had not come to her room when she'd needed water or to use the bathroom. A couple of young, punk, resident doctors had screamed at her, as if every elderly woman they'd come across couldn't hear. She'd been annoyed with almost everyone.

If she could just talk to Howard, she knew she'd feel better. Her breathing struggles had gotten much better. She'd pulled out the oxygen tubes from her nose more times than she could remember and her breathing had been fine without it. She wanted to go home.

She had to be sure she never forgot to take her medicine again. Despite all the care her sister needed, she couldn't forget to do that again.

As she turned off the television and her bed side light, she listened to the sounds around her. Beeping noises from other rooms. Nurses talking at the station just outside her room. Looking out the window, by her bed, she thought of Irene. Her sister was now her friend. Her companion. Whether she knew things or not, she did know she appreciated her company.

She sighed as she realized she'd have to be without her soon. Life just stunk. She spent years of her life avoiding her sister. They'd fought. Disagreements had separated them for decades. And this pact with her sister would probably be the hardest thing she'd have to do. Ever. She knew her sister was ready, but was she? For once in her life, thinking of being all alone again made her sad. There was only one answer to that problem. Howard needed a wife.

Chapter 30

Kathleen called five assisted living homes that morning after she managed to get her mother up and moving for the day. Some had single room openings, but most did not have two available rooms. Perhaps she'd better get her mother settled first and then worry about Aunt Louise later. The woman had never liked people to make decisions for her in the past. She called Brian with two available places and then talked to Edna about coming to stay with her Mom.

Soon they were sitting down at the first home and talking through the details of her mother's care. The lady in charge was chipper. Friendly. After talking through their mother's care issues, the woman told them a little more about the home and what they could expect from having her mother stay at this particular care facility.

"We have daily events for all our residents which includes exercise time, book reading, even a time for crafts from time to time. We assess what the resident can do before they are admitted and then adjust their schedule to what they can understand and take part in."

Brian nodded. "We want her to be stimulated every day."

"That is a definite. We find dementia patients do much better when they are having activities each day."

"What about hairdressers. I've heard that sometimes you provide that as well?" Kathleen shifted in her chair and wrote down the name of the woman who came into the home on a weekly basis to cut, curl and wash the resident's hair. Her mother would like that.

"Well, we have one more home to visit today." Kathleen added after the director told them of the costs of the care at this home. She wasn't sure how she'd pay for her care. She'd probably end up selling her mother's home just to pay for her to be in a facility like this one. What about Aunt Louise? Where would she live? Would she have enough money of her own to take care of herself? A headache began to form in her forehead. The decisions she was about to make would affect both of her loved ones. For the rest of their lives.

Brian took her arm and they returned to the car. "We'll figure this out. Don't stress."

Kathleen grew more tense. Not only were they needing to make quick decisions, but they still needed to visit one more home and pick up Aunt Louise from the hospital that afternoon. Anxiety over planning a wedding was nothing compared to this.

The price of this assisted living home was much lower than the other. The care seemed just about the same and Kathleen breathed a sigh of relief. The trip to visit their mother would be farther from their home, but close enough they could visit her on a regular basis.

After all the formalities, answered questions and concerns, Kathleen knew this would be the home for her mother.

"We have only one room left and there is a woman waiting for it right now. We haven't heard from her caregiver in a while, but I'll call her today to find out their status. If she doesn't take the room, it's all yours."

Kathleen knew this was their only option. "Put us on the list for the next room, either way."

The director of the home nodded.

"Can I call you this evening?"

Brian nodded. "Here's my number. Call me. We have to go get my aunt out of the hospital and my wife might be busy."

Kathleen was so blessed to have Brian. He tried hard to shoulder her worries.

"I'll let you know as soon as I know for sure." The director stood behind her desk. "It was so nice to meet you and I'll look forward to meeting your mother and possibly your aunt in the near future."

Kathleen and Brian stood. "Thank you." Kathleen held out her hand to shake the woman's hand.

"Let me know if there is anything more I can do for you. If you have any more questions, feel free to call me." The woman escorted them to the door of her office. "Oh, by the way, what's your mother's name?"

"Irene," Kathleen answered as she pulled on her jacket.

"Oh my," the director added, "Really?"

"Yes," Kathleen turned to the woman who now held a suspicious look on her face.

"Why?"

"Just a coincidence, I'm sure. The woman waiting for the next room has the same first name."

Kathleen laughed. "If she's as wonderful as my mother, you'll have some great Irene's here then."

The director nodded. "Yes. We will. Thanks for considering our facility for your mother. We'll provide her the best of care."

Aunt Louise was determined to walk out of the hospital instead of riding in the wheelchair provided for her. She insisted, "I might be sick, but I'm not dead yet."

Brian did his best to help her by holding out his arm to her. She took it and hung onto him as if her life depended on him to walk. He knew she was weak and didn't really realize it. "Aunt Louise, if you were dead, I'm sure they wouldn't take you out in a wheel chair."

Louise smiled up at him, "You're right, Brian."

On their way home their Aunt was fairly quiet. Kathleen began telling her about their day. "We visited some assisted living homes today, Aunt Louise."

"What?" She appeared startled.

"Yes. I think it's time, don't you?"

"You made that decision quickly."

Kathleen turned to her aunt in the back seat. "Are you upset by that?" Louise was pale, but she was breathing well on her own now.

"How soon?" Her aunt seemed a little more agitated than just minutes earlier.

"Soon. We are waiting to see if a room is available for Mom. There could be someone ahead of her. If they take the room, then we'll have to wait until the next room opens up."

"What's the name of the place?"

Brian looked at Aunt Louise in the back seat in his rear view mirror. She seemed much more uncomfortable. Perhaps the walk to the car hadn't been a good idea. "Are you okay, Aunt Louise?" Brian reached over and patted his wife's hand in her lap. He gave her a look to tread carefully with her words.

"Sunrise."

"Sunrise Assisted Living in Okemos?"

"Yes, how did you know?"

Brian again glanced back at his aunt. Her face was even more pale than before.

She shifted in her seat, but seemed to regain her composure. "Lucky guess."

She had to work fast. When she returned to her room she found her phone was plugged into the charger. She didn't remember doing that. But there were sketchy things she hadn't remember from the day she lost consciousness. For instance, her medicine.

She was thankful her phone was plugged in. She glanced at the phone and found several calls from Howard. He was probably worried sick.

She also saw two calls from Sunrise. They'd called her. Twice. She breathed in and held her breath. What if she was too late? What if they'd given the room to her niece?

She sat down on the edge of the bed. Their sister pact seemed to be unraveling. They'd never planned on Louise getting sick. She never thought, in less than two days, Kathleen would seek out a place for her sister, and find one so quickly.

Thinking about Irene she envisioned how easy it would be to just let Kathleen take over. Would Irene really even remember the pact now? Just now, as she came into the kitchen with Kathleen and Brian, she had to be told that Louise had been in the hospital. Surely someone would have told her where she'd been.

Life would be easier if she could just forget about the pact. Ignore it. Her niece and nephew could take better care of Irene than she could right now.

Louise looked over at a recent photo of her and her sister she'd just placed on her bed stand. It was from Taylor's wedding. She liked it. She looked at the pleasant smiles of two old women.

At that instant Irene walked into her room and came over and sat beside her on the bed. She looked into her eyes.

"Look at this nice photo of us, Irene. Isn't it nice?"

Irene took the photo in her hands and looked at it. "Yes."

"I like it. Do you?"

Irene nodded. "You have a nice smile."

"You do, too."

Irene handed her back the photo. "We have to hurry, Louise."

"Hurry?"

"It has to be now."

Louise placed the photo back on her bed stand.

"You promised." Irene reached for her hand and squeezed it. "Please."

Louise knew exactly what she was asking her. "Are you sure?"

Irene nodded and said again. "You promised."

"Okay." Louise knew one thing she couldn't do at that exact moment. She couldn't ignore the pact. Her sister was counting on her.

"Oh Howard!" Louise couldn't believe how much she'd missed her friend.

"Louise? Where have you been?"

"In the hospital."

There was silence for a few seconds.

"Howard?"

"Are you okay now?"

"I forgot my medicine for a day. It's getting so bad that even if I miss a day, it doesn't turn out well. I'm bad off."

"I need to come be with you."

"In Michigan?"

"Yes. Before the snow falls though. Not sure I can come when the weather is cold and horrible."

Louise laughed. "I understand that completely."

"I'll come. We'll get you packed and then you can come back to Florida with me."

"You mean that?"

"Absolutely."

Louise's lungs filled with sweet air as she thought of her friend.

"Are you ready?"

"Give me a few days. I have to take care of Irene. I promised."

"Okay, but I'm going to look up tickets tonight. We'll ship everything back here. You can live with me. I'll take care of you."

Louise began to cry. "Howard. You are the best."

"So you will? You'll come back with me?"

"Of course."

"Great."

"What will you tell your kids?"

"Maybe I won't. I have a life. It doesn't always revolve around them."

"But, you'd want their blessing, wouldn't you?"

Howard was silent on the other end.

"Howard?"

"Let's be together for awhile. Move to the east side, in my winter home. Then we'll figure out how to tell them. Okay?"

Louise desired nothing more right now than to be with Howard. She agreed.

Louise planned to ask Greg to move the boxes with Irene's possessions to her car. She had about five large boxes packed, sitting in her bedroom. Hopefully, they weren't too heavy.

She decided to use her own suitcases to pack most of Irene's clothes. She'd buy more for herself later. Packing Irene's clothes had been difficult. She had to be careful to pack clothes which wouldn't raise suspicion from Kathleen, if or when she'd find them missing. She stood in Irene's bedroom that afternoon trying to sort her pants, shirts and 'unmentionables.' Choosing half of everything seemed doable. That would still leave half for Kathleen to sort through after she put Irene in the home.

Irene walked in, finding her sorted piles on her bed. "Is it almost time?"

Louise found Irene's perspective of what they were doing to be somewhat assured and positive. She often helped Louise pack her things, making choices of what to take and what to leave.

Louise needed to rest for a bit, so she sat down on the bed as Irene took her chair by the window. "Irene, do you remember why I'm doing this?"

"The pact." Irene's memory never seemed to fluctuate on the details of their plan. For that, Louise grew more tense.

"They might catch on. We might not pull it off as we planned."

"But, can we still try."

Louise sighed. There was nothing she could do to change her sister's mind. And, a promise was a promise. She nodded, "Okay, Irene. Okay."

Her sister's gaze left the clothes stacks on the bed and moved to looking out her bedroom window. "It will be winter soon."

"Yes, the sooner this is over, the sooner I can get out of here."

Irene's attention jerked back to gaze at her sister, "Where are you going?"

"Florida."

"But Kathleen will be here. How will she be able to help you, Louise, if you move back to Florida?"

"Irene, you are changing every single part of your life, even your death, to cause your daughter to not have a burden. To be able to get on with her own life. Why would I stay and be a burden to her myself?"

"I hadn't thought of you."

Louise stood again and waved off her sister, "I'll be fine."

"But who will care for you?"

Louise wasn't sure she should share her new adventure with Irene. What if she were to spill the beans? If Kathleen were to find out about her escape, would she stop her from going back to Florida? No. She needed to keep Howard a secret. Even from Irene.

Max slinked into the room. He looked up at Louise and then headed to Irene. Soon he was in her lap. Irene patted his head and smoothed down his coat.

"Irene, Max will be fine. Perhaps Greg and Violet could adopt him."

"Poor Max. We didn't think of you." Irene leaned her head back on the chair. Her dementia had taken over again. "Don't worry, Max. You'll be okay."

Louise gazed at the calico cat in her sister's lap. Another issue she could definitely leave for Kathleen.

Irene's luggage now packed, Louise went to the cupboard to find the new bottles of hygiene products she'd bought just a few weeks before. It should hold Irene for quite a while. She'd be sure to leave enough money for the home to buy her essentials such as shampoo. For however long God deemed it to be.

She thought through the funeral process and how they had planned it all. Her acting abilities hadn't been rigorously used since high school, but Louise knew she could put on a show again. But would it all be a show? She'd dearly miss her sister. These past few months had been a rekindling of their relationship. Their friendship. She sat down at the table in Irene's kitchen and wrote down the day's events.

A production. That's what it was beginning to feel like. Would it work out as they had planned for so many months? Would it work out how Irene made her promise at the grave of their mother? Could Louise really pull it off? She'd soon find out.

Chapter 31

Greg picked up one of the boxes from Louise's bedroom and grunted.
Louise asked, "Is it too heavy for you Greg?"

"No, I got it. No problem, Louise."

The sweat began to form on the man's forehead. Louise worried she'd asked him to do too much, but he continued to pick up the boxes and load them in Irene's car.

"I have some luggage upstairs. Can you get those for me, too?"

"Sure," Greg carried the last of the boxes out of Louise's bedroom. "No problem, Louise."

She patted the man on his back, "Thank you so much for this, Greg."

"No problem."

Violet met Greg as he made his way out the back door, followed by Louise. "Louise, what is all of this?"

"Donations. I've cleaned out our bedrooms. Should have happened a long time ago." First lie. First notch in the plan. "I'm so thankful Greg has agreed to help us."

"He works hard," Violet nodded to her son. "He is happy to help."

"Yes he is. I'm grateful."

"How is Irene today?"

"She's taking a nap. Not a good day."

"How are you feeling?" Violet stopped her by holding her arm.

"I'm tired, but okay. Just need to remember my medicine."

"Well, don't do too much."

Louise nodded.

"I'll go up and get those suitcases now."

"Suitcases?"

"We have way too many. So I packed some of our clothing donations in the suitcases. Easier to carry and we get rid of the suitcases as well."

"What a great idea." Violet smiled.

"Yes. Irene thought of it."

Violet walked out the door, "I'm going home now. Tell Greg to come home for lunch when he's finished, would you Louise?"

"Yes. Thanks Violet."

Violet waved over her shoulder and shuffled off to her own house.

Louise sighed at the kitchen door and folded her arms. She'd fooled the neighbor. It gave her hope that she'd succeed in much more by the end of the week.

"The car is loaded," Louise told Irene that night at dinner.

"Okay."

Louise looked at her sister who looked tired tonight. "Are you okay, Irene?"

Irene nodded.

They both sat in silence for awhile, eating their dinners. Louise had managed to just reheat some leftovers from Sunday's lunch. There wasn't much food left in the house, another plan working out well. No sense wasting food. She could go to the store at the end of the week, just after she'd taken care of Irene.

She waited to hear back from Howard, who now seemed unfamiliarly quiet. No phone call in over two days. She wondered if he'd changed his mind from telling his children. Or, had he changed his mind about having her come back? To take care of her?

She stopped eating, wiped her mouth, and noticed Irene staring at her.

"Do I have something on me?"

Irene continued to stare.

"Irene?"

"I wish we'd planned a time to talk to Kathleen."

Louise was skeptical. Did she know what she was saying? "What?"

"To say goodbye."

Louise shook her head, "But that wouldn't work. She'd ask why you were telling her goodbye."

"I know."

Irene bowed her head. She stopped eating.

"Are you having second thoughts?"

Irene didn't look at Louise but shook her head. "No."

"We can stop, right now. I can call Kathleen to take over. You know that, right?"

Irene nodded.

"Tomorrow. It will be tomorrow."

Irene nodded again.

"But you need to decide now. Tonight, if you want to change your mind." Louise touched her sister's hand, "Irene, you can change your mind, but it has to be now."

Irene looked up and for a moment Louise was sure her sister aged. More gray hair, a few more wrinkles appeared. Oh how she'd miss her sister's companionship. Perhaps she'd change her mind.

"For Kathleen's sake, I have to do this. I want her to continue to love me, especially after I'm gone. Not be happy that I'd passed away, but just able to remember our sweet memories of being together."

Louise nodded. "So?"

Irene nodded. "We have to do this. For them."

Louise smiled, "This is what you've wanted since Mother died. Right?"

Irene nodded and smiled back. "Thank you, Louise."

Sleep didn't come easy that night. Louise just laid in her bed and thought of all the times her sister and her had shared. She recalled the giggles before bedtime they'd shared as children. The fights when boys were more important than the sibling bond. They'd allow too many years to pass by and they hadn't kept in touch. It was probably more her fault than Irene's.

A stiff wind blew outside her window. Leaves fell from the trees, and tomorrow a whole new layer would be on the ground. In the distance, Louise could hear a thunderstorm brewing. She thought about how she could have prevented all of this. What if she'd denied her sister's wishes?

She could still do it. She could forget this whole plan and just call Kathleen. Tell her. Reveal her sister's wishes.

Louise got out of bed as lightning lit up her room. Rain would soon follow. She closed the window and turned back to the chair beside her bed.

Instead of sitting, she picked up the bathrobe draped over the chair and put it on. She stood for a moment, and had a strong desire to be with Irene. It seemed silly but she gave into the impulse and left her room. A crack of thunder penetrated the house as another flash of lightning brightened the room.

As she ascended the stairs, she heard the rain hitting the windows on the west side of the house. Another crack of thunder seemed to shake the house as she lifted foot after foot up the stairs. She got halfway up and stopped to catch her breath. She almost went back down the stairs, but something made her take the last four steps.

Irene's bedroom door squeaked as she slowly pushed it open. A flash of lightning revealed her sister in bed, covered and still. She approached her as another crack of thunder sounded outside.

She pulled back the covers and got under them. Picking up her feet, she placed her head on the pillow beside her sister. As she did, Irene stirred.

Louise scooted herself closer to her sister. Her breathing labored for climbing the stairs. Irene startled a bit and turned to her as a flash of lightning lit up the room again. "Louise?"

Louise patted her sister's shoulders, "It's just me. It's a thunderstorm."

Irene sighed. "It will go away soon." Irene's right hand came over her shoulder, "Give me your hand."

Louise obeyed. Just as she did when she was the little sister. Her sister took her hand. "Go to sleep, Louise. It will be over soon."

The sisters fell asleep in the storm, just as they used to do nearly seventy years ago. Caring for one another.

Chapter 32

Louise slept for just a few hours. When she woke, the house now quiet, the thunderstorm over. Darkness penetrated the room. It was time. The plan needed to happen now.

She left her sister's room and went back to her own room. Flipping on the light, she dressed and did her best to primp her hair and freshen her makeup. She brushed her teeth.

She glanced at the clock by her bed. Nearly four in the morning. She wondered how she could manage to get Irene up so early. Her sister had a hard enough time arousing by eight each morning. They needed to leave within the hour.

She went to the kitchen to fix them some breakfast, starting the coffee pot and breaking some eggs into a bowl. Time couldn't be wasted. They had to leave before dark. She couldn't take a chance of Greg or Violet seeing them driving away.

Ascending the stairs the night before had been laborious. To do so again this morning brought Louise great trepidation. But this would be the last time. She'd let Kathleen and Brian do it from now on.

To her surprise, Irene came out of her bedroom in her pajamas. She called up to her, "Irene. Can you get dressed?"

"Yes," Irene went back into her bedroom.

"Bring down your hair comb and toothbrush. You can finish up down here."

"Okay," she heard Irene call from her bedroom.

They ate their breakfasts in silence, by candlelight, so even the kitchen light would remain off. No clue for the neighbors. Surely, Violet would see a light on and be suspicious if she saw it.

She could clean up once she returned home. As she thought through her day, she realized it really didn't matter if she cleaned up or not. Any sign of both of them eating needed to be erased, but her dishes could remain. Would Kathleen even pay that close of attention? The day would be tragic for her. She'd probably not notice dishes in the sink for two instead of just one.

"Are you ready?"

Her sister nodded. "I've left my Bible for Kathleen. I want her to have it. I've taken Frederick's Bible instead."

Louise nodded. "I'll be sure she gets it."

"Where is the home?"

"Okemos. Close to Lansing."

Irene nodded.

"If I forget to tell you, Louise, thank you. You have proved to me that our sisterhood is much more important than anything else. And..."

Louise watched her sister struggle with words.

"I love you Louise. I really do."

Louise reached out and took her sister's hand. "I love you, too. I need to ask your forgiveness for my stubbornness. I should have been a better sister to you down through the years."

"It's the way it was. But this will make up for all of that. I can never thank you enough."

"I'll miss you."

Irene nodded. "But we'll be okay. We'll see each other again. Right?"

Louise wondered if Irene had forgotten the pact details. They'd never see each other again.

Irene then asked her, "You haven't forgotten how to make your life right, have you dear sister?" Irene was speaking in a spiritual sense.

"Oh Irene. You know I've gone about my own way of living. Too many years of selfishness. Not thinking of anyone else. "

"It will all go away. If you confess it and change. Change for the better. Only Christ can change a heart, sister. You know all of this."

"Yes."

"Remember to love the Lord your God with your whole heart and soul. Serve Him before anything else the world has to offer. Because one day," Irene looked around her kitchen. "It will all go away."

Louise nodded. "Old things have fallen away, all things will become new."

"Yes," Irene smiled.

"I know it all. I've asked Christ into my heart. Once when I was scared by a thunderstorm and crawled into bed with you. You've always made me feel closer to God."

"I have?"

Louise smiled, "Always. In that, you've done your job, Irene. Well done."

Back at work, Kathleen went out to lunch with a coworker. As they ate, Kathleen told her about their feverish attempt to find a room for her mother.

"Sad to say, someone in the home will probably have to die for my mother to get a room. Kinda morbid to wish that on anyone."

Her co-worker nodded. "I'm sure your aunt will gain strength each day to continue caring for your mother."

Kathleen nodded. "I hope so."

"Are you finished? I have a ton of reports to complete this afternoon."

"Glad you got that house on the west side sold. How long have you been sitting on that one?" Kathleen took her coat off the back of her chair, and put it on.

"A long time," her co-worker put on her own coat. "That thunderstorm last night put a real chill in the air."

"The lightning was crazy." Kathleen's phone rang. She pulled it out of the side pocket of her purse and looked at the number, "Oh, excuse me a minute, it's my aunt."

She swiped the phone, "Aunt Louise?"

"Kathleen?"

"Yes. Everything okay?"

"No, Kathleen. You need to come home. Right now."

"Mother?"

"Yes, you better get Brian. Come to the house."

"Aunt Louise, what's wrong?"

"Kathleen. Your mother's gone."

Kathleen sat back down in the chair at the table. "What? Did she go on a walk again?"

"No, Kathleen. She's *gone*. In the middle of the night."

"What?"

"In her sleep."

"Kathleen, I'm sorry.

"The funeral home just came for her body." Kathleen dropped her phone. She felt her body go numb. Her mind reeled. Sobs overtook her body.

Her co-worker came over and hugged her. "Kathleen, what happened? What's wrong?"

Brian couldn't believe his mother-in-law was gone. He'd just gotten the call and left his office as fast as he could. He wanted to be with Kathleen. He met her in front of her mother's home. "What did she say to you?"

"She said Mom died in her sleep." Kathleen sobbed in his arms.

"I don't believe it," Brian wrapped his arms around his wife and held her tightly. "Who would have thought?"

For a few minutes they just stood in the middle of the driveway as Kathleen cried. Violet came out and stood by them.

Kathleen turned to her, and the woman held out her arms and held her. "Louise just told me. I can't believe it. I didn't hear anything this morning. She said they came for the body before dawn. I didn't hear a thing."

"Before dawn?" Brian looked at the neighbor through his own tears. "Why did it take Louise so long to call us?"

"I don't know, Brian. I'm so sorry for your loss."

"Thank you, Violet, for all you did for mother. We appreciate you and Greg and your friendship to her. Let's go inside, Kathleen. Talk to Aunt Louise."

Louise was standing at the door, her face ashen and red with tears streaming down.

"What happened?" Kathleen blurted out.

"I awoke early this morning. I had a hard time sleeping through the thunderstorm. I heard her call for me. By the time I got up the stairs, she was gone." Kathleen's aunt wiped her tears. "I'm so sorry."

"Why didn't you call us this morning? Before the coroner came?" Brian asked.

"It was so early. I managed to take care of it all. No worries."

"What?"

"I hated to bother you. It's better this way. Your mother wouldn't have wanted you to see her like that."

Brian was puzzled. Who did his aunt think she was? This was Kathleen's mother. Why would it have been a bother?

"What home, Aunt Louise?" Kathleen asked.

"Watkins."

Kathleen nodded, "Okay. What did they say to do?"

"Well, your mother has preplanned most of it. We went a few months ago and took care of the details. They will cremate her this afternoon."

"Cremate?"

"Yes." Aunt Louise's tears now subsided a bit. "That's what she wanted, Brian."

Brian shook his head. He had never heard of this wish from his mother-in-law. Nor had he heard Kathleen say anything about it.

Kathleen looked at him as if she knew what he was thinking, "We never really took the time to talk to her about what she wanted." Tears again filled his wife's eyes. "Why didn't we? I was just too busy. Too busy to ask her."

Aunt Louise wrapped her arms around her niece. "It's okay. I did. We've had this settled for a few months now. You know your mother hasn't been thinking straight. She just probably forgot to tell you."

"What about the service?"

"All planned."

"All of it?"

Aunt Louise sat down in the chair at the table and nodded. She looked exhausted. No sense causing a scene by asking too many questions. The loss surely was hard on her, too.

"I'm sorry. I should have shared with you when we did it. I just didn't think of it at the time."

Brian pulled out a chair for his wife and sat her down. He needed to do something, so he went for the stove and picked up the tea kettle to start water to boil. Even if no one wanted anything, it gave him something to do.

"We can meet with the funeral director in the morning. He'll share with us what to do next. I gave him my cell phone number," Aunt Louise said.

"Okay. But are you sure? She planned everything?"

Louise nodded. "Yes. All of it."

"I better call the children. They'll need to get time off work for the funeral." New tears filled Kathleen's eyes.

Brian took his wife's cell phone, "I'll do it, Kathleen. I'll tell them."

Kathleen and Brian stayed through much of that day. By evening, Louise had grown so tired she could barely hold up her head, let alone keep track of all her lies. She knew if she didn't get them out of the house soon, they'd find a detail missing or become suspicious.

She knew just how to get them out and began to breath heavily, "Brian, I need to get some rest. It's been a long, tiring day." She did her best to pretend to struggle with her breath.

Kathleen seemed concerned. "Do you want me to stay with you tonight, Aunt Louise?"

"No." Louise pushed herself up from her chair in the living room. "I just need to sleep." She thought she could just ask them to lock the door on the way out, but then grew doubtful they'd leave. What if she'd left something undone? She needed to get them out of the house.

"Please, head home. You both are tired as well. We can call the director tomorrow and schedule the funeral. How about tomorrow afternoon?" Louise knew she'd need the morning to get the urn ready for the funeral home director.

"We can schedule that, Louise." Brian began putting on his coat.

"No!" Louise shuddered, "No, Brian. I mean, let me call him. He knows me. He knows our plans."

"Are you sure?" Kathleen asked.

"Positive. Now head home. Get some rest."

Kathleen put on her coat. "Call us if you need anything, Louise?"

Louise nodded, "Yes. Yes I will."

Brian grabbed Kathleen's hand, "Let's go."

"Can you lock the door, on the way out?"

Brian answered, "Yes, thanks for all you did today, Louise."

"You're welcome."

The couple left the living room and headed toward the kitchen. She stood and waited to hear the kitchen door shut. When it did, she sighed. Done. Finished. She'd been able to keep up the charade all afternoon. She hadn't been kidding when she told the kids she was tired. She thought she'd be able to sleep for a week, but set her alarm for the morning. She had to get the urn to the funeral home director before anyone suspected anything.

Before she fell asleep she thought of her sister, and, for the first time in a long time, she prayed. She prayed that Irene's first night at the assisted living home would go smoothly, and be easy on her. They'd both been so emotional saying a final goodbye to each other. Thankful they'd planned it this way, she could truly mourn along with the rest of the family.

Tears fell on her pillow as she listened to the now silent house. No more creaks from her sister's bedroom upstairs, or water draining from the upstairs restroom. She was all alone now. If she didn't have Howard and his proposal, she was sure her tears would be worse.

Much worse.

Chapter 33

The funeral was scheduled for Thursday. The director had everything prepared the way Irene had asked. Irene's church was contacted and many church members stopped by the house with food and condolences. The church offered to provide a meal after the service. The pastor reminded Kathleen that Irene had often helped with other funeral dinners down through the years.

As photos were chosen and mounted on bulletin boards and even made into a video memorial of her life, Louise knew Irene would have been pleased. She had led a noble, good life.

Perhaps she could snap a few pictures and take them to the home to show her. No. The pact was clear on this point. Not even Louise could visit her again, for fear someone would find out that she was still alive. Louise had promised. Faking her death would keep her hidden. From everyone. Forever.

Louise had worried that Irene become lonely, without anyone in her life to go and visit her, but she met friendly people at the home. Irene would make a new circle of friends, and soon wouldn't remember her own family.

Louise hadn't heard from Howard in nearly four days. She tried to call him, but each time she dialed his number, it went straight to voice mail, as if his phone wasn't even being charged. If she hadn't been so busy answering the door, talking to Irene's friends, and greeting those who called her, she'd go crazy.

She wondered to herself what could possibly be the problem. Fear set when as she imagined the worst. What if something had happened to him? No one would know to call her because no one knew she existed. She found the whole situation a bit ironic.

The day of Irene's funeral arrived. Louise dressed herself in black. Stuffing her purse with tissues, she turned to get her coat. The weather was sunny, but the cold winds of fall brought down many of the yellow oak leaves from the tree out front. Winter would soon be upon them. She thought of how she'd make her own getaway. She refused to spend another long winter here in the north. She longed for sunshine.

She took her medicine and, sat down at the table waiting for Brian to come for her. She looked at her phone several times and decided to turn it off for the day. If Howard called, she'd have to call him back. This day was to remember her sister's life. To give her a proper goodbye.

"Aunt Louise, are you ready?" Brian appeared at the door, and startled her. She hadn't seen him pull into the driveway.

She stood and put her purse strap over her arm. "Yes."

They walked in silence. She took Brian's arm as he led her to the passenger side of his car. She thanked him as she got into the car.

He pulled out of the driveway and headed to the funeral home. It was only a five-minute drive, so conversation consisted of how she'd slept, what she had for breakfast, and if she was feeling well for the day.

Cars were parked everywhere around the building. Brian let her off at the door and went in search of an empty parking spot. She soon found a family friend to help her get up the stairs of the funeral home.

The room smelled of carnations and roses and seemed to be packed beyond capacity. The urn she'd chosen at the store, which was filled with five pounds of sand and a couple of scoops of Max fresh kitty litter mixed, was ornate and decorative. It sat on a table at the front, with flowers surrounding it. She smiled when she saw it. Irene would have loved it.

Many came to her, offering condolences and wishing her well. Kathleen had waited for Brian at the door and now they were receiving the same amount of attention from their friends. Louise made her way to a couch in the center of the room and sat down. A rendition of "How Great Thou Art' played in the background. The pastor from Irene's church got up and began the service.

God was the focal point of the sermon and eulogy, just as Irene would have wanted. She was praised as a woman of high esteem. Praised as a hard worker and a kind heart. Louise smiled to think of everyone praising her sister. She was a good woman. Had always been utterly kind to people. The pastor gave opportunity for those attending the service to speak and tell about their friend. Many commented on how they always were warm in the winter due to the mittens and caps she crafted from yarn. Some talked about having her as their Sunday school teacher for years. Loving others had been a hallmark of Irene's life.

Greg even got up and said something with encouragement from the pastor. "I found her," he'd commented, referring to the day she got lost. Violet watched her son from the corner, clearly filled with pride. He finished his eulogy by saying, "She was a good friend."

The service ended with one of Irene's friends from church singing one of Irene's favorite songs, "Great is thy Faithfulness."

Guests silently filed out of the funeral home and entered the processional to head to the graveside service. The line stretched out behind Kathleen and Brian's car. Louise sat in the back with Kathleen's daughter and new son-in-law. They commented about burying Irene next to her own mother and also her husband. Kathleen seemed very pleased with the funeral.

"It was so lovely. Mother would have loved it."

"She planned it," Louise added, "Of course she would have liked it."

"I'm glad you two had enough sense to plan it before this happened, Aunt Louise."

"Me, too." Louise added and looked out the window. She recalled how Irene had tried to convince the funeral director to follow Jesus. It made her smile.

At the graveside, the fact of losing her sister forever finally hit Louise. She couldn't stop crying. It was hard to believe that just over a summer she'd have grown so close to her sister again. She thought back to the day when she'd surprised her sister by walking through Irene's door. She grinned a bit remembering the look on her face. Yet that day had proved to be a huge blessing to Louise. They'd shared things she never imagined could be shared again.

Their life together now ended. She remembered standing at this same gravesite so many years ago for their mother. At that time, she was fairly certain that she would be the first to die. She never imagined she'd have to hold to Irene's silly agreement. Though she still wasn't quite sure it had been the best idea, she knew now that they'd been able to pull it off. She'd kept her promise. Despite that fact, she mourned for her sister. Louise was sure that spending these last few months with her had been some of the best times of her life.

As the pastor said the last of the farewell, she remembered what Irene had tried to help her remember just a few days before. *They could be together again. Someday.* Louise bowed her head and prayed to the Lord who had brought her back to her sister. She thanked Him for her congestive heart failure for because of that, she was standing here today. She also thanked Him for salvation and the opportunity to change her heart.

Then she asked Him to be a major part of her life again. She wanted a legacy like her sister. She wanted people to know her as kind, loving and caring. Life wasn't just about her anymore. Life was also about God and family. She'd do her best to live for Him from now on.

Before she opened her eyes again, she asked Him if she could be with her sister again. In heaven. As she opened her eyes, she looked up to see two birds sitting on a stone just a few feet away. They were crowded close, seeming to keep one another warm against the cold, fall wind. Soon one took flight and left the other all alone on the stone.

Louise watched the bird fly away until she could no longer focus in the afternoon sun. As she looked back to the single bird, left alone on the

283

stone, she knew she would dearly miss Irene, but she also knew Irene was right where she had asked to be. She'd be fine. Until the two of them could be together again.

Chapter 34

Violet came over one afternoon. Louise sat in a lawn chair on the back porch. The cold from the week before had allowed just one more warm day. The thermometer on the porch read seventy five degrees. With less than a week before November, this day had been proceeded by what Michiganders call an 'Indian summer.'

"Isn't it beautiful out today?" Violet approached Louise.

Louise startled, "Violet, my soul! Be careful. I about swallowed my teeth." She then remembered her promise to be a kinder, gentler soul, and made a mental note to read her Bible more to accomplish that goal, having solidified bad habits in her life for so long.

Violet opened up another lawn chair that had been leaning against the house. Irene's chair. "How are you today?"

"Tired. My heart isn't getting any better. I've been trying to do a little fall cleaning. Get the house ready to sell for Kathleen."

"Where will you go?"

"I'm not sure," Louise felt her soul drop. Lying was a way of life now. Certainly God wouldn't approve of that either, but it was necessary to keep her sister's secret. For the first time in many years, Louise felt guilty.

"You could move into an assisted living place," Violet meant kindness, but often her matter-of-fact tone set Louise on edge.

"I could." Louise wanted that answer to be sufficient.

"Greg and I could help you find something."

"Oh Violet, that isn't necessary. I just need to concentrate on getting the house ready for Kathleen. She's so busy."

"Yes, she is."

"Louise, do you have any children?"

Louise shook her head.

"They are such a blessing when it comes to this part of our life. I don't know what I'd do without mine."

"Do you have other children, besides Greg?"

"Oh yes. Two daughters."

"I'm sure they bring you much joy."

"They don't live close, but if I needed them, they'd be here."

"We never had any children, my husband and I. At that moment, Louise thought of Howard. It had been almost two and a half weeks since she'd heard from him. Perhaps he'd changed his mind about their plan. Perhaps Violet's idea of an assisted living home would be appropriate for her, too. But she wouldn't look close by to find one, for fear Kathleen or Brian would end up finding Irene. Discovering their secret. She needed to look elsewhere.

"We make so many bad decisions in life. We can't have regrets." Violet patted her arm. "It could eat us up inside and cause us more heartache than helping us."

For a moment, Louise held her breath. Did Violet suspect something? Had she forgotten something she'd said to hint of Irene's whereabouts?

Violet just smiled. Louise immediately changed the subject. "Do you think we will have another hard winter?"

"I'm shocked you are back so soon," Kathleen's co-worker, Linda pulled her into a hug. They'd headed out for an early lunch. Kathleen was struggling to concentrate.

"I need to keep busy. Sitting at home makes me just want to question everything."

"I was that way when my mother died. It all happened quickly for us, too."

"Like one day she's here. Her mind is bad and she is struggling trying to get through a day. You wonder how long she'll remember your name and the next day," tears began to erupt again. "I'm sorry." Kathleen rummaged through her purse for a tissue. She was pretty sure none were left.

Linda handed her one. "I know. I'm so sorry."

Kathleen blew her nose and sighed, "I just can't sit at home. Too many things running through my head."

"I understand," Linda looked over her menu, "For me, it was too many things I wanted to say and didn't. So many things I wished I would have told her. Why did I spend...?" Linda stopped and just looked at her.

Kathleen nodded, "Exactly. No need to stop yourself. Why didn't you spend more time with her?"

Linda nodded.

"Why didn't I? I'd been so caught up with Taylor's wedding. It's been such a busy summer. I was thinking about planning a vacation for Brian and myself. Why wasn't I thinking more of her?"

"Do you think she'd have wanted you to do anything less?"

Kathleen looked at her friend and thought. "I don't know."

Linda put down her menu and patted Kathleen's hand. "Of course she wanted you to live your life. You couldn't be there anymore than you were. You did well."

"Then why do I have so many regrets?"

"Why don't you just mourn? Stop worrying about what you did or didn't do. Be thankful for your mother and how much she meant to you."

Kathleen nodded. "I know. She was a wonderful mother. She cared so much about us. I guess I just assumed that now that her sister was living with her, she was well taken care of."

"And she was."

"I hope so. Aunt Louise can be so mysterious sometimes."

A waiter approached their table and Kathleen did her best to just rattle off something she knew was on the menu. She hadn't eaten well. For the past few days, she'd forced herself to just eat.

Linda asked, "Are you suspecting something?"

"What?"

"When you were talking about your Aunt Louise. It sounded as if you suspect her of doing something. Or not doing something?"

"I guess it all just happened so fast. No warning. The coroner came for her body before I was even able to see her. Should we have done an autopsy. Other than the dementia, I didn't know of any other physical ailments."

"It was probably her heart."

"Of course. It had to be. But what if...?"

"What?" Linda looked at her.

"Oh," Kathleen shook her head, "Never mind. Aunt Louise wouldn't have..."

"What are you thinking?"

"That's the thing," Kathleen put her hand over her mouth before a sob could erupt from deep inside her gut. "I don't know."

Linda sat back in her chair and folded her arms. "Do you think she could have...?"

Kathleen shook her head, "I don't want to think of Aunt Louise doing anything to hurt Mother. But there are just so many unanswered questions. It's just that...they've always been at odds with each other."

"I often remember you saying that."

"But I just don't think," Kathleen gazed into the eyes of her friend, "that she could harm Mom. And even if, God forbid, she did," new tears emerged, "why? What could she possibly gain from something as horrible as that?"

Linda pulled another tissue out of her purse and handed it to Kathleen. "Not to make things worse for your thoughts, but didn't you say your aunt had just started taking over your mom's finances?"

Kathleen didn't want her thoughts to go in that direction. She'd lose her mind. She shook her head, "My mother wasn't a wealthy woman. She was barely getting by. That can't be it." She wiped the tears off her cheeks, "It just can't be."

Brian walked into his house that evening and called Kathleen. He wasn't sure if she would be home this early, but the previous week just

289

made him keep an extra cautious eye on his wife. She had been so distraught.

He entered the living room and looked around. There she was, in her favorite chair, gazing out a window.

Dropping his briefcase he headed for her and tried to quietly greet her, for fear he'd frighten her. She seemed deep in thought. "Sweetheart."

Her head turned sharply and he saw she was crying. He went to her chair and sat down beside it. He took her hand and she turned away. Stroking her hand, he kissed it. "Kathleen, how long have you been home?"

She didn't answer him, but she withdrew another tissue from the box on her lap and wiped her face.

"What's wrong?"

"I think," his wife's shoulders slumped more, "I think I should have been there more for her. Why did we allow Aunt Louise to come live with her? We could have made room here."

Brian wanted to refute and tell her the reasons why, but he held his tongue. Better not to add to her misery.

"Can we trust Aunt Louise? You don't think she would have harmed Mother, do you?"

"Kathleen," Brian got up and sat in the chair opposite her, but kept holding her hand. "She didn't harm your Mom. She died in her sleep."

"But...what...if...?" Kathleen choked out the words.

Brian shook his finger at her, "No what ifs. She died in her sleep. We have to believe that. Why are you thinking Aunt Louise would harm her?"

Kathleen picked up her tissue and wiped her nose, "She hasn't been sick. Other than the dementia. How will we ever know what happened to her? Without an autopsy?"

Brian let go of her hand, sat back in the chair and studied his truly rare, hysterical wife. "What are you suspecting?"

"I don't know," Kathleen sorted through the wadded-up tissues now accumulating in her lap, then looked up to face Brian, "I just can't believe this happened. I guess my mourning is coming out in accusations."

Brian nodded, "Mine, too. Your Aunt Louise wasn't a charmer, but I highly doubt she'd do anything to hurt your mother." He sat forward again, "They were getting along just fine. Look how they interacted at Taylor's wedding. They trusted each other. I can't even imagine, even Aunt Louise, harming your mother."

"I guess I'm just not thinking straight."

Brian nodded. "I think mourning can do that to people."

Kathleen nodded in agreement.

"Why don't you go upstairs and wash your face? I'll take you out for dinner. Do you want to go get Aunt Louise? She's probably lonely herself."

Kathleen looked into her husband's eyes.

"You trust me? Right?"

Kathleen nodded.

"Then go get washed up. I'll call Louise and see if she wants to join us. Perhaps talking with her, will ease your pain."

As Kathleen arose to leave, Brian sat back in her chair and rubbed the afternoon bristles on his chin. All of Kathleen's worries had been on his mind since her mother's-in-law death. He didn't want to worry Kathleen by saying anything to her. But this whole thing just seemed sketchy somehow.

Chapter 35

"An autopsy? Why would you bring that up now?" Louise knew this conversation would happen. She was ready for the questions. She'd planned how to answer the question and perhaps even accusations.

"We were just wondering, why you wouldn't have thought of asking for that?" Kathleen shifted in her chair.

"I guess, it wasn't at the top of my list after I found your mother dead. I assumed you'd want the body taken care of. Your mother asked me to be sure she was cremated after she died." This answer seemed to set Kathleen on edge.

"She never told me that."

Louise pretended to be naive, "Did you ask her?"

Kathleen shook her head, "No."

"Well then, how would you know?" Louise decided tears would help this situation. She wasn't one to produce them, in an instant, but knew if she didn't show some kind of vulnerability, they'd continue with the accusations. She reached for her handbag and rummaged through it for a tissue, blinking her eyes hard to produce some kind of moisture.

Kathleen stopped the questioning. She was buying it. Louise put the tissue to her eyes to catch whatever tears she had produced.

"I'm sorry Aunt Louise. I don't mean to sound like I'm accusing you of something."

"It was a horrible morning. How would you feel if you found your sister? Dead? In bed? The whole thing continues to give me nightmares."

Brian patted Kathleen on her hand. Kathleen nodded to him.

"I'm sorry. I know it has been a shock to you as much as to us."

"I'm lonely."Tears would erupt on her face faster if she showed some of her true feelings, "I miss her." It felt better to not have to lie.

Brian answered, "I know. We all miss her."

"I'm sorry it happened this way. But I lived with her. Ninety-nine percent chance it would have been her to find me. Don't you think?"

Both Kathleen and Brian nodded.

Louise sighed. Subject averted. But for how long?

"Aunt Louise. I need to get Mom's death certificate."

Louise startled. This was one thing she'd totally forgotten about. "What for?"

"We need to get into her bank accounts, send one to the insurance company, and I'm pretty sure we have to have one for social security as well."

"I've taken care of all that."

"You have."

"Yesterday."

Brian and Kathleen looked at each other suspiciously. "Well. Okay. But where is her money?"

"It's in her account. There isn't much, but it's still there."

"What about the house?"

"You can sell it. I'm going back to Florida."

"You are? When?" Kathleen looked startled.

"Soon. I've started to pack up my things. It won't be long."

"Okay." Kathleen seemed more unsure. "I'll take a few days off next week and get packing things up."

Louise nodded. She hoped that would be enough time.

Louise lay in bed that night. She was exhausted. She hadn't slept well in the past few nights. The house was so eerily quiet. She hated it.

Howard hadn't called for over three weeks. It was as if he had disappeared, just like Irene.

She picked up her phone and looked at the front. It was twelve thirty. Normally, she would have been asleep for the past two hours. Instead she just lay in bed, wishing for sleep.

Thoughts of her sister filled her mind. She'd been okay with all the plans and how it had turned out, up until she left her at the home. She'd had a bad dementia day that morning. Her sister was tired, which didn't help. But as one of the workers carried her sister's boxes and belongings into the home, she'd had to convince Irene that this is what she had wanted to happen. Irene's frightened eyes scared Louise. She even considered taking her back home. But she remembered her promise.

She'd taken Irene by the hand and led her into the home. A nurse was waiting for them and helped her, on the other side, to lure her sister into her room. Once in the room, Irene seemed to calm down a bit. But she still looked at Louise as if she were making her do something she didn't want to happen.

She'd wanted to take Irene by the hand and back out to the car. But she knew, if she did, Irene would wake up the next day or the day after that, and make Louise promise again to go through with her wishes. She'd made a promise to her sister. If she ever did anything right, it had to include this.

She'd tried hard to tell Irene goodbye, but the nurse was doing a great job of distracting her. They showed her around the room and told her about the pull cords and how to activate them if she needed something. Her sister was so tired and unsure of things, that morning, Louise wasn't sure if she even understood what to do.

Tears now wet Louise's pillow. She never realized how hard it would be to walk out of the room that morning, leaving her sister's care to strangers. Irene had looked lost and alone. Louise knew she had to get that image out of her thoughts or it would haunt her forever.

Just at that moment, Max decided to jump onto her bed from the floor. Louise jumped in fright. The cat looked at her as if to ask, *Where's Irene?* Louise patted his head.

"I'm sorry, Max. I miss her, too."

Max then turned around and around and settled into a crook left behind her knees on the bed. He settled down and began to softly purr. She reached down and stroked his soft fur. He could sleep with her. Tonight, she didn't care. He was the only other breathing soul in this big lonely house. Where was Howard? It was so unlike him to neglect her.

She rolled over in bed, trying hard not to disturb Max. She couldn't believe she hadn't remembered to figure out how to get a death certificate issued. Perhaps the funeral director could help her with that. She'd call him in the morning.

###

"Irene is all alone," murmured the nurse. "No one has come to visit her since she arrived."

"What was the date?" The director of the assisted living home glanced in the room at the woman, in a corner, rocking.

"Nearly a month ago," the nurse added, "it's just so strange."

"Do you think she realizes it?"

The nurse shook her head, "I don't think so. Occasionally she will ask about someone named Kathleen."

"I'll go look at her chart. I'm pretty sure it was her sister who put her here."

The nurse felt as though she was just about to cry, "She's such a sweet thing. Always kind. Often not even knowing where she is, but she'll smile and tell me that it's okay."

"Perhaps we need to contact her sister."

"What if something happened to her and Irene was her only living relative? That would be so sad."

The director shook her head as she headed back down the hallway. "Her chart should show next of kin. I'll look into it."

Kathleen entered her mother's room and looked around. It had been almost a month since her mother's passing, but tears still emerged. She walked to her rocking chair, looking for her favorite afghan. Her mother rarely sat in the chair without her purple, green, and orange blanket covering her legs. If it was in her mother's room, she couldn't find it. Perhaps it was downstairs in her chair there.

She found Louise in the hallway, coming out of the bathroom. "Aunt Louise? Do you know where Mom's lap blanket went? Taylor was asking about it the other day."

Her aunt looked down for a moment as if to gather her thoughts. "Oh for goodness sakes, Kathleen. Are you wanting me to keep track of all the blankets your mother owned? Almost all of them got scattered around the house somewhere. Just before she died, Irene began hiding things. Perhaps she hid the blanket, too." Her aunt stopped talking and looked to Kathleen for a response.

"Well then, okay. I'll keep looking for it." She motioned upstairs. "I'm going back up to start sorting through mother's things."

Picking up a box, Kathleen opened the flaps and set it down on her mother's bed. She crossed her arms. Where would she begin? Clothes? Knickknacks? She should probably take the comforter, sheets, and blankets off her mother's bed. Washing them was probably the best place to start. Shaking the pillows of their cases, she was startled when Aunt Louise entered the room. She didn't know Louise could get up stairs anymore.

"Can I help?"

Kathleen was reluctant to have her aunt help. She easily tired, making her breath come short and rapid. "I can manage, Aunt Louise."

Her aunt seemed relieved. She went to her mother's rocking chair and sat down. "I'm sorry I haven't gotten up here sooner to take care of these things."

"That's okay. I'd prefer to do it myself."

Louise grew quiet. She sat back in the chair and closed her eyes.

297

Kathleen continued to strip the bed.

"I never realized how much I would miss your mother."

Kathleen pulled off the comforter and then each sheet. She wadded them up and placed them near the door. "It's hard for me to believe she's even gone." Kathleen looked over at her aunt. "Sometimes I pick up the phone to call her, only to remember after dialing that you'll be the only one answering it."

Her aunt nodded. "I keep trying to fix two meals instead of one."

"I go to the store and pick up her half gallon of milk and last week I was to the checkout counter before I caught on that she wasn't here to need it anymore."

"Life sure has its surprises."

Kathleen folded her mother's comforter and then decided to tackle the contents of her mother's dresser. "Mom used to call them God interruptions."

Her breathing now calmed after climbing the stairs, her aunt stood and came over to the dresser. "Why don't you let me help you pack this up?"

Kathleen pulled out undergarments and some pajamas. She carefully folded them and handed them to Louise who put them in the box on the bed. "What will you do with all of this?"

"Probably end up throwing the undergarments away."

"Well then, why are we packing it up? Head down to the kitchen for a garbage bag. No sense packing things you are going to toss anyway."

Her aunt was right. Kathleen left the room and headed downstairs for a trash bag. She couldn't help it, anger grew in her heart.

Louise had checked and rechecked her sister's drawers. She'd placed things just as her sister had them. Most of the things here were old. She'd purchased many new items for her to take to the assisted living home. She wondered if Kathleen would grow more suspicious. If she were to pack up her winter shirts, perhaps Kathleen wouldn't notice any of them missing.

She pulled out the bottom drawer and began putting the items into the box on the bed, hurrying before her niece returned to the bedroom from her errand. She placed the last shirt in the box as Kathleen walked back into the room.

"I've packed her shirts. She has a few left in her closet."

"Thank you, Aunt Louise."

"You could put some of her breakable things into this box as well. Tucking them in her clothing would prevent them from breaking."

"That's a good idea. Taylor wanted to go through those kind of things to see if there was anything she could use for her new home."

Louise felt herself grow weak from working and stopped. She sat back down in the chair. "Why don't you have her come over? She can go through the whole house. Perhaps there is some furniture or dishes she might like from the kitchen."

"Thank you, Aunt Louise."

"I'm sorry, I'm not much help. I get out of breath so easy." She didn't want to head back downstairs. The lonely, old house seemed to haunt her.

Without realizing it, she put her head back on the chair and for the first time, in a long time, Louise closed her eyes. Just for a moment.

299

Kathleen gazed at her aunt now sleeping in her mother's chair. It was as if she hadn't slept in months. Her mouth fell open and she began to snore. Kathleen shook her head.

She hadn't really paid that much attention to her mother's wardrobe for awhile. There was far less clothing to sort through and put away than she imagined. Her closet held many empty hangers.

Looking into the drawer of her mother's nightstand, she found candy wrappers. Empty ones. She smiled as she threw away the papers from her mother's favorite candy. Her mother always did have a sweet tooth. Under the candy wrappers were church bulletins. Most had her Mother's scribbled handwriting on them. She found notes from church services as far back as 1970.

She sat on the edge of the bed and read through a few of them. Her mother's handwriting was precise and clear. She'd even jotted notes to herself about bringing a treat for the ladies the next week or a prayer request from one of her friends.

Edna's name was jotted down more than any other. She hadn't chatted with Edna since the funeral. It had been hard to have any real conversation with people at her mother's funeral. She'd been dealing with her mother's sudden death. She needed to call Edna. Besides Aunt Louise, Edna was just about the closest friend her mother had, besides Violet and Greg.

She stopped for awhile and gazed at her aunt. She'd finally stopped trying to decide if Louise would have the nerve to harm her mother. Brian and she had talked extensively about it now for a few weeks. Their conversation never got beyond reasoning that there wasn't a possibility of Aunt Louise doing anything that horrific. If she had, there wasn't any indication of it anywhere.

Kathleen picked up her mother's clock radio, unplugged it, wrapped the cord around it, and put it in another box on the bed. She added a few books and the bed lamp as well. As she shuffled through some papers on the night stand, she found a receipt from what appeared to be the grocery store, a bookmark, a thank you card from Taylor for one of her shower presents and a pamphlet.

Kathleen threw those things away, but as she did, she noticed what the pamphlet was advertising. She reached back into the trash can and pulled it back out. It was for the assisted living facility she'd recently visited. Perhaps she should call the home and inform them of her mother's passing.

She sat down on the bed and began to wonder why her mother would have had the pamphlet. She'd not shown her the home beforehand. Was she looking for a home before Kathleen was?

Kathleen gazed over at her aunt who now had stopped snoring and was looking up at her. She held up the pamphlet. "Where did Mom get this, Aunt Louise?"

Her aunt's face blanched. She stared at Kathleen with bug eyes.

"Aunt Louise?"

"Oh my dear, did I just fall asleep?" Her aunt wiped the spit from the corner of her mouth with the back of her hand.

"You were sleeping like you haven't slept in weeks."

Her aunt sat up straighter in the chair. "I feel like I slept hard."

She held up the pamphlet again. "Aunt Louise, what about this?"

"Oh my, what time is it?"

If she didn't know any better, Kathleen would have sworn her aunt was trying to avoid the question.

Chapter 36

Kathleen left shortly before dinner. She hauled box after box of Irene's things out to her car. Louise hoped nothing that might mean something to Irene would be donated or given away. She shook her head, *Did it really matter?*

She looked down at Max by her feet as she poured a can of soup into a pan. The whole conversation regarding the pamphlet had put the fear of God into her. Why hadn't she seen the pamphlet herself? It was a huge clue. Would Kathleen suspect something? What if she were to go out to the home and just check?

Louise shook her head, "Why would she do that, Max? For what reason would she suspect anything?"

Louise had hoped to have dinner with Kathleen and Brian tonight. This eating alone was getting old. She'd been used to it in Florida, but during those days, she'd at least eat out for lunch. Getting out of the house. Enjoy the company of some of her friends. Now she was stuck in the house. In Michigan.

She sat down at the table, waiting for her soup to boil. Where could Howard be? She'd tried his number several times in the past few days and kept getting his voice mail. If she were to leave a message, perhaps one of his children would find it. She didn't want them growing suspicious. It was Howard's responsibility to tell them about her.

She sighed and looked out the window. The days were growing shorter. The air chillier. Almost all of the leaves were now off the trees. She dreaded the winter, and really thought she'd have gotten back to Florida by now, but with Howard gone and her condo no longer available, where would she go? Would she have the energy to find another place to live?

Max rubbed against her legs. He was now her only company. Looking out the window at the leaves blowing around the browning grass, she just couldn't believe how much she missed her sister. She was so busy making plans to ensure their pact worked, she'd never thought of how lonely it would be.

She looked down at Max. He looked up at her as if he hadn't had anything to eat in days. Louise looked over at his water bowl and food dish. She'd fed him today. She noticed his empty water bowl, and she pushed herself up from the table and reached down to pick up his bowl. As she did she felt her head grow warm. Grabbing for the counter, she stood up too quickly and the blood rushed into her head with a surge.

She was on the verge of fainting. This was all she needed, to faint, with no one to find her.

Steadying herself, she closed her eyes and did her best to concentrate on holding onto the counter and breathing in and out slowly. Her senses returned and she opened her eyes.

As she filled Max's bowl with fresh water she thought back to the conversation she'd had with her doctor just a few months before. His warning, to not live alone, was even more needed now.

Now she had no one. She bent at the knees to return Max's bowl to his eating place and then slowly stood back up, being careful not to bend over.

"Oh Howard. Where are you?" Tears formed in her eyes as she looked back to the soup now boiling on the stove. She hated soup from a can.

The director of the assisted living home had looked through all of Irene's papers. The only living relative was the sister who'd brought her in. There was no one else listed. The lonely, old soul in her care had no one else. She wondered where the sister was. Why hadn't she even been to visit her?

Picking up the phone book, the director decided to look through the listing of the name *Fredericks*. Perhaps there was someone, with the same last name. If she were to call them, maybe they'd know Irene.

There were days when Irene was alert. She'd be the most quiet on those days. If asked about family, she would smile, lay her head on the back of her rocking chair and shake her head. She didn't give them any indication that she had anyone else but her sister.

On her bad days, she would keep mumbling about someone named Kathleen. One day, she'd asked a nurse about another person named Taylor. "So pretty," was all she would say about Taylor.

The nurse had tried so hard to pry something out of her, but then she'd get off on a tangent unrelated to family and the dementia would take over.

Soon they'd have to resign themselves to the fact that the woman had no one. The director would put her name on the church list. On a monthly basis, a church group would come into the home and sit and read to those who had no one to visit them. Irene was a great candidate for this program.

"Have you gotten any financial stuff from Aunt Louise yet?"

Kathleen shook her head. "I thought she'd offer it to me, but no. I go in, pack up mother's belongings, and leave."

"Well, ask her. Tell her you need her checkbook."

"I can't."

"For goodness sake, why not?"

Kathleen sat down at the table opposite her husband. "What if she doesn't want to give it to me?"

"What? It's your property now. And you just have to find your mother's will."

"Brian, I don't even think she has one."

"Are you kidding me?"

Kathleen shook her head. "Unless she went out and got one done up herself, I don't think one has ever been made."

"What about when your father died?"

"Mother took care of all of that. I had no clue about what was left or to whom." Kathleen shook her head. "What can we do?"

"I don't know. Let me call someone tomorrow. I have a friend in Lansing who is a lawyer. Perhaps he can help us to know what to do."

Kathleen began to cry. "This whole thing is so strange. So odd. This is not how I thought this whole death thing would happen. How was I to know my mother would die like this? Even more than that, I have to worry about Aunt Louise, too?"

"Why?" Brian folded his arms. He grew frustrated with her, she knew.

"Her health isn't getting better. I worry about her living alone now, too."

"Let's kick her out. Make her move to a home."

"Brian, that's horrible."

"Well then you could get into the house. We could put it up for sale. One less thing to worry about."

"I know, I know, but I will not put Aunt Louise out on the street."

Brian shook his head. "Then there really isn't anything we can do. We'll wait until she kicks the bucket and then we'll figure out what to do with everything. Until then, let's just hope and pray the old biddy doesn't kick the bucket without us finding her for days. It would be horrible to get a stink like that out of the house."

Kathleen stood up, but before leaving the room she gave him 'the look.' He had been leaning up against the counter and now he stood up straight.

"What? What did I say?"

"I will not put my aunt out of that house. Mother would want her to be taken care of. She'd not want me to claim a house over caring for someone." Kathleen stomped out of the kitchen. "Especially Aunt Louise."

Louise pushed the off button on the remote control that night. The house's silence brought tears to her eyes. She was tired. So tired. She looked over at Irene's chair and just sighed. The ache in her heart for her sister was almost more than she could bear.

She thought back to their talks at night. They'd often turn off the television and find a puzzle or something to add a bit of flavor to their evenings. Now there was only Max who now took up residence on Louise's lap each night. She stroked his fur. She scolded herself for falling in love with a cat, but there wasn't anyone else.

Standing up, she placed one stiff foot in front of the other and headed to the bathroom. Her legs ached. A hard rain fell on the roof and hit the west windows of the house. Her bedroom faced west, so the sound grew louder as she made her way into her room, shutting off lights in the house as she went.

A wind caused the windows to whistle. Soon winter would be here. Could she endure another winter in this cold, frozen north?

She'd almost given up on Howard. Something must have stopped him from calling her. A fear, struck her heart, as she envisioned him in a car accident, falling down a flight of stairs or worse yet, just plain dying. She shuddered to think of him gone, too.

Kathleen and Brian had kept their distance since Irene's death simulation. Louise was actually surprised they'd accepted it so easily. They came into the house only on occasions to take more things to their own home. Taylor had come, one afternoon, for her Grandmother's hutch. Kathleen had bundled up Irene's china and boxed that as well.

After they took the hutch, Louise found herself daily gazing at the mismatched, faded part of the hardwood floor where it once sat. The thing had been sitting there for over sixty years. It had been a gift from Irene's husband when they were newly married. The room seemed bare without it.

All of Irene's friends had stopped visiting. They didn't know Louise that well. Why would they stop and talk to a woman they barely knew? The only one faithful to speak to her these days was Violet, but she and Greg had been gone the last two weeks to visit her daughter in South Carolina.

Louise had never felt so alone. In Florida, she had friends to visit. She felt better then, and was able to go to Bingo every Monday night at the community building. Even this past winter, until she moved to Michigan, she'd done her best to stay active by going to the activity center to play cards.

Here, she had nothing. No one. Not even Howard to call anymore.

After crawling into her bed, she listened to the mysterious noises of the house. She'd heard them now for almost a year, but when the wind blew, like it did tonight, the noises were more pronounced. Louder.

She often felt she heard someone enter the house. She'd lay as still as possible. Images of murders and abductions would fill her thoughts. The darkness of night now seemed ominous and frightful. Living alone for such a long time, she rarely had been afraid, but during the past six weeks without Irene, she had many sleepless nights.

She would lay awake and long for the morning. As soon as the light would rise in the Eastern sky, she'd be able to fall asleep for awhile. She often didn't get out of bed until noon. How long could she live like this?

As tears wet her pillow for another night, Louise began to imagine what it would be like to just go get her sister and bring her home. The thought made her sit up in bed. That was it. It was a great idea. Could she convince Irene to change her mind? Stop trying to hide and just come home?

Louise would bring her home to spend the winter with her again. They'd be able to just go back to how it was before.

A shopping trip. They could go shopping again. The thought put hope in Louise's heart. Even though the wind continued to blow against her windows and the rain beat the glass, Louise soon found herself cuddling up again with Max and even smiling a little.

That was the answer. She'd just bring her home. If Irene fussed, she'd tell her how lonely she'd become. Her sister would understand. She was sure of it. She'd continue to help care for her. They'd live out the rest of their days, together. Stupid pact. She was wrong to agree to it in the first place. Irene would just have to deal with it. She'd convince her that her lie was a sin and how wrong it had been to lie to Brian and Kathleen. That would fix her relationship with them as well.

For the first time, in a long time, Louise fell asleep just around midnight.

Chapter 37

Louise woke up and recalled her idea. She'd slept the entire night. The wind had died down and now the morning light woke her up by shining through her curtains and into her face. She smiled. She felt wonderful. She hadn't slept like that in weeks.

Scooting out of bed, she glanced at the time on her cell phone she'd left by the door to charge. Why she charged a phone which never rang was beside her. But she did it every night. What if she needed emergency help? It was the only phone in the house now. She'd cancelled her sister's phone after she'd left.

Going to go get Irene. It was a masterful idea. Thinking of Kathleen and Brian made her want to do it all the more. What a wonderful gift for the upcoming holidays. They'd scold them, but forgive them both. And they could tell everyone how the sisters had come up with such an absurd plan. This had to work. She needed Irene back.

She went into the kitchen to find Max waiting by his bowl. Louise could head to the store before going out to get Irene. She'd get what they needed. Perhaps buy a roast. Irene loved roast beef and potatoes.

Plans formed in her thoughts and lined up like scenes from a Passion play. Wouldn't everyone be surprised to see Irene come into the church that next Sunday? She'd even go with Irene. It would be hilarious to see the expression on people's faces. Her sister would be like Jesus now. She'd arise from the dead. They could celebrate Easter just a few months ahead of time. The thought made her laugh right out loud.

Louise turned to find Brian standing at the door. He had on a winter coat. Last night's storm, must have brought in more cold air. November was breezing in. She smiled at him and opened the door.

He seemed nervous and fumbled with his keys. "Aunt Louise, I hate to bother you this early, but I was on my way to work and well, I just think we need to talk. Can I come in?"

Louise looked behind him to find Kathleen, but she wasn't to be found. "Are you alone?"

Brian nodded, "Yes Kathleen doesn't know that I'm here."

Louise back up to allow her nephew inside. "Has the temperature dropped?"

Brian smiled, "About twenty degrees. I'm afraid winter is breathing down our backs."

"Well sit down, Brian. I was just going to start breakfast. Do you want some coffee or something?"

Brian shook his head, pulled out a kitchen chair, and sat down. "I can't stay long and I had coffee before I left."

"Well, do you care if I have mine?"

"Of course not, be my guest."

Irene poured her coffee, carried the cup to the table and sat down. "Well, what brings you out on such a cold morning?"

"I need to discuss something with you. And I don't want Kathleen here when I do it." Brian seemed agitated. He picked up his keys again and began fingering each one.

"What is it?"

"The reason we haven't been over here very much is..."

"Yes?" Louise looked forward to hearing this one. She'd been wondering.

"We're mad."

"At me?"

"Yes." Brian's matter-of-fact tone seemed patronizing.

"Why?"

"I don't want to pull in a lawyer for this, so I'm just going to come out and tell you." Brian leaned into the table, "I want you to find everything that has to do with Irene's estate, a will, her checkbook, her bank statements, everything. I want you to get it all together for Kathleen. When she comes later today, I want you to hand it all over. Do you understand?"

Louise sat back in her chair now. She wasn't sure why he had to have this particular tone with her. It wasn't an enjoyable moment, but she knew it would come.

"I want everything. Kathleen is Irene's daughter. You may have come in here like you owned the place, but it isn't yours. None of this," Brian waved his hand through the air, "is yours. Do you understand?"

Louise stood. "How dare you? Why would you even think that I wouldn't hand over anything of your mothers? Kathleen has barely talked to me, let alone asked me to provide any of those things for her yet."

"Well, I just did. So give it up."

Louise wasn't really all that shocked, but she never imagined Brian would have the courage to say it.

"And," Brian added, "If you don't, I have plans to take you to court. My lawyer is drawing up papers, as we speak."

"How dare you? How dare you march into this house and act like I haven't been gracious to you or to Irene. I loved my sister. We had great times together these past few months. I would never keep Kathleen from getting anything and everything from your mother's estate." Louise stood up as straight as she could. She needed this to look as good as it sounded.

"Well good." Brian stood. "Just so we're clear."

"Oh we're clear all right. Now get out."

"We're done with your games, Aunt Louise."

"I have not played games."

"Okay then." Brian walked out the back door. "By the way, don't mention to Kathleen that I've been here."

Louise slammed the door behind him. She watched as he glanced back over his shoulder just once to give her a stern look. It was all she could do to not burst into laughter. If only they knew. If only they knew that by this afternoon, she'd produce far more than just her sister's checkbook.

Louise felt light again. As if a burden had been dropped by the roadside and she'd slammed the door on her car and driven off without it. Free. Wonderful.

She hummed as she got ready for the day, thinking through carefully the steps to take to get things back to normal. As she sat down to put on her shoes, she wondered how things would unfold. After straining to put on her shoes and then tie them, she sat up, winded. She breathed in through her nose and out through her mouth. There on the end table beside her bed, she saw her phone. Should she try to call Howard, just one more time?

Picking up the phone, she swiped the screen. No calls. No messages. "Oh Howard, what has happened to you?" Did it even matter anymore? She'd stay here for the winter, take care of her sister, and then perhaps try and relocate Howard in the spring. The only thing that would prevent him from getting in touch with her was if...

She couldn't think of that now. She placed the phone in her sweater pocket and went to find her winter coat. It was time to bring it out again. They'd have to go and buy another coat for Irene. She'd donated all her winter things to charity. What hadn't been donated, Kathleen had taken.

She smiled, thinking of Kathleen's reaction to seeing her mother still alive. Perhaps she could invite the entire family over for dinner. Or maybe she should wait for Thanksgiving. What a surprise for Kathleen and her children. Even Brian. She just couldn't remain mad at Brian. He was just caring for his wife. She only wondered why it had taken them so long to get the courage to face up to her. Was she really that horrible?

As she left her bedroom, Max came and circled her legs. "Oh Max. In my excitement, I forgot to feed you today. I'm so sorry." Shuffling into the kitchen, Louise went to the cupboard to find it bare. "Oh dear Max. I forgot. You need more food."

Looking down at the cat who now gazed up in anticipation made her cringe. "I hope you can wait until I go and get Irene and then head back to the grocer." The whole ordeal seemed a long and arduous one. "I don't think you'll starve." She picked up the cat and, scratched him on the head. "Be patient, my friend. You'll have Irene back tonight to give you the food herself." The cat purred.

Louise stooped down and dropped the cat to the floor then looked around the kitchen for her purse. She hadn't driven for a couple of weeks. She again felt out of breath. Sitting down for a minute, she considered just calling Kathleen and having her go with her to the home. She could help get Irene back home. Then Louise wouldn't have to do it all herself.

She shook her head, "No. This is my responsibility. My job to fix this."

She stood and grabbed her purse. She rummaged through the brown bag finding all kinds of goodies there, but no keys. What had she done with them? Dumping her purse contents on the kitchen table, she pilfered through the items. Still no keys. "Where did I put those things?" Louise rubbed her forehead.

Did she leave them in her bedroom? She turned toward her room. Maybe they were still here, in the kitchen somewhere. The last time she'd driven the car was to visit her doctor. When was that? Louise's hand went to her mouth. "What if I've lost the darn things?"

If she didn't hurry, Kathleen would show up. How would she explain her venture out today without letting out the secret?

###

"Dad, we've been over this and over this. You are not going back to the Gulf Coast to live. Not now, not ever. We live here. You need to live close to us." Howard's son shook his head when he brought up the subject one more time.

Weeks had gone by since his last conversation with Louise. He couldn't call her and tell her the bad news. He also couldn't bear to even talk to her and let her know his family refused to allow him to leave them again. Even for just a month or two in the winter.

It had just been a mini-stroke. The doctor confirmed it many times, but his children were adamant. The next stroke, if it were to come, could be much worse than the one he suffered just a few weeks before. They weren't taking any chances of allowing him to go back to the Gulf Coast.

Should he explain his love for Louise to them? If they knew about her, would it make a difference?

"Michael. You have to listen to me." His son was a reasonable man. He'd understand. Wouldn't he? "Please sit down here for a minute."

"Dad," Michael sat down on the chair opposite him in the living room. "We've talked about this. You know how I feel. We're not going to allow you to go to the other side of the state right now. Maybe in the spring, when you are feeling better."

"Michael, I have something to tell you."

"Nothing will change my opinion. What if you were to have a stroke over there? You might die in an ambulance bringing you back home."

"It's not just me."

"What? What are you talking about?"

"I've met a woman. A beautiful woman."

Michael stood. "A woman? What are you talking about?"

"We met last winter. Son, I'm in love with her."

"You fell in love with a woman when Mom wasn't even dead yet?"

Howard looked down. It wasn't something he was proud of, but he wasn't going to lie to his son either. He nodded.

"Dad. Really?"

He looked up into his son's eyes, "Your mother died years ago. You know that. She hasn't known you, me or any of us for years."

"That doesn't mean you go out and cheat on her."

Howard gazed into his son's eyes. "I didn't cheat on her. I didn't even kiss the woman. We were just friends."

Michael shook his head. "Dad. I'm sorry. Even if there is a woman, you cannot leave here." Placing his hands on his hips he just looked at Howard. "That's final."

"I think she should come here?"

"Oh Dad, really? No. I have enough to just take care of you."

"Michael. You've forgotten one thing." Howard stood and looked into his son's eyes. "I'm your father, not your son. If I want Louise to move here, she can. Do you understand?"

Michael crossed his arms, but nodded. "Dad, please reconsider. Mom just passed away. Less than a month ago. Do you want people to see you shacking up with a woman so close to her death?"

"At my age Michael, I really don't give a rat's behind what people think about me." He pushed past his son and headed for the kitchen. "Even you." He turned halfway to the kitchen. "I'm calling her tonight. I'm not sure when she can come, but when she does, we're gonna be married. And that's all you need to know." Howard turned his back on his son.

Chapter 38

Louise still couldn't find her keys. She searched the house. Max did his best to trip her, several times. His hunger was getting the best of him. The keys weren't in the house.

Louise decided to carry a bag of garbage out to the trash container in the garage. Maybe the walk would help her remember where she'd put the keys. She stepped off the porch to see Greg walking toward her. "Where you going, Louise?"

"Oh Greg. Thanks be to God. Can you lift this bag and put it in the trash container in the garage?"

"Sure Irene. I mean, sure Louise." He giggled, "I just called you Irene. I'm sorry Louise."

Louise shook her head, "It's fine Greg. I'm proud to be called by my sister's name."

"I miss her, Louise." The young man lifted the bag and began taking it to the garage. "Are you going somewhere, Louise?"

"Yes Greg. But," Louise looked back toward the house, "I can't find my car keys."

"They're right here," Greg pointed into Irene's car, parked in the garage. "Remember, you told me to leave them there when I moved the car the other day for you."

Louise sighed and then headed back inside the house to grab her purse. "You're right Greg. I can't believe I forgot that. What would I do without you?"

Greg shook his head, "I don't know, Louise. I just don't know."

She came back down the stairs of the back porch, hanging onto the handrail as she went. "Thank you."

"You're welcome Louise." The young man stood in the driveway with his hands on his hips. "Where are you going?"

Louise stopped and looked into his eyes. She reached out and patted his hand. "Don't worry Greg. I won't be long. And..." Louise smiled at Greg, "I'll bring you back a big, big surprise."

Greg laughed, "Really?"

Louise nodded. "You keep watch over the driveway and when I return, you come out and help me, okay?"

Greg nodded. "Okay, Louise. Be safe." The man turned and went back into his own house.

"I will Greg. Have a good afternoon."

It was all Louise could do to get into the car, fasten her seat belt, and turn on the car. She was so out of breath she sat in the garage for a bit to try and regain her strength. Breathing a short prayer, she hoped Greg had gotten out of the way because for her to turn around while backing out would doom failure.

She had to keep her wits about her. Once she got Irene home again, she'd go right to bed. This day was already taking a toll on her and she'd just gotten out of the house. Soon she had the car in drive and began cruising down the street.

The bare trees along the road waved now in the strong breeze of the oncoming winter. Leaves littered the yards and the road gutters. More leaves fell into the street as the wind blew. It was sad to think of another winter coming.

Louise stopped at the first stop sign and sighed, looking out for oncoming traffic. She'd finally managed to catch her breath a bit better. As she turned and cruised down the Saginaw Street of their town, she thought back to the moment when she'd taken Irene on this drive just eight weeks ago. It'd been so early that day that the sun had yet to come up.

Irene had seemed so calm about the whole thing, but Louise had noticed her hands shaking when they entered the home that morning, just after the sun came up. The director had made some comment regarding their early arrival, but Louise had explained that some of Irene's best times were in the morning. That explanation had satisfied the woman.

She wondered what the director would do now. Would she allow her to just come in and take Irene? She chuckled at that thought, as if her sister was some kind of property. Perhaps she could just tell the director to think she was taking her sister on a day's adventure. She didn't really need to explain herself. Irene was her sister, for heaven's sake.

Thinking back over the last few weeks made Louise just feel thankful. She never realized what kind of effect their sister promise would have on her. While in Florida, she'd lived alone. It wasn't that big of an issue there. But here, the situation made her uncomfortable, frightened and lonely. She wondered if Howard were still calling her, if it would have been enough to change her loneliness.

There were so many things she missed about Irene. Silly things which she never imagined missing. She had a hard time praying for her meals now. She did her best to do it, but it just didn't sound as gratifying and sincere as Irene's prayers. She missed all of Irene's friends from church dropping by at various times of the day. Edna rarely visited her. Despite the fact that the woman drove her crazy at times, not having her stop by anymore, just made the house seem dull and boring.

She hadn't minded Max taking up residence on her bed, but whenever she would move in her sleep, she could feel him. It just reminded her that her sister wasn't with her any longer. She was growing tired of having to feed him every day and cleaning out the litter box. Well, that was exactly the chore Irene could take over once she returned home.

Violet had been kind, but for some reason, even her visits weren't as fun after Irene left. Violet and she would chat about many things, but the talks about God between her sister and the neighbor lady were amazing. She wanted to hear more of these and would do her best to listen better once she got her sister home.

Her stomach growled. She wasn't sure if it was because she was passing all the fast food places or if it had taken so long to find her keys that it was almost lunch time. She looked over at the clock on the car's dash. Yes, it was indeed eleven thirty. Almost time for lunch. Perhaps she and Irene could stop and get a bite to eat before heading home.

Louise smiled as she turned down another street. She laughed at the thought of telling her sister about her decision to follow Christ at her fake burial. If any of this foolishness regarding her sister's stowaway were to make sense in a few months, surely her decision to change her life had to be the reason why it had taken place.

Now they'd be able to watch the news and, perhaps, she could see Irene's point of view easier. Maybe Irene would do a Bible study with her. She decided to breathe a little prayer as she approached the highway toward the assisted living home. Her mother had taught her to pray. At a young age. Yet her communication with God had been a bit strained during her life. She now revisited the prayers of her younger years. It felt good to pray again.

The trip to the home was just over a half an hour and soon Louise was on the off-ramp just a few minutes away. She was almost as excited as they had been as children, waiting for Santa to arrive. Today would be a great day. She hoped Irene was having a good memory day. She would hate to have to convince her sister that she belonged with her. At home.

A ring from her cell phone in her sweater pocket interrupted Louise's thoughts. She fumbled for a minute but realized she'd have to open her coat to get the phone out. As she unbuttoned her coat, the sound grew louder. Who would be calling her?

She pulled at her jacket and reached inside her sweater pocket. The phone slipped out and fell into her lap. Glancing down, she saw Howard's name on the screen. "Howard?" She pushed at the screen. She had to answer this. What if she never had the opportunity to speak to him again?

Of all times for him to call. Louise looked up again to check the road, just in time to see another car coming right at her. She jerked the wheel to the right as she heard, a loud grinding, noise. It was the last thing Louise heard in this world.

###

Howard listened to a fumbled noise on his phone. He said Louise's name, but stopped when he heard the crashing noise. The phone went dead at the other end. What had just happened? He had been so eager to finally talk to her. What he heard, scared him. He hoped it wasn't what he imagined it to be.

Howard waited for Louise to call him back. Perhaps she'd just fumbled with the phone as she was picking it up. She'd probably dropped it while trying to answer it. But somehow, Howard had a bad premonition about this. As the afternoon drifted on and he sat down for supper that evening, he couldn't get Louise off his mind. Why hadn't she called him back? What could have happened? Her phone went to voice mail, when he tried to call her again.

Worse of all, how would he know? If something horrible had happened to Louise, he would probably never know. For she and he were the only people to know about their relationship among the people she knew in Michigan. He was pretty sure she never had told anyone about their friendship.

He breathed a silent prayer for his friend.

Chapter 39

"I'm going to put Irene on different medicine." The doctor handed a prescription note to the director.

The director nodded and added, "She's been so confused since being admitted."

"When was that?"

"Around eight weeks ago now. Not one person has come to visit her since her admission."

"No one?" the doctor looked puzzled.

The director shook her head. "I have been given complete permission to care for her. Changes of medicine is in my hands."

"We'll try her on this for at least a week and see what happens. Perhaps after being on it for a week or two, she'll be able to tell you more about her situation."

The director nodded and took the note. "I hope so. Poor dear. She doesn't say much. It's as if she has a big secret and she isn't about to tell anyone about it."

A knock at Kathleen's front door stopped her from finishing up the dinner she was making. She set the spoon down on the stove and turned down the burner. Hopefully dinner wouldn't burn before she could return.

She was expecting Taylor and her husband for dinner, but they always used the kitchen door.

Wiping her hands on a towel, she headed for the front door. People rarely came to the front door, so she knew it had to be a stranger. Opening the door, she saw two police officers who immediately took off their hats.

"Yes?" The brisk air from the November day made her bristle. But it was not the temperature, but the sight of the Michigan State police officers, which sent fear through her.

"We're sorry, ma'am, but do you know anyone by the name of Louise Williams?" The man behind the first officer coughed.

"Um, yes. Why?"

"How is she related to you, Ma'am?" The officer took out a pen and wrote down something on his paper.

"She's my aunt, is something wrong?"

"I'm sorry to have to tell you this, but your aunt has been in an automobile accident."

Kathleen put the towel to her mouth. The cold air coming through her front door now made her body ache.

"May we come in?"

Kathleen backed away from the door, "Of course. Sure. Come in."

Brian came into the house as quickly as he could. A Michigan State police cruiser was in his driveway. What could they possibly be doing? He set his briefcase down as he made his way into the kitchen. Something on the stove smelled like it was burning. He turned off the burner and headed into the living room where two officers sat on the couch opposite his wife. She sounded upset.

One officer stood as he walked into the room. He wasn't sure why he did it but he put up both his hands and said, "I'm her husband," and pointed to Kathleen.

The officer held out his hand, "My name is Officer Kendall. This is Sergeant Malcolm. We're here to notify your wife of the death of her aunt."

"Aunt Louise?"

Kathleen looked up at him with tearful, red-rimmed eyes. She was dabbing at them with a kitchen towel.

"What happened?"

Kathleen grabbed his hand and pulled him closer to her in the chair, "It was a car accident. She swerved into the path of another car."

"I'm sorry sir. But she died instantly at the scene."

Brian couldn't believe what he was hearing. He sank onto the arm of Kathleen's chair and put his head down. He'd just seen his aunt that morning. Then he remembered how angry he'd been with her. "Where was the accident?"

"Okemos. She was heading down Marsh Road."

"I just don't know why she was in Lansing. She rarely leaves her home, let alone our small town. I wonder where she was going."

"When was the last time you spoke with your aunt, sir?"

"Brian. My name is Brian. Um, just a few days ago." He wasn't sure why he lied to cover up the visit with his aunt that morning. Kathleen was visibly shaken. If he told the police he saw her that morning, that may upset her more.

"We saw her a few days ago. We ate lunch with her."

"Well, I don't think we need to ask any more questions. These are some of her belongings. We have her purse and an emergency identification card along with her cell phone. We've checked it and it appears that she might have received a call just prior to the accident. Perhaps she was trying to answer it. We found the phone on the driver's side floorboard."

"Who was calling her?"

"Um, you can look." Brian took the phone, which now had a broken screen, and pressed a button. The phone lit up. "It still works." He'd look later to see who might have called Louise. He put his arm around Kathleen who leaned into his shirt and cried.

"We'll be going now." The officer on the couch now stood. "We are sorry for your loss." Both officers put on their hats at the door. "We'll let ourselves out."

Brian hugged his wife. Guilt began to penetrate his thoughts. Had he caused the accident? But where was Louise going? He meant her no harm. He just wanted Kathleen to have access to Irene's important papers. He wasn't sure he could live with himself if the cause of any of this had something to do with something as superficial as a checkbook.

Greg and Violet came out to greet Kathleen and Brian as they got out of their car.

Greg came toward Brian and Violet came toward Kathleen. Almost at the same time, they both exclaimed, "Do you know where Louise is? She's been gone since yesterday."

Kathleen took Violet's hand. "She won't be coming back."

Violet looked shaken. "What? Where did she go? Back to Florida?"

Kathleen shook her head and fought back tears again. This whole ordeal had taken its toll on his wife. He wasn't sure if it she was mourning for Aunt Louise or if this just reminded her that her mother was gone, too.

Violet looked at Kathleen and then at Brian. "Was she the woman in the traffic accident yesterday?"

Brian looked over the car at Violet and nodded.

"Oh my."

"What Mother, what's wrong?" Greg went back to his mother's side. She grabbed his hand now and looked into his soft, blue eyes. "Mother, where's Louise?"

Kathleen smiled at Greg. "She's with my mother now."

"In heaven?" Greg asked.

Kathleen nodded. "Yes Greg."

"I guess she won't be bringing back the surprise then."

Violet looked over at her son. "What surprise, Greg?"

"When she left yesterday. She said she was bringing me back a big surprise and to watch for her so I could help her."

Violet glanced at Kathleen, "I don't know what he's talking about. I didn't even see Louise yesterday. I'm so sorry, Kathleen. Brian. Sweetheart, if Greg or I can do anything. Anything for you, please let us know." She then led Greg back into their house.

Kathleen came around the front of the car and stood gazing at her mother's back door. "It will surely be quiet around here now."

Brian took her hand, "Let's go in. Everyone will soon see the news report and we won't have to worry about having to tell everyone."

"Maybe we will find something telling us what Aunt Louise wanted for a funeral service." Kathleen wiped her eyes.

Soon Kathleen and Brian were going through every drawer in her mother's house in search of her mother's will, bank statements, or anything regarding Aunt Louise's death wishes.

Kathleen wandered into Aunt Louise's bedroom. The scent of her aunt's perfume still hung in the air. Other than her unmade bed, the room was quite clean. Kathleen felt as though she were invading her Aunt's privacy. She remembered all of those boxes that used to be sitting in the corner. There were at least five or, six of them when she'd stayed here while Aunt Louise was in the hospital. They were gone. Louise must have found a better place to store them.

"Brian. Come in here," Kathleen called to her husband in the living room.

He called, "Be there in a minute."

She sat on the edge of the bed and pulled out her aunt's end table drawer. In it was a book and some letters. The letters were recent and still in their envelopes. She pulled out one and looked at the return address. Someone named Howard Miller had sent them to her aunt, at this address.

Brian came into the room, "What Kathleen?"

"There were some boxes in the corner when I stayed with Mom when Louise was sick. They're gone now."

"Well maybe she found a better place for them."

"She couldn't have carried them herself. They were large and full of things."

Brian shrugged his shoulders and handed Kathleen a checkbook, "Here's Mom's checkbook. There isn't really anything written in the register since last year."

"Last year?" Kathleen took the checkbook from her husband and looked at the carbon copy of the last check written. The date was November of last year. The scratching was hard to make out.

"How has she been paying the bills?"

Brian shrugged. "I don't know, but wasn't with this checkbook." Brian handed Kathleen some bank statements. Money balances had remained the same, except for her monthly social security deposits. Other than that, only about a hundred dollars each month had been removed since April.

"Do you think Aunt Louise was paying the bills with her own money?"

"We'll have to find some bank statements, or her own checkbook or something, but what it looks like right here, Aunt Louise was paying for most of the bills around here."

"Look at this letter," Kathleen held up the letter from someone named Howard. "Looks like Aunt Louise has had someone writing to her. From Florida."

Brian looked at the envelope. "Should we read it?"

Kathleen shrugged, "She won't care now."

Brian opened the note and read through the first few lines and then sat down beside Kathleen on the bed. "Sounds like this guy really liked her."

"What does it say?"

Dear Louise: So happy to get your letter this past week. I've been missing you so much. Life here is duller now than before. I have nothing to occupy my life. No one to visit. No one to look after. I just want to be back on the gulf coast. With you.

"She had a boyfriend?"

Brian nodded, "It appears so. Who would have thought?"

Kathleen took another letter out of the envelope and read the first few lines of it. Also from Howard. He talked about the weather and his children. "Sounds like he may have just lost his wife. Read this part." Kathleen handed the letter to Brian and pointed to the paragraph about a funeral.

"Oh my. I think Aunt Louise had a few secrets," Brian stood up and looked around the room, "Kathleen, what did you do with Aunt Louise's phone? Do you still have it?"

She pointed in the direction of the kitchen. "It's in my purse. On the kitchen table."

Brian left the room and Kathleen counted about twenty letters stashed in the drawer.

Brian walked back into the room, "Bingo."

Kathleen looked up, "What?"

"Guess who called her yesterday?"

"Howard?"

Brian nodded. "Yup. Maybe we should call him and let him know."

"How sad, Brian. If he's recently lost his wife and now, his girlfriend."

"But, what a player. When I get old, I want to have that kind of talent. Keeping two old women on the line," Brian laughed, "At the same time."

Kathleen shook her head. "You'd better not. I'll come back and haunt you."

Brian searched the house for other clues as to the whereabouts of the most important missing document: the death certificate.

"Maybe Aunt Louise never applied for the death certificate," Kathleen told him as he rummaged through the last drawer in the living room desk.

"That's unlikely. Doesn't the funeral director take care of that?"

"How am I supposed to know?"

Brian nodded, "We haven't had to deal with a death in the family. I just assumed,"

"That's the problem, Brian. We just assumed."

"Wait," Kathleen pulled out a small stack of papers from the bottom drawer, "here they are."

"The death certificate?"

"No, Aunt Louise's bank statements." Kathleen's face turned white. "Brian, look."

Brian glanced over the statements for the past few months. "Kathleen, your aunt has been paying all the bills. From her own money. The electric bills, water bills..." He flipped through more statements. "She paid all of the property taxes as well. Look."

He handed Kathleen the statements. She glanced over each one. "There seems to be no massive transfer of money from Mom's account. Brian, Aunt Louise was taking care of everything."

Brian shook his head, "Let me look at the last month's statement."

Kathleen handed over the October and November statements. "Look at this amount." He handed the October statement over to her.

Kathleen looked it over and said, "What's this?"

"It's a withdrawal. A large withdrawal from Louise's account."

"It's nearly all the money she had."

"It doesn't say where it was sent to, but Kathleen, wait," Brian bent over the desk and looked at the calendar on top of the desk. "It happened the week before your mother died."

Kathleen looked at him, "Did she pay for the funeral?"

"The week *before* she died? How would she know it was going to happen? And above all, how much do funerals cost? This is nearly a hundred and fifty thousand dollars."

"How's the medicine working?" The doctor stood in the hallway outside of Irene's room.

"Better. She seems to be responding, but she still doesn't talk much."

"Dementia does that sometimes, but not often. I thought maybe her cognitive skills and her surroundings would become more familiar."

The director shrugged her shoulders, "If you mean she'll tell us why she's all alone and no one comes to visit her, it hasn't happened yet."

"I feel so bad for her. Family issues can be so frustrating some times. But why in the world, would someone put a loved one in a home and never come visit them."

The director turned to go back to her office, "Unfortunately, it happens more than you'd think."

###

Brian called the funeral home that they had, used for his mother-in-law, to arrange for Aunt Louise's body to be transferred there from the morgue. He chose to identify Louise, rather than have Kathleen go through the process so soon after losing her mother. After identifying the body, Brian went out to his car and cried. He hated the way he'd treated Louise just before her death. If only he'd have known. He couldn't stop chiding himself for the horrible accusations when he realized she'd been paying all the bills since last year.

After looking through Irene's bank statements, he never realized how much of her finances were gone. The only income left was a few social security checks, which Louise hadn't even used. And the house. Why hadn't he kept better track of things for his mother-in-law? Perhaps he could have helped her invest a little to at least have some money left over to bury her. But Louise had paid for even that.

He would have never believed that the woman who came to them in the spring from Florida, would be more of a godsend than he could ever imagine. She had been so helpful in caring for his mother-in-law that Kathleen and he didn't have to worry about Irene's care. They had been able to really enjoy Taylor's wedding and live their lives almost fully. Maybe a little too much.

Kathleen and Brian had talked about Louise's funeral arrangements. They wanted her to have just as nice as funeral as she had graciously provided Kathleen's mother. They arranged to meet with the director the next morning.

On the way, they went to the impound center to arrange for the disposal of Irene's car. The mangled mess sat in a far corner. The front of the vehicle, including the passenger side facing Kathleen, was completely crushed in. White airbags covered the front seats. It appeared that the driver's side door had been pried off with a heavy tool.

Brian offered to gather Louise's belongings from the car. Kathleen could just watch through the window of the impound office. She couldn't bear to go out and look inside it. As he made his way across the parking lot, with a box in his hands, Kathleen cried.

She watched as Brian set the box down in the back seat and began to fumble with items in the front seat. He placed a few things in the box and then stood back from the car. Kathleen saw him sigh and then go back into the car. He picked up a few more things and placed them into the box.

He made his way around to the other side of the car and then stopped. He placed the box on the ground and tried to open the back door. He pulled so hard that he nearly fell backward when the door finally gave way and opened.

Steadying himself, he reached into the back seat and pulled out what looked to be a grocery shopping bag. He looked inside and then back to Kathleen through the window. He added the shopping bag to the box, and carrying it all to the office where Kathleen stood waiting.

As he walked into the door, Kathleen asked, "What did you find?"

"Looks as if her purse spilled out onto the floor in the front seat: a tube of lipstick, a change purse and some old grocery receipts.

Kathleen nodded, "But what did you find in the back seat?"

"That's the oddest thing. Look." Brian pulled the bag out of the box and opened it for Kathleen to look inside.

She pulled out a magazine. It was one of her mother's favorites. There were two or three fairly recent issues. "Maybe she was taking them to a recycling center or donating them to a home or something."

Brian nodded and sighed, "Yeah. You're probably right, but they're recent issues."

Something fell to the floor before Kathleen could put all the magazines back into the bag. She bent down to pick it up and noticed it was the pamphlet from her mother's funeral.

Brian reached into the bag and said, "Wait, here's something else." He pulled out a tube of hand lotion. "What's this?"

Kathleen took the tube from him and looked at him, "It's mother's favorite hand lotion." Brian handed her a small, plastic-wrapped box. "Tea. Mom loved this kind." She held up the box, "I'd often get her some for the holidays."

"If I didn't know any better, it's almost like this bag was meant for your mother."

"I'm so sorry for your loss. So soon after your mother's death, too. You just never know how life will change, do you?" The funeral director sat behind his desk, opening up a folder on which Louise's name had been penciled in at the tab.

"We're still in a bit of a shock. We had to go through her car this morning." Kathleen couldn't seem to turn off the tears. She reached for a tissue from her purse.

"It's never easy to get through a funeral for one, but two loved ones so close together. I'm so sorry."

Brian shifted in his chair. "We were wondering if you could help us with something else, while we are here. We can't seem to find a death certificate for Irene. Could we get that from you?"

The director looked at Brian with an odd look. "Let me look." He got up from his chair, went to a filing cabinet behind his desk, opened it, and fumbled through some of the folders. "Fredericks, right?"

Brian nodded, "Yes."

The director flipped through a folder, then sat down again at his desk. "I'm sorry, Brian. I have no death certificate. Mrs. Williams told me she would be getting those from the director who cremated Mrs. Fredericks."

"You didn't cremate her?

"No, I'm sorry."

"Then who did?" Brian sat up straighter.

"Um," the director flipped through the papers in the folder. "I don't think she mentioned his name."

Kathleen reached out for Brian's hand. "Why didn't you cremate her?"

The director took off his glasses. "I thought you'd known about this arrangement. Mrs. Williams had your mother's ashes delivered to us the day of the funeral. In fact, she brought them herself."

Brian grimaced. "What?"

"Yes. She and Mrs. Fredericks came into the home just a few weeks before. Mrs. Fredericks was adamant that her body be cremated at another funeral home across town. I didn't really question it, because they said they'd gotten a two for one deal after your father died."

"My father died almost twenty years ago. I was pretty young then, but he wasn't cremated."

"Well, I don't know then. It was just something special they requested. You saw the urn. I assumed she'd gotten it from the other home. Whoever did the cremation would be in charge of the death certificates."

"What other home could that have been?"

The director rattled off two or three other funeral homes in the area. None sounded familiar to Kathleen.

"You can always bypass the home and go right to the county offices in Corunna. They'd have a certificate there as well. They could get your copies."

Kathleen felt even more disturbed. Why hadn't she paid more attention when her mother died? She'd left too many of the arrangements in the hands of her aunt.

Brian looked at Kathleen, "This is so weird. Why would your mother want her ashes from another home? Why hadn't they discussed this with you? I wonder if Louise's boyfriend in Florida can shine a little light on some of these things for us."

"How would someone in Florida know about all of this?"

"Because he's your aunt's boyfriend."

"We don't know that yet."

"Well, it won't hurt to get him on the phone. Talk to him."

Chapter 40

All of the family and friends they'd seen for Irene's funeral came back for Louise's funeral. Taylor and her new husband came from Chicago, as did Jade from his first semester at Michigan State.

The flowers filled the room with scents of mums and the colors of fall. Much of the service resembled Irene's. The same pastor, many of the same friends. Less than what they'd had for Irene. The pastor mentioned that Louise had approached him the last few weeks and had come to the church alone, after Irene passed away. Brian hadn't known about that, either.

"She confessed to me that her life had changed considerably since her sister's funeral. She said that somehow she knew the importance of getting back into church, seeking God for things in her life again." The pastor recalled some sister memories that Louise had shared with him. "They were quite the pair. I have no doubt in my mind that today, they are with each other again in heaven."

Brian chuckled to himself. Kathleen gave him the look. He was pretty sure he knew where Irene stood with God, but Aunt Louise was a different story. She'd always been independent. Free from control. A free spirit. He wondered if the pastor had her confused with another older lady in the church.

Still, he couldn't get the bank statements, and what they said about his wife's aunt, out of his head. She hadn't been obligated to pay anything for

Irene, yet she had. He would have deemed it fair if they would have evenly shared the expenses, but Aunt Louise paying for everything made no sense to him.

After the funeral dinner that afternoon, as Brian carried some of the leftover food to his car, he realized he couldn't manage all that he'd loaded on his arms. He saw Greg coming up from downstairs, so he motioned for Greg to help him before he dropped the box and food spilled all over the church's foyer carpeting.

Greg nodded. "I got it, Brian.

Violet called out to Greg as he took a box, "Greg. Be careful of your back."

Brian assured her. "It's the lightest one, Violet."

"I'm sure it's fine, but Greg hurt his back a few weeks back."

As they made their way to the car, Brian asked Greg about it. "What happened to your back, buddy?"

"Oh it's nothing." Greg lagged behind him a bit.

"Did you do something to hurt your back?" Brian asked.

Greg shifted the box in his arms and said, "I helped Louise move some heavy boxes. My back got hurt moving the boxes. It still kinda hurts."

"Heavy boxes? Where did you put the boxes?"

"In Irene's car."

They reached his car. He pulled keys out of his pocket and pushed the unlock button on the fob.

"Do you know what was in those boxes, Greg?"

Greg shook his head and handed Brian his box, which he set in the back seat of the car. "Nope."

"Did Irene tell you?"

"Nope. She wasn't outside. Just Louise."

"So you didn't see what was in any of the boxes?"

"Nope." Greg turned. "I gotta get back to Mother Goose."

Mother Goose was a name Greg often called his mother when he was out of ear shot of her. Brian laughed.

"I hope your back feels better soon"

Greg waved as he went back into the church.

Boxes? What did Louise move that they knew nothing about?

Kathleen came out of the bathroom, pulled back the covers, and crawled into bed that night. Brian had been reading, but he just couldn't seem to concentrate on the plot of the book. Or even the writing for that matter. He kept re-reading one paragraph over and over. He finally put a bookmark in the spot and put the book on the end table.

"Kathleen, I talked to Greg."

"I saw Violet, but I don't think I got to talk to Greg today."

"He told me he'd strained his back helping Louise with some boxes a few weeks ago."

"Boxes? What kind of boxes?"

"That's what I asked him," Brian pulled the covers over his wife's legs and up to her shoulders as she scooted closer to him in bed.

"Aunt Louise probably had things she wanted to donate or something. She had so many things delivered to the house this spring from her house in Florida. It was probably just things she didn't need any more. What's so important about that?"

"Nothing really."

"I'm so exhausted. I don't think I would ever say this, but I'm eager to get back to work. To a normal life again."

Brian nodded. "Yeah. It's gonna take me a month to get through all my e-mails." Brian turned to his side, reached up, and turned off the lamp beside his bed. The room went dark.

He pulled the covers up to his shoulders as Kathleen snuggled in behind him. "I'll go tomorrow and see if I can get somewhere with your mother's death certificate."

Kathleen patted his back. "Thanks. You're a great guy, did you know that?"

"Even when I do this?" Brian pushed his cold feet back onto his wife's legs.

Kathleen let out a squeal. "No! Stop it. You're feet are freezing."

After their giggles, the room became quiet. Brian could hear Kathleen's heavy breathing within minutes. He knew she hadn't slept well since the accident. He was thankful she seemed calmer tonight.

Brian gazed out at the moon, lighting up their window. He wished he could fall asleep as easily as his wife. But for some reason, all he could think of was the bag from the car. It had been wrapped up and tied shut, the same way Irene had tied many plastic bags she'd sent through him to Kathleen.

But mostly, the bag contained so many items that seemed designated to one person, his mother-in-law. Where would Louise have been taking that bag? And why?

The hairdresser put down her brush and turned the woman in the chair around a bit before doing the other side of her hair. "How do you feel today, Irene?"

"Very well. The nurse told me they put me on some new medicine. It does make me feel better and I have remembered a few things like...putting the top back on the toothpaste."

"Don't worry," the hairdresser smiled, "I often forget that myself. Irene, do you have a family?"

Irene grew quiet.

"I don't mean to pry. You are just such a kind, nice woman. I rarely see anyone come to visit you." The hairdresser was in the home almost every single day. Her parlor was just in the next room from Irene's living area.

"I do, but they are all gone now."

"No children?"

Irene grew quiet again. The director had been talking to the hairdresser about Irene and her lack of visitors. Everyone working at the home had been encouraged to bring up the subject. They all hoped someone would be able to find a bit of information about the kind lady in room 601.

Irene slowly shook her head.

"No children?" Irene looked into the mirror, opposite the chair, and again slowly shook her head.

The hairdresser looked into the sad eyes of the woman looking back at her through the mirror in front of her chair. "Do you like your hair like this?"

Irene smiled again. "It almost makes me look just like Louise."

"Louise?" Irene's face now grew stone-like and pale. "Who's Louise?" Irene looked down and said nothing.

The hairdresser kept doing her hair. She knew it really wasn't any of her business and she hated to see Irene purposely try to be quiet, so she changed the subject. "So, do you think we'll get snow before Thanksgiving this year?"

Irene looked up and smiled, "Oh probably. Isn't that typical for Michigan?"

The hairdresser peeked in on the home's director before heading out that night, "No luck with Irene today."

The director smiled, "She seems better though, doesn't she?"

"As long as you don't bring up her family. But she knew where she was today. She said Michigan always has snow before Thanksgiving. Last week she swore she was in Florida."

The hair dresser laughed.

"Yes. The caregivers are all saying the same thing. The new medicine is helping."

"We'll just love her as family should. Perhaps someday, her sister will even come back. By the way, what is her sister's name?"

"I'm really not supposed to divulge that information to you, but..., for Irene's sake. Maybe someone will know her. It's Louise Williams."

"Wow, that name sounds familiar, but I don't have a clue why."

"Well, don't tell anyone I told you."

The hairdresser shook her head, "Mum's the word. I'll just keep loving her as best I can and maybe someday, somehow, someone may know her."

"I hope so. For her sake."

Brian had the opportunity to look through a few of his e-mails the next morning before heading off to the courthouse in search of Irene's death certificate. He'd encouraged Kathleen to not only sleep in, but to head to work when she woke up. "It will do you good to get back to work. Let me worry about the certificate."

Kathleen gulped another mouthful of coffee, "Thanks Brian. We won't be able to do anything with the house, until you find it."

"Are you going to sell it?"

"I hate to do it, but the kids don't want it. It's a beautiful old home. I can't imagine having to hand over the keys, but what would we do with it?"

Brian shook his head. "We have enough here to take care of."

"I'm gonna get ready to list it by spring. Lots of packing and things to figure out before we can put it on the market." Kathleen kissed him on the lips. "Thanks for doing this errand for me before you get back to work yourself."

"No problem." Brian stood up as she walked out the door. He picked up his keys, slipped on his coat, and locked the kitchen door behind him as he headed off to the courthouse.

Chapter 41

"What was your mother's-in-law name again?" The clerk looked up at Brian over the glasses perched on her nose.

"Irene Fredericks." Brian coughed. "F-R-E-D-R-I-C-K-S."

"Fredericks, Fredericks...And the date of death?"

"October second. This year. She was cremated in a funeral home somewhere close to Durand."

"I have Freders, Freirs...but I'm sorry, no one with the name Irene Fredericks during that time frame."

"What are you saying?" Brian couldn't believe their luck. This had to be some kind of mistake.

"Are you sure she passed away in Shiawassee County?"

Brian groaned. "Positive."

"Well sir, I think you have a problem. We have no death certificate for anyone named Fredericks for this year. Do you want me to go back a year or two?"

"She was alive on October first, ma'am. I saw her myself."

"I suggest, you talk to the funeral director. He should have filed the paperwork. If he didn't, there's no death certificate."

Brian sighed, "Okay. Well thank you for your time"

Brian left the courthouse. As he descended the steps he grew more anxious. How would he break this to Kathleen? What in the world had Louise been thinking? Why hadn't she just used the crematory of the home where Irene's service was held? Irene had never told Kathleen she wanted to be cremated anyway. It just didn't make any sense. Either there was a major mistake by the funeral director who cremated Irene, or worse yet, she'd never been cremated. So what happened to her?

So many questions with Irene's death. The next thought made Brian stop dead in his tracks. Louise hadn't allowed anyone to see her mother after she passed away. Not even look at the body. That had bothered Brian as he watched Kathleen not able to mourn over seeing her mother dead. She'd mentioned many times that she wished she could have seen her mother in a casket. That look often helped a person deal with death.

Kathleen had voiced it many times since her mother's funeral. "I just have a hard time believing she's really gone," Brian took another step and another down the stairs of the century-old court house. He stopped again when he thought it through. *How could they be certain she'd really died? Especially now, without even a death certificate to prove it.*

"Look at this," the hair dresser put the small, cut-up newspaper clipping in front of her boss as she rushed in to start work the next afternoon.

"What is it?"

"It's a news story. After you told me Irene's sister's name, I couldn't help but think I remembered that name from somewhere. I racked my brain, which honey, isn't so hard to do, but I just couldn't get her name off my mind. Then it hit me. I pulled this out of the garbage. Last week's garbage. Thank God it hadn't gone to the landfill yet."

"What does it say?" The director did her best to smooth down the paper and read it.

"It was stuck between some of my leftover fruits and vegetables from last week. But look right here, at the name."

"Officials released the name of the elderly woman who was killed in the automobile accident on Marsh Road. Her name is..."

The director looked up at the hair dresser. "...Louise Williams."

"Irene's sister. That's why she hasn't gotten visitors lately. She died. But read more."

The director mumbled through much of the article.

She leaves behind her niece, Kathleen (Brian) Moser and great niece and nephew, Taylor (James) Matthews and nephew Jade Matthews."

The director looked up again. "She had a niece."

"Could be on Louise's side of the family."

"Or it could mean, Irene has a daughter."

"It gets better. Keep reading."

Louise was preceded in death by her sister, Irene Williams.

The director stood up from her chair. "What?"

"Honey, someone on this side of the family believes Irene Fredericks is dead."

Chapter 42

"Kathleen, we need to talk." Brian wasn't sure how to tell his wife that his search for the certificate came up short. He moved his cell phone to his other ear as he fumbled with his keys in the door lock.

"Honey, can it wait until tonight? I have so much here to catch up on."

Brian shook his head, "No. We need to meet right away. Let's meet for lunch."

"Did you get the certificate?"

"I'll pick you up."

"Brian, why aren't you answering me? Stop scaring me."

"We have to talk. Right now. I'll be there in ten."

"Look in this one." The director held out another phone book for a co-worker.

"We've looked through every Lansing book we have. Have you Googled it?"

"Brilliant! That's why I pay you the big bucks." She pulled open her computer and clicked on Google. "What's her husband's name?"

"Brian. Brian Moser."

"Barry, Larry, Tom...Oh here...Brian and Kathleen Moser. They live in Durand."

"Does it list a phone number?"

"Wait." The director scratched her head. "Brian Moser and here it is. Hand me my phone."

"What are you going to say?"

"I'm not sure yet, but there has to be a connection. Somehow. If not, then Irene will live the rest of her time here alone. I can't allow that to happen."

"Is this legal?"

"Probably not, but I don't care. If I lose my job over resurrecting someone from the dead, then so be it."

"It's ringing?"

Both sat in anticipation. "No one is answering. Oh wait, it went to voice mail." The director hung up. "I can't say this in a message. I'll have to try again later."

"This is so weird. Like a plot to a really, really great novel. I mean think about it. You think your relative is gone, dead and, suddenly, an assisted living home calls and tells you that your loved one isn't dead. Like you said, it's like some kind of resurrection or something."

"Or something like that." The director added, "Why would someone want to pretend a death for someone like Irene? She's nothing but sweet."

"Maybe she's loaded."

"Well I hope so. Cause I can't see any other reason for doing it." The director hung up her phone. "Wait a minute. That name sounds familiar as well."

"Which one?"

"Moser. Wait...wait a minute." The director grabbed a file from off the front of her desk. She opened it up. "That's it."

"What?"

"A week before Irene moved in a couple came to my office inquiring about a room for their mother. I remembered because their mother's name was Irene, too."

"What happened with that?"

"They called a week later and said. She died. It can't possibly be,"

"I think so."

"The same Irene?" She looked up smiling. "It is. Look at this phone number. It matches the one I just called."

Kathleen climbed into the passenger seat of Brian's car. His color was ashen and he seemed especially nervous. "What is wrong with you?" Brian turned around to back out of his parking space.

"We need to go somewhere and talk."

"About what? Did you get a certificate?"

"I'll tell you about it when we can sit and talk without distractions."

When they got to the restaurant, Brian took off Kathleen's coat as she sat down. "Are you thirsty?"

"No. Stop it. You are making me nervous. I've never seen you like this. Sit down and talk to me."

A waitress came up to the counter and asked if they wanted something to drink. "Two Arnold Palmer's please."

Brian put his jacket on the back of his chair and sat down. He picked up Kathleen's hand and kissed it. "Brian, what's wrong?"

"Sweetheart, I went to the courthouse today."

"I know that. What did you find out?"

"There is no certificate."

"What do you mean?"

"What I think I mean is, there is no death certificate for your mother. Sweetheart, I don't think we know for sure, but maybe she never died."

Kathleen looked at Brian in disbelief. "You're crazy. What are you talking about?"

Brian shook his head. "I don't know, but one thing's for sure. She didn't die at home. Not in Shiawassee County? Not in October?"

Kathleen began to tremble and she put her hand to her mouth. Tears welled up in her eyes. "Brian, what are you thinking?"

"I'm not sure yet. We've found a few clues. I can't stop thinking about the bag in the back of Louise's car."

"It's just a bag full of things Louise was going to donate somewhere." Kathleen shook her head, "Brian, stop it. You're scaring me."

"Your mother always sent you bags like that. Filled with stuff you'd left at the house or plastic containers from food you sent over. Remember?"

"Yes, but..."

"Then the lack of death certificate. Something's up. Perhaps we need to get the police on this matter."

"You're crazy. You've watched too many detective shows."

"Maybe."

Kathleen had never seen Brian so suspicious.

###

"Irene, how are you tonight?"

The elderly woman smiled back at the director and answered, "I'm fine. How are you?"

"Great, just great. Thanksgiving will be here soon and I was wondering if you would like anything special for the holiday? Do you have a special tradition you always liked to do? Something like that?"

Irene shook her head. She grew quiet again.

"Irene? Can I ask you a question?"

Irene looked up, but didn't answer.

"Who's Kathleen?"

Irene's face went blank. She shook her head. "I don't know that name."

"Irene," the director prodded a bit more. "What about the name Brian?"

Irene turned her face away and looked out the window. This time she didn't answer.

The director turned her face toward her. She had tears in her eyes. "Irene. It's okay. Why won't you talk to me?"

"I don't know anyone by that name." She turned her head again and refused to talk anymore.

Kathleen's phone rang as they left the restaurant. A woman's voice asked, "Is this Kathleen Moser?" Kathleen nodded and answered, "Yes."

355

"This is Lauren Andrews. I work at the Sunrise Assisted Living Home here in Lansing. Do you remember me?"

"Yes, I think I do. We thought about that home for my mother, just before she..." Kathleen stopped. Why was this woman calling her? Especially after Brian's news at lunch.

"I need to ask you a few questions. Is that okay?"

Kathleen nodded. "Of course."

"Do you know an Irene Fredericks?"

"Well, of course. That's my, was, my mother."

"Why do you say 'was'?"

"She passed away. In October."

"This is going to sound very odd, Kathleen, but...are you sure?"

Kathleen nearly dropped the phone. She looked up at Brian and handed him the phone as she put her hand to her mouth and began to cry. Brian took the phone and said, "Hello, who is this? Yes. Are you sure? We'll be there in about a half an hour. You could be right. Yes. Yes. By the way, thank you."

Brian set the phone down on the seat between them. Soon they were heading down the highway. Kathleen was crying. Brian reached out and held her hand. "It's okay, sweetheart. This is good news."

"Why would she do this? What could Aunt Louise possibly gain from doing something like this?"

"I don't know."

"If it's true, how...will...we...ever tell everyone?"

"Slowly." Brian nodded. "Carefully."

356

They exited the freeway and soon were on Marsh Road. Brian veered off into a nearby parking lot and he stopped the car.

"What are you doing?" Kathleen looked at her husband. He pointed to the side of the road. "She died right there. Look at the glass by the side of the road."

Kathleen strained to look over him to the side of the road. "I've been wondering why in the world she was headed this way. She rarely got away from Durand. She hated driving in traffic..." Kathleen stopped talking.

"Are you thinking what I'm thinking?"

Kathleen looked at her husband.

"Kathleen, remember the bag? In the back seat of her car?"

Kathleen again put her hand to her mouth. "Brian. Do you think it's true?"

"We don't know yet," Brian hoped his intuition was correct. If it wasn't, his wife was going to go through more heartache again. "We'll just have to go and see. Perhaps this is just a whole mix-up."

Chapter 43

Brian held tightly to Kathleen's hand as they made their way into the home. She couldn't stop the flow of tears. What if it was true? What if her mother was here? Living at the very place she'd wanted to put her in the first place. But why would Aunt Louise do such a thing? So hard to imagine anyone thinking up such a selfish act. But what if it was true? It would be as though her mother had come back from the dead. Questions flooded her thoughts like an endless train through Durand.

The director greeted them at the door. "I know this is awkward for you, but you need to remember how hard it might be on your Mom. Can we sit a few minutes and I'll tell you a few things?"

Kathleen blurted out, "What if it isn't her? We've had her funeral. People sent cards. Who, or what, did we bury in the cemetery across town?" Brian wrapped his arm around her, whispering to her to sit down.

Kathleen sat on the couch and Brian sat beside her. The warm tones of the room and the smells of lit candles felt relaxing and serene.

"Our Irene came to us in October. A woman named Louise brought her. I had no idea what they had planned, especially without any of you knowing about it. I thought they were just sisters who were doing their best to care for one another."

Kathleen swallowed hard, but her tears just wouldn't stop. Brian leaned forward, rubbing his forehead with his thumbs. As shocking as her mother's death was, her resurrection held doubt, fear and intense anxiety. He wasn't sure Kathleen could handle more shock in her life.

"She's been so quiet about family. About ten days ago, the doctor put her on some new medicine. She perked up almost immediately and began doing things again on her own, like brushing her teeth. She started remembering her caregiver's names and what she'd had for lunch. The change was remarkable. We began asking her more questions about her family. No one has been to see her since Louise dropped her off. It was disturbing seeing her all alone."

"What did she tell you?"

"Nothing. Never anything about you. At first I thought it was just the dementia. Now, I know that for some reason, she wanted to forget all of you. She would acknowledge she had a sister, but never any children or grandchildren."

Brian looked up, "Then how did you figure it out?"

"Your aunt's accident report in the newspaper. A hair dresser we have here brought the article in. We knew Louise's name. Then we just put two and two together."

"Why do you think she didn't want to tell you about us?" Kathleen wasn't sure she wanted to know the answer, but she'd grown tired of suppressing all her questions.

"I just don't know. I really don't."

Kathleen shook her head, "I don't get it."

"Perhaps we'll find out now. Now that you're here. But just know, she might get a little angry."

Kathleen nodded. "It's as though she wanted to hide from us."

"I think that's it exactly, but I don't know why. But first, before we get the cart before the horse, we need you to identify her. We can't let you go in without knowing for sure. We have laws concerning people's privacy. Look into her room through the open door. Tell me first if this woman, our Irene, is your mother."

They stood. Kathleen's legs felt like rubber. Grasping Brian's arm, she stumbled down the hallway behind the director.

"This is Irene's room. Go ahead. Tell me who you see."

Kathleen's knees shook. She let out a sigh and gazed into the room. She saw a woman by a window. Without having her see face, she stepped back and looked up at Brian. Tears streamed down her face. She didn't have to tell the director anything. The director nodded her understanding.

The director motioned for her to go into the room. Kathleen reached out and grabbed Brian's hand. Tears were in his eyes. Even seeing her mother now couldn't stop her from remembering how they'd mourned for her during the past months.

Kathleen slowly walked into the room. Her mother turned. Her eyes grew wide and she stood up. Kathleen walked closer. "Mother?"

"What are you doing here?"

Brian came up beside Kathleen, "I think that should be our question to you, Mom."

The director slowly shut the door behind them.

360

Kathleen clung to her mother for a long time. Soon, her mother tightened her grip in return and began to sob. She whispered, "I'm sorry, Kathleen. I've missed you. I've missed you so much."

Kathleen looked into her mother's tearful, red eyes. "Mother, why did you do this?" She held back her anger as best she could, but she couldn't believe her mother had put her through such grief needlessly. "Why did you lie to me?" She could feel her mother grow weak in the knees. She motioned for her to turn around and sit back in her chair. "Sit down. Let's talk about this."

Her mother reached out for Brian's hand as she sat down and then grabbed Kathleen's hand with her other hand. "How did you find me?"

"That's a long story, Mother, but why did you do this? Did Louise make you come here?"

She looked down at her lap and then up, "This is how I planned it."

"You? *You* planned all of this? Aunt Louise didn't make you do this?"

"No. Louise tried to stop me several times. She tried hard to talk me out of it. For months. I think. I haven't been thinking clearly, you know, for this past year, but we made this pact. Louise promised me she'd do this for me, years ago."

"Years?" Brian asked.

"Yes, years. I made her promise me. At Mother's grave."

Kathleen couldn't believe what she was hearing, "But why? Why would you plan something like this?"

Her mother shook her head. "For years, I watched as my mother dwindled away to nothing. Slowly. Dementia, such a slow death. It erodes so many things. Years of memories are remembered on some days, but on others, they seem like strange ideas. Mother's care went on like that for years. By the end, she hated me. She accused me of all kinds of horrible things. She said I took her money. She told people that I hated her. She said I beat her. I never laid a hand on her. Ever. I only cared for her. The best way I knew how."

"I know that, Mother. I watched you."

"Day after day went by. One year, then two. Four years and then six. It took some of the best years of my life. I missed out on your high school prom. Do you remember that? Another mother had to take you to get your hair done."

Kathleen nodded.

"I missed out on family events. The last years of my husband's life. So many things."

Brian sat back. Kathleen looked at him. He shook his head.

"So many days gone. The day I buried her, I looked in the mirror and I had aged. I wasn't young anymore. I was old. I'd even missed out on helping you with my grandchildren. All because of my mother."

She looked Kathleen in the eyes, tears moist on her cheeks. "I didn't want that for you."

She squeezed Kathleen's hand, "I made your Aunt Louise promise to do this for me. At first, she refused, even on that day beside Mother's grave, but she also knew how much I had given up to be there for Mother. I guess she felt guilty, so she promised."

"But Mother, why would you think that faking your death would be a good thing? Do you realize how much we've been through?"

Irene shook her head. "I just thought it was better this way. A quick death. You would grieve, but your lives would go on. You'd feel free to live your own life. Not be burdened with a mother who couldn't care for herself. When Aunt Louise finally came to visit me, I knew it was a sign that God probably thought it was a good idea, too. I didn't ask her to come, but she just showed up. Ready to go through with the plan. Even though, she told me many times to rethink it and to change my mind. But I couldn't. I just couldn't."

"I thought it would be easy, until last week. The doctor must have given me something different, because I haven't thought this clearly in months. I even remembered why I was here and who put me here."

Kathleen stood up. "Of all the selfish things to do in your life, mother. This beats it all. Your mother didn't mean to take away your life. She was sick. She needed you. And despite the fact that you gave up so much to be with her and care for her, think of all the blessings you had while she was here."

"Kathleen, don't twist this."

"Don't twist it. Mother! It's you who has done the twisting. How dare you hide like this? How dare you put us through all of this? This is so out of character for you."

Her mother look at her, stunned, as if she didn't think of it as something she was doing wrong, but as something she was doing right.

"I understand why. It makes sense that you didn't want me to give up my life to care for you while you were going through this, but look what could have been prevented. You've been bad almost since the middle of the summer and now a new medicine has helped you to think clearer. If you'd have let me care for you, perhaps we could have found this drug sooner. Don't you understand, Mother, this was a purely, selfish act. Even against Aunt Louise."

Shock now shown on her Mother's face.

Irene looked up, "But Kathleen, how did you find out? Louise promised me she wouldn't tell you."

Brian knelt beside his mother-in-law's chair. He gripped her hand tighter. Then he gave a look to Kathleen. Kathleen knew he was asking her to allow him to tell her mother. She nodded. "Mother, Louise didn't tell us. I'm sorry to have to tell you this now, Mother, but Aunt Louise isn't with us anymore."

Horror now accompanied the look on her mother's face.

Irene looked at Brian, "What?"

Kathleen bent down. "Mother, she was killed. Last week. In a car accident."

"Not her heart? She didn't die because of her heart?"

"No," Brian added. "And, we think, she died trying to come see you."

"No!" A sob seemed to come from the deep recesses of Irene's soul. "She wasn't to come and see me ever again. That was part of the promise."

Irene couldn't believe what she was hearing. Louise had kept her promise. To the end. She covered her mouth with her hand and gasped, "Did she suffer?"

Brian leaned in and hugged her. "No. I really don't think she knew what hit her."

"I did my best, in the last few months, to remind her from where she came. How our parents raised us. Helped us to see an awesome Creator. Someone who would be with us through our life's ordeals. Help her to stop having all those crazy liberal beliefs. I don't know if any of it helped. I may never know now."

Kathleen stood and went to the room's eating area. She came back with a tissue box and handed it to her. She wondered how long Kathleen would be angry with her. Kathleen knelt beside her chair and put her head in her lap. Irene began to stroke her daughter's hair.

What had she been thinking? Why would she give up so easily? She'd put her family through unnecessary heartache. Her plan had backfired and now she would have to pay the consequences of her sinful heart. Her agony now doubled with guilt.

As the three family members reminisced about Louise, it helped to ease the grief. They even began to laugh about her stubborn, obstinate ways. How she'd speak her mind in the midst of any discussion. How much she hated Max. Brian assured her that Max had been well fed and loved since Irene left home.

Irene reached out and took her daughter's hand again. "Kathleen. Please forgive me. I didn't think through how much sadness this would bring you. I just wanted to protect you, which I have never been very successful at. From the time you were a little child I would imagine how I'd keep you from harm. Keep the bad things from happening to you and then I slowly realized how that is completely impossible. You'd ride your bike and fall or you'd stumble on a sidewalk and skin your knee. Protecting you has been my goal in life and now, I realize again, that I can't do any of that. It's God's job to protect us. Please forgive me."

"Mom. I love you. Please don't ever feel as though you are a burden to me, or to Brian or to our children. We need you. I'm sorry for neglecting you so much this past year. I'll try harder to be there for you."

"You know what, Kathleen? Living here isn't all that bad. I like it here. I feel safe. It isn't nearly so big or lonely as that old house of mine. And now, once others know the truth, maybe they'll forgive my selfishness and come visit me from time to time. I think this would be a wonderful place to spend the rest of my life. As long as you all come visit me."

"Well maybe, but for now, we need you home. You need to give us a chance to be your helper. Take care of you. And then, we promise, when the going gets rough and you need better care, we'll bring you back here. Okay?"

"I'll think about it. I promise."

Kathleen and Brian left after sharing a meal with Irene and spending the evening with her. They'd even allowed her to talk to Taylor on the phone. As she heard Taylor cry through the phone she began to realize how selfish she'd been during this whole ordeal. She thought she was saving everyone from pain, but her desire to protect them only made them more vulnerable and hurt.

The director stopped in to visit her after her family left. She sat down in a chair opposite Irene. "How are you, Irene?" She reached out and touched her knee. "Are you doing okay?"

"I did this whole thing to protect them. Help them through a difficult time. I wonder if I caused more harm than good. Yes, they didn't have to worry about my needs and the care I required, but I took away so much more. I remember how happy I was at Taylor's wedding. She was such a beautiful bride. But if I would have gone away, like I did, I might have missed out on other things in her life. What about her first baby? Her second? Maybe she will make me a great-grandmother. I would have missed out on holding her children. Jade hasn't gotten married yet. What about his wedding?"

Irene began to cry. "I didn't mean to cause them so much heartache and now, now I find out I missed out on being with Louise more. Showing her Christ more. Sharing my love for Him with her. That was also selfish of me."

"In trying to protect my family, I did just the opposite. I kept them from learning about old age, dementia and having an elderly mother. To learn to care for others and finding that you are stronger than disease. You are strong as a family, not just as individuals. "

"You know, my mother died of cancer when I was thirty-four." The director looked out the window of Irene's bedroom. "I never got to see her grow old. Never got to share special moments with her as a married woman. She didn't see me in my wedding dress or shop for my first-born baby."

"Oh, my dear, I'm so sorry."

"I think you better make this up to your family. Do your best to be with them. Times will get hard. Sometimes you won't remember or you may even accuse them of doing things, but you'll be together. Being alone is a whole 'nother hardship that many of us have to do, no matter what." The director stood. "You do what you think is best, but maybe just going home for a few weeks will help smooth things out with your family. Sleep well, my dear friend."

As the director stood to leave, Irene reached out her hand. "If I go home for a little time, can I still stay here? I do like it."

"Don't worry about the details, Irene. We'll make it work."

As Irene lay in her bed that night, she asked God for forgiveness. She'd acted as if she were a perfect Christian in front of Louise for months now. As she prayed she realized she'd also asked her sister to lie. To her family. That was not a part of God's plan. It was Irene's plan. Not His. What if her plans had prevented her sister from finding God again in her life? Irene began to cry out to God. She understood a little better. Her mind was clearer and she realized the sin she'd done to get to this point. This whole plan had done only one thing: it showed her that she still clung to bitterness regarding the care of her mother.

She had blamed God for taking away those ten years of her life. Crawling out of bed, Irene tossed a pillow to the floor and got on her knees. For the first time in a long time, she looked at her life through God's eyes. She had pretended to be this wonderful, godly woman, but deep inside, she'd harbored bitterness. She confessed it to her heavenly Father.

Crawling back into bed, she cradled her legs and cried for her lost sister. What had she done? Had her own issues come before her sister? Yes, they had. She cried out to God to help her sister, but then realized, it was too late. Her sister was gone. She wished she could go to an assisted living home and find her, find her hiding, but she knew that wouldn't be how it would turn out. Irene began to mourn. She couldn't change the past, and now, for Louise, it would never be fixed.

Brian sat down beside his wife after dinner one night. "I hope you don't mind, but I took Louise's phone and found Howard listed among her contacts."

"You did?"

Brian nodded. "I called the number today. A man answered and I told him who I was."

"So who was he?"

"Your Aunt Louise was in love."

"What?"

"Yup. Howard lives in Florida. They spent last winter together before she came to Michigan. They met at a local diner. They took walks, went out to dinner. He even helped her sell her condo and he's the one who sent all her things up here to Michigan."

"He told you all that?"

Brian nodded.

"How did he take the news about Aunt Louise?"

"At first he was silent for a while and then I realized he was crying. He told me that he had just asked her to marry him."

Kathleen was shocked. "What?"

"They were planning to get married as soon as Louise went back to Florida. He sounded like a very nice man. He said that his heart broke to hear the news. That Louise was a light in his world of darkness."

Kathleen laughed. "Really?"

Brian nodded, "He offered his condolences to the family. And then said that it was probably better this way, but he would never forget the time he spent with your aunt. I think he truly loved her."

Chapter 44

Kathleen was finishing up her mother's dishes one night soon after they'd brought her home. She glanced out the window to see Violet heading over. Soon she was tapping on the back door. Kathleen went to let her in.

Violet stood at the doorway and asked her if Irene was up to visitors. Kathleen nodded. "She's in the living room, Violet. She's been so sad since we brought her home. She misses Aunt Louise so much."

"Can I talk to her?"

Violet could calm the deepest heartache. Soothe anyone's soul. Kathleen smiled and pointed to the living room. "Absolutely. I'm just going to finish up these dishes."

Irene sat in silence in the living room. For another night, guilt penetrated her soul as she sat gazing at her sister's chair next to her. She felt a light hand on her shoulder. Startled, she looked up to find Violet smiling down at her. "Hello Irene. Can I sit for a while?"

Oh how Irene loved her neighbor. They'd been so close for so long. She smiled, "Of course, Violet. You are always welcome. Come sit."

Violet made her way to Louise's chair and sat down. Irene tried hard not to look upset, but she couldn't hide her grief from her friend. Violet looked across at her and smiled. "Are you feeling okay, dear?"

"I feel fine." Irene assured her but then realized that Violet would be the best person to pour out her heart to. "But my heart hurts. My heart hurts like I've never, ever really felt it before."

"Do you want to tell me why?" Violet smiled.

"I've been so wrong. I did something so utterly selfish and have confessed it to the Lord, but Violet, I can't seem to get over what I've done to my sister. Before she came I asked the Lord what it was in my heart that I needed to take care of. What sin kept me from being the kind of Christian He would want me to be? He kept showing me that I needed to love others more."

"But you do that so well, Irene."

Irene shook her head. "I do it well to those who give me love in return. For the others who bother me or antagonize me, like Louise used to do, I didn't love them enough. I know this is hard to believe, Violet, but that woman would drive me absolutely crazy sometimes."

Violet smiled. "I know."

"You do?"

"Of course. We all have people in our lives who are hard to love. But I think, dear Irene, that all Louise wanted from you was your love. She wanted you to love her despite how she was."

"I tried. I really did. But I tried with my own power. Not God's. And now, dear Violet, it's too late. I've wasted the time God gave me and for some reason, even though I've confessed it, my heart just hurts over my sin."

Violet rested her head on the back of Louise's chair. "I think we've all done that from time to time, Irene. We've missed chances God has given us to share Him with others. I know I have. But that doesn't mean that the time with them was wasted."

"Oh, but it was. Did my sister really know how much she meant to me? Did she know how thankful I was to have her here with me, the past few months? There were so many times I could have set this foolish idea of mine aside and just concentrated on loving my sister. Showing her Christ with my life, instead of revealing my true sinful and bitter heart. The time is gone. These past few months with her were just a waste."

Violet shook her head. " Irene, I need to tell you something."

They'd been home a few days before Irene had the courage to enter Louise's bedroom again. She stood in the doorway of her once sewing room and gazed at the way Louise had made it her home. She always had taste when it came to decorating. The souvenirs from her trips were exquisite and perfectly placed. Irene sat on the edge of the bed. She picked up a tiny doll figurine on a table beside Louise's bed. Turning it over, she noticed it was from Norway. Oh how she would have loved to have gone there with Louise. They would have probably so enjoyed it together. Irene smiled.

Kathleen came to the doorway, seeming to be in a bit of a rush. Irene held up the doll for Kathleen to see. "Isn't it beautiful?"

Kathleen nodded. "Mother. I need to show you something."

"What is it?"

Kathleen came toward her with an envelope in her hand. "We found this in a bag Aunt Louise was bringing to you before her accident. We missed it before, but I just found that bag again and this was tucked inside one of the magazines Aunt Louise had put into the bag."

Irene held out her hand and took the envelope from her daughter. "I'll let you read it in privacy." She turned to leave, but stopped at the bedroom doorway. "If you need me, I'll be right out here."

"Kathleen, just stay. We'll read it together." Irene patted a spot on the bed, right beside her.

"Are you sure?" Kathleen hesitated, but came back to Irene.

Irene nodded and held out the letter. "You can open it and read it. I'll listen."

Kathleen sat down and took the envelope from her mother. She pulled open an edge and slowly tore it open. "It's addressed to you."

"That's okay. I want you to read it to me. From this point on, I want you to be a part of everything in my life."

Kathleen smiled and unfolded the piece of paper she'd found in the envelope. She sighed and then began:

'Dear Irene.'

Kathleen paused. Irene looked back and nodded. "Go ahead."

I miss you so, Irene. I didn't realize how hard this was going to be faking your death. I was so busy with the process of making it all work that I just didn't imagine how hard it would be to go on without you. There is hardly a second that goes by that I don't want to talk to you. Sometimes I just say something. All I hear back is silence. This house is so uncomfortably quiet. The whole thing reminds me of how I got when Mommy and Daddy put me in my own room for the first time. We'd slept together all our lives. Do you remember that? That first night without you, I couldn't stop crying.

Daddy would come in every so often and scold me. He'd tell me to be a big girl and stop crying. Then he'd hug me and leave the room. That would make me cry all the harder. Until, my door creaked open again. I hid under the covers because I was so afraid it was Daddy there to scold me. But soon, I realized it wasn't him. The steps coming toward me were too quiet. I peeked out of the covers and who was standing beside my bed, but you. You put your finger to your lips and told me to stop crying and move over. You pulled back the covers and got right into bed with me. I never felt so loved. You stayed right there, all night. Praying. You prayed for me to stop crying and you prayed that God would keep us safe while we slept. I fell asleep to your words to God.

I will never forget that night. As long as I live. So now, each night, as I lay in that big old bed in your sewing room, I listen to the squeaks and groans of the house. I hear the trains going through town, in the middle of the night. Sadly, I was just as afraid as I was back when Daddy made me spend that first night without you. And again, I would cry myself to sleep. That was until...

Irene turned to look at Kathleen who had stopped reading. Kathleen wiped her eyes and looked at her mother. She smiled and continued.

...until I talked to Violet. Violet read to me out of Ecclesiastes. I'm sure you know which part. A time for every event under heaven. A time to give birth and a time to die. A time to plant and a time to uproot what is planted. And on and on it goes. Until it says, "He has made everything appropriate in its time." And then, "I know that there is nothing better for them than to rejoice and to do good in one's lifetime. I know that everything God does will remain forever; there is nothing to add to it and there is nothing to take from it, for God has so worked that men should fear Him."

Irene put her hand on Kathleen's arm, "She's quoting scripture." She then put her hand to her mouth and the tears began to flow.

I'm writing this to tell you that I now trust God. From your example my whole life. I realized that it was you who took away much of my fear, it was you who helped me fall asleep when I was afraid, it was you who took care of our mother without me so that I could keep living my life how I pleased. You have always been there for me. So much so, that I guess I never thought I needed God. But now I do. I feel so alone. My life is about over and yes, I did many, many wonderful things in my life...But all of it was for me. When I had the chance to come back up here to Michigan to help you, I thought it would be the first time in my life that I could do something for you! I'm so happy I did. I also knew that there was no way that I couldn't keep our sister promise. I had to do that for you. But Irene, I just want you to know...I still think it is a stupid, silly idea.

Both Kathleen and Irene laughed right out loud. "For once," Irene wiped her cheek, "I agree with her."

Your family loves you. They won't think of you as a burden. Because that is how you treat everyone around you. With love. I was always a burden to you, but you rarely showed it. Through that sacrificial love, you showed me how much God loves us. Because of your example, I have come to believe in Him as you do. I remembered how Daddy used to tell us to talk to Jesus and that's what I did. I want you to know that.

Tears were now flowing down both Kathleen's and Irene's cheeks as they finished Louise's letter.

Like Ecclesiastes says, you had a purpose in all that you did, Irene. Your purpose was to sacrificially give to everyone around you. Just as Christ gives us salvation. For whatever it is worth, you are an amazing example of God's love to me. Thank you.

Kathleen folded the letter and, placed it back in its envelope, and wiped her tears with the back of her hand. "That is you, Mother. You have always given to others. Aunt Louise is in heaven now. She'll be waiting for you."

Irene nodded and took the letter from Kathleen.

"Mother, what did you pray when you crawled into bed with Louise? Was it the same prayer you'd tell me when I was afraid of the dark?"

Irene looked at her daughter and nodded, "God promises us, Louise. He promises us that every night sky will change to morning. In just a few hours."

Kathleen smiled, "Promise at Daybreak."

Irene nodded, "And God's promises never fail."

Another Book by Elizabeth Wehman...

This contemporary romance is set on Mackinac Island, Michigan. This coming-of-age story finds Kenna hiding from her family in order to find her own way. She soon finds out that her way isn't always the best route to growing up. Available on Amazon.com or by e-mailing Elizabeth at elizabethwehman@yahoo.com.

Dear Reader:

Thank you for reading "Promise at Daybreak." I would love to hear your feedback. You can get on Amazon.com and post a review by searching my name or the book title and leave a review there or you can just send me a note at elizabethwehman@yahoo.com.

Don't forget to like my author page on Facebook at Elizabeth Wehman/Author and keep up with my writing career on my website at www.elizabethwehman.com.

Thanks again for all your encouragement and kind remarks. I appreciate each one.

Elizabeth